SCHOPENHAUER'S PORCUPINES

By
Lynn Bushell

Strategic Book Publishing and Rights Co.

Copyright © 2013.
All rights reserved by Lynn Bushell.

Book Design/Layout by Kalpart. Visit www.kalpart.com

No part of this book may be reproduced or transmitted in any form or by any means, graphic, electronic, or mechanical including photocopying, recording, taping or by any information retrieval system, without the permission in writing of the publisher.

Strategic Book Publishing and Rights Co.
12620 FM 1960, Suite A4-507
Houston TX 77065
www.sbpra.com

ISBN: 978-1-62857-465-4

By the same author: *Remember Me* (2009)

For
Jonathan

*Like Schopenhauer's Porcupines we rush together
because we are chilly
and rush apart because we are prickly.*

PROLOGUE

Nathan stared into the black hole opening up below him. This was the vantage-point that God had. There was nothing special in it, he reflected. Only that the scene beneath him looked dispiritingly dingy in the dull light and it seemed to be a long way to the ground.

He rested one hand on the bannister and felt the residue of tackiness that had been left behind by other hands. He drew his fingers back, fastidiously. He abhorred this kind of accidental contact with the human race; he felt contaminated by it. That was what was so appalling about Mitzi's revelation. Not the fact that she had sinned; she didn't seem to realise that she had, but that the sin had been committed here.

Oh Mitzi, Mitzi....

He sighed irritably as the light switch clicked off and the hall was plunged back into darkness. It was an economy of Wanda's: 'After all, cats find their way home in the dark,' she'd pointed out, as though there was some virtue in arriving there without the benefit of light.

He crept past Mrs Pampanini's door and heard the reassuring murmur of the BBC World Service. On the top floor landing, he reached automatically into his pocket for the key and then withdrew. The hand hung limply at his side. He didn't live here. This had never been his home.

He started to remove his clothes. He took his shoes off, first, and brushed a scuff mark from the toe, before aligning them beside each other. Then he draped the Astrakhan coat carefully across the bannister. Next came the waistcoat, then the trousers. He had thought of emptying the pockets, but to do that would have brought back memories of the fate of others he had known. He did not want to feel that he had been deprived of everything.

He carefully unhooked the bow tie, laying it with an exaggerated gentleness inside one of the shoes. The process of undressing had absorbed him totally until this moment; it was almost as if he were watching someone else. And then he noticed that a speck of dirt had found its way under the cuticle of one of his immaculately manicured nails. He attempted to remove it with the index finger of the other hand. His fingers were like those of a musician, long and pale. It was the one advantage he had over Gregor; he *was* a musician, but he had the podgy fingers of a pugilist. He played the violin like somebody possessed. But then, thought Nathan, his son *was* possessed.

The rim of dirt next to the fragile pink flesh brought him back to the reality of where he was. The light went out again. A button popped off in the darkness and he let out an involuntary yelp. He gripped the rail and climbed onto the narrow ledge. A rush of cold air from the stairwell mingled with the scent of cabbage, which his nostrils registered nostalgically. His palms were skidding on the rail. He let go with one hand to wipe it on the shirt-front and immediately felt his heel begin to slide. He clawed the rail behind him, but his body was already giving in to gravity.

He couldn't have said afterwards if he had jumped or slipped, and probably the truth was somewhere in between. He only knew that this was one decision he would not be able to go back on. As he fell, he was aware of something in the space behind him, of a presence that had not been there before. He registered the fuzzy outline on the second landing as he passed it, diving through the beam of light that came from Mrs Pampanini's flat, masked by the ample figure in her dressing gown. Their eyes met for a fraction of a second before Nathan heard a roaring in his ears and felt the heat behind his eyelids. And then there was silence.

***

Twenty Years Later

'Come on, Gregor, put a bit more effort into it. I've got a seminar in half an hour.'

'We are on the seventh round, you know.'

'I've known you go ten rounds and still be up before the count was over.'

'I was young then.... Jesus, Gloria. I'm done for.' He rolled over on his back. He noticed that the ceiling, though it had been painted white like others in the block, had greyish-yellow patches from the Turkish cigarettes that Gloria smoked constantly and handed out to students when they came for seminars. There were some women in the faculty who doubled up as mother-substitutes but Gloria had made it clear she wasn't one of them.

'You haven't given up?' The sharp point of her elbow made a sideways sally.

Gregor levered himself up onto his elbow and rolled sideways off the bed. 'I've got a train to catch. Christ, what's this?' He picked up a leaking Biro from between the sheets and rubbed the black stain on his chest. 'I hate to say this, Gloria, but you're a real slut.'

'I hate to say this, Gregor, but it's none of your business.'

'I still care about you.'

'Please don't bother.'

Gregor swung his legs onto the carpet and picked up his trousers. A cascade of small change shot out of his pocket. He went down onto his knees and grubbed around whilst Gloria looked on dispassionately. 'You're my next of kin. That must mean something.'

'I can't be your next of kin if we're divorced.'

He scooped the loose change back into his pocket and pulled on his trousers. 'All it means, to be the next of kin, is that you get one bloody phone call when I'm dead.'

'Oh well, in that case....'

He went over to the window, buttoning his shirt over the tight little belly with its fuzz of dark hair. Gloria turned on her side and bunched the pillow underneath her head so she could keep him in her line of sight. She couldn't help feeling a frisson of affection for this ugly little man she'd spent a large part of her academic life in bed with.

She had overheard a colleague liken her to one of Goya's duennas, dragging dwarves around with them to make themselves look beautiful by contrast. Unlike Gregor, Gloria was tall and she did nothing to disguise the fact. Inside the university she always wore her academic gown; she did not want to be mistaken for a woman.

Gregor boasted of her as a siren that had lured his ship onto the rocks and wrecked it, although his proposal eight years earlier had nothing of the ship-wrecked mariner about it.

'We've been happy, haven't we?' he'd argued.

'I'm not sure that happy is the right word. We've been manic, loud, hysterical, abandoned, wanton and disgusting. Does that count as happiness?'

'I think in our case probably it does.'

'Quick, Gloria. Here!' Gregor bent over the sill and rubbed his handkerchief across the pane.

'You want to make love to me across the windowsill?'

'It's her again...outside the buttery.'

Gloria climbed out of bed, unhurriedly, and joined him at the window. She gazed out across the quadrangle. A young girl in a drab brown mackintosh, with what looked like a file of papers underneath her arm, had stopped a student coming in the opposite direction. He looked round and pointed to the block where Gloria had rooms. The girl looked up and Gregor stepped back quickly. Maybe as a consequence of going through life blindly doing what he wanted, he disliked the feeling he was being watched.

'She looks a bit like you,' said Gloria who, unlike Gregor, rather liked it when she was the object of attention. Students passing underneath her window sometimes got a fleeting glimpse of Gloria without a stitch on, staring back at them. They put it down to wish-fulfilment. There weren't many undergraduates of either sex who wouldn't willingly have swapped with Gregor at a moment's notice. With her Amazonian appearance and her autocratic air, she was an object of unbridled fantasy.

'She's nothing like me.' Gregor found himself drawn back towards the window.

'She's got your chin.'

'From here you can't even see her chin.'

'That's what I mean.'

'Did you see that?' The girl had taken a step back onto the lawn that fringed the path. She took a pencil from her pocket and wrote something on the file. 'She's making notes.'

'You think she's researching a thesis on the brilliant Schopenhauer scholar Gregor Silver? Dream on.' Gloria went back to the divan and started searching for her dressing gown amongst the tangled sheets.

When Gregor looked again, the girl had disappeared. 'I wouldn't have these fantasies if we were still together,' he said, grumpily.

'Oh, let's not start on that again. I said I would divorce you if you were unfaithful and you were.' She checked her watch. 'I thought you had a train to catch.'

'Damn.' Gregor pulled his sleeve up. 'I've already missed the ten fifteen.'

'Where are you going, or would it be better not to ask?' Whilst she affected to have lost all interest in what Gregor did when he was not with her, she still preferred to know what she was missing.

'Carter-Brown is taking me to lunch, to talk about the book. I need to call in at The London Library and be in Primrose Hill by six. It's papa's anniversary.'

'You mean today's the day he topped himself. Your mother's organised another of those gruesome dinners, I suppose? No doubt she's doing goulash, so that you can all feel terribly Hungarian.'

'We're Polish, actually, as you well know. These traditions have more weight when you're an exile, Gloria.'

'You'll always be an exile, Gregor. You never bothered joining the human race and now it's too late.' She pulled up the blankets and bumped both the pillows into shape. 'You want someone who understands you and that person happens to be me. Unfortunately, I understand you so well, I would rather not have any more to do with you.'

'That wasn't what you said last night,' said Gregor, petulantly.

'I was drunk,' said Gloria, disarmingly.

'No doubt you would prefer to think I took advantage of you.'

'Yes, I would. It wouldn't be the first time.'

'And it wouldn't be the first time you've been more than happy to be led astray.' He pulled his jacket on. 'I'll pop across when I get back tomorrow. I shall be in need of therapy by then.' He bent over the dressing table to examine his reflection in the mirror. He smoothed out his eyebrows and then looked on as the terse hairs sprang back into their original position, like a thicket halfway up a cliff. The pupils gleamed like lasers underneath them, ready to zap anything that came across their beam. There were whole areas of Gregor's body, he reflected, that were rebel garrisons. He looked at Gloria. The eyebrows were the least of it. It crossed his mind that he might miss the next train, too, and have another go at salvaging his reputation.

'If you mean by 'therapy' what I suppose you mean, I'm sorry but you'll have to look elsewhere for it,' said Gloria. 'I've managed to go back to being normal since I left you.' She piled up the loose hair on her head and stuck a clip in it.

'Gloria, that's most unfair. A lot of what we did was your idea.'

'I don't care whose idea it was. I don't want to do it any more. Anyway, I'm busy tomorrow. I'm expecting somebody.'

'Chol-Mon-Doolally, I suppose?'

She made a hissing sound. 'It's Cholmondeley, as you know full well. 'Chumley,' if you want to pronounce it properly.'

'What's the point of spelling your name Cholmondoolally and then calling yourself Chumley?'

'Anyone who's English knows that you pronounce it 'Chumley.'

'Are you accusing me of being foreign?' Gregor stuck his chin out.

'Frankly, Gregor, I'm not certain what you are, but by the farthest stretch of the imagination you could never pass for English.'

'He does know that you and I still have an understanding, does he?'

'I'm not sure I'd call it that.'

'What would you call it, Gloria?' said Gregor, with a patience that was slightly menacing.

She slipped her arms inside the dressing gown, unhurriedly, and looped the belt so that the last glimpse Gregor got was of the downy furrow in between her legs: 'I'd call it final orders.'

'Meaning?'

'Meaning that was it. From now on, Gregor, if you want to see me it'll have to be in office hours.'

'You'll fit me in round the odd seminar?'

'I'm not concerned to fit you in at all.' She pulled the two halves of the dressing gown together.

'Is this you getting your revenge because for once I couldn't go the full ten rounds?'

'It's typical of you, Gregor, to assume that sex is what this is about.' She sat down at the desk and pulled a pile of notes towards her.

'It's not very typical of you, Gloria, to assume that you can do without it.' Gregor stood his ground, reluctant to depart until he'd won on points.

'Who says I'll be doing without it?' Gloria said, coolly.

'I doubt that CholMonDoolally would be good for anything except the missionary position. You'd soon get bored with that.'

'At the moment, the missionary position would be something of a novelty.'

'You can be a real bitch sometimes, Gloria.'

'I'd get yourself to Primrose Hill if I were you. I'm sure that Wanda will look after you. It is a mother's duty, after all.'

***

'You're saying you will not be here this evening?'

'Yes, of course I'll be here, Wanda.' Mitzi's fingers fluttered nervously up to her neck.

That flimsy scarf she had on, Wanda thought; it was exactly like the one she'd taken out of Mitzi's room a fortnight earlier – a yellow, chiffony affair with purple splashes running through it. It was loosely knotted round her sister's throat and as with everything that Mitzi wore, it seemed to mould itself around her, whereas Wanda felt she had a battle on her hands if she so much as stretched her fingers out towards an object she desired.

'Is anything the matter, Wanda?'

'That scarf….' Wanda spread the butter thinly on a slice of toast and took a prim bite out of it. She wasn't hungry but she needed to go through the motions. She did not want Abel or her sister thinking she was nervous.

Mitzi's fingers wandered to the scarf, self-consciously. Too late, she realised what she'd done. She rubbed the ends between her fingers, as if hoping she could make them vanish.

Wanda eyed the scarf obliquely. Maybe Mitzi had replaced the one she'd taken, or perhaps…. No, it was probably just similar in colour. Mitzi had a drawerful of them – little bits of frippery that had so little substance, they served merely to reflect her sister's own transparency. If Mitzi knew about the sewing room, she would not be so reckless as to wear the scarf in front of her.

'Is that the costume you'll have on, this evening?' she said, critically. 'It's rather colourful, I would have thought, considering the circumstances.'

'Yes, of course. I'll change when I get home,' said Mitzi.

'Which is when?' asked Wanda, going back to the discussion they'd been having quarter of an hour earlier.

'I should be back by half past six, if I can get away on time. It's only that the students are expecting me. I wouldn't want to let them down.'

'But you do not mind letting me down?' Wanda got up from the table. She moved Mitzi's plate to one side, to make space, and went to fetch the tray of cutlery for polishing. She needed to be doing something. She eased out the drawer in short jerks. It stuck halfway and she thumped the dresser, to release it.

Abel put his cup down. Wanda saw the glance that passed between her sister and her son. She took an inward breath and held it. It was no use. She was feeling agitated and the day had barely started.

'Eat your breakfast, Abel.'

'I am eating it.'

'You vill get indigestion reading at the table.'

Abel closed the book. He pulled up his sleeve to check the time. He wished that Mitzi wouldn't endlessly keep trying to excuse herself. It only made things worse.

'It's just a pity that this year the anniversary is on a Monday when the students have their evening class,' said Mitzi, meekly.

Wanda tossed her head: 'Perhaps if you had asked him, Nathan would have died on Tuesday to fit in with your arrangements. Gregor can come all the way from Oxford and be here by six o'clock, but you will not be here until six thirty. Well, so be it.'

Mitzi didn't answer. If the letter hadn't come she might have got one of the other models to stand in for her. This one was different from the others she'd received. The words themselves weren't threatening, but beneath them Mitzi sensed a growing agitation.

This one would require an answer. If she hadn't been distracted by the letter, she would never have selected that scarf from the drawer this morning.

'I must go. I'm sorry, Wanda.' She took Abel's plate, to stack it in the sink.

He handed her his cup. 'I'll walk down with you,' he said quickly. He had also registered the scarf and wondered briefly whether Mitzi was deliberately trying to provoke her sister.

'You'll be home in time this evening, Abel?' said his mother, sharply.

Abel hesitated. 'I've arranged to have a drink with Cressida after the library closes. I was wondering whether to invite her over.'

'You would ask a stranger to our anniversary?'

'She's not a stranger. We've been friends for ages. It would be an opportunity for you to meet her.'

'But the anniversary,' said Wanda, trying not to let the anger creep into her voice. 'Is this the right time?'

'It's the only chance she'd have of meeting Gregor,' Abel pointed out, although he was aware that this might not be such a good idea. His brother would enjoy her company, but that was not the point. He knew from past experience that Gregor usually took possession of the things he liked.

'You've mentioned the reunion to her already?' Wanda looked at him, accusingly.

'It isn't that exclusive, is it? Gloria's been several times with Gregor.'

'Gloria was family; we had no choice.' She laid the knives out in a row, exerting pressure on them like a parent anxious to impress upon a child the need to stay exactly where it was. Her lips were drawn in. 'She will come to gawp,' said Wanda, as the funnel of her anger rose up from her lungs into her throat. She tipped the drawer up on its end and the remaining knives slid out onto the table with a clatter.

Abel calmly took his jacket from the armchair. 'All right,' he said, carelessly.

She looked up: 'What?'

'All right, I'll tell her not to come.' He slipped his book into the pocket.

Wanda cast about her, looking for a way out. 'You cannot invite her and then tell her not to come.'

He shrugged. 'Why not? I'll say that you're uneasy about having strangers in to join us.'

'No,' said Wanda, darkly. 'You cannot say that.'

'Of course I can. That is the reason, after all.' He wound the scarf around his neck.

'It would be rude to say so.' Wanda turned towards the dresser. Abel saw her face reflected in the glass and registered the battle going on behind it. He would let his mother off the hook, but not before he'd turned the screw another notch. 'There's no point in her coming if she's made to feel uncomfortable.'

'Why should she feel uncomfortable?'

'She might get the impression that you didn't want her there.'

There was a pause. 'You are making a big thing of this, Abel.' Wanda shrugged dismissively. 'You have invited her; she must now come.' She looked towards the landing as if half-expecting to see Nathan standing there. 'We have to hope your poor dead father will not mind.'

***

Outside the flat door, Abel waited whilst his aunt pulled on her jacket. Normally he kept his gaze turned from the shrine when he was going in or out, but he was drawn towards the covered table with its photograph and candles, in the way that empty houses draw the living to them out of loneliness. In spite of being on their doorstep, Nathan's shrine had a forsaken air about it. The red ribbon tied around the bannister was faded, like those flags on buildings that have weathered wind and rain. But this one hadn't been exposed to anything. It was the lack of contact with the elements that had destroyed it.

When they came back in the evening, Wanda would have lit the candles and the hall would reek of incense. Did he really want this to be Cressida's first introduction to his family? He went on down the stairs and Mitzi clattered after him, the sound of her heels reverberating like the rat-tat-tat of a machine gun in the silence.

When he was a small boy, Abel used the vast space of the hall for roller-skating. He was not allowed to play outside without a chaperone and this was the nearest he could get to being free. He sped in circles round the stairwell, working up fantastic speeds till all he was aware of was air rushing past him and the vibrant rumble of the wheels under his feet.

After his father's suicide, he couldn't play there any more. He'd tried, once, but the harsh sound of the metal wheels on their exposed ball-bearings, once so thrilling, conjured up an image of his father's body being trampled underfoot. Conversely, he imagined the sound adding to his father's torments in the draughty halls of Purgatory, to which those who had cheated death by meeting it half-way, were relegated.

Mitzi had caught up with him. She slid her arm through his companionably as they crossed the landing outside Mrs Pampanini's door. 'It would be nice if you could bring your friend this evening.'

'Would it?'

'Don't take too much notice of your mother, Abel. She's just anxious.'

Given how much notice Mitzi took of her, thought Abel, it was rather rich of her to counsel him. 'I don't know if she'll come or not,' he said. 'She was a bit vague.'

'Have you known her long?'

'About six months. She came into the library. She's a student at the art school.'

'Really' Mitzi said, excitedly. 'Perhaps I know her.'

Abel instantly regretted passing on this confidence. He wasn't sure that Mitzi was the best ambassador between himself and Cressida. 'Perhaps,' he said, 'But it's still early days. I wouldn't want to frighten her away.'

'No. No, of course not,' she said, wistfully. 'I won't say anything.'

'I didn't mean that.' He saw Mitzi had been wounded by the inference and he tried clumsily to make good. 'If she comes this evening, I can introduce you properly.'

'That would be lovely.' Mitzi smiled.

They parted at the bus-stop. Abel gave his aunt a quick peck on the cheek. She glanced up at the window of the flat and then took off along a side-street to the college. Mitzi never walked. She might not know where she was going, but she was always in a rush to get there. Abel wished that he could summon up the same enthusiasm.

***

Wanda watched as Abel and her sister crossed the road together. She was trembling on the inside of her skin. But maybe after all, she had been wrong about the scarf. And was it really likely that a total stranger would choose an occasion like tonight to introduce themselves? I'm getting upset over nothing, she thought. Abel said these things to tease her, sometimes. She felt calmer now that she was by herself, although she always felt a trace of panic as the door closed and she listened to the footsteps disappearing down the staircase. Maybe this time, like her husband, they would not come back.

But Nathan had come back. For twenty years he hadn't left the house. He was more hers now than he had been when he was alive. When Wanda thought about the rendezvous she was about to keep with her beloved husband, she felt almost skittish. She had spent the whole year looking forward to this day and she would not let it be spoilt by anyone.

She crossed the hall to Abel's room. She needed to reclaim the space inside the flat as hers, before she launched into the preparations for the evening. Abel's bedroom hadn't changed much since he was eleven. On the shelf above the desk there was a model aeroplane that he had made with Nathan's help when he was seven. There were half a dozen reproductions on the pin-board and a

London Transport poster he had brought home from the library, with a 1930's couple gazing from the window of a train across the sand dunes of a seaside town. Two rows of pens were lined up neatly on the desk beside a file of papers. Wanda gave the notes a brief glance. Abel had no secrets from his mother. On the bedside table was a single library book. The shelves were neatly stacked with others. Even the waste-paper basket had an ordered air to it.

By contrast, Mitzi's room resembled a theatrical costumier's. There wasn't an uncluttered surface anywhere. Clothes – blouses, skirts, odd stockings, pumps, leg-warmers, belts and scarves spilled out of drawers. The dressing table was awash with lipsticks, perfume bottles, bracelets, creams. When Wanda pulled a drawer half out, the contents seemed to swell and overflow as if they'd come to life and were intent on sharing the anarchic freedom of their comrades.

Wanda stuffed them back inside the drawer and closed it briskly. Mitzi's wardrobe had the same propensity as some sea creatures. If a star-fish lost a tentacle, it simply grew another one. If Mitzi noticed there was something missing from her wardrobe, she would just assume that she had left it in the dressing cubicle inside the studio, or on a bus. She wouldn't think to look inside the sewing room, which was the place of ultimate retreat for Wanda. She kept this space strictly for emergencies, aware that like a friend whose sympathy might finally run out, she ought to ration her demands on it.

She stepped back, closing Mitzi's door, then opening it a fraction, as she'd found it. Stopping to collect a broom, she went onto the landing and began to briskly sweep the floor around the shrine. She nudged the pile of dust towards the edge and then with one quick movement pushed it through the iron bars of the bannisters and watched the dust motes slowly and majestically float down into the stairwell, tumbling through a beam of sunlight from the lantern in the roof as they descended. She imagined Nathan's body floating earthwards on the dust-motes, like the Holy Spirit from a cloud in a Renaissance painting. She enjoyed this moment in the ritual. It seemed to sanctify the mindless horror of her husband's action that night twenty years ago.

She brushed the stray dust off the ribbon, tightening the bow. The loops appeared to perk up for an instant, only to subside again. Soon she would have to think about replacing it, but she did not like change and she was sure that Nathan, too, would rather be without it. Reverently, she picked up the shoes and carried them into the flat. She laid a sheet of paper on the kitchen table, placing the shoes side by side, the heels towards her. Moving slowly and deliberately, she fetched the polish from the kitchen cupboard and put out two dusters. Dabbing a little polish on the cloth, she slid her hand into the right shoe and began to smooth the polish on the toe. She felt a tremour of excitement, thinking of her hand inside the shoe where once his foot had been. It was as if a part of her had entered him.

'Well, Nathan,' she said, 'here we are again. There's not a great deal to report. It is a year since we saw Gregor, but that's no great loss. At least he won't be bringing Gloria this year. It seems that Abel has a girlfriend, but he does not talk about her much. I do not think that this is serious. Next week he will be thirty-one; too old for girlfriends. As for Mitzi, well what can one say?' She rubbed the shoe a little harder. She could see her face reflected in the patent leather uppers, now. The shoes were still in good condition. He had taken great care of his clothes. When she first met him, Wanda had assumed it was because he only had the one suit and a pair of shoes to match it, but she found that it was in his nature to take care of things.

So why had he not taken care of her? She pressed her lips together. If she gave vent to her spleen now, he might turn away from her, the way he had in life. She finished polishing the shoes in silence and then, carrying them back on to the landing, she aligned them side by side, exactly in the spot where she had found them that day twenty years ago. The candles in their holders waited one on each side of the large framed photograph. She'd never liked the photograph, but she had not been able to find anything more suitable. It had been taken on their wedding day. The eyes seemed to be sliding sideways, as if they were trying to avoid her, and the fleshy lips emerging from the auburn beard reminded Wanda of a well-bred satyr.

'You betrayed me, Nathan,' she said, trying unsuccessfully to catch his eye. She couldn't stifle her resentment any longer. 'Why?' She bunched her fist against her heart. The eyes looked vaguely back at her, as if the question were irrelevant.

'Tch'. She uncurled her fingers in a gesture of dismissal. If he wouldn't tell her at the time, it wasn't likely he would tell her now. She aimed the spray at him and scrubbed the glass as if it were a scratch card with a winning number underneath. Each year it was the same; as if the past had held itself in check for twelve months and was rattling the cage bars to be let out on a rampage of attrition.

As she let go of the photograph, it shuddered and collapsed onto the table with a muted 'thwack'. She jerked her hand back. With exaggerated self-control, she propped it up again, and then her fingers curled around the frame and she leant forward, as if her whole body needed its support.

'You were the only man I ever loved!' she uttered, helplessly. He didn't answer. Wanda closed her eyes a second and then briskly she restored the photograph to its original position, giving it a final curt flick with the duster before moving on. 'You could at least have kept your trousers on to jump. Imagine letting Mrs Pampanini see you in your underwear like that. A good thing she is half blind.'

She smoothed out a wrinkle in the cloth. The hyacinths at each end of the table were already giving out their slightly rancid scent. The first year, Mitzi had brought home a bunch of poppies that had shed their black seeds and provoked an argument that escalated out of all proportion. As she ranted, calling up oaths in her native tongue that she had not heard since she left the ghetto, Wanda knew that it was not the spilt seeds on the clean white cloth that had provoked her outburst. They were just a catalyst. Her rage had been for Nathan, for the ease with which he had slipped off out of their lives and left them: Wanda, doomed to celibacy for the rest of her existence, shackled to her sister; Gregor who was living proof of the abomination that had spawned their marriage; and the fragile Abel, product of a single night of love, in whose sad eyes she saw her husband's.

'They are weeds' she'd shouted, banging her hand down onto the table so that any seeds remaining in the poppies were immediately shaken out onto the cloth. 'And they are dying! Look! They shed their seeds!' She'd glared at Mitzi's shocked face. Abel, terrified by this eruption of his mother's anger, whimpered in the background.

Gregor had come sauntering past: 'Nice poppies,' he remarked, before he disappeared into his own room.

'Take them!' Wanda had insisted. 'Take them to the rubbish bin. I will not have them here.'

There was a pause, then Mitzi gathered up the poppies in her arms and carried them away into the scullery. The next year nobody had interfered. The hyacinths stood bobbly and erect, like sentries on each side of Nathan's photograph, their prissy flowers with their tiny stamens like pursed lips. She'd known that Mitzi hated them and she rejoiced. The shrine was hers.

***

There were no vacant seats inside the bus and Abel held onto the rail with one hand, folding back the pages of his 'Madame Bovary' so he could hold it in the other. It had rained that morning and the dampness mingled with the cheap scent emanating, like a misty sauna, from a woman in a raincoat standing next to him. The smell reminded Abel of the heavy, oak interior of Mitzi's wardrobe and the afternoon he'd spent in there with Gregor. After quarter of a century he could still smell the perfume of her dresses, tinctured with the bitter smell of camphor.

It was Gregor who had started it, of course. For weeks his brother had been disappearing into Mitzi's room when she was out. When Abel asked him what he did there, Gregor had invited him to find out. Mitzi left the college at five-thirty unless she was booked to stay on for an evening class. That afternoon, when Abel was supposedly completing an assignment on The Hundred Years War for his homework, Gregor put his head around the door and gestured him to follow. They crept down the corridor to Mitzi's room. Occasionally, Abel had spent afternoons with Mitzi in her room when he was little. She would let him try on clothes of hers and listen to the gramophone, but he had never been in there without an invitation.

Gregor had gone over to the wardrobe and pulled back the fur coats on their hangers, to make space. They sat there in the darkness, Abel wondering if he wouldn't rather having been finishing off his assignment in his own room.

'I can't breathe,' he whispered.

'Shut up,' Gregor felt inside his trouser pocket for an aniseed ball, which he shoved in Abel's mouth. For the remainder of his life he would associate the company of women with the mustiness of cupboards and the heady scent of aniseed. After a pause that seemed to Abel to go on forever, they had heard the bedroom door click open. In the darkness, he had just been able to make out his brother with his eye pressed up against a fissure in the wood. He saw there was a chink of light next to his own head and looked through the gap. He heard the scratchy melody of a Rossini overture, with Mitzi's voice accompanying the libretto. She stood for a moment at the window before throwing down her coat. She did a few twirls round the room and sank down in the armchair.

Abel felt uncomfortable. What if she had decided to hang up the coat instead of throwing it across the chair? Apart from shock at finding her two nephews in the wardrobe, Abel knew she would be disappointed. He had never known her angry or censorious. She wasn't bitter like his mother or resentful because life had let her down. She wouldn't point out that it was bad manners to go into someone's room when they weren't there and then not to declare themselves. She would just look at him with that expression of bewilderment she'd worn when they discovered Nathan's body in the stairwell, as if it was she who was at fault because she hadn't understood. He wondered whether he would be less guilty if he closed his eyes.

A moment later, when he opened them again, he saw that Mitzi was no longer in the armchair. She had moved out of his line of vision, but now she moved into it again. She'd started to take off her clothes. There was a full-length mirror in the wardrobe door and Mitzi stood in front of it.

She threw her head back, gazing sleepily at her reflection with her eyes half-closed. The blouse she had been wearing, slid provocatively from her shoulders and she let it fall onto the floor. Her fingers moved down to her waist and Abel heard the faint 'whoosh' of the zip before the skirt slipped down over her thighs and joined the heap of clothes at Mitzi's feet. She let her left leg sag a little, emphasising the prolonged curve of her body on the right side.

'Gosh,' said Abel, weakly. Suddenly he felt an urgent need to pee. He'd looked at Gregor crouching next to him, his face a mask of stillness with the concentrated stare he wore whatever he was doing, even if he wasn't doing anything. He'd pressed his eye up to the crack again. He wasn't sure what any of it meant. It brought back memories of the pantomimes that Mitzi sometimes took him to at Christmas, which he'd never liked much. He'd suspected that the characters dressed up as women, were in fact men. One year, he had noticed that the Dame had a moustache. He'd tugged at Mitzi's elbow: 'It's a man,' he whispered.

'Yes, dear,' Mitzi had responded, smiling, as if men pretended to be women all the time. After an hour, he had felt like crying. When the audience began to shout and throw their popcorn at the Dame, he'd wanted to go home.

As Mitzi went on swaying to and fro in front of him, he'd focused on the pendulating breasts and raised pink nipples that were not quite level. They'd looked suddenly like eyes that squinted in two different directions. Abel knew that if they came much closer to him, he would scream.

There was a pause whilst Mitzi put another record on the gramophone. She did a final turn before the mirror and then, reaching for her wrap, she'd left the room.

The bus lurched round a corner and the sudden jolt threw Abel forwards. He clutched blindly at the rail and fumbled for his season ticket. The conductor nodded. Abel went back to his book, but didn't bother turning any of the pages. He pretended to be reading so that nobody would speak to him. There had been one appalling morning when the senior librarian, Miss Quettock, had got on the same bus and he'd had to talk to her for four stops. He would rather spend a month in Mitzi's wardrobe in the dark than go through that again.

It was odd, Abel thought, how one's life seemed to hinge upon a scattering of moments that had no significance to anybody else. He didn't think that Gregor had the least compunction about what they'd done, but from that day on Abel felt he had lost Mitzi as an ally. You could not confide in someone you had spied on secretly, whose fantasies had been laid out before you like a scattering of gewgaws on a market stall. After his father's suicide, she had seemed even less approachable. She was a wraith inside the house where once she had been an amazing splash of colour. He had felt her anguish as a mute but tactile presence in the air. Confronted with such steadfast grief, he felt inhibited. He spoke to nobody and neither, he supposed, did Mitzi.

***

Mitzi ran along the corridor and turned into the studio. It was a vast, light room with benches ranged along the walls. She saw that Mr Harpur was already there, arranging a green cloth on the podium to look like grass. The project of the day was Manet's 'Déjeuner sur l'Herbe.' She had been looking forward to it all week. Mr Harpur had explained the plot to her. She was to be the naked woman at the picnic. They would have to do without the two male figures in contemporary costume. Mr Harpur pointed out the toad beside the picnic hamper in the reproduction and the chaffinch flying through the trees above. They symbolised the spirit and the baser passions, he said.

Mitzi loved these stories. She clung onto them long after she had stepped down from the podium. She sometimes thought the unseen pull of gravity had drawn her in under the drop stone portico that day as she went past the college on her way home from the council offices. Although it added half an hour to her journey in the evening, Mitzi often made the detour simply for the pleasure of imagining herself a part of the community she caught a glimpse of as she passed the swing doors.

She had seen the models come and go. They stood out from the students with their dyed hair and their raucous laughter. They had a determined swagger, a defiance that she rather envied. They were neither young, nor beautiful, and this had given Mitzi courage. Following them up the steps one day, she'd found a world that mirrored perfectly the one inside her head.

'I've got a new job,' she'd said, cautiously, a few days later.

Wanda had continued ladling food onto their plates. The fourteen year old Gregor sat in silence, frowning at the salt as if he were engaged in working out the square root of the grains. 'I've signed up as a model at the art school. You remember, Wanda, it was where I'd hoped to study.'

Wanda's serving spoon had seemed to levitate above the casserole. Was there some criticism of herself implied in Mitzi's use of the past participle in reference to her hopes? All Wanda had done was suggest that art was not a proper path for her to follow and that, since she was responsible for Mitzi's welfare in the absence of their father, she hoped that would be the end of it. She handed round the plates and took her place at table. 'Go on.'

'They have tableaux, reconstructions of the great works of the past. You know, the 'Odalisque,' the 'Primavera'...'

Wanda smoothed the serviette across her knees: 'And what will you be wearing in these tableaux?' she'd asked, pointedly.

There was a long pause. Mitzi drew her top lip in between her teeth. 'I won't be wearing anything,' she whispered.

Gregor had let out a short, ferocious laugh that Wanda countered with a slap around the ears.

'The students need to draw the figure, Wanda. It's a useful occupation.'

'You were doing something useful in the council offices.'

'Anyone could do that,' Mitzi said, resentfully.

'You're saying that not everyone can take their clothes off? Are there men in this class?'

'Yes, of course.'

'And are you not ashamed to speak of this in front of Abel.' She had glanced at him protectively whilst Gregor kicked him underneath the table. 'When do you begin this...new job?'

'I've already started. I've been there since Monday.'

'You did not think it would be appropriate to let us know?' She looked at Mitzi coldly. 'Nathan you agree with me. She must give in her notice. You can say you were mistaken, Mitzi, that you thought the job was something else.'

'No, Wanda, I can't do that.'

'Don't forget that you are living now in my house,' Wanda had said, ominously.

Nathan looked up sharply. 'Wanda, I don't think you need to threaten Mitzi. She should be allowed to choose her own career.'

'You think that taking off the clothes is a career?'

'I wish you wouldn't keep on talking like that,' Mitzi broke in, 'as if that was all it was. If Marthe hadn't taken off her clothes for Bonnard, we would not have had his painting of her in the bath. If Rembrandt's wife had been too busy keeping house to pose for him, we wouldn't have his picture of Diana...'

'They were married women,' Wanda interrupted. 'They were working for their husbands. It was not a prostitution.'

'Are you saying that's what I am?' Mitzi had half-risen from the table. She heard Abel whisper to his brother.

'What's a prostitute?'

'It's a woman who wears clicky heels and bright red lipstick. They have handbags that they wave at you. And then they ask you if you want a good time. But you have to pay them.'

'Gregor you will stop that!' Wanda had commanded.

But for Mitzi it had been the final insult. Scraping back her chair, she'd rushed out of the room.

The only person who reflected Mitzi's own conviction that to be an artist's model was a noble calling had been Mr Harpur. Listening to him paying tribute to the contour of her ankle or the hollow of her neck, she felt the separate parts of her had an aesthetic value even if the whole did not.

'Ah, there you are, Miss Brzeska.' Mr Harpur went to stand up.

'Please don't get up, Mr Harpur,' Mitzi urged. 'I'll go into the changing room. Do carry on with what you're doing.'

She took off her coat inside the cubicle and hung it on the nail. The changing room was small and only separated from the studio beyond it by a fraying curtain, but she felt a calmness when she entered it, like a dog in its kennel finally in control of its own small world. She started to undress and hang her clothes up on the hanger, smoothing out the little waistcoat with its vivid cross-stitch. She had been discouraged from appearing in such outfits in the council offices. 'We're trying to impress the public with our seriousness, after all,' the head clerk had said one day, asking her if she could 'tone it down a bit.' But toning down was not in Mitzi's nature. She was drawn to colour like a bee towards a flower. At twenty-four, her wardrobe had a slightly risqué air about it; by the time she got to thirty, she was like an orange-crested hoopoe, a rare, antiquated bird of many colours threatening to become extinct.

She stuffed the scarf under the cushion on the chair. It would be better if she wasn't wearing it when she went home that evening. Hopefully, her sister would have been too busy with the preparations to remember it. She eased her feet into the little Chinese slippers and gazed for a moment at the pattern on the worn red carpet Mr Harpur had provided. He'd been very kind to Mitzi in those early days. She'd hoped to have a chance to speak to him about the letter before anybody else arrived, but she could hear the students shuffling chairs and easels outside. She would have to wait.

She slipped the envelope into the pocket of her dressing gown and drew the curtain back. She didn't feel the least qualm about taking off her clothes; she'd found that being naked left you free to put on any skin you liked. As soon as she took up the pose, she would be Victorine Meurent. She climbed onto the podium and sat down on the grass, one elbow on her knee, the other leg bent at an angle underneath her, gazing out defiantly at the spectator as her predecessor had.

'If you could move your big toe just a fraction to the right,' said Mr Harpur, looking at her with his head on one side. 'It's important that it's in the centre. It's the axis, so to speak.' She moved her foot obligingly.

A couple of the students wandered round the platform looking at her first from one side, then the other, as they might have wandered round a buffet before choosing what to put onto their plates. She heard the soothing sound of Mr Harpur humming snatches from 'Die Rosenkavalier.' The sound reminded her of insects gathering at dusk. She liked it, but the students found it irritating. When he wasn't there, they mimicked him and when he was, they laughed behind his back. How many generations had passed by this podium since Mitzi first stepped onto it, a quarter of a century ago? And all of them had treated Mr Harpur with the same contempt. There was a rumour that he had been married once. The students speculated that his wife had died of boredom on their honeymoon in some Byzantine chapel in the Caucasus.

Once, when she'd been invited to his house in Golders Green for afternoon tea, Mitzi had been shown a photograph of Mr Harpur as a young man with a woman standing next to him whom she supposed must be the lost wife, but she hadn't liked to ask. She'd seen the look of absolute devotion that the camera had intercepted, though. She knew that Mr Harpur's wife would not have left him unless death had taken her away. Here, Mitzi sensed, were those two forces – tragedy and romance – that had wrecked her own life so decisively.

She'd moved on round the room, occasionally picking up an object to admire at closer quarters and then carefully replacing it. The parlour overflowed with just the kind of knick-knacks that were irresistible to Mitzi and anathema to a cleaning lady - shells and fossils from the coast of Italy, volcanic rocks from Ischia, trays of pumpkins, gourds and lacquered fruits, their colours muted by the dust that lay across them.

Wanda wouldn't have such things in Primrose Hill. 'What is the point of food you can't eat?' she'd protested.

'But they're beautiful to look at, Wanda.'

Wanda's look implied that Mitzi was a child who did not know the way the adult world worked. So the flat in Primrose Hill was bare of anything that could not justify its presence. Mitzi had begun to wonder whether this might be a category that she fell into. After Nathan's death, her presence in the flat had seemed increasingly precarious. She felt she was there under sufferance; that in some way Wanda blamed her for her husband's death.

And why not? Mitzi thought. It had been her fault after all.

Exactly twenty years ago, she'd stood on this spot with tears rolling down her face. That morning they'd been doing Botticelli's Venus, borne ashore by wind gods. She'd been practising the role all week, rehearsing in the full-length mirror in her bedroom. She knew Botticelli had been hounded for his decadence. He'd had a nervous breakdown at the end of his career and gone back to Nativities.

'There were a lot of artists like that,' Mr Harpur told her. 'They were thrilled by the discoveries of the Renaissance, but they had a medieval attitude to God. They couldn't cope. Poor Michelangelo was just the same.' He'd said 'poor Michelangelo' as if he were a close friend. Mitzi almost felt she knew him.

She had tried to occupy her mind with thoughts like this, to put a barrier between herself and what she'd done. But it was no use. She had felt pain everywhere. Her heart had splintered and the separate shards had taken root inside her head, her breasts, her legs. A lump had started forming in her throat. I mustn't cry, she'd thought, but it was too late. Tears had started running down her cheeks.

***

When she had finished on the landing, Wanda took the dusters and the jars of polish back into the flat and set about preparing for the evening as if she were putting on a banquet for a Head of State. She waxed the great oak table in the parlour and then took the silverware she'd put out earlier that morning, wiping each piece individually before aligning it. Then came the cruet and the oil, the water jug, the glasses, finally the plates, all carefully positioned on the table. Wanda was incapable of leaving anything to chance. She'd seen how easily things slipped away from you. Trust no one, she'd decided. Put your faith in things, in rituals.

She still felt agitated by the thought of Abel and that friend of his. Ought she to lay a place for her, or not? In ramming home the message that this was a family affair and not a free for all, she risked upsetting Abel, the one person whose support she could not do without.

Whilst she would normally have been preoccupied to wonder how she could get rid of Abel's latest girlfriend, it occurred to her that this year she could probably rely on Gregor to achieve this for her if he wasn't bringing Gloria.

'You won't be bringing Gloria?' she'd asked when Gregor telephoned, her voice betraying her relief.

'No.'

'Why not?' Wanda asked suspiciously, prepared to be insulted if she thought the circumstances called for it.

'She doesn't want to come.'

'She doesn't want to come. What is this? She is family. She is obliged to come.'

'She isn't family and so she's not obliged to come.'

'What do you mean?'

'She isn't bloody coming. What more do you need to know? Just count on one less for the goulash.'

Wanda smiled triumphantly into the telephone receiver. She did not hold with divorce but Gloria was the exception. Wanda found her daughter-in-law's brusque air and her healthy appetite repellent and that name 'Van Arend' clearly had a German root.

She'd overheard them on the landing that day when he'd brought her down the first time. Peering through the spy hole in the front door, Wanda saw her fingering the hyacinths to see if they were real and sizing up the shrine, incredulously.

'Are you saying this is where he did it? Christ Almighty, Gregor, it's bizarre.'

'Don't look at me I didn't have a hand in it.'

'What's in the pot?'

'His ashes.'

'Can I look?'

'For God's sake, Gloria, you're making a career of this.'

She'd gazed into the stairwell, as if still expecting to see Nathan lying on the pavers down below. 'What do you suppose it's like, to kill yourself?'

'I should imagine it's quite thrilling, till you hit the bottom.'

'How long would it take?'

'About three seconds.'

No, thought Wanda, she did not like Gloria. She did not warm to any of her son's friends. And she warmed to Gregor least of all. She wasn't certain why he still came every year to the reunion. It wasn't as if he held any of them in affection, or that he revered the memory of his father. She did not think he was capable of either feeling and she was surprised when he capitulated to her wishes and still more surprised when he continued doing so. It was a penance she exacted, an expression of the only power she had over him.

He took revenge in other ways, of course. She'd heard him goading Abel one year when he came down, after Abel's sixteenth birthday.

'Time you got away from here,' she had heard Gregor say. 'The place is getting to you.'

'But I can't leave mutti,' Abel had protested.

'Oh, for God's sake, Abel. She's got Mitzi.'

'But she's always criticising Mitzi.'

'That's the way they are. That's the relationship they have with one another. They had it before you came and they'll have it after you've gone. They'll get by, Abel. Do you really want to stay here all your life and rot?'

'The trouble is she loves me,' Abel had said, innocently.

'Are you sure?'

'Of course I am. She would be lost without me.'

'Bunny, you can be lost if you turn the wrong way down the High Street.'

In the hall, the clock struck nine with an emaciated echo. Wanda went into the kitchen and turned on the radio in time to hear the final chimes. She fancied she could hear the sound of Big Ben drifting from Westminster, echoing a fraction of a second later on the radio.

She stood beside the window, waiting for the pause that always followed. She was glad they'd settled on the top floor when they came to Primrose Hill; she liked to stand there looking out without the threat of anybody looking in. Officially, the block of flats was in the curtilage of Camden, but when Wanda heard that only half a mile away the residents were living in a place called Primrose Hill, she switched the boundaries to incorporate the flat. To live on 'Primrose Hill' after the horrors of the Warsaw ghetto was like waking from a nightmare to discover that the sun was shining.

Wanda held her breath and waited for the calmly modulated voice. 'This is the nine o'clock news and this is Alvar Liddell reading it.' She did not listen to the News in order to discover what was happening in the world; she didn't care about the world. But there was something in the voices of the people reading it that made her feel secure. They were so imperturbable, so unemphatic, even when they relayed news of terrible disasters. She remembered hearing on the BBC World Service that the ghetto where she had last seen her mother, had been sealed off and was under siege. There was no comment on what this might mean for those inside, no outrage in the voice, no sense that this was an event that called for action.

It must be all right then, she thought. Later, when they'd talked about the weather, it was in the same voice. Wanda had been lulled by it. There might be earthquakes, genocides and coups in Africa, eruptions of volcanoes off the coast of Italy and hurricanes in the Pacific. Any danger had been siphoned off before it got to her. The flat was Wanda's refuge from the world. The house had more rooms than they needed, but political uncertainty and sitting tenants on the first two floors had brought the price within their reach. She'd known the minute she set foot in it that here the past was safe.

How different it might all have been, she thought, if Nathan hadn't died. But once you started saying 'if' there was no end to it. If their mother hadn't disobeyed her husband, she might still be with them. If their father hadn't left America before the war to travel back to Poland, they would not have been there on the station that day, fighting to get on the last train out of Warsaw. No one in their right mind left America in 1930, least of all to travel back to Eastern Europe. On the quay, they had met knots of immigrants who looked at Jakob with a fascinated incredulity when he revealed that he was going in the opposite direction. Even as a seven year old, it occurred to Wanda that perhaps this wasn't such a good idea.

When Jakob saw the poverty and dullness of their chosen city, she'd felt even his enthusiasm start to waver. Warsaw had an edginess about it. There were riots in the streets; political campaigners demonstrated rather more assertively than they had done in Iowa. The skills he had brought back with him were highly valued, but he found that as a Jew he was restricted in the application of them. In America he had got used to thinking of himself as middle-class and he was hurt that anti-Semitism seemed to be a middle-class phenomenon. Disenchantment made him restless. It was Sophie's family, after all, who'd come from Warsaw. His had moved into Bavaria a century before. He didn't even speak the language properly. His name was Polish, but beyond that he epitomised the Wandering Jew. Wherever Jakob was, after a year or two he would decide that it was time to move on.

Wanda's mother was the opposite. The minute they stopped anywhere, she would begin accumulating things around her, humping chairs back from the flea-market, a carved wooden cradle for the next child, paintings that purported to be antique, from which paint flaked indiscriminately, china dogs that flanked the clock at each end of the mantelpiece. 'You shackle me with your possessions!' Jakob raged and Wanda, overhearing him, knew that the time had come again to move on.

'Wanda, take the coat for mutti'. Those had been her mother's last words. They were almost at the station. It had still been dark when they set out, but now the streets were packed with hoards of sweating, overloaded families, crying babies, young men carrying their cases on their heads and frail old people clinging to each other for support. Her mother suddenly let out a wail. They stopped. Her father's case slid off his back onto the pavement.

'Halt mich fest,' he growled. 'What is it now?'

'The letters, Jakob. papi's letters. They're still in the bureau.'

Jakob rolled his eyes. 'Forget the letters. Let's get on.' He bent to heave the suitcase back onto his shoulders.

Sophie gripped his arm: 'Please, Jakob. I can't leave without them.'

'Are you mad? You want to go back three kilometres, to fetch a pile of letters? No!'

But Sophie was already taking off her coat. 'I'll run.' She'd turned to Wanda.

'Sophie, I forbid it.' The exasperation in her father's voice was laced with fear. 'There might not be another train. Don't do this.'

Wanda looked between them. Jakob might have been the stronger of the two, but he was no match for her mother. Sophie was already backing off into the crowd, her eyes bright, her face vacantly expectant, like a page that she was waiting for HER story to be written on. For as long as Wanda could remember, they'd been going somewhere, but this was the first time Sophie had gone on her own.

She's leaving us, she thought, instinctively. She's leaving us for a pile of letters that aren't even hers. Her mother handed Wanda her fur coat. She wore another one beneath it. In the cardboard suitcase Wanda carried, there were spare vests, pens, a waterproof, an English phrase book, socks. In Mitzi's small attaché case, there was a doll, a spare frock and a comforter. She'd brought an extra set of clothes, but these were for the doll. A piece of string attached the case to Mitzi's wrist. Another, on the other wrist, attached her to her sister.

Wanda took the coat and slid her arms into the sleeves. The fur coat trailed along the ground. She'd felt like some old dowager. Her mother disappeared into the crowd. Wanda went on staring after her unblinkingly, as if her fixed gaze were a rope to which her mother would stay tethered. No one spoke. They waited, Jakob muttering to himself, Mitzi sucking the finger she had managed to poke through a loose stitch in her mitten, Wanda listening to the ticking of the clock in Sophie's suitcase. It had been passed on to them by Sophie's grandfather. The clock did not like travelling and had stopped twice on the way to Europe. Jakob had been all for leaving it behind. The laboured ticking with its slight whirr, like a chuckle, undermined his confidence.

They heard a whistle in the distance. Wanda saw her father struggling with himself. He caught her eye and glanced away. As people pushed past, it became more difficult to hold their ground. At last he picked the suitcase up and hoisted it onto his shoulders. Once they'd joined the crowd, there was no going back. Feet trampled on the hem of Sophie's coat as Wanda pressed on, holding desperately to Jakob's jacket with her free hand, tugging with the other at the ribbon joining her to Mitzi's mitten.

When they reached the station, Jakob forced his way onto the platform, pushing the cases through the carriage doors and lifting Wanda and her sister in behind them. He stood with his fingers wrapped around the handrail and one foot still on the platform, staring out over the sea of heads. A man behind him shoved him forward and a guard yelled.

Jakob roared his wife's name. As the sound spread outwards, it was swallowed up. He went to yell again, but had the air forced out of him by someone's elbow. Guards were moving down the train, securing doors. A whistle blew. He swung himself inside. The door slid shut behind him.

Wanda looked up at her father: 'Mutti didn't come,' she whispered.

Jakob pulled his daughters to him. 'Maybe she got on the train a little further down,' he murmured. 'Let us hope.'

But Wanda knew that Sophie wasn't on the train. When Jakob showed the guards his papers and she saw her mother's papers were there too, her first concern was that her mother would be cold without the fur coat. Looking up, she saw the red mark underneath her father's chin where he had caught himself that morning on the cut-throat razor. Something had gone wrong with time. Already there were bristles growing round the wound.

Her mother hadn't just been left without her fur coat. She'd been left behind in Warsaw without money, without papers, in an empty flat that would be commandeered within the week. As the train ploughed through the countryside and Mitzi chattered on, unconscious of the unexpected shift their lives had taken, Wanda silently adapted to the role that she would have to play from then on.

***

Abel turned his collar down as he went through the side door. There were limits to Miss Quettock's tolerance. He wore the same clothes he had worn when he was eighteen, a black polar-neck or sleeveless pullovers with different coloured stripes, brown corduroys and hair that slightly overlapped his collar. If he'd been allowed to go to university he'd probably have cast the whole lot off in favour of a suit by now. If there was something that you should have done and didn't do, you never quite moved on from that point.

When he first came to the library he had been afraid Miss Quettock had designs on him. Although there was at least ten years between them she'd affected a flirtatious giggle when she spoke to him that was at odds with her appearance, but when the relationship progressed no further she appeared to lose all interest in him, not just as a suitor but as an employee.

Aileen, the assistant, nodded as he hung his rucksack on the peg. She was a rung below him in the pecking order, but because she had ambitions she'd already taken on responsibilities that had been his. 'Miss Quettock's asked if we can photocopy this lot and collate them.'

Abel hesitated. Jobs as menial as that should have been hers.

'Unless you're busy,' Aileen added brightly.

Abel took the documents. He noticed Aileen's finger had a ring on it. She flashed a smile at him.

'You like it?'

'Is it an engagement ring?'

'Yes.'

'Aren't you rather young to be engaged?' asked Abel, innocently. He had no idea what passed for normal these days.

'Nineteen's not young. I'll be twenty-five before I know it.' Aileen held the ring in front of her as if it were a member of the Royal Family. She'd lost a shoe and gained a prince.

He felt himself drawn briefly into the enthusiasm of the moment. 'Well, congratulations,' he said, giving her a quick hug.

'Thanks.' She nuzzled at his neck. They'd had more contact in the last two minutes than they'd had in three years. There was Romance in the air.

'Good morning, Abel,' said Miss Quettock. 'Maybe you could open up.'

He smoothed his hair down, slid the bolts and levered back the doors. There was invariably someone standing on the doorstep stamping their feet, resentful that whilst they were outside in the cold, the library staff were inside in the warm.

'Good morning, ladies,' he said, pleasantly. They simpered past him. Abel had the distant glamour of a 1950's film star.

'Isn't it about time you got married?' Aileen said as she sat down at her computer. Abel gave a wan smile. 'After all you're not bad looking.'

'Thank you.' Abel wondered whether he should mention Cressida, but he could hardly pass her off to Aileen as his girlfriend. Aileen had stamped more of Cressida's overdue library books than he had, with the difference that he let her off the fines and Aileen didn't. It meant that she waited now till he was serving, before coming forward, and felt more or less obliged to speak to him, if only to say thank you. When he found she was a student at the art school, he'd asked after Mitzi. 'I'm her nephew,' he'd explained. 'She models for the life class.'

Cressida was vague. She gave him the impression that like Chinamen, all models looked the same. But still, it was a link of sorts. They'd had a drink together in the pub after the library closed one evening and she let him buy her lunch, occasionally, in the café down the road. He'd mentioned the reunion, but had stopped short of saying that it took place each year on the date his father had committed suicide. He was still torn between an impulse to present her to the family, thereby making her officially his girlfriend, and the fear that if he did it might lay waste whatever hopes he had of her. He wasn't certain what he meant by 'hopes'. He had avoided having them as far as possible. Since Wanda's devastating intervention between him and Mrs Allerton a decade earlier, his appetite for happiness seemed to have withered. He expected nothing and that, by and large, was what he ended up with.

'You could always get a girlfriend on the Net,' said Aileen. Now that she was spoken for, she seemed less interested in the library and more interested in securing somebody for Abel.

He smiled faintly. Even had the Net existed in his youth, he doubted that he would have been inclined to use it. He imagined googling Mrs Allerton and wondered what might have come up upon the screen. He felt a flush spread upwards from his neck and so that Aileen wouldn't notice, he picked up the pile of documents and hurried down the corridor.

***

Gregor rushed onto the platform as the train was pulling out. He managed to secure a corner seat in a compartment that was empty and subsided into it. He felt inside his pocket for his cigarettes and found he'd left them on the bedside table next to Gloria's divan. He cursed. She would have finished off the packet by the time he got back. Although Gregor much preferred his cigarettes expensive and refined in contrast to the muck that Gloria smoked, it remained another of the questionable habits they enjoyed together.

Though she was by no means the most biddable of Gregor's conquests, he'd rejoiced in the discovery that Gloria was someone who regarded most things, and particularly sex, in much the way that he did. When she first took off her clothes in front of him, he'd wondered for a moment whether she had been replaced by someone else. His eyes passed down the body from her head, which was the kind of head you saw on all the female academics: handsome as opposed to beautiful, with slightly horsey features, hair drawn back into a roll, a mouth that was a checkpoint rather than an avenue. He'd felt obliged, out of politeness, to start at the top and work down, but as he had taken in the full breasts with their captivating nipples, the firm outline of the stomach and the touching triangle of hair that looked a bit like the lawn outside, well-trimmed and waiting to be trampled on, he'd felt an unexpected rush of joy.

She'd gripped his cheeks and planted a ferocious kiss upon the thick lips that had so much suction in it, Gregor wondered if she was about to swallow him. He'd felt her hand go down between his legs. For one appalling moment, he thought Gloria was going to emasculate him. She was kneading him between her fingers in a way that bordered on the painful, but was also giving him exquisite pleasure.

Despite the multiple erections of the night before, the memory was causing Gregor's trousers to feel rather tight. He fidgeted. The longing for nicotine was having an unfortunate effect on his libido. All his life his energy had arced from one end of his body to the other. He'd off-loaded his virginity when he was fifteen, clumsily and without much reciprocated pleasure, to a girl who worked behind the counter of a chemist's shop. She would have brought the curtain down on the performance earlier, but it was not in Gregor's nature to let anybody off the hook before he'd done with them.

His earlier experiments had been on Abel, who agreed because he didn't know what was involved and Gregor hadn't bothered to explain. He'd picked an afternoon when there was no one in, but Abel's shrieks had percolated down the stairs till Mrs Pampanini came and hammered on the door and Gregor had to put his trousers back on rapidly and answer it.

He'd told her they'd been playing tag and Abel kept on getting caught. Mrs Pampanini had encompassed Gregor's bland smile with suspicion: 'Maybe you would like to come and sit downstairs with me until your mother or your aunt get home,' she offered.

Gregor had smiled enigmatically and raised his eyebrows.

Abel bit his lip: 'No, thank you.'

'We'll find something quiet to do,' said Gregor, ominously, edging the door to. 'Toad,' he muttered, cuffing Abel round the ears.

'You hurt me, Gregor.'

'It's supposed to hurt, you dummkopf, that's the point of it.'

'But it was only me it hurt.'

'It can't hurt both of us at once,' said Gregor. 'Someone had to do it. You can be the one to do it next time.'

'I don't think I want to,' Abel sniffed.

'You're such an insect!' Gregor had flounced off into his own room. 'Christ, I don't know why I bother with you; you're so boring.'

'Can't we play that other game instead, the one where we watch Mitzi get undressed?'

'I'm bored with that. And anyway, she isn't here.'

'She'll be back soon'

'I can't be bothered. You can watch her if you want to.'

'What will you do?'

'I think I'll go and bugger myself.'

A few weeks later, Gregor had succeeded in persuading the boy who shared his Bunsen burner in the chemistry laboratory to help him with his research. This time the experiment had worked so well they'd carried on with it throughout that term and half way through the next. The boy had started passing notes to Gregor and waylaying him when they came out of school. He looked at him with doe-eyes in Assembly and presented Gregor with a cloth bag full of marbles, which he'd managed to exchange for tennis balls.

Not having been in love with anybody but himself, it took a while for Gregor to see what was happening and by that time he was ready to move on. He'd been convinced that there were other practices that might provide a passing entertainment. Certainly he wasn't interested in touching hands across a Bunsen burner for the next three months.

His hunger for enlightenment had been unquenchable. The first time he'd seen Mitzi, had been accidental. He had spent the afternoon inside her wardrobe, wrapped in Mitzi's lace and taffeta, exploring the sensations that were newly opening to him, basking in the dense warmth and cheap perfume of her clothes, the air around him drained of oxygen, his breathing laboured. I could die in here, he'd thought, exultantly.

A group of young men off to watch a football match, exploded noisily into the carriage. Gregor groaned. He picked up the paper lying on the seat beside him and pretended to be reading. Soon the print began to blur. He dozed and dreamt the girl he'd seen outside the buttery had come in and sat down opposite him. Gloria was right. There was something in the small chin and the way she held her head that was familiar. She leant forwards, as if she were making up her mind to speak. Well, all the better, he thought. Let her make the running. It was years since he'd had an adventure on a train. He rarely travelled on one these days. He'd determined long ago that he would not observe the Jewish New Year, Yom Kippur, or any other ceremony when the family might have come together. Once he had decided that his future lay as a philosopher, Gregor had felt more or less obliged to call himself an atheist. He'd never felt particularly drawn to God. He was by nature too competitive to easily subscribe to the idea of something greater than himself. Philosophy had freed him from the need to be subservient to anyone. He was expected to defy authority, which suited Gregor very nicely.

'Don't you worry that you will be damned?' said Wanda.

'I suspect that God's already noticed I'm an atheist. I don't want to be damned as a hypocrite as well,' said Gregor.

He was jolted back to consciousness as the consoling rhythm of the wheels over the sleepers locked into a single drawn-out whine. The train had juddered to a halt and was now moving slowly into Paddington. The young men had departed with their flags and rattles, leaving empty plastic cups and cartons strewn across the seats. He glimpsed a pack of Marlboro Lights amongst the debris and his eyes moved quickly past it. He had certain standards.

He got up and flexed his shoulders optimistically. He might be heading for a miserable evening, but he planned to have a splendid afternoon first.

***

Wanda looked up, startled. What was that! The radio was still on in the background, but the sound had come from somewhere else. She listened, all her senses focused like an animal that hears a twig snap half a mile away. She got up quietly and went out into the hall. Someone was out there. How had they got past the front door? If they'd rung the outside bell first, she would not have let them in. She crept towards the spy-hole. She could never quite believe that if she could see out, the person she was staring at could not see in. She saw a badge pinned onto a lapel. A man in uniform! Her legs felt weak. He couldn't know she was inside the flat. If she stayed silent, he would go away, unlike those other men in uniform who did not go away. She stared back at the spy-hole. This was England. She was safe here.

When she looked again, the man had turned away. He wandered over to the shrine and picked up Nathan's photograph. Her hand slid to the chain inside the door and she secured it silently. She waited till she heard the front door slam and then went quickly down the passage to the living room. She stared out of the window, watching as the flat cap passed beneath her. At the far end of the road she saw a blue van waiting.

Wanda fetched the fur coat and a shopping bag. It would be better if she went out now, in case the man came back. She'd heard of people being tricked by conmen who wore uniforms and managed to get into peoples' houses by pretending they had come to read the meter.

The fur coat felt heavy on her shoulders, but the weight of it was reassuring. Wanda rarely went outside without it even in the height of summer. In the early days, when they first came to Primrose Hill, she'd used it as an eiderdown. She liked to huddle underneath the bedclothes, basking in the heavy, aromatic scent that was all she had left of her mother. In the fifties, fur became less fashionable and this one looked more like a dead mule than a fox, but she would not be parted from it.

In her mother's absence she'd slipped seamlessly into the role of matriarch. It was as if the only way she could accommodate her mother's loss was by becoming her. She'd cooked and cleaned and washed and ironed. She went to school and when she came home in the afternoon she would begin again, preparing supper for the three of them, positioning herself inside the front door when she heard her father's footsteps on the stairs so that she could relieve him of his coat and guide him to the armchair, kneeling at his feet to ease his slippers on.

'Your nose is on the grindstone, papi,' she said, showing that she was attempting to improve her English side by side with managing a house and looking after everybody in it.

Jakob gave a sad smile. 'To the grindstone, kätchen.' Wanda nodded.

Every evening after supper she prepared a bath for Mitzi, keeping to the usual routine, down to the reading of the bedtime story. But her mother's ritual of turning Mitzi upside down and tickling her and then when she was no more than a squealing puff ball of pink flesh, smothering her with kisses and endearments, this she had not done. When Mitzi cried occasionally for her mother, Wanda patted her half-heartedly and told her not to fret. She'd waited to see whether Mitzi would become disconsolate or clingy, but she had turned elsewhere for the love she needed.

'Cuddle, papi!' she demanded, burying her small head with its blond curls in her father's sagging cardigan. And he had stopped whatever he was doing, melting in the aura of affection Mitzi generated round her.

Wanda looked on stoically. She envied Mitzi her ability to cry when she was sad and laugh when she was happy. Wanda had not cried once. With each year she had become more introspective. She remembered that her mother had been left behind because she had refused to leave without the things that mattered to her. Wanda understood this impulse absolutely. She had found the English psyche lightweight. Any notion that you could be jollied out of centuries of suffering, or put the past behind you, was abhorrent to her. She had no desire to put the past behind her. It was like a second skin.

She'd come across her mother's documents one day inside a drawer, tucked underneath a pile of handkerchiefs. The photograph was blurred. Her mother's eyes stared innocently back at her. She couldn't have been more than thirty when the photograph was taken. What must she have felt when she arrived that morning at the railway station and discovered that the train had left? Would she have gone back to the flat, now empty with its windows boarded up, the furniture and carpets sold, the stove bereft of fuel, and stood silently like Wanda as the world slid sideways on its axis and she tilted with it.

***

Mitzi started counting backwards from a hundred. The leg folded underneath her was becoming cramped. If Victorine Meurent had sat there on the grass like this whilst Manet painted her, it was no wonder that she had that fixed expression on her face.

At heart she knew the romance she wove into her existence in the life class was as much a fantasy as all the other aspects of her life. The mattress underneath the fake grass hadn't been replaced since she'd first started working there. The sheets were only washed if Mitzi took them home and washed them. She could hold the same pose for an hour if required, but after fifteen minutes she felt pain in every joint. The students barely seemed to look at her when they were drawing. Only if she moved did they complain that she had lost the pose and blamed her for the shortfalls in their drawings.

'Thank you, Miss Brzeska.' Mr Harpur flipped the lid back on his pocket watch. There was a clattering of easels being scraped back and the thin sound of a regiment of pencils falling on the wooden floorboards. Mitzi felt the pins and needles in her lower leg.

Reaching for her dressing gown, she hobbled over to the cubicle and sat down on the ledge. She waited until Mr Harpur joined her. He took out the flask. The tea had not improved over the years. She wondered if he left the tea bags in there.

They talked amiably about the weather, the geraniums that Mr Harpur was about to bring in for the winter, the disturbing increase in the price of coal, the exhibition in the sculpture court. 'Not quite my sort of thing,' admitted Mr Harpur. 'On the whole I still prefer Giotto.' Mitzi smiled. She took a cookie from the packet he held out to her. She wondered why it was so easy to tell Mr Harpur things she wouldn't have told anybody else. It was strange, given that he had been witness to the single most defining moment of her life, that she continued to refer to him as Mr Harpur and that he continued calling her 'Miss Brzeska' in the studio.

'It's so the students aren't encouraged to take liberties,' he'd said once.

She knew Mr Harpur's Christian name was Charles, but she had never called him that. In quarter of a century she had discovered nothing other than that Mr Harpur had a sister and a cottage on the seafront down in Deal and that he was that rare phenomenon, a gentleman.

Once, as they sat talking in the corner of the studio, she'd seen them for an instant from the vantage point of someone coming on them for the first time: Mitzi with her dyed hair and her gaudy costumes, Mr Harpur with his fussy gestures and his irritating hum, his florid pink face sandwiched in between the white hair and the white suit, like a drawing rubbed out and then arbitrarily restored to colour with the only crayon in the box. She knew that what united them was not so much the things they had in common as the things that separated them from other people. Mr Harpur, with his linen jackets and his bow ties, his unfailing courtesy and his enthusiasm for Giotto, was a relic in the same way she was. In his quintessential Englishness he was as much a foreigner as Mitzi.

She'd tried not to mention him outside the life class. Wanda had a way of asking questions that put things into perspective – that was her term. What it did was make you think you'd been mistaken in the emphasis you'd put on something, that another person would not see it in the same light. 'Is that all?' her tone inferred. 'No more than that?' She hadn't wanted Mr Harpur to be rendered down in this way.

'I've received another letter,' Mitzi blurted out. 'I wondered if...well, if...' She tailed off. Mr Harpur's eyes regarded her with mild inquiry. Mitzi rummaged in the pocket of her dressing gown. The letter was beginning to resemble something that had passed through several hands already. She smoothed out the edges, trying not to let her fingers tremble.

Mr Harpur fumbled for his glasses. He adjusted them. 'Don't worry, Mitzi. I'm sure we can sort it out.' He grunted as he scanned the contents and then settled down to look at it more carefully. His lips pursed. When he'd read the letter, he was silent for a moment. He removed the thin-rimmed spectacles and rubbed his eyes. There was a stub of charcoal poking through a small tear in his pocket. Mitzi felt an urge to reach across and rescue it before it fell onto the floorboards.

'I suppose it was inevitable this would happen, Mitzi,' he said, quietly 'Were you not prepared for it?'

'Perhaps. I'm not sure,' Mitzi said. 'I told myself that it was better not to think about it. It was all so long ago. Our lives have moved on.'

But the moment she said it, Mitzi knew their lives had not moved on. Each of them in their own way had become stuck in a time warp brought about by Nathan's suicide. Even Gregor now seemed stuck. His intellect was razor-sharp still, but his wit was bitter rather than incisive. Then there was poor Abel. In his late teens she had felt him fretting, fearful that unless he got away, he would be there for life. The tussles that went on between himself and Wanda were the more disturbing because, as in silent movies, the spectator had to work out from their gestures and expressions what was going on between the characters and gauge the moment when the final crisis would occur.

Once, when he had discovered that an envelope of university prospectuses had been ripped open and then dropped into the rubbish bin, she'd seen his anger suddenly erupt.

Her sister had shrugged airily: 'Well they are only brochures; they are not important.'

'Yes, but they're addressed to me!'

'You want I put them all back in the envelope?'

'No,' Abel had said, sulkily. 'It's too late.'

Wanda had gone through the motions of continuing to clear the table. 'No doubt when you have decided, you will tell me what this is about.'

'I want to go to university. I'm going to apply to study English Literature.'

'You're saying you will leave home?'

'Everyone leaves home at eighteen, mutti. Gregor did.'

'But you are not like Gregor. Are you used to doing for yourself?'

'You know I'm not. But that's because you never let me. I expect I'll soon learn. Other people manage. Half the class is going.'

'Half the class is not as delicate as you are. It does not have asthma or a weak chest. It has not been suffering rheumatic fever.'

'Those things won't be any worse in Leeds or Sheffield.'

'Well,' said Wanda, 'we will see.' She'd turned away deliberately.

Mitzi knew and so did Abel, that when Wanda told him she 'would see,' it meant she had already seen. He'd rounded on her.

'Couldn't I at least apply? Then I would know if I was good enough to get a place.'

'I see,' said Wanda, coolly. 'You pretend to do what I want, but in fact you do what you want.'

'Well, why can't you want what I want!'

'Want, want. You are like a spoilt child. I have spared the rod and this is the result.'

When she was in her twenties Wanda had enrolled down at the library on an Adult Education Course. Each week she'd brought home lists of English proverbs and had got into the habit of resuscitating one or other of them when she could not find the right word to describe her feelings.

'Oh, by all means go,' she snapped. 'You think that out there is so wonderful? No doubt you think you'll find a girlfriend. Like your brother and his Gloria.'

'I wouldn't want a girl like Gloria. She terrifies me.'

'All girls terrify you,' Wanda had said, narrowing her eyes.

'What's that supposed to mean?'

'Is true, I think? You are not easy in the company of girls.'

'That's just because I didn't have a sister. I know lots of girls. I'd introduce you to them if you weren't so hostile.'

'You are saying I am hostile? I have never met your friends. Who knows, they may be very nice.' She shrugged. 'If they exist.'

'Why are you so unreasonable?' he'd shouted. 'It's a small thing, going off to university. Why do I have to beg for everything? Why can't I be like everybody else?'

'Because you aren't like everybody else. You think that you belong here, but you don't. You are a foreigner, you will remain one. You will find the English never really let you in. They think they are so reasonable, so fair, they give you space inside their country, but they watch you all the time, they hear your accent and they do not give you jobs, a crime it is committed and if you are there, of course, you are responsible. You think they will accept a Pole to study English Literature in England? No,' Wanda had said lightly with a crooked smile. 'I do not think so.'

'You don't think he ought to be allowed a little freedom?' Mitzi ventured, after Abel had gone out and slammed the door between them.

Wanda had looked mystified: 'What freedom? Have I not said he should go? Of course he should. Go, I have said.' She'd waved her hand.

'But he knows, when you say it like that, Wanda, you would rather he did not go. He needs friends his own age.'

'He has friends at school.'

'Yes, but they go off in the evenings and he can't. He feels obliged to come home.'

Schopenhauer's Porcupines

'He is not obliged,' insisted Wanda. 'Abel wants to go out in the evening, he can go. He wants to bring home women, let him. You see,' Wanda gave a terrifying smile. 'I want the best for him.'

It was the last time Mitzi had tried speaking up for Abel. Till the letters started to arrive, she had assumed that her life too, was fixed. She wasn't as capricious now. Her tragedy had calmed her, as it sometimes does with an erratic nature. Mitzi knew the twilight that lay waiting for the day. Occasionally, when she looked at pictures of herself at seventeen or eighteen, she could see what people meant when they said she had been a pretty child; she had that fragile beauty that does not withstand the ravages of time. The owner of it must die young or look back with nostalgia to a bygone era. It was not a beauty that matured.

She sighed and Mr Harpur looked up. He returned the letter: 'I'm not sure how to advise you, Mitzi. Is there no one in the family you can talk this over with?'

She hesitated. Had he known her family better, he would not have asked. Her fingers curled around the envelope. 'It's just that you were so kind all those years ago,' she said, 'and no one else knew.'

'Do you mean they still don't know?' said Mr Harpur, curiously. Mitzi shook her head. He looked at her a moment: 'Twenty years is a long time to keep a secret, Mitzi.'

'Yes, it is.'

***

Wanda glanced up at the dark clouds gathering above. There would be rain before long, but at present there was just a dampness in the air with every now and then a pallid ray of sunshine breaking through the cloud. She turned along the narrow alleyway beside the flat and came out at the top end of the row of stalls. She wandered down the central aisle, occasionally stopping to pick out an onion or tomato from the piles of fruit and vegetables and test it in her hands before she moved on. Sometimes, she asked Mitzi to bring back the things she needed from the supermarket. She'd avoided going there since that unpleasant business with the tea. But she would not have trusted Mitzi when it came to buying vegetables or fruit. She always got an extra plum, or two or three tomatoes that she hadn't had to pay for, but what was the point of that, said Wanda, if they were inedible?

She reached the end stall and began to make her way back slowly, her head still inclining first to one side then the other, as if she had not yet come to a decision which of them would have her custom that day. It was part of an elaborate performance. Wanda always bought fruit from the same stall at the top end of the market. She'd been going there since they first came to Primrose Hill. She paused and breathed the sharp scent of the lemons and the sweeter, rather melancholy scent of Cox's orange pippins. A faint beam of sunlight fell across the pavement at her feet and Wanda turned her face towards it gratefully.

As she drew level with the stall, she saw the tray of peaches…..Peaches. In November! The sun cast a yellow-orange patina across the skin of one peach in particular. She gazed at it, entranced. She had been ten before she'd even seen a peach. No, in America she must have seen one. In America there were no shortages.

If we had stayed in Iowa, I might have been a housewife, Wanda thought, one of those pink-cheeked, healthy-looking women who wore little frilly pinafores and advertised the latest household gadgets on the television. She could have been living in a white-washed, single-storied house out in the suburbs with a tidy garden and a husband whose idea of a fulfilling weekend was to mow the lawn.

If Jakob hadn't had the mad idea of going back to Poland, Wanda wouldn't be here at this moment, standing in the chill of a November morning at a market stall in Camden Town. Suppose her father had been someone else? She tried to think of Jakob as a fair-skinned, innocent American, full of that irritating openness and good will. It was no use. Jakob was a foreigner whatever country he was in.

If he had not had Wanda to contend with, he might have moved on again or formed a partnership with someone else. He wasn't even forty when they came to England and he had that tragic caste that English women liked so much. He sometimes went out in the evenings and did not return until the early hours, but he always came back on his own. There was a heaviness about him when he came home in the middle of the night. She wasn't sure if it was going out that made him sad, or coming back. Once, when they'd been in Primrose Hill for four years, he had hinted that they might find somewhere else to live, but Wanda had been horrified. What if their mother traced them all the way to Primrose Hill and then discovered they had gone. 'We have to stay here, papi, just in case.'

He'd looked at her beleaguered face and nodded: 'If you say so, little one.'

The stallholder looked up as Wanda made her way towards him down the line. His smile had more respect than liking in it. After quarter of a century, they hadn't reached the stage of speaking to each other. He accepted her determination to get value for her money; he did not, as with his other long term customers, put one more in the bag when he had weighed the fruit. He knew that Wanda would despise him for his generosity. She would think he was trying to ingratiate himself. And so he didn't. Wanda got exactly what she asked for.

There were several women in the queue in front of her, but he leaned over, handing her a clutch of paper bags. She never let herself be served. She would examine every item before dropping it into the bag and then wait. She did not fret if she had to stand for quarter of an hour, or the woman in the queue in front of her was more than usually demanding. Wanda had got used to waiting. It was something she was good at.

Her eyes passed over the vegetables within reach. She might slip the peach in with the carrots, or conceal it underneath the apples. It did not occur to her to buy it. That would have been an extravagance. It was the sort of thing her sister would do, spending money on a bunch of daffodils to brighten up the house or on some luxury she fancied for herself – a little scarf, a belt, a sugar mouse.

She thought of the real one Jakob had brought home one evening from the social club for Mitzi. It was in a little cage and it was running round in circles, either in excitement or in desperation to discover a way out. Her sister's squeals of joy had drowned the racket that the mouse was making.

Wanda threw her head back. It was time to put her foot down. The next day the cage stood empty, its floor peppered with the tiny droppings that had been the mouse's only legacy. But as she told her father 'After all, a mouse is vermin, papi.'

Mitzi was distraught. A fortnight later, Jakob had brought home a kitten. 'Is not vermin, after all,' he said to Wanda.

Wanda, who would have adored a kitten of her own, looked darkly at the mewling lump of fur that scratched her every time she tried to pick it up. It clung instead to Mitzi, digging its small, razor-sharp claws into the lace-work of her frocks so that she carried it from room to room like an extension of herself. Occasionally, when Wanda saw her playing with the cat, she had an urge to stamp on both of them.

The friends that Mitzi brought home barely seemed to notice Wanda. When they did, they treated her with an exaggerated deference. They were more at ease with Jakob, who appeared to find their rowdiness engaging.

'Gruss Gott!' he roared from his study as they tumbled down the hall and soon they started shouting back 'Gruss Gott, Herr Brzeska.'

'Give the boys a Pils,' yelled Jakob down the corridor to Wanda. She pretended not to hear him. She resented having to go round the sitting room and clear away the metal beer tops afterwards. The social club they went to at the weekends had been Wanda's only taste of life outside the flat, but it was very much a family affair. They sat at tables, playing cards or talking about funerals or weddings. Sometimes someone put a record on the gramophone and there was dancing. It brought back exquisite memories of the throaty voices on the gramophone her mother had brought home one morning to the flat in Warsaw. They had waltzed together round the cramped apartment. She could smell the wood smoke from the stove.

The men who danced with Wanda on the social evenings smelt of pipe tobacco and their beards left blotches on her neck. She'd reached the age of twenty-one without having been kissed by anyone except her parents and her sister, although Mitzi, who swamped everyone she met with hugs and kisses, rarely showed the same enthusiasm when it came to Wanda. She would peck her on the cheek each time she left the house or came back and she never went to bed without the statutory kiss, but Wanda knew that this was merely a politeness, not a need. If anybody had a need now, it was Wanda, but since no-one knew about it, it continued unfulfilled.

'You know that none of Mitzi's friends are Jewish, papi,' she said once.

The look that Jakob shot at her suggested that whatever drawbacks this presented, it was better than not having friends at all. 'We have to integrate, my Wanda,' he said, gently. 'We are now in England. It is like America. We have to show that we are not superior.' His lips curled mischievously. 'Even if we are,' they seemed to say.

'She isn't serious,' insisted Wanda. 'Mitzi doesn't understand the world. She will meet people who will take advantage of her.'

'Yes, we have to keep her in her gymslip for as long as possible,' her father had responded with a chuckle.

Wanda felt a sickness in her stomach that was partly jealousy and part revulsion. She had barely thought of Mitzi as a person, let alone the object of desire. Her eyes passed to her father's slightly fleshy fingers as they flicked cigar ash in the grate. She had felt suddenly remote from him.

'I'll talk to her,' he said. But they were both aware that it would be like trying to rein in a butterfly. She might as well go straight into the jar of chloroform.

The peach was within reach now. Wanda started filling up the bags. Her fingers shook as she selected the tomatoes that she needed, kale, potatoes. Twice, three times, her fingers hovered in the air over the tray of peaches and moved on. She looked round to make certain nobody was looking, but in doing so she'd drawn attention to herself. She saw the sullen gaze of women in the queue behind her. She picked up the peach, defiantly, and held it in her hand a moment, breathing in the agonising sweetness of the flesh. The peach pulsated with the warm sun of the south. She squeezed it slightly, then she put it back. There was a dark smudge on the skin where she had fingered it. It would soon turn into a bruise, thought Wanda, satisfied.

***

Abel flipped the sleeve back on the Xeroxing machine. The brief exhilaration and the burst of bonhomie that followed Aileen's news, had given way to gloomier reflections. In a week's time I'll be thirty-one, he thought. He'd never quite been able to forgive his father for committing suicide a week before his birthday. He had known that morning when he went into the living room and saw his mother wailing, that the celebrations would be muted. Mrs Pampanini had an arm around her shoulders and was murmuring incessantly, as if it were a mantra 'There, there, Wanda.'

A woman in a gaberdine coat, sitting with her back to him, had looked round and his eyes met hers. 'You must be Abel,' she said, kindly. 'My name's Mrs Allerton.' She came across to him and bent down. 'Let's go back into your room a moment, shall we, dear?'

She took his hand and led him back into the bedroom, easing herself next to him on the divan. When Abel's mother held his hand it was as if the two of them were chained together, but with Mrs Allerton his hand felt like a small bird safely in its nest. There was a faint scent of gardenia about her and a light flush on her cheeks, which looked as if it might be rouge. It matched her lipstick. Abel found the regularity of colour soothing. Mitzi was the only member of the household who wore make-up, but the way his aunt applied it was so indiscriminate it seemed to go off like a firework. There were small eruptions miles from the original explosion. It was difficult to know where Mitzi started or finished and in this respect her face reflected her personality. He could remember hoping Mrs

Allerton's reflected hers. They went on looking at each other for a moment.

'How old are you, Abel?' Mrs Allerton said, softly.

'I shall be eleven next week.'

'Well that's quite grown-up and you're going to have to be very grown up now, Abel, because you're going to have to look after your mother.'

'Why can't papi do it?'

'I'm afraid your father had an accident last night.' She rubbed her thumb against his palm. 'He fell into the stairwell.'

'Is he dead?'

'Yes, I'm afraid he is.'

No birthday celebrations, then. His eyes passed to the door and back to Mrs Allerton. 'Is my daddy still there, in the hall?'

'No, dear. The ambulance has taken him away but there are men in white coats downstairs, looking round to try and find what happened. You don't remember anything from last night, I suppose? Your father didn't come into the flat before he....went out?'

Abel didn't answer. Instinct told him that the less he said, the better. 'Who are you?' he asked.

'I'm someone the social services send round to families when there's a crisis. We'll be seeing quite a lot of one another in the next few weeks.' She smiled encouragingly. 'You might find you feel all sorts of things you might not have expected. Sometimes we feel angry when a parent dies, because they've left us. Even if we know they didn't mean to, we still wish they hadn't gone and sometimes we think if they'd only loved us more, they wouldn't have.'

'Where's Gregor?'

'Gregor is your brother? I expect he'll be arriving later on today. Do you get on with Gregor?'

'Sometimes.'

'Well, I dare say it will be a comfort to have everybody in the family together.' She smiled reassuringly. The wailing from the sitting room had reached a peak. 'Your mother's obviously upset,' she added, as the noise continued.

No she isn't, Abel thought.

There had been only one occasion in the past when Abel had come close to knowing what it felt like to be free. He'd gone with Mitzi on a shopping trip and she had left him in the playground that adjoined the store. He had played happily for half an hour and a little less contentedly for half an hour after that. Then he had sat there on the swing as dusk fell, until Mitzi suddenly remembered him. He'd seen her running down the pathway through the twilight, like a harpy at a Halloween feast, drawing him towards her as she reached him in a helpless show of love and terror. 'Abel, I'm so sorry.'

He had not felt any trepidation, sitting there in darkness on the swing, his small feet in their lace-ups scuffing at the pebbles underneath. He had experienced the space and silence of aloneness, which he'd found was not the same as loneliness. He'd wondered at what point this might have turned to fear and panic and a part of him wished he had been allowed to find out and that Mitzi had gone on forgetting him a little longer.

For the three weeks following his father's suicide, he walked home through the park each afternoon from school with Mrs Allerton. His mother always took the bus or did a detour to avoid the playground area, but Mrs Allerton seemed perfectly content to sit whilst Abel queued up for the slide or clung onto the rubber tyres fixed by chains that swung deliriously out over the grass. The other boys jumped off when it was at its highest, scarifying knees and elbows as they tumbled to the ground. If she had glanced up, Abel would have felt obliged to show off that he was as tough as they were. But apart from turning his way every now and then to smile, she put no pressure on him either to be reckless or to take care. He could please himself.

He had to make sure that the ice-cream tubs she bought him went into the bin before they reached the flat and once, when he spilt some onto his blazer, Mrs Allerton took out a handkerchief and scrubbed the dark stain, spitting on the handkerchief and, when her eye met Abel's, pulling down the corners of her mouth, conspiratorially. On an impulse Abel threw his arm around her neck and kissed her on the cheek. He licked the powder off and smacked his lips together. 'Yummy.'

'Have you got a little boy?' he asked once, thinking that she couldn't know so much about them otherwise.

'No,' she said, sadly. 'I'm afraid not.'

'I can be yours if you like,' said Abel, thinking what a shame it was that people like his mother managed to have two, when others far more suitable, like Mrs Allerton, had none at all.

She smiled and cupped his chin. 'I'm not sure that your mother would be very keen on that.'

'She wouldn't mind.'

'Well, maybe I could borrow you from time to time, if you think that would be all right.'

He hoped she wouldn't feel obliged to ask his mother. It would be their secret. If his mother's secret was the sewing room, why shouldn't he have one too?

On his birthday Mrs Allerton had taken him to see a Star Wars film and afterwards they'd gone back to her little house in Belsize Park for tea. The sitting room faced south and sunshine flooded through the windows. Glass doors gave onto a ragged garden wild with meadow grass and daisies. Abel thought he was in heaven. She had made a special cake with icing on the top and 'Happy Birthday, Abel' in pink letters. In the middle was a pink and white striped candle.

Mrs Allerton had lit the candle and told Abel he must make a wish and Abel wished that he might stay forever in the sitting room of Mrs Allerton's chaotic little house in Belsize Park with its faded cushions and the dusty sunlight picking out the threadbare pattern on the rug.

A fortnight later, she had gone.

***

The stallholder had started weighing up the bags. Each time he shouted out the prices, Wanda's lips moved, as if she were adding up the sum inside her head. And then she saw the peppers. She'd forgotten them. She hesitated. Could you make a goulash without peppers? Mitzi wouldn't notice. Abel might, but he would not say anything. Gregor would not miss an opportunity to point out there was something missing from the meal, of course. And what about that friend of Abel's, if she came? She might think that, in Poland, that was how they did things.

'I need peppers,' Wanda said. 'I take these.' This time she did not hold each one to the light to check for blemishes. The women in the queue behind her were becoming hostile. She could hear them muttering, the way they had that morning in the supermarket when she found herself surrounded suddenly by people who had never given her a second glance before. She had pretended, for the first time since she came to England, that she didn't speak the language. She had failed to understand their customs. Once she had identified herself as foreign they'd begun to talk amongst themselves about her. Wanda felt her skin crawl with humiliation. Was this how they treated guests? Was it for this that they had left the ghetto, only to be ridiculed and persecuted somewhere else?

She started counting out the small change from her purse. There seemed to be a lot of coppers. Even after thirty years, they were confusing. At the end she found that she was five pence short. She searched the other pockets of her purse. The metal clasp had caught against the chain around her wrist. She tugged at it. Her hand jerked and the pile of small change balanced on the ledge beside her, toppled. Half a dozen coins fell to the ground, along with the two halves of the broken chain and those charms that had been attached to it and which had fallen through the gap.

She gave a small cry and dropped down onto her knees to search for them. She didn't care about the coins now, but she could not bear to lose the charms.

Her father pressed the box into her hands. 'Your mother would have wanted you to have them. They're for you and Mitzi.' He'd kissed Wanda on the head and left the room.

She'd run her fingers over the encrusted surface of the box before she opened it. She took a necklace out and held it up against her throat. Her colour wasn't right for jewellery; her face was not enhanced so much as thrown into the shadows by the necklace. Mitzi had her mother's creamy pink complexion. Wanda took after her father. She had fine, strong features; when she got to forty, she would be a handsome woman. But the one thing she would never be was beautiful. Men would not pursue her with their greedy eyes as she walked past them down a corridor, or crossed a dance floor. They would go on talking, arguing or pouring drinks, untroubled by her presence.

Mitzi, on the other hand, had pounced upon her mother's jewellery as soon as she could stand up and their mother, laughing, had adorned her younger daughter like a Christmas tree till Mitzi, squealing with delight as she was lifted up to look at her reflection, wet herself in her enthusiasm.

No, thought Wanda. Better not. But Mitzi had come in before she had a chance to hide the box. She'd leant across the table.

'These are mutti's,' she said, trailing one hand through the box. 'Did papi give them to you?' Wanda nodded. 'Maybe he would like it if we wore them.'

Wanda had glanced sharply at her, but the look on Mitzi's face was not acquisitive. 'Of course he wouldn't. Do you think he wants to be reminded of her every time he looks at us?'

'It must remind him anyway,' said Mitzi, reasonably.

Perhaps, thought Wanda, when he looks at you. 'How can you be so thoughtless, Mitzi. Don't you care how papi feels?'

'Of course I do,' said Mitzi. She had rested one hand on her sister's shoulder. 'What do you think happened to her?' she said, quietly.

'I expect she would have been arrested and then taken to Treblinka.'

'You don't think she might be still alive somewhere?'

'Of course not. We'd have found her if she had been.'

'Yes,' said Mitzi, quietly, 'I suppose so.' She'd continued staring at the open box a moment. 'We still miss her, don't we?'

Wanda glanced at her. She'd known that this was one of those unlooked for moments when the opportunity arose to change the way things were. She might have got up, hugged her sister and thrown off the sorrow she had buried for a decade. They would finally have come to terms with one another and their loss. They would have ceased to be on different sides and faced the world as allies. All it needed was a single gesture. But she couldn't make it.

'Yes,' she'd said, 'but it is no use living in the past. We have to carry on.'

Her sister looked at her, surprised. It wasn't Mitzi who was living in the past, thought Wanda. It was her. In Warsaw she had had a family she could relate to and a language that she understood. She might have gone to university and trained to be a teacher or a doctor, married into an adjoining family, become a matriarch in a society that valued women of her kind. In Warsaw Mitzi would have been the outcast. She had closed the lid down on the box decisively.

A young man in the crowd bent down to help. She pushed his hands away. 'No thank you,' she insisted, scrabbling at the earth and picking up the last link off the ground. She gave up trying to sort out the bits and tipped the whole lot back into her purse. Whilst she was waiting for her change she glanced about her warily, but nobody was looking at her. She had ceased to be of interest.

Then her eyes locked onto something in the crowd. Her knees began to give way under her. No. Surely not. She looked away. It hadn't been the face, she recognised; the woman was too far away. It was the gaberdine coat that had caught her eye and, by the same sign, Wanda realised that she would be recognised inside the fur coat.

She held out her hand impatiently. 'I must go,' she insisted. 'Please to let me have my change.' She took the notes and coins and, without bothering to put them in her purse, she turned and hurried quickly up the hill towards the safety of the flat.

***

Schopenhauer's Porcupines

The telephone rang shrilly at the other end. As it continued ringing, Gregor felt the ire begin to bubble up in him. He hadn't lied to Gloria about his schedule, but he'd decided to postpone his lunch engagement so that he'd have time to drop in on a recently divorced economist he'd met when she came up to give a lecture at the university. It was too good an opportunity to let slip.

Gregor was in charge of hospitality. It was a role he gave some weight to. When the college entertained he always reckoned on a gap each side of lunch of half an hour. Never more. He always made it clear to anyone that he was making love to, that the action wasn't open ended. He would leap up, energised, say thank you, tell them there was no rush in a voice implying that there was, and close the door on them. He couldn't think with women strewn around the place. Their scent confused him, their affection bothered him and their demands defeated him.

He knew that he was talked about within the university. He always picked the brightest students in the group and then demolished them, with argument, initially, and then with an insinuating charm. Occasionally, it was 'him,' not 'her,' but on the whole he favoured women. They were not as complicated. He behaved towards them in the same way he had done to Wanda, carefully removing them from ground they thought they occupied, onto a No Man's Land where they would wander blindly till they found another trench.

'I'll be in London next week', he'd said, airily, to the economist. 'I'll look you up.' She'd given him her number. It was tantamount to an agreement.

Gregor rang again in case he'd got the number wrong. He was in half a mind to take a rain-check on the whole day. The derailment of his plans infuriated him. He saw it as an Act of God, which was ironic in the circumstances.

He took out his pocket book and flipped the pages back. Some of the numbers went back years. A couple of the women on the list were dead. He called up a receptionist in Panton Street and an assistant at The London Library, but there was no response from either. He debated whether it was too late to call up his publisher and reinstate the lunch and then discovered he was out, too. He went through another half a dozen numbers before giving up and then, because he felt a violent need to make somebody else the victim of his irritation, he phoned Gloria. A man picked up the phone.

'Have I miss-dialled, or is that Gloria's apartment?'

'It's her number, yes.'

'Then why the hell are you there?'

'Gloria is in the kitchen,' Cholmondeley answered, vacantly. 'I only picked it up because I thought it might have been important. You can leave a message if you like.'

'I don't like. Put me on to Gloria.'

'I'll let her know you're here.' He came back, minutes later. 'Sorry, George, she doesn't want to speak to you. She's busy.'

'What's she doing?'

'Putting a lasagne in the oven.'

'Are you having lunch there?'

'That was the idea.'

'Then what?'

'I don't think that's any of your business.'

'This is my wife we're discussing, Cholmondeley.' Gregor wedged his foot against the door. The mirror in the kiosk was already misting up.

'Your ex-wife, I believe.'

'I still regard her as my wife.'

'There's not much point in getting a divorce, if you continue thinking that you're married.'

'The divorce was never my idea.'

'I know.'

'Has Gloria been telling tales?' asked Gregor, coldly.

'She did say you were a pain to live with and she wishes you would take the hint and go away.'

There was a pause. 'If it's not putting too much of a burden on you, Cholmondeley, I would be obliged if you would take the phone out to the kitchen and stick the receiver under Gloria's right ear.

There was a whispered conversation and some interference on the line.

'I thought CholMonDoolally wasn't due back till tomorrow.'

'Change of plan.'

'I don't know where you find the energy.'

'I noticed yours seemed to be running down.'

'I reckon I could still compete with Cholmondeley, even as a vegetable.' He heard the rattle of saucepan lids and pictured Gloria and Cholmondeley taking it in turns to stir the pasta whilst the mince and onions bubbled in the frying pan seductively. He felt an overwhelming impulse to smash Cholmondeley on the nose.

'I take it that you're only criticising Cholmondeley, knowing that he's standing next to me. It won't work. He's here, you're there. That's the way it's staying.'

'You do realise what a bloody awful day I'm having?' he said, hotly.

'If you mean the anniversary, I don't know why you bother going. Your mother can't stand the sight of you.'

'That's why I go; to remind her that it's mutual. At least it takes a bit of the heat off Abel and Mitzi....spreads the misery around a bit.'

'I'm not surprised your father dived off the top floor landing. He must have been desperate to get away, and so am I. If you'll forgive me, Gregor...'

'Listen, Gloria.' He noticed that the dial had suddenly gone down to ten pence. He had one coin left. He made a grab at it and found it stuck onto the shelf with chewing gum.

'I'm going, Gregor.'

'Don't. I'm putting in more money.' Gregor got his nail under the twenty pence piece, levering it off, but the remains of gum prevented it from dropping down into the slot. He bunched his fist and banged it twice against the box. The coin dropped down just as the final pip went.

***

'Don't forget the house in Deal is always there for you.' For several minutes, neither of them had said anything. The letter lay in Mitzi's palm like a foundling no one quite knew what to do about.

'That's very kind of you,' said Mitzi, gratefully.

'I'm privileged to have been trusted with your confidences.' Mr Harpur gave her hand a light pat. 'I had no idea that, after so long, I was still the only one who knew.'

Not quite, thought Mitzi. She had told one other person and she was still living with the consequences.

'No-one uses it,' insisted Mr Harpur. 'As you know, my sister has her own house; I have mine. Because the cottage was our parents' house, we keep it on for sentimental reasons. Having someone in it, goes some way to justifying its existence.'

Mitzi swirled the tea leaves round inside her cup. The winter she had spent in Mr Harpur's cottage, twenty years before, had been one of the calmest of her life. Not happy. In the circumstances it was strange that she looked back on it so fondly. She had known that in the course of time she would be on her own again, but that was in the future and the future seemed a long way off.

She'd spent weeks walking on the beach and later, when the days grew short, she lit a fire and curled up in the armchair with a book until the daylight faded. In the past her concentration span had been so limited that though she often started books, she rarely finished them. She sometimes picked a different book up, thinking it was one she'd started, and continued reading from the middle. If the characters mysteriously changed their names, their sex, their occupations, she accepted it as she accepted everything in life.

At the beginning, it had been her saving grace. Although she'd been too young to realise what had happened to her mother, she had sensed that she would not be seeing her again and that she must look elsewhere for the things she needed. Later, when her sister married Nathan, she'd accepted that too. At sixteen she was too young for him. At twenty-eight, he'd been too old for her. But in his eyes she'd seen a passion that flared briefly and subsided into wistfulness.

She hadn't realised she was lonely until she was well into her twenties. Given her accommodating nature it was something of a miracle that Mitzi had got through her teens and early twenties without losing her virginity. Perhaps it was the presence in the house of Nathan, or more likely Wanda, that deterred petitioners from pressing their advantage. And then there was Mitzi's vulnerability. She'd brought out in the men she met, a latent courtliness. They felt they couldn't take advantage of her.

Mitzi in her own way had loved all of them, but none as much as she loved Nathan. As time passed, the number of young men surrounding her had tailed off. Sometimes, if she needed company, she'd gone to places: tea dances and clubs, that she would not have gone to previously. Here she'd met a class of man less principled than those she had been used to, anxious to ensure that their investment in her, paid off. There were one or two unpleasant incidents that Mitzi had got out of more by luck than judgement.

She'd become increasingly uncertain. When she looked into the mirror, she still saw the same face, only in the eyes there was a frightened and perplexed look which had not been there before. The blond curls that cascaded round her face insouciantly when she was sixteen, still had a wilful heedlessness that made her look a little mad. She wandered, neither old nor young, along a narrow pathway of acceptability, aware that even this might soon be snatched away.

She felt the same uncertainty at home. She'd sensed her sister's disapproval even as a three year old. The string that tied her wrist to Wanda's had become increasingly distressed over the years. She'd been aware of it that night when she returned to Primrose Hill after the months in Mr Harpur's cottage.

She had been about to let herself into the flat and then stopped. She knew she could not assume too much. She'd rung the bell. The sisters stood there on the doorstep, looking at each other. Wanda's dark eyes travelled down from Mitzi's pale face to the scuffed shoes, taking in the battered suitcase on the way. She did not move aside to let her in. She merely went on looking at her. Mitzi had begun to feel weak.

'Please, Wanda,' she said, desperately. 'Could I come in?'

She had stepped into the hall as Wanda moved aside reluctantly. She didn't know if she should cross the passage to her room, or wait to be invited. She remembered Wanda tugging on the string that tied them both together that day on the railway station, tugging not because she wanted to keep Mitzi with her, but because she hoped the string might break and she would be relieved of the responsibility for looking after her.

It seemed that she was destined to be on her own, no matter where she was.

'You're welcome to stay on a little longer,' Mr Harpur had insisted as she'd been preparing to return to London. 'No one comes here. You are quite safe. And you know the life class will be there when you return. You will be able to put all of this behind you and take up your life again. You must look forward.'

Mitzi had experienced a foretaste in that instant of the separation that was imminent. She was about to lose one half of her completeness. She could not have borne to go on living in the cottage afterwards. The emptiness she sensed around her, seeped like cold into her bones.

'I do have pleasant memories of that time,' she said. 'Despite the circumstances.' She returned the letter to its envelope. The urge to turn away from life was stronger now. Two decades earlier she would have fluttered helplessly towards the flames, but she had had her wings singed once.

He nodded. 'So tonight is the reunion? The family get-together. I expect you'll want to get away on time.' He screwed the top back on the flask. 'We'll see what we can do. I dare say Victorine could do with a night off.'

Mitzi would have been quite happy to continue sitting there on Mr Harpur's fake lawn with the picnic basket next to her, until the sun went down, but whilst they had been talking, she had come to a decision. She would speak to Gregor that night.

***

As she reached the top floor, Wanda heard the telephone inside the flat. She threw the bag of shopping down and rummaged for her key. The ringing stopped abruptly as she crossed the hall. The sound disturbed her, but the silence grated on her even more. She stood with one hand hovering above the telephone. After a pause she picked up the receiver, listened to the dialling tone and then replaced it, curtly, and went out onto the landing to retrieve her shopping.

I expect it was a wrong call, she thought, but she felt perturbed. The unexpected was what Wanda dreaded and she had already been the victim of it twice that day: the man in uniform who had called earlier, and then that woman in the gaberdine whom she had caught a glimpse of in the market. It was Mrs Allerton; she was convinced of it. She had pretended not to notice her and Mrs Allerton had done the same, but the encounter had unsettled her. What she had seen that afternoon in Mrs Allerton's small house in Belsize Park, was there again in all its gruesome detail.

She went through into the kitchen, put the kettle on and emptied her pockets of the small change, broken links and charms. She spread them out over the kitchen table, pushing the coins aside so that she could begin to loop the charms onto the bracelet. For the moment, she would have to use a length of cotton to secure the broken link. It only had to last the evening, but she couldn't go through the reunion without it. It was as essential to the ritual as Nathan's shrine. It symbolised not just the little love she had been able to extract from him, but Nathan's first betrayal, the first Station of the Cross that led them to their Calvary.

She'd wondered even at the time at the apparent ease with which he had allowed himself to be absorbed into the family. One day there were the three of them as usual; the next day there were four. Her father had brought Nathan back with him one night after a visit to the club. She had heard voices in the hall and left her room to ask her father if he wanted coffee. Nathan had his back to her. As he turned round, she caught a brief whiff of the dense, expensive scent of aftershave. 'Come, Wanda,' Jakob had said, amiably. 'Come and meet my good friend Nathan Silver.'

From then on the two men either met up at the club or Nathan came to Primrose Hill. They spent their evenings in the study, talking politics. Occasionally he stayed to supper. He deliberately held back when he ate and never took a second helping, but she sensed that he was hungry. When they ate together, he was always careful to include her in the conversation. He seemed genuinely interested in her point of view and gradually she started to confide in him. One evening when her father had gone back into his study for a book, they heard him coughing. He had had the cough for several months and no amount of medication seemed to be improving it.

'I'll bring some whisky with me when I come the next time,' Nathan said. 'We'll make him up a toddy. It's a Scottish recipe for colds.' They made the toddy up together in the kitchen. Wanda giggled as he raised a teaspoon to her lips. She thought that she had never been as happy as she was that night. She flapped her hand in front of her. 'It's burning me!' she cried.

'That's why it does you good,' said Nathan. 'It burns out the virus.'

Jakob drank it and a thimbleful was poured for Wanda that set up a buzzing in her head and made her feel a little as if she were levitating. She heard Nathan and her father talking to each other, but they seemed to be a long way off. She stumbled as she got up and her elbow caught an empty cup and tipped it over. 'Is my daughter schwips?' said Jakob, laughing.

Wanda's face burned. She did not like feeling that she wasn't in control and that the men were laughing at her. She decided alcohol was not for her and was surprised that it affected everybody else so little. After two weeks there was no more whisky in the bottle. But her father went on coughing and the cough became more guttural as time went on. He still smoked his cigars and sometimes when she went into the room the atmosphere was so dense she could hardly see the two of them in there.

It irritated her that Mitzi did not comment on the cough. When he had first been introduced to Mitzi, Wanda had sensed Nathan's curiosity. He'd glanced between them. Wanda knew what he was thinking. Mitzi is the grasshopper, she thought. I am the ant. But without me, the household could not carry on.

In Mitzi's presence, Nathan showed the same degree of courtesy that he had shown to Wanda, but he did not talk to her. He sat and smiled whilst Mitzi chattered on inconsequentially about the frocks she'd bought, the dances she had been to, and the films she'd seen that week. Her laughter tinkled like a harpsichord against the drab monotony of their existence. Mitzi laughed at everything. Her nature was entirely superficial, Wanda thought. She simply did not see what tragedy existed in the world.

As Nathan left the flat one night, she'd handed him his scarf as usual and he had hesitated: 'Thank you, Wanda,' he said, softly. She was conscious suddenly that he had noticed her. The next week Wanda took more care to plait her hair before she brought the tray into the study. She avoided catching Nathan's eye, but she knew he was watching her and so did Jakob. An agreement had been forged between the three of them. A rough, dull joy began to grow in her. She had grown up accepting that the most that she could hope for, was to hold on to the little that she had already. Her security lay in her lack of expectation. If you did not hope for anything, then you could not be disappointed when you didn't get it.

She took out the sewing box and hunted through it for a reel of cotton strong enough to hold the broken links together on the chain. That it should break today, of all days, seemed to Wanda like an omen. She had known somewhere inside her that day, when she went back to her mother's jewel box, that if she opened it she would be letting out a genie.

'You look very nice this evening,' Nathan had said, with that velvet voice of his, the next time he was there. His eyes had lingered on the necklace and she wondered briefly whether he was trying to assess its value.

Wanda fingered it. 'The necklace was my mother's,' she explained. 'She had a bracelet that went with it. She was wearing it, the day she disappeared. She used to say it was her good luck charm.'

'Ah.' Nathan nodded. Slowly his eyes rose to take in Wanda's face above the necklace. 'Are you like your mother?'

'No,' said Wanda. 'She was beautiful.'

'Well, then,' said Nathan, with a charming smile, 'You are like her.'

He said that I was beautiful, thought Wanda, wondering how soon she could escape back to her room and unwrap the amazing compliment he'd paid her, lay it out and look at it again, examine it from this side and the other, turn it over, put her ear up close to it. Until that moment, she had based her dowry purely on her value as a human being, not on what she would have called contemptuously 'sex appeal.' But with her mother's necklace, she appeared to have acquired her other assets. If her mother had been there, she might have cradled Wanda's face between her two hands and said, lovingly 'My darling child, my lovely creature,' in the way that Wanda heard her sometimes when she lifted Mitzi from her cradle.

It was possible to make a human being beautiful by telling them that's what they were. She knew this. She was not condemned by fate to linger in the shadows. She could metamorphose from a grub into a dragonfly, an ugly duckling to a swan. She could.

***

Abel crossed the square and pushed open the iron gate of the gardens. Sometimes in the winter, when he couldn't eat his lunch outside and didn't want to spend an hour in the stockroom talking to Miss Quettock, he threw Wanda's sandwiches away and walked down to the café on the corner. In the months after the reappearance in his life of Mrs Allerton, he'd sometimes sprinted over to the house in Belsize Park and had his lunch there. He had been delighted to discover that her door was always open. Wanda kept the flat door permanently bolted, even when she was at home.

He was still agonising in his own mind whether to go down the road and look for Cressida. She spent her lunches in an underground refectory at the college, called The Catacombs. The noisy informality, the low light and the dense and smoky atmosphere, were something Abel found exciting and intimidating at the same time. Although outraged at his mother's interference in his life, he doubted that he would have gone to university in any case. The library was where he felt safe. There, he had as many books as he could ever hope to read and if he wanted to reclaim one that was missing from the shelves, the sewing room was where he looked. He'd spent a large chunk of his childhood watching from his Moses basket as his mother spread across the desk whatever loot she had acquired that morning. Her lips moved laboriously as she read the titles of the books she'd brought back, or the labels on the packets. Abel saw the pink tip of her tongue poke out between her teeth as she eased off the date sheet from the inside cover of the books. It sounded like a plaster slowly being torn off someone's knee.

He'd realised even then that Wanda didn't eat the contents of the tins or packets, or bring home the books to read. She turned the pages slowly, muttering to herself, but what she muttered wasn't on the page; it was inside her head. The sound was like a mantra. Abel found it soothing. He would often doze and when he woke up, Wanda would still be there at the sewing table with the book in front of her. When he was not yet old enough to read, it was the pattern of the words that fascinated him, the calming sense that when he turned the page there would be more words on the other side just like it. He soon learnt to recognise which books came from the library and which ones Wanda had decided were not going back there. In his mind, the library was a vast and overflowing treasure-house of words.

He had no wish to be promoted; to go off to other branches or to sit inside an office all day doing paperwork. He wanted to be where the books were. His job served a secondary purpose in that he could monitor the traffic in between the library and the flat. Occasionally, once he'd started working in the library, he retrieved books from the sewing room, replaced the date sheet and returned them to the shelves. His mother seldom took the same book twice. She had a preference, she said, for books that 'told you something.' She particularly liked ones with a moral edge to them, although she only knew from what was on the fly leaf whether what was inside had a moral edge or not. She'd picked up 'Tropic of Cancer', thinking that it was a medical encyclopaedia.

When he was little he would sometimes take a pack of biscuits or a chocolate bar, to curry favour with his brother. Gregor never asked where these things came from. He would have delighted in exposing Wanda, but although he had no qualms about invading other peoples' privacy, the sewing room had somehow passed him by. The only reference he had ever made to it, was one day when he'd had an argument with Wanda and she had retreated into it. He'd shouted after her that he hoped she would be locked in and found years later with a bobbin on her finger and a half-darned sock beside her.

Abel crumbled the remaining sandwich in his fingers, scattering it on the gravel for the pigeons cooing round his feet. He watched them trying to transform the meat paste into something they could swallow, but their beaks kept sticking. He brushed off the loose crumbs from his trousers. It was too late, now, to go and look for Cressida. He pictured Wanda's face when he turned up that evening on his own: relieved, triumphant, ready to assume that Cressida had not existed in the first place. So there would be just the four of them this evening. And his father.

A young woman on the bench across the path from him smiled. He had seen her in the library. If she took her lunches here, she must work nearby. Worried that she might decide to speak to him, he got up from the bench and threw the paper bag into the bin. He walked back briskly down the path and looking at his watch, broke suddenly into a run.

***

'What have we got here?' Gregor stabbed the brownish-yellow circles on his plate. The waitress glanced over her shoulder, insolently. They'd already had a run-in over a miss-spelling on the menu.

'Are you sure the steak is feminine?'

'You what?'

'You've spelt it 'tournedose'. It's either female or not very lively, in which case 'dose' needs a 'z' in it and not an 's'. Of course if 'dose' is what you mean, it doesn't sound particularly appetising. You would not refer, for instance, to 'a dose of oysters.'

'Did you want to eat, or are you only here to criticise the menu?'

'I just wanted to be clear what I was ordering. I think I'll have the sirloin, to be on the safe side. Are the roast potatoes cooked in goose fat?'

'I don't know; I'd have to ask the chef.'

'Is there a choice of vegetables?'

'Today it's cauliflower.'

'What about tomorrow?'

'Wednesday's green beans.'

'Couldn't we pretend it's Wednesday?'

'No, we couldn't.'

'Cauliflower it is, then.' Gregor handed back the menu, holding onto it a second before letting go. The waitress eyed him, coolly. She had fluffy brown hair springing up around the starched white cap. 'Nice crown. I don't suppose you keep that pinny on in bed?'

'Sod off, creep.'

When the plate arrived, he pushed the doughy yellow circles to the edge. 'Well? Are you going to enlighten me?'

'They're Yorkshire Puddings.'

'Did I order them?'

'They come with the roast beef.'

Gregor looked over his plate. 'You've got a very decent pair of legs.'

'They don't come with the roast beef.' She turned on her heel.

'I'll have some mustard, if you don't mind,' Gregor called out after her.

A family sat down at the table facing him. The waitress came back, left the mustard on the table and went over to the new arrivals.

'Don't expect a tip for service,' Gregor muttered.

'It's included,' said the waitress, shortly, taking out her notepad.

One of the two boys at the table opposite leant sideways to look past his father. He watched Gregor whilst he ate. When Gregor stared back with the same wall-eye, he made a face. His father leant across and clipped his ear, then turned to Gregor to apologise.

'Don't mention it,' said Gregor. When the man turned back again, he thumbed his nose. The boy protested and his father clipped his ear again.

Ah, the injustices of childhood, Gregor thought. No wonder by the time we're adults we're such monsters. Plato was right; we should be separated from our parents for our own protection. Not that his had ever got the better of him. From the start he had regarded Wanda as a sparring partner. Physically, when he was young he sometimes came off worse, but intellectually he'd always had the measure of her. When he was thirteen he had decided that he would no longer call her 'mutti.'

'What was that you just said?' Wanda had her back to him, but she'd inclined her head in sharp anticipation.

Gregor stood his ground: 'I called you Wanda. Isn't that your name?'

'I am your mother.'

'Oh yes, I forgot,' said Gregor blithely. Once he'd made a stand, he never back-tracked. Wanda knew it. A direct approach from her would only lead to all-out war. She'd brought his father in, to tackle him.

'Your mother would prefer it, if you called her 'mutti',' Nathan had said, casually, one evening. They'd been playing chess together after supper. Abel had gone back into his room to do his homework. Gregor had already finished his. Although she criticised his lack of application, Wanda knew that Gregor wasn't lazy; he was just too clever for his own good. Things that would have taken anybody else a day to do, he could knock off in half an hour.

He would win the game, but Nathan had a more strategic mind. As adversaries they were well-matched. In a war he would have been the general, planning his attack meticulously. Gregor would have been the reckless subaltern, impatient to advance, intent on victory and glory, never for an instant reckoning the cost in terms of life.

'Unless it goes against your principles,' said Nathan, weighing up the option of securing Gregor's castle with the loss of one knight. 'After all, you're only giving her the name that best describes her.'

'Doesn't 'Wanda' best describe her? It's your name for her.'

His father's fingers moved towards the castle and withdrew again. He hated sacrifices. Any gain was matched by loss. 'I have no other option,' he said, mildly.

'You could call her 'Mrs Silver'.'

'That would sound ridiculous towards my wife.'

'It's what they do in Dickens all the time. Mr Squeers refers to 'Mrs Squeers,' for instance.'

Nathan glanced at him, obliquely. He knew Gregor was deliberately trying to distract him from his move. These were the kind of games they played with one another. 'Are you saying you are doing it for literary reasons?'

Gregor grinned: 'No, actually, I'm questioning the concept of her as my mother.'

Nathan briskly swept the castle off the board. He'd left himself more vulnerable in consequence, but suddenly he felt the game had gone on long enough. 'You're criticising her capacity in that role, I think we are all aware of that. She's certainly aware of it, which is why it is cruel of you to do it. You are telling her that she has failed in the only job she's ever had.'

'Yes,' Gregor said, relentlessly. 'You'd think with nothing else to do, she would have made a better job of it.' He picked up Nathan's knight and threw it in amongst the dead pawns, as if tossing it into a common grave.

'You can't hold her responsible for what you are.'

'All this because I happened to say 'Wanda' once, instead of, well, that other word.' He'd clamped his jaws together in a mock show of resistance.

'I do not wish to discuss it any further,' Nathan said, impatiently. 'I'm merely pointing out that, what to you is just a principle, is deeply wounding to your mother. That is doubtless your intention. If it is, then I am disappointed in you. I thought you had more humanity'.

'Come off it, papi, you know I have no humanity at all. That's why I think I'll end up studying philosophy.'

He'd eked out lunch by ordering plum pie with pastry, that he commented would have served equally to insulate his study. He discovered that the waitress had charged double for the pudding and subtracted it when he made out the cheque. She looked as if she were about to take him on and then thought better of it. Gregor's mouth curled as he got up from the table. She looked after him, vituperatively.

'Have a nice day.'

'You too.'

***

Mitzi saw him come into the cafeteria. She had been sitting at the models' table which ran down the length of one wall opposite the door. There was no policy of segregation, but the models always gravitated to this table and the students never used it.

Mitzi always got dressed before going off to lunch. Some of the other models didn't bother, clumping down the aisles between the tables in their high heels and their dressing gowns, but Mitzi felt this was a bridge too far. She knew that Mr Harpur didn't like such informality and never went to the refectory himself. Sometimes, he brought in tubs of houmous and tzatziki from the little deli on the corner and invited her to share a picnic lunch with him. They sat in Mitzi's cubicle and spread a napkin on their knees or, as had happened yesterday, they took advantage of the fake grass on the podium and sat beside the picnic hamper. She had taken up the pose of Victorine Meurent as Mr Harpur handed her a blini and he had responded by adopting the reclining pose of Manet's brother,

Eugène, who'd sat opposite her in the painting. They had laughed companionably at the little joke and Mitzi felt her heart lift. This was the closest she could get to living in a painting and to have the company of Mr Harpur was an added bonus.

He had needed to call in that lunch-time at the travel agents, he said, and so Mitzi had gone downstairs to The Catacombs. When she saw Abel standing in the doorway, for a second she could not think who he was. You rarely had an opportunity to look at members of your family; you were too busy interacting with them, although lately Abel seemed to have stopped interacting altogether. Mitzi felt in some way she had let him down. Since that appalling denouement with Mrs Allerton, so long ago now, Abel seemed to have withdrawn not only from the family but from everybody else.

Poor Abel. She had tried to warn him but his happiness had given him away.

'Guess who I met this morning in the library,' he had said, as they sat down to supper one night, '..... Mrs Allerton.'

'And who is Mrs Allerton?' said Wanda, pointedly.

'You know, the social worker who came in when dad died.'

'Ach yes, I remember. She was always interfering.'

Abel smoothed the serviette across his knees, defensively. 'That was her job.'

'I did not like her. That is all I'm saying.'

Abel had retreated back into himself. There was a long pause.

'Well?' said Wanda.

'Well what?'

'What did she say, this Mrs Allerton?'

'Not much. I asked her how she was. She asked me how I was.'

'And how is she?'

'She's all right.'

'She must be quite old, now,' Wanda said.

'She isn't old at all,' said Abel hotly. 'She was only twenty-eight then.'

'You remember this from when you were eleven?'

'Yes. Why shouldn't I?' Too late, he saw the warning look that Mitzi shot at him. His mother had regarded him, acutely.

'There is no need to leap off the handle, Abel,' she said, coolly.

'Fly.'

'What?'

'You fly off the handle, mutti.'

'Well, for all it matters,' she said, testily.

He scanned the rows of students. Mitzi wondered for a moment whether it was her he'd come to find. She got up, but before she could squeeze down the row and out into the aisle, he'd turned to someone in the food queue, who looked round and shrugged. She watched as Abel scribbled something on a piece of paper and then gave it to him.

She was anxious not to compromise him. Life might be egalitarian inside the college, but there was a pecking order there, too, and the models ranked as one up from the janitors. She wondered sometimes whether Wanda wasn't right about them. One or two talked openly about the men they slept with. Sometimes, they'd be seen with one or other of the students. Mitzi was appalled. There wasn't one of them below the age of forty. But then, who was she to judge? If they had known what she was guilty of herself, they would reject her out of hand, or maybe they would laugh and welcome her wholeheartedly to their cabal. She wasn't certain which would be the more disturbing.

Two of them were laughing next to her about their husbands' lack of drive. Presumably they meant their sex-drive. Mitzi overheard the women, sometimes, telling jokes with innuendoes, some of which she guessed the meaning of and some which she would rather not have understood. She noticed that they never talked about art. Once when she had tried to start a conversation about Raphael's 'Galatea', whom she'd been impersonating every Wednesday that semester, her companion had looked mystified.

'Who?'

'Galatea.'

'No, the other one; the bloke she's with. It is a 'she', I take it?'

'You mean Raphael? Raphael painted her.'

'Oh, I see. It's a painting?'

'Yes, of course,' said Mitzi.

'Well, you should have said,' the woman threw back, tartly.

People always seemed to blame you for their ignorance, thought Mitzi. She had thought at first that she might find friends at the art school, people who were more like her. But she had come reluctantly to the conclusion that when it came down to it, there wasn't anybody else like her.

'That's nice, a lovely bit of stuff.' The model nearest to her, in a nylon dressing gown, pinched the reveal of Mitzi's waistcoat in her fingers, rubbing it between them as if testing it for durability.

'You like it?' She felt genuinely pleased in spite of the assault. 'I got the waistcoat from the market, but the pattern's mine. I sewed it on myself.'

'I'd never have the patience,' said the woman, carelessly. The dressing gown hung loosely from her shoulder. Mitzi saw the stretch marks on her breast. Another millimetre and the breast would pop out.

' 'like the scarf too. Get that in the market, did you?'

'No, I've had it twenty years.'

'Christ, I wish I could keep things that long. Mine end up in shreds.' She stubbed the cigarette out in the ash-tray and reached in her pocket for another one. Her nails were bitten to the quick. They had been painted red, which drew attention to them. She had dark rings round her eyes and smudges underneath the lashes where the Kohl had run. She looked tired. Mitzi suddenly felt sorry for her. On an impulse, she unwound the scarf.

'Why don't you have it?' she said, bunching it in one hand. 'It looks nice with the kimono.' Mitzi held it up against the dressing gown. She couldn't wear the scarf again in Wanda's presence and she didn't want to leave it languishing inside a drawer.

The woman stared at her, suspiciously: 'You're giving me your scarf?'

'Yes.'

'Why?'

'I don't know.' Mitzi shrugged. 'You said you liked it.'

'You don't give away stuff just because somebody says they like it.'

Mitzi draped the scarf across her knees. 'It was a present. I was given it by somebody who died.'

The woman's eyes locked onto Mitzi's face. This was the sort of tragedy she couldn't get enough of. 'Go on,' she urged.

Mitzi looked up, startled. For an instant she'd been somewhere else. 'That's all,' she said. She might be giving up the scarf, but that was all she would be giving up.

'Your boyfriend, was he?'

'Not exactly.'

'Not exactly?'

'We were kindred spirits.'

'Oh yeah?' She looked sceptical. 'Still, I don't see why you would want to give the scarf away.' She touched it covetously with her fingers.

'I just felt I'd like to give you something.'

'Why?'

'Because I think you need it.'

Suddenly the woman's face banged shut against her. 'What the fuck is that supposed to mean?'

'I'm sorry. I just....'

'What would you know about my needs?'

Those on either side of them, were looking round now, eagerly.

'You said you liked it,' Mitzi uttered, helplessly.

'I might have said I liked it. What's that got to do with anything? I might admire your fanny..... doesn't mean I fucking want it.'

Mitzi got up, hurriedly. 'Of course not. I do see...' She started making her way down the row towards the door. She wanted to get back into the studio. She noted with relief that Abel was no longer there. As she went out, she heard the models' voices clamouring behind her.

'Lady bloody bountiful. I wouldn't mind, but she looks like a sodding peacock when she's dressed. Makes you wonder what she's like without her feathers on....' They laughed and Mitzi, hot with shame, still with the scarf clutched tightly in her fingers, ran along the corridor towards the studio.

***

'The kitten's name was 'Homer'.'

Wanda saw that she had captured his attention. 'It was grandpa Jakob who gave this name to the kitten because every time it went off, always it came back.' She glanced up from the napkin she was darning. 'Home-er'. You see?'

Abel's face broke out into a smile. He laughed and Wanda laughed, too. So many years ago, she thought. There was no reason to resent the cat now. She paused, staring into space as she remembered.

'That's not why he called it 'Homer',' Abel said. He went on filling in the sky with blue above his drawing of a cat. It wasn't like the kitten Jakob had brought home. This one had eyes like Abel's – searching, timid, although she had noticed lately that there was a certain wilfulness about him which had not been there before. No doubt it was the school. They were encouraging her son to have his own ideas.

She gazed at Abel. He was frowning slightly as he bent over his drawing. Wanda wanted to reach out and smooth the frown away. She felt an overwhelming need to touch him, to reclaim him as her own. Sometimes when they were in the sewing room together, he seemed so completely hers that she wished she could leave him in there, lock the door and go away, secure in the knowledge that whenever she went back he would still be there.

Abel put the crayon down and sifted through the box. He took another one and tested the point against his finger-tip. 'He named it after Homer, the philosopher,' he threw out, casually, as if this were just one of many facts he had acquired during his long life. 'He was Greek. He wrote a book he called 'The Odyssey'. We studied it at school.'

'You think your grandpapa would call a cat after a Greek philosopher?' said Wanda, disbelievingly.

'The Odyssey's about a journey,' Abel said, with childish certainty. 'When grandpa called it 'Homer', I expect it was because the kitten went on journeys.

Wanda looked at him. He held the drawing up to study the effect. He didn't ask her what she thought of it. He changed the crayon for a purple one and traced a line around the outside of the cat's head and the sharp points of the ears. He had forgotten all about the other cat. But Wanda hadn't. Now she wasn't only haunted by the cat, but by her ignorance. Of course, she thought, it would be just like Jakob to do something like this and not bother telling her. Was that not how he had disposed of her to Nathan, after all?

Her fingers stuttered suddenly over the charms. She felt the moisture draining from her mouth. One charm was missing. Frantically, she went out to the hall and searched the pockets of the fur coat, digging down into the lining that was separating at the seam. She found a couple of receipts and then her fingers closed on something round and hard. She threw her head back, laughing with relief, until she brought it out and saw it was a five pence piece. She sank down on the kitchen chair again and started rocking. She was kneading the remaining charms between her fingers, as if hoping she could conjure up the missing one by dint of effort.

Should she go back to the market now and search the ground next to the fruit stall? Was it likely that the charm would still be there? Or maybe she had picked it up and it had fallen from her pocket on the way home. In her head, she saw it lying on the pavement, trampled under foot, abandoned. Her charm.

On the evening of her twenty-second birthday, they had gone to Berlingot's. Her father had put on a bow tie, as an indication that the evening was a special one, and Nathan wore the suit that Wanda had decided was his only one. A brief glance would suggest that he was doing very well. His carefulness to detail, his fastidious appearance, trimmed beard, leather gloves, immaculately cleaned shoes and his quiet air of confidence all reassured those meeting him that he was sound, that he could be relied on. It was only Wanda who had looked more closely, who for months had thought of nothing else, who could have reproduced his profile as he sat inside her father's study simply by retracing her way round the image burnt onto her retina, who'd sensed his loneliness, his diffidence, his fear of poverty and failure.

That night at the restaurant he'd been especially attentive, pulling out her chair, adjusting the shawl around her shoulders, filling up her wine glass. Wanda put her hand over her glass, but Mitzi held hers out. She'd tossed her fair curls at the room coquettishly; her laughter punctuated the subdued sounds coming from the other tables. Wanda wished that it had just been her and Nathan in the restaurant.

When they had finished and were waiting for their coffee, he had taken out a small box from the pocket of his coat and laid it on the cloth in front of her. She touched it fearfully. He reached out for her hand and kissed it: 'Happy birthday, Wanda.'

Jakob smiled. The men had ordered brandies. Jakob reached for his cigars.

'What is it?' Wanda asked.

'Why don't you open it?' said Nathan, gently. Wanda fumbled as she took the paper off. She looked down at the small, black box. 'Go on,' he smiled, encouragingly. Wanda pressed the catch. There was a moment's silence. 'A companion for your necklace, Wanda.' Nathan lifted out the silver bracelet and secured it round her wrist. 'To make up for the one you left behind.' The pause had lasted seconds, but it seemed to Wanda to go on forever. Then her father clapped his hands. 'Good fellow,' he'd said, bluffly.

'Thank you,' Wanda murmured.

Nathan sat back, satisfied. He'd raised his glass of brandy in the air. 'To Wanda.'

***

As he looped his scarf over the peg inside the library, Abel saw Miss Quettock glancing at her watch. He was ten minutes late. He looked at Aileen and she gave a warning grin.

'I'm sorry, Miss Quettock,' he said. 'I was on an errand.'

'You weren't buying tickets for the cinema by any chance?' She gave a thin smile.

Abel sat down at his desk. The question was rhetorical. It seemed to give Miss Quettock satisfaction to refer back to that incident whenever Abel came in late, although since then he'd rarely given her an opportunity. In retrospect, he was surprised he'd got away with it for so long. As so often happens after a disaster, he could see the signs were there from the beginning.

He'd been spending Wednesday afternoons in Belsize Park for three months when Miss Quettock had decided it was time to reel him in. 'I'll need you to stay on, this Wednesday, Abel,' she had said, one Tuesday. Abel held the label he had just glued, in his fingers. 'You had better stick that label in before the glue dries,' she suggested.

Abel smoothed his hand across the label carefully, to give himself a chance to think before he answered: 'Wednesday is a little difficult,' he'd said.

'The auditors are coming in a month's time. We must be prepared. The fact that we are closed on Wednesday afternoons, does not mean you are automatically at liberty to go.'

'It's just that Wednesday is my mother's birthday. I said I would take her to the cinema, you see. I've got the tickets.' He had prayed Miss Quettock wouldn't ask him what the film was.

'Very well, we will postpone it till the next week. But your Wednesdays will be taken up from now on.'

Abel rarely glanced up from the books when he was stamping them. Occasionally, he would note the title of the book and form a mental picture of the person who had chosen it before he looked at them. There was a Catherine Cookson face, for instance, and a kind of sombre eagerness in those who chose forensic thrillers. That day he had looked down and seen Mrs Gaskell on the counter. 'Better than a sleeping tablet,' someone once remarked when they returned it.

He had been aware of something in the air, a faint scent of gardenia, and was already searching backwards in his memory for the source of it when he saw that the hand beside the book was pale and peachy-coloured, with a thin band on the middle finger. He had raised his eyes.

She hesitated: 'It's not Abel, is it?'

Seeing her again had been so unexpected that it took a moment for him to adjust. The years had left their mark on Mrs Allerton, but whereas Wanda's face had tightened and grown sharper, Mrs Allerton's had softened and spread out. Her cheeks still had that faint bloom, as if lit up from behind, the auburn hair swept carelessly into a loose roll.

'Yes, it is.'

She smiled: 'You won't remember me. I'm.....'

'Yes, I know. You're Mrs Allerton.'

'Good heavens, what a memory.' She laughed, bashfully. 'It must be over ten years since we met.'

'It is. I was eleven.'

Her eyes searched his face, as if the little boy behind it might still be there. 'So you're twenty-one now; grown up.....Sorry,' she blushed. 'What a thing to say. Of course you're grown up. You were grown up then.'

'I never grew up,' Abel felt like saying. 'After those three weeks with you, I didn't want to.'

'Twenty-one.' She shook her head. 'How are you, dear?'

'I'm very well. And you....?'

'Oh....you know. Can't complain.'

He nodded at the gaberdine. 'You still work for the social services then?'

'I'm afraid there's not much else I'm good for. It's the only job I've ever had. Too late now to take up the piano.' She laughed, cheerfully.

They went on smiling mutely at each other. Mrs Allerton looked past him. She had heard Miss Quettock clear her throat.

'I mustn't keep you,' she said, quickly, reaching for the book, which Abel found himself reluctant to let go of. 'It's been lovely seeing you again, dear. I'm surprised we haven't come across each other earlier, you being in the library. It's not far from where I work, so sometimes I come here instead of Belsize Park.' She slipped the book into her bag and moved along the counter.

Abel moved down with her. 'You're still living in the same place?'

'That's right. Clintock Avenue.'

'I came to tea there.'

'So you did.' She smiled.

'You used to make a special sort of chocolate cake with bits of ginger in it.'

He saw Mrs Allerton's eyes register the longing in his own. She hesitated. 'Maybe you would like to come to tea one afternoon,' she said. 'It would be nice to have a chat. But I expect you're busy.'

'No, I'm not.' His face lit up. 'I'd like that.'

'Well, perhaps next week....'

He nodded. 'Wednesday's half-day closing.'

'Let's say Wednesday, then. About three-thirty? I'm afraid I'll still be in my uniform. I don't leave work till three.'

'That's all right,' Abel said. 'I like you in your uniform.'

She laughed. 'It's not exactly fashionable, but after all these years I'm used to it.'

'I'm glad that nothing's changed.'

As she went through the swing doors, Abel saw her trying to secure a strand of loose hair in the roll behind her neck. She seemed to ebb and flow inside the gaberdine, her body leaking out in unexpected places. She had not secured the flap over the shoulder bag and Mrs Gaskell peeped out from between the ragged files of other peoples' lives.

Once someone else had fixed you to a moment in the past, thought Abel, they became as stuck in it as you were. Every time he turned up late, Miss Quettock would refer back to that Wednesday afternoon when Abel's mother had decided to come looking for him. If this time he'd said 'I went to find my girlfriend at the art school, but she wasn't there,' he might have stopped the needle sticking in the groove and relocated it. 'I dare say you've been looking for your girlfriend, Abel,' she'd have said, the next time he was late. For her, what mattered was to make it clear he hadn't got away with it. But Abel knew that anyway.

***

The wave of passengers was funnelling towards the exits. Gregor had already let one train go through. Although there were a dozen ways in which he might have spent the afternoon, he felt the day had been entirely wasted.

After lunch he'd wandered round Trafalgar Square and spent an hour in the National Portrait Gallery. He didn't want to risk arriving at the flat and finding Wanda there alone. The intervals between their meetings seemed to aggravate their natural antipathy. His feelings for his father were more complicated. Nathan had tried hard to get on with his eldest son, but Gregor didn't want a father he could get along with; he was looking for a hero. Seeing how his father kept his patience, Gregor's natural response was to be more assertive, more aggressive and to push his parents to the limits. By his eighteenth birthday, his relationship with Wanda had reached breaking point. He had left home and she'd made no attempt to stop him. Given her propensity for hanging onto things, her willingness to let him go had seemed to Gregor all the more provocative.

He had pre-empted any birthday celebrations by announcing that he'd made his own arrangements. Gregor had decided it was time he went to Madame Julienne's. He knew his father went there and if it was good enough for Nathan it was good enough for him. The only kind of sex that Gregor hadn't had yet, was the sort you had to pay for. He was not sure how much, or if there were limits to what he could ask for. On the one occasion when he'd been approached, he'd only had a fiver on him and the woman wasn't open to negotiation.

'You have made your own arrangements?' Wanda uttered, scandalised. 'What does this mean?'

'It means that you won't have to bother giving me a party.'

Wanda had had no intention of arranging anything for Gregor's birthday, other than a cake, although his father had slipped fifty pounds to him the night before and told him to enjoy himself.

'You do not think your eighteenth birthday should be spent at home? Here, with your family?'

'Good God, no.' Gregor looked at her as if she had suggested he dine out on cabbage water. 'Isn't that the point of being eighteen, not to have to make do with one's family?'

Abel shot a look of envy at him. Even then, he had suspected he would still be 'making do' at thirty.

'But the next day you are going off to Oxford.'

'That's right. If you'd only held on for an extra day, I could have celebrated there.'

'Well,' Wanda said, abruptly. 'It is good that you are doing something else. We will not be here, anyway. There is a dinner at the club that evening.' She had glanced at Nathan.

He looked back at her with mild surprise. They rarely went out in the evenings. Wanda did not like the club. She blamed the smoky atmosphere for killing off her father. He knew this was Wanda's way of dealing with the slight she felt and he relented.

'If you're sure you won't be here,' he said to Gregor, 'then you won't mind if we have a night out?'

'Not at all,' said Gregor, genuinely.

Abel lingered in the doorway, whilst his brother smoothed his hair down and examined his reflection in the mirror. 'Where are you going?'

Gregor touched his nose.

'Can I come?'

Gregor snorted. Abel wandered over to the suitcase on the bed. 'I've brought you something for your birthday,' he said.

Gregor eyed him in the glass: 'Come on then, hand it over.'

'Only if you take me with you.'

'Where to? Oxford or the house off ill-repute? You're too young.'

'What's a house of ill-repute?'

'A place where you buy happiness.'

'You can't buy happiness.'

'Who told you that?'

'Mutti.'

'She would know,' said Gregor, straightening his tie.

'If you could buy it, everybody would.'

'Most people can't afford it and a lot of them would rather going on being miserable.'

Abel fingered the package in his pocket. 'Once you've bought it, is it yours forever?'

'I'm afraid not. I believe you get an hour's worth and that's it.'

'Does it mean that when you come home, you'll be miserable again?'

'No doubt and I expect I'll have a head-ache, too, but I'll be richer in experience and that's what counts.' He stepped back, to admire his own reflection. Abel caught his brother's eye and Gregor held it for a second: 'Do you want a bit of advice, old chap?'

'I don't know.'

'When you get to eighteen, let me organise your birthday for you. Don't let Wanda do it.'

'Why?'

'Because there's more to life than blowing out a candle.'

Abel handed him the parcel. 'Here's your present.'

'Well now, what could this be?' Gregor fingered it. 'I think I recognise the shape.... rectangular and flat; hard corners...'

'It's a book.'

'You don't say.' Gregor tore the wrapping off. He turned the volume over in his hands. Inside the cover were the faintest marks of glue where something had been torn out. Gregor laughed. 'Cold Comfort Farm!' He rifled through the pages, giggling to himself.

'It's very good,' said Abel.

'Hasn't anybody told you, Abel, it's bad form to read a book you're giving someone as a present.' He came up to Abel, waving the book under his nose. 'And it's a criminal offence to pinch books from the library. You could get me thrown in clink for being in receipt of stolen property. What sort of a start would that be for my glittering career at Oxford?'

Abel bit his lip: 'I didn't get it from the library.'

'Ah. The Oxfam shop?' He shook his head. 'Please, Abel, promise me it didn't come from Age Concern.'

'It didn't.' Abel felt a twinge of panic. 'Don't you like it?'

Gregor laughed. 'I love it.' He slapped Abel on the shoulder.

'Were you joking when you said it was a criminal offence?'

'Who cares, in any case? When it comes down to books, I'm all in favour of free trade. I must say I'm impressed. I didn't think you had it in you.'

Abel was confused. He didn't know if what he'd done was laudable or criminal, but he was vaguely conscious that what happened in the sewing room was not straightforward and that he had better not tell anyone about it.

Gregor took his red and white striped jacket from behind the door and tucked a red cravat into the pocket. He'd let Abel try the jacket on once and been peeved because in terms of height it fitted Abel perfectly.

'Shit,' he'd complained. 'You're such a handsome bugger, Abel, it's a pity you've not got a bit more going for you in the other areas.'

'What time will you be home this evening?'

'God knows. When the money runs out, I suppose.'

'You mean the happiness?'

***

'I happen to go past the library this afternoon,' said Wanda casually. 'I look in. I don't see you, so I go away. I think, perhaps my son is taking stock.'

'Stock taking is the word.'

'It is the same thing.'

'No it isn't, mutti. I'm not taking stock.'

'More fool you,' Wanda said, a little too acutely.

'I was in the back room, I expect. You should have tapped against the window; I'd have let you in.'

'Next time, I tap.' She gave a hard smile. 'If I don't disturb you.'

'No, you won't disturb me,' Abel said. 'But sometimes I go off to other branches. I can't guarantee I'll be there.'

'No, of course you can't,' said Wanda. 'He is busy, my son, now that he controls the library?'

'I wish you wouldn't use that term,' said Abel. 'It sounds fascist. And I don't control the library, I just work there.'

'Well you will control it. In the end.'

The end, thought Abel, dismally. It sounded like a prison sentence.

'You look sad, my Abel.' Wanda laid her hand, consolingly, across his shoulder. He inclined his head towards it. She was waiting for him to reach up and put his own hand over hers, to reassure her that he wasn't straying.

But I am, thought Abel, smugly. I have sinned with Mrs Allerton, not once but many times. And next week I shall sin again.

The afternoons he'd spent in Belsize Park with Mrs Allerton were probably the happiest he had spent anywhere. Each Wednesday afternoon as he went up the path, he smelt the dizzying aroma of the cake she'd popped into the oven half an hour earlier. Sometimes they ate it in the parlour. Mrs Allerton would ask him what he had been doing in the library that day and he took advantage of the opportunity to off-load his frustration with Miss Quettock or the foibles of the old aged pensioners who wanted Abel to explain the plot or give a résumé of books before they borrowed them.

She never interrupted him, or hurried him, or gave him the impression she had other things to do. They laughed together about human nature, something Mrs Allerton had seen a lot of in her time.

Occasionally, they dispensed with the preliminary chat and took the cake into the bedroom where they made love on the crumbs that crackled underneath them. Abel had not had a sexual encounter since the afternoon his brother had experimented on him. He'd associated his pain with Gregor's pleasure and assumed that this was what sex was about. The longer he held off, the harder it became to let go. Now he found that there was nothing easier. Their love making was merely an extension of a tea time ritual. In Mrs Allerton's warm, undemanding body, Abel had at last found peace.

'You don't seem very happy, Abel,' she'd said gently, that first afternoon when they were having tea together. They'd been talking casually about the separate paths their lives had taken.

'Your poor father. Such a tragedy. And you so young.'

'It's just that we were never certain why he did it.'

'Yes, it's hard to come to terms with someone leaving like that, isn't it?' She'd looked at Abel. 'You were such a lovely little boy, so serious. It was as much as I could do to stop myself from hugging you whenever I was there.'

'I wish you had.' He gave a wry laugh.

'They were rather strict about that in the rules. I can't think why; it's not as if a hug did anybody any harm.' She caught his eye and flushed. 'I was surprised to find you in the library. Is that what you thought you'd end up doing? I remember, when you were eleven, you said you would like to be an archaeologist.'

'I don't remember that. But it's a phase you go through, isn't it? Gregor had just gone to Oxford and I thought that that's what everybody did. He's still at Oxford. He's a don, now. He's the bright one in the family.'

'But you're the nice one,' Mrs Allerton had pressed another slice of cake on him. 'You're still young, you don't have to go on working in the library all your life, you know.'

'That's what my brother says. He's always needling me to get out, leave home, get a life. Only people who already have a life say that. They don't appreciate how difficult it is to get one, if you haven't.'

Mrs Allerton was gazing at him. He felt something start to rise in him and fought to get a hold on it. He'd been aware of a displacement in the air as she got up and lumbered round to his side of the coffee table. It was as if he had catapulted back in time and they were perched uncomfortably on the divan in Abel's room with Mrs Allerton's arms round him and her sweetly perfumed handkerchief against his cheek. His world was suddenly reduced to the consoling canyon of her cleavage.

Abel realised instantly that this was where he'd always wanted to remain, secreted between those two breasts whose magnanimity and generosity made up for all the meanness he had suffered, all the paltriness of Wanda's suffocating love, his brother's spitefulness and the desertion of his father. Whilst he stayed there, nothing could go wrong, no harm could come to him.

***

When Mitzi went into the sewing room, she was surprised how cold it was. The Moses basket that was Abel's day-time home until he got too big for it, was still there in the corner. Had it been in Mitzi's room, she would have filled it with dried flowers or cones, but here it had stayed obstinately empty.

Opposite the basket was the sewing table with its treadle and the scissors, pinking shears, chalks, bobbins, all lined up in neat rows. There was no sign of the sewing basket. She did not want Wanda to think she'd been rummaging. Already she felt guilty. Wanda was particular about the things she felt were hers, but it was just a needle, after all. The one she had been using to embroider one of her thick linen belts, had snapped. She needed something more substantial.

In the cupboard, there were piles of sheets and blankets, odd socks waiting for a partner, shirts of Abel's without buttons. In the days before they came to Primrose Hill, this would have been a dressing room. It lay beyond the master bedroom, occupied by

Jakob whilst he was alive and then by Wanda and her husband. It was windowless. It had been commandeered by Wanda as a sewing room from the beginning. Nathan had to make do with a wardrobe in the bedroom. He let Wanda have her way in most things.

Mitzi saw the sewing box at last. It had been pushed back on a shelf above her head. Beneath the tray of cottons, she found what she wanted. When she'd finished her embroidery, she put the needles back exactly as she'd found them and returned the box to its original position on the shelf. She pushed it to the back but there was something in the way. She gripped the shelf with one hand, searching with the other, and felt something round and hard. It was a tin. She brought it to the front. Condensed milk.

She reached further back and found two tins of sardines and a jar of coffee essence. On the label was a dark-skinned man in yellow turban with a tent behind him. She had not seen this brand since the 1950's. She replaced the jar of coffee and the tins and then, on impulse, she went to the next shelf down and edged the pile of blankets sideways.

She felt breathless suddenly. Behind the blankets, stacked in rows three deep and occupying all the space between the shelves, were tins, jars, packets, boxes, all with contents ten or fifteen years beyond their sell-by date. She found a stack of books which came, she realised, from the library and then she found a box of trinkets – bracelets, brooches, scarves, a choker, decorative hair-bands…

For a moment she could not remember where she'd seen these things before and then she realised all of them had come from her room. Every now and then, when Mitzi went to look for something and it wasn't there, she would assume that it was buried underneath the piles of clothes she left haphazardly around the room or that she'd left it in the studio. She didn't grieve for objects in the way that Wanda did. The scarf she had received from Nathan on her birthday, was a token of their fondness for each other. It was an expression of a sentiment but it was not the sentiment itself. Because he knew how she delighted in such things, whenever he saw something she might like, he bought it for her.

She did not think Wanda knew about the gifts, but as she ran her fingers through the contents of the box she realised most of them were here. It seemed her sister had been systematically despoiling Mitzi of whatever souvenirs she might have of her husband. Mitzi closed the box. Poor Wanda, she thought. Did she think she could steal back her husband's love by stealing back the loose change he had left in other peoples' pockets? If the other things in Wanda's hoard had also been appropriated, this was dangerous. Supposing she got caught? But she could only stop it by exposing Wanda and what would the consequences be, then? She removed a bangle from the box, one she had been particularly fond of, and replaced the piles of linen.

She had not said anything to anyone about the sewing room but every now and then, if she discovered something missing that she'd planned to wear, she simply took it back. That's how she'd come to have the yellow scarf around her neck, that day. Her sister wouldn't normally have noticed, but today she was alert to everything. Since she could not risk putting on the scarf again, she'd reasoned that she might as well get rid of it to someone who'd expressed an interest in it. She liked giving presents and she thought that Nathan would approve. She hadn't realised she was being clumsy. Now, the models would close ranks against her. It would be no use apologising. From now on she would be forced to take her lunch breaks in the studio or sit alone in the refectory.

She hoped that Mr Harpur wouldn't be there, but she found him sitting by the podium, a pile of brochures spread out on the floor in front of him. He glanced up with a smile and then looked queryingly at her. 'Mitzi?' He still only used her Christian name if he felt that the circumstances called for it. 'Is anything the matter?'

Mitzi shook her head. 'It's nothing,' she said. 'Just a silly argument between myself and someone else in the refectory.'

'A student?'

'No, a model. I spoke out of turn. I'm sure it was entirely my fault.'

'I'm quite sure it wasn't,' Mr Harpur uttered, knowingly. 'I hate to say this, but the girls don't always live up to their calling. I occasionally feel like pointing out that Rubens or Tiepolo would not have been impressed by their behaviour.'

Mitzi blew into her handkerchief. Already, she felt better. She could count on Mr Harpur to put things into perspective. Since that morning twenty years ago, when Mitzi realised she could not continue standing on the podium pretending to be Botticelli's Venus any longer, he had been the yardstick by which Mitzi gauged the temperature of her relations not just with the living but the dead.

She'd stood for several minutes with tears running down her cheeks before the students noticed. They were concentrating on the other bits of her. Few bothered with her face, in fact some drawings started at the neck. The student nearest to her whispered to the person next to him. A ripple passed along the line. This was the first time some of them had realised they were drawing from the life.

'We'll have a short break.' Mr Harpur's voice had broken in on them. 'We shall resume the class in twenty minutes.' He'd picked up the wrap that Mitzi draped around herself when she stepped off the podium, and held it out to her. 'Come, Mitzi,' he said, quietly. 'Let us go and have a cup of tea.'

'I can't apologise enough,' said Mitzi, sniffing into Mr Harpur's handkerchief. 'I feel so unprofessional.' The handkerchief was large and red, like the ones Gregor tucked into his blazer pockets, only he would never lend you one of his, thought Mitzi; he would let you use your sleeve first.

'Why should it be unprofessional to cry?' said Mr Harpur, gently. 'One is still a human being.' He put down a mug of tea in front of Mitzi.

She reached out and picked the cup up, shakily. The tea was so unpleasant that it shocked her into life. She shook her head and took a deep breath, shuddering as she let out the air. 'No, no, this won't do.' She returned the handkerchief, which Mr Harpur stuffed back in his pocket carelessly, in an attempt to show her that he didn't mind it being wet through. He sat with his hands clasped in between his knees, whilst in the studio the students shuffled chairs and shared jokes, unaware of what was going on behind the faded curtain of the cubicle.

He hadn't seemed surprised by Mitzi's grief. Nor did he pressure her to tell him what the matter was. He merely sat there silently, his presence giving her whatever comfort she could take from it. She'd never entered the confessional, but she imagined this was what it might be like – a kindly, patient figure who would listen to her story and afford her absolution at the end of it.

***

'The witch put one hand through the bars and prodded Hansel with her fingers. 'Too thin!' The boy clapped his hands, delightedly. His mother jabbed his midriff. 'Feed him up and when he's fat enough......' She bared her teeth. The boy stared, wide-eyed, rocking with excitement in his mother's arms. 'We'll eat him!'

At his age, thought Abel, if his mother had made out she was a witch he would have pressed both hands against his ears and screamed. She'd never read to him. He had decided that books must be valuable because his mother wanted them, because the cupboard in the sewing room was full of them. But nobody had teased the content out for him like this. They were a treasure he had to unearth himself.

He busied himself putting books back on the shelf, so he could watch them. The boy held his chubby hands out, patting at his mother's cheeks and pulling at her lips. She growled and he let out a peal of laughter.

Abel laughed, too, and she turned: 'I'm sorry, are we making too much noise?'

'No, not at all. There's no one else here.'

'Yes, there is. There's you.'

'Don't stop for me, please. I'm enjoying it.'

She smiled, but now she was self-conscious and the link between her and her son was lost. The boy looked up at him, resentfully. He turned back to the shelves. If he went back into the body of the library he would have to find something to do and he did not see why he should be driven out because one small boy did not want to share his mother with a stranger.

He'd been twenty-one before he had been held like this in someone's arms. He wondered how things might have turned out if he'd gone on seeing Mrs Allerton whilst he was growing up, if their association hadn't ended so abruptly.

'That's the way they do things, I'm afraid,' she told him. 'We're instructed not to say goodbye, in case the client makes a fuss and gets emotional.'

'Is that the way you thought of us, as 'clients?'' Abel said, resentfully.

'Not you, dear. You were always special. I'd have gone on seeing you, but Mrs Silver thought I ought to stop. She didn't like you coming over at the weekends. She felt I was taking too much interest in you, that it wasn't healthy.'

Abel stared. 'My mother stopped you seeing me!' He felt blood rushing to his head. 'You mean that if it hadn't been for her....?'

'You mustn't blame your mother, Abel. She was acting for the best. And maybe she was right.'

'She wasn't. How could it be right, to stop me seeing you? It was the only thing I had....'

'Oh Abel.' She screwed up her face in anguish. 'It was hard for me, too. I looked forward to you being there. I felt so lonely afterwards. Your mother thought I'd taken you away from her. I didn't mean to, but that's how it must have looked. I thought me being in a uniform would reassure her, but I had the feeling that was what upset her most.'

'She has a phobia about them.' One that seemed to have rubbed off on him too, he reflected.

'I was worried that it might be personal.'

It is, thought Abel.

Once, when he arrived at Belsize Park and she had found the time to change into a dress, he had felt unexpectedly intimidated. He had never seen her in a dress before.

'I bought it in a sale,' said Mrs Allerton. 'I don't buy new things very often, but it's nice to have a change.' She saw the look on Abel's face. 'I liked the colour,' she said, doubtfully, and then when he did not respond. 'Perhaps it wasn't such a good choice after all.'

He gave a weak smile. He could not get rid of the impression that in casting off the uniform, she'd jettisoned her whole persona.

'You don't like it,' she said, and he heard the disappointment in her voice.

'No,' he said, hastily. 'It's very nice. It's just that....' He cast round him for an explanation that would be acceptable to both of them. 'It's just that I'm not used to it. I've always known you in your uniform, now suddenly....' He stopped himself in time, but it had dawned on both of them what Abel meant. In putting on the dress, she had become a woman. Previously, Mrs Allerton had either worn her uniform or she had not worn anything. In either case, her 'dress' did not define her in the way that it defined Miss Quettock, or his aunt, or Cressida.

They looked at one another silently a moment and then Mrs Allerton had nodded. 'I'll go next door and slip into something that's a bit more comfortable,' she murmured.

'No,' insisted Abel. 'Please don't. I'm just being silly.'

She reached out and patted him. 'You're not.' She squeezed his hand. 'We understand each other, dear. That's all that matters. I can wear the dress some other time.' She got up. 'Help yourself to more cake. I won't be a tick.'

Although she wore a plain ring on her wedding finger, after twenty years it had become embedded in the flesh. It was for Abel just another one of the anachronisms, like the green hat with the upturned brim and the old-fashioned upright bicycle, that rounded off the picture Abel carried in his head.

'Is there a Mr Allerton?' he had inquired, once, thinking that perhaps he should have asked this earlier.

'There was, but he's been gone a long time,' Mrs Allerton said, cheerfully. 'He was a merchant seaman. He went off on long trips round the world and came back for a week or two, then he was off again. I got so used to it that it was months before I realised that he hadn't come back from the last one. He'd jumped ship in Bali.'

She had cupped his chin inside her palm and pressed her thumb against the dimple. 'You had that when you were little,' she said, fondly.

'Yes, you used to put your thumb in it and then say: 'Oops, I've made a dent in you. I'd better kiss it better.'

'Oops, I've made a dent in you,' said Mrs Allerton, her voice like buttermilk. 'I'd better kiss it better.'

***

It was no use, Wanda thought. She could not wear the bracelet if the charms weren't all there. It was like a rosary with one bead missing. Agonisingly, she combed her fingers through the separate pieces one more time and then took down a bowl and swept them into it. She had not kept their contract to the letter all these years, to compromise now.

She had worn the bracelet each year on the anniversary, not as a love-gift but because it symbolised the contract Nathan and her father had drawn up between them, one she was determined he would honour. Wanda's disappointment in the restaurant had been so palpable she feared that Nathan must have been aware of it. She'd made a show of turning the bracelet on her wrist and showing it to Mitzi, but as soon as they got home she'd disappeared into the kitchen. Later, as she took the tray along the corridor, she'd overheard them talking in the study.

'My dear chap,' she heard her father say, 'I understand what you are saying. I am not unsympathetic, but you must see that it isn't possible.'

'I would take care of her,' insisted Nathan. 'I'd be like a father to her. Trust me.'

'That is not the point. It isn't just a question of the age she is. I have to think about her sister.' Wanda wasn't able to decipher the response, but then her father had cut in: 'And she will make a good wife.' Wanda held her breath. 'She is reliable. She will look after you the way she has looked after me. You will be well served.' She had listened to the list of virtues. They were not the ones she prized the most. They sounded almost like a plea. 'And you pay court to her, too,' said her father, testily. 'You are a businessman, yes?'

Nathan sighed. 'Your daughters are both dear to me. I have respect for Wanda.'

'It will do. Respect is not so bad a thing to bring into a marriage.' The remainder of the sentence had been lost under a fit of coughing.

Wanda had stood, paralysed. She'd wondered whether she could make the short trip back along the corridor, but if she moved she risked discovery. She had rapped loudly on the door and entered. Instantly, the conversation ceased. She put the tray of coffee in between them and bent down to kiss her father, muttering 'Goodnight,' as she retreated, without waiting for an answer. In the silence of her room she climbed into the iron bedstead, wrapping the fur coat around her, burying her forehead in its muffled warmth and ancient scent. What she had overheard had chilled the last remaining embers of spontaneous affection in her.

***

It had come as no surprise to Jakob to discover he was dying. He had heard the sound his lungs made when he coughed and realised that a fuse had been ignited. He could feel it burning through him, sparking in his arteries. He wasn't sure when the explosion would occur, but it would not be long in coming. When he looked at Nathan, he knew he was looking at a young man on the make, but what the hell, weren't all men on the make? He had been one himself when he had courted Sophie, picking out the prettiest, the most alluring girl amongst the crowd in Iowa, but also, shrewdly, he had picked the girl whose parents owned the biggest house, who had the most expensive cars and who did not have other daughters to dilute the dowry. If I struck lucky, Jakob thought, why should I mind if he does? There had been a moment when he thought that Nathan might choose Wanda of his own accord. He saw how Wanda lit up in his presence. Once or twice she laughed and at those moments she was almost pretty, but she lacked the kind of carelessness that Mitzi had in such abundance. She was solid and reliable, but she was not much fun. If even I can see that, Jakob thought, I dare say he will.

When he'd seen the look in Nathan's eyes, that night, he felt quite sorry for him. This was not how it was meant to be. He knew enough of Nathan's circumstances to be confident that he would not be able to refuse. The boy needs Wanda, Jakob thought. I shall be doing him a favour. He saw Nathan's mouth twitch wretchedly as he perceived that he was caught. His willingness to play the gentleman, had let him down.

'Imagine,' Jakob whispered, 'how hurt Wanda would be if she thought that you preferred her sister.' It was pointless to suggest that Mitzi might be just as hurt by his decision to take Wanda. Nathan knew it didn't work like that. Mitzi would just flutter off and settle on another flower; Wanda would retreat into her citadel.

'Of course, I've told him the decision will be yours.' He'd smiled. 'I married for love and so must you.'

'You think that Nathan loves me?' Wanda had replied.

'I think that he is fond of you and that he would be conscientious as a husband. You may not be rich, but you will certainly be comfortable. I shall make sure of it.'

'How will you make sure, papi?'

'I'll make this house over to him as a wedding gift. The income from the two flats is not great, but it will give you some security. I know that I can count on you to let your sister live here till she marries and of course I hope that you will let me go on living here a little longer, too.' He had laughed, throatily.

So that's the deal, thought Wanda. I get Nathan, Nathan gets the house.

'You can have time to think about it,' said her father. 'Nathan doesn't need an answer straight away. It would be better not to take too long, however. He's already twenty-eight and he is an attractive man. The ladies like him.' He'd subsided in his armchair. 'Think about it, Wanda.'

'I have thought about it, papi.'

Jakob nodded: 'You like Nathan, am I right?' He laughed. 'You reckon you can do the business, as they say.'

***

For quarter of a century, she'd kept the secret of that eavesdropped conversation. Her acceptance had the same hard edge of pragmatism to it as her father's proposition. She was twenty-two. If Nathan didn't value her for what she was, then she could not be sure that anybody else would.

Following the wedding, she and Nathan had gone down to Hastings for a week. The honeymoon, when they had found themselves alone together for the first time, had not been as difficult as she'd expected. Nathan never gave her cause to think that he would rather have been marrying her sister. As for Mitzi, she seemed unaware of any awkwardness connected with her sister's marriage. She'd engaged in preparations for the wedding with her usual enthusiasm.

Wanda bore the ceremony stoically affecting to be happy, even though she knew that with the wedding, she had sacrificed her chance of happiness forever. She could never trust herself to Nathan and, now she was married to him, she had forfeited the right to trust herself to anybody else. Her only consolation was that so had he. A bargain had been struck and she would make sure it was honoured.

She'd observed her duties as a wife, unstintingly. The shyness that so crippled her in company, could easily have melted in the warm embrace of somebody she loved. It struck her that if she had only not been party to that conversation in the study, she and Nathan might have been entirely happy.

Anybody less acutely sensitive might have forgotten what they'd heard, or relegated it to history. But Wanda had preserved her pain as if it were a nugget of discrete gold that could not be dented or devalued. Every time she lay in Nathan's arms she forced herself to think back to the scene outside the study door.

The only men that she had ever loved had both betrayed her.

***

'I'm not sure that I can manage Wednesdays for a bit,' said Abel. 'I think I've been rumbled by Miss Quettock.'

'I suppose we couldn't hope to carry on like this for ever,' Mrs Allerton said, wistfully.

He sank down in the bed until his head was resting on her stomach. 'Why not?'

'Someone's bound to find out in the end,' she sighed. 'They always do.' She'd known, when she ran into Wanda in the street that day, that Abel's mother had her in her line of sight. She might have walked on past her, but their eyes met at the crucial moment. Mrs Allerton had no alternative but to acknowledge her. Inevitably, Abel's name came up in the ensuing conversation.

'He's a fine young man,' said Mrs Allerton. 'You must be very proud of him.'

'Yes, Abel is a good son.'

'I expect you'll miss him when he leaves home,' Mrs Allerton said, guilelessly, and stopped as Wanda's face slammed shut against her.

'Abel has no plans to leave home, I believe.'

'No, it was just…..I'm sorry. I assumed that being twenty-one…' she tailed off.

'He has said this to you?'

'No. Good heavens, no.' Did Wanda know about their meeting in the library? He had not said anything to her. She saw they were in danger. Shame had not played any part in her relationship with Abel until Wanda had imposed it on them, writing 'guilt' in capitals across their foreheads, poisoning their innocence with knowledge. She was conscious of the pink flush spreading upwards from her neck and knew that Wanda had observed it too.

'But I don't want to stop,' said Abel, turning on his side to look at her. From where he lay, he saw the contours of her breasts, the rolling outlines of her neck, the fulsome cheeks, the generous brown eyes that radiated kindness. He felt as if he had wandered in this Eden all his life. He couldn't bear the thought of his expulsion from it.

'Well, we'll have to see,' said Mrs Allerton. 'Perhaps there'll be another day.'

But there would not be any other days. That morning Wanda had determined to discover what it was that Abel did on Wednesday afternoons. She wasn't certain what it was about the meeting she had had with Mrs Allerton that had disturbed her. Whilst they stood there talking in the street, her eyes kept finding Wanda's and then shooting off again, like small, magnetic filings scattered by a centrifugal force. She's lying, Wanda thought. But why? At thirty-eight, she hardly counted as a threat.

As Abel left the library that afternoon, he hadn't seen his mother lurking on the far side of the road, although Miss Quettock had. She'd signalled Wanda over.

'Abel has just left. You'll catch him, if you hurry. He was keen to be back early for the cinema.'

'The cinema?'

'Your birthday present. I hope I've not spoilt it for you. Abel didn't say it was a secret.' She'd smiled, cynically.

'Excuse me, I must catch my son,' said Wanda.

Abel had already disappeared, but as she reached the corner Wanda saw him disappearing down a side street. Quarter of an hour later Abel stopped outside a small house with a ragged garden set back from the pavement. He went up the path and let himself in through the front door.

Wanda had stood silently for several minutes. She risked being seen if she went down the path, but there did not seem to be any other way in. She would have to make it look as if she wasn't snooping. Her gaze moved towards the windows. On one side, she saw into a sun-drenched parlour with untidy piles of cushions littering the floor and armchairs. On the other side, the curtains had been drawn.

She went to knock and then her hand dropped to the door knob and she turned it, silently, between her fingers. She could hear low voices and the sound of laughter coming from a room off to the left. She moved along the passage quietly, trying to blot out the memory of the study door that she had lurked behind that evening twenty-five years earlier. She paused outside the door and with her finger tips, she pushed it open.

It swung back, obligingly, and Wanda saw her son encased in such a broad expanse of flesh that it was hard to know how many bodies she was looking at. The faces separated and she saw that one of them belonged to Mrs Allerton. She'd felt a bleak self-satisfaction.

Abel stared at her. The silence in the room was so complete that it was like another presence. Mrs Allerton had raised her head. Her eyes searched Abel's face. She didn't want to look in the direction of the door. She knew what she would see there.

Wanda drew breath and released it in a long sigh. She threw Abel one last glance, in which she poured as much contempt as she could muster. And then, turning on her heels, she'd left the house.

For Abel it would have been a relief to perish at that moment, not to have to think beyond it, to be found at some point in the future decomposing, with his skeleton and Mrs Allerton's conjoined in death. He had been lying naked on the bed, a plate of melon sandwiches beside him on the pillow, rapturously looking on as Mrs Allerton drew petals round his nipples from the little well of brandy she had poured into his navel. It was one of those ridiculous and paltry rituals that lovers think belong to them alone, deliciously primeval, wild and savage, smacking of the rituals of slaughter and regeneration, Bacchus and the Mass, the holy and the not so holy.

Abel, glancing at his stomach, noticed that a little lake of brandy still lay in his belly-button, an oasis waiting for a passing nomad. He'd had the desire to laugh, but he was not sure what would happen to the sound as he expelled it.

They continued lying there for several minutes and then Abel had got up and started putting on his clothes. When he had finished, he picked up his jacket and went over to the door without a backward glance. He closed it with a soft click after him and made his way back down the path. For several hours he had walked the streets. He'd gone back to the park where he and Mrs Allerton had wandered all those years before. He pressed his face against the window of the ice-cream parlour where she'd watched him eat two Knickerbocker Glories one after the other. He walked passed The Odeon, where he had sat through 'Star Wars' half a dozen times. And then, because he didn't know what else to do, he'd gone home. It was ten o'clock. He had been wandering the streets alone for seven hours.

'We were worrying about you,' Wanda said, her face inclined towards him through the open doorway of the kitchen. 'There is still some stew left on the table. Go and eat.'

Although he wasn't hungry, Abel had responded automatically to the authority in Wanda's tone. He spooned the food onto his plate, mechanically. His jaws were stiff and he felt little shudders rippling through him.

Wanda pushed the bowl of vegetables towards him. He did not look up. She noticed that his hair was wet. She was about to let her hand rest on his head, consolingly, till she remembered whose hand had been there. She drew back. 'Afterward, you run yourself a nice hot bath and then you go to bed,' she said. She'd known he was defeated. It was over.

The few encounters he had had since then, invariably ended up with Abel backing off. Either the woman was the wrong sort (Wanda's judgement), or she was too much like Wanda (Abel's judgement). After two or three affairs like this, he'd started to withdraw into his own shell like a tortoise that, let loose in an allotment, has discovered it does not like lettuce and would rather starve than chew its way through any more. There was a space behind his eyes that Abel kept deliberately empty. Gregor, like Nature, loathed a vacuum but this was Abel's last retreat, the one place where he could still be himself or what remained of him. He was amazed that he was courting somebody like Cressida at all. He would be even more amazed if he got through this evening without either Wanda or his brother bringing down the curtain on his hopes. It was the only time the two of them showed any common purpose.

***

It was starting to get crowded on the station. If he'd not been early, Gregor would have flagged a taxi down. He didn't like the anonymity of travelling on the underground, the sense that he was just a drone like everybody else.

That evening outside Madame Julienne's had been the only time in Gregor's life when his self-confidence had wavered. Nothing on the outside of the building indicated what was going on inside. He didn't know which bell to press, so he pressed all of them. Because the top step would have brought him face to face with anybody coming out, he'd waited on the next step down. It put him at a disadvantage when he realised he was looking up into the woman's face.

'Yes?'

Gregor rattled the loose change in his pocket. 'Am I in the right place?' he asked, diplomatically.

'Depends on what you want, dear. Are you looking for your mother?'

'Christ no.' Gregor snorted. 'Anybody under forty-five, but that's the limit. Thirty would be ideal.' Gregor raised his eyebrows. 'Anybody in there fit the bill?'

She stared at him a moment and then laughed. 'I'm sorry, dearie. We don't do school outings.'

Gregor tried to get onto the top step but there wasn't room for both of them. 'I must have pressed the wrong bell,' he said, irritably.

'Doesn't matter what you press,' she answered, pleasantly. 'The answer's 'No'. She seemed to find his lack of height amusing. 'Come back when you're tall enough to reach the knocker. I'll remember you.'

'You know my father, I believe. He patronises this establishment from time to time.'

'You don't say?'

'Silver is his name. It's my name too.'

'Well, yes, it would be, wouldn't it?' She stood with one hand on her hip. He heard the sound of laughter from an upstairs landing.

'I'm the eldest son. There is another one a little farther down the line. You could do rather well out of our family, if you play your cards right.'

He looked past her down the hall. A chandelier hung from the ceiling and an ornate alcove with a chaise longue and a tray of glasses on a small, round table, welcomed those who'd managed to get past the door.

'You wouldn't like to sign your mother up, as well?' the woman uttered, cheerfully. 'Come on love, I like little men myself, but there are limits.'

'I'm eighteen,' insisted Gregor. 'As it happens, it's my birthday.'

'Happy birthday,' she said. 'Now, if you'll excuse me….'

'I thought you existed to provide a service?' he said, petulantly. He was starting to feel seriously rattled.

'It's a club, dear. Members only.'

'So? I'll join.'

'You can't unless you're nominated.'

'Nominated!'

'By another member.'

'You want me to go back home and ask my father whether he's prepared to nominate me!'

'I just want you to go home.'

'This is ridiculous,' said Gregor. 'I'm eighteen. I want a bloody tart. You've got a shedful of them.' He restrained himself. The woman had backed off into the hall. She held the door with one hand and looked back over her shoulder, as if she were getting ready to call out. He didn't want to have to wrestle with a bouncer. 'Sorry,' he said, 'but I don't see what the problem is.'

'I've told you,' she said, shortly. 'You're not eligible.'

'Trust me,' Gregor said, ingratiatingly. 'There's nobody more eligible on the planet. Christ, I'm gagging for it.'

She leant forward: 'Piss off, or I'll call the fuzz.'

'Let me get this right,' said Gregor. 'Are you saying no one under 5'6" is eligible?'

'What I'm saying is that, in the first place you're not eligible if you're not a member. In the second place, you're not eligible if you're a minor. In the third place, I don't like your attitude, so even if you weren't a dwarf I wouldn't let you in.'

'You don't think that's a trifle prejudiced?' said Gregor, simmering. 'Perhaps you don't take Blacks or Irish. Maybe cripples aren't admitted. What about mutilés de guerre or old aged pensioners? What do you have to do these days to get a whore?'

There was a struggle as she tried to close the door and found that Gregor's foot was in the gap. She brought her heel down on it and he yelped. The door slammed.

'I suppose you think I can't pay, you old slag,' he shouted through the letter box. There was a muffled answer. On the upstairs landing, a door slammed, decisively. He stepped back, staring up at the façade. The blinds were drawn on every window. For the first time in his life, he hadn't got his way.

***

As Wanda stacked the dishes in the sink, her hand shook suddenly. She nudged a glass left on the draining board. It tilted and before she could retrieve it, it had toppled sideways in the sink and smashed. She stared at it, dismayed. Her hands were trembling as she started to pick up the fragments. It was just a beaker, Wanda told herself. It had no value. But it represented something she had had a moment earlier and which she had no longer.

When her father died, less than a year after her marriage, it had seemed to Wanda to release the chaos back into their lives. She'd always been fastidious, but now her tidiness became obsessive. She could not endure a miss-placed serviette ring or a missing book that left a gap along the shelves. She swept the flat out every day; the kitchen pans were burnished till they shone. And she had started doing jigsaws.

First of all they were the usual country cottages and river scenes, but soon she'd graduated to more complicated and sophisticated subjects. It would take the best part of a day to turn the pieces over and to sort the edges from the middle. Then she started working from the outside in, methodically completing each part with a growing sense of her authority. To anybody else it would have seemed a frivolous activity but Wanda knew what she was doing. She was like a general on the battlefield.

For months she had been working on a puzzle titled 'The Awakening Conscience', of a young girl in the costume of the nineteenth century endeavouring to free herself from the embrace of her seducer. It had been there on the coffee table in the dining room for eight or nine months. On the box it had looked fairly simple, but the quantity of detail was deceptive. Not that Wanda minded searching for the pieces that eluded her, provided she was certain they were there. She couldn't bear games where the odds were stacked against her. She had played those games before.

When they were children, Gregor had amused himself from time to time by taking out a piece or adding one. She always knew. Her eyes would linger for a moment on the gap whilst Gregor sank his head ecstatically between the pages of a book and Abel looked on, sick with fear. He'd flinched as Wanda's hand came down across his brother's ear:

'You will not touch the jigsaw,' Wanda hissed. 'You will not interfere with anything of mine. You hear me, Gregor?'

Gregor looked at her in mock bewilderment.

'You hear me, Gregor?' she repeated, menacingly.

'Absolutely.'

Wanda swept the broken glass into a dustpan, running her hand carefully across the draining board, to make sure she had not left any shards. All day she had been haunted by a sense that things were slipping from her grasp. She'd found a photograph of Gregor at his graduation which would go back to its usual position, lying face down in the dark, as soon as the reunion was over. Not for the first time, she had noted the resemblance to his father. Gregor's smile did not have Nathan's flaccid generosity, but it betrayed the same vain sensuality, the same assumption that the world was there to gratify him.

She had placed it next to one of Abel on the dresser. The comparison was not in Gregor's favour, although when you saw the two of them together, you knew which of them would always manage to come out on top. She had the disagreeable impression as she stood there that the eyes were watching her. The smile appeared to waver, then she thought she saw the right eye blink. It was an insect crawling up the face. She grabbed a handkerchief and pressed it on the glass, maintaining the compression of her fingers long after the insect had expired. The black smudge in the centre of the forehead looked like a demonic third eye. Gregor stared malignly at her. She bent down to wipe the insect off the glass and stopped. She could not bear to bring her fingers into contact with that face again. She felt as if she had let something new and terrible into the space around her.

Instinct had alerted Wanda to the very instant when the cataclysm that was Gregor came into existence. The ensuing pattern of his life had been mapped out at his conception. That night Nathan had come home late from the office, or perhaps he hadn't been there after all. He'd knocked over a stool as he climbed into bed. She smelt the brandy on his breath. The scent revolted her, reminding her of that night when she'd overheard the two men sitting in the study, packaging her future, carving up the territory between them.

He had been less sensitive than usual, as if the need had come upon him suddenly. He'd turned her clumsily towards him, foisting himself onto her without the usual preliminaries, unaware of the resentment seething in her. Afterwards he fell asleep at once, a low snore coming from his throat.

So this is it, thought Wanda. Now I have him. She'd experienced a dullish pleasure at the thought that, even if he changed his mind now, he was bound to her by other, more enduring ties. She would be bound as well, of course, but Wanda understood herself sufficiently to recognise that she would not know what to do with freedom if she had it.

She knew, in the moment when she saw her son, that there could be no truce between them. He had fought his way into the world without a backward glance. His tiny, screwed up face exuded rage. He did not look as if he was connected to the human race at all. For months before his birth she'd felt him underneath her diaphragm and braced against her pelvis, bent on taking up as much room as he could. She spent her mornings retching and her afternoons in grey exhaustion. After five months she could think of nothing but the end of her confinement, when she could expel the foreign body that had taken residence inside her.

"Would you like to hold him," said the midwife, who did not seem keen to go on holding him herself.

"No," Wanda shook her head. She'd been in labour fifteen hours. Given that they had a common aim, she was amazed that it had taken him so long to leave her. Now she saw why. This child was determined not to give her any latitude. He was her nemesis, the product of a union that was dishonest from the outset. He had fed on her resentment for the past nine months and now he had his own agenda.

When she fed him, he clung onto her as if he was determined to drain every last drop out of her. Four, five times in the night, she would be woken by his horrid, rasping cry, a wail of neediness, but not the sort of neediness that called up your compassion. His was more the sort that made you want to pass by on the other side because you knew that, once you'd stopped, he wouldn't only have the shirt off your back, but probably the trousers and the shoes as well.

Mitzi was the only one who seemed to have the wherewithal to calm him. She danced round the room with him or rolled him on the floor and tickled him and Gregor's howls of rage subsided into howls of laughter. When she left the room, his brown eyes followed her and when she came back, he held out his arms to be picked up again.

'He seems to get along with Mitzi,' Nathan added, thoughtfully.

'She will give in to him,' said Wanda, a remark that turned out to be horribly prophetic.

***

The train doors slid open and then closed, with bits of arms and legs extruding from the gaps like suitcases that had been badly packed. Somebody nudged him in the back and Gregor half turned. He heard snatches of the conversation going on behind him.

'What you doing? Get yer paws off me!' The woman pushed the man back and he held his hands up, grinning. She made little sallies at him with her handbag, as he tried to back off.

Gregor glanced between them. She was in her thirties, some years older than the man, and her peroxide hair was dark brown at the roots. The man was handsome in a greasy kind of way, with olive skin and dark eyes, and he wore a T-shirt underneath a dark striped jacket, looking simultaneously smart and casual. He ducked his head from side to side. The woman made small pecking gestures with her mouth. The man laughed.

'Fucking A-rab,' she said.

Gregor, who would not have dreamt of interfering, wondered whose side he would have come down on if the situation called for it. His natural inclination would have been to give the woman his support, not out of chivalry so much as with a long-term view of what he might get out of it. Although he liked the absence of commitment that was one of the advantages of sex with call-girls, Gregor didn't see why he should pay for something if he didn't have to. He still sometimes went to Madame Julienne's when he was up in town, but more because he wanted to establish that he had a right to go there, that he'd always had a right to go there, that indeed his father went there and had done so on the night he died.

The police had made a big thing of the visit, to his mother's horror. Neither Mrs Pampanini nor Miss Zellwig had referred to it, but Wanda was convinced they must have seen the findings of the inquest in the local paper. She'd insisted she knew nothing of her husband's visits.

Gregor had his own opinions, but he couldn't feel much over Nathan's death. He was aware that what had not been said between them, never would be, but he doubted that they would have said much to each other anyway. Convinced that he had never had a mother and was not therefore obliged to offer her support, he felt free rather than bereft. You didn't miss what you had never had.

At Baker Street, he changed trains. Whilst he waited, he allowed himself a quick swig from a quarter bottle of Jack Daniels he'd bought earlier. An old man on a bench a little further down the platform raised a mittened hand in a salute that Gregor felt obliged out of politeness to acknowledge.

'There but for the grace of God...' he thought.

He'd used the last of his small change to ring the flat in Primrose Hill. Had Wanda answered, he would have hung up. He didn't want to speak to her, but he knew that receiving calls unnerved her and he felt like passing on a little of the aggravation he had suffered that day.

He avoided looking at the tramp, who was amusing himself by repeating out loud some event involving Princess Margaret and himself. It would be better not to stay there too long, Gregor thought. He didn't want to end up as a character in someone else's past. He looked at his watch. These pilgrimages were a bit like visiting a Pharoah's tomb. You could decipher the inscriptions; on the surface it was colourful and vital, but you knew that ultimately there was no hope of the people in there coming back to life. He'd given up on Abel years ago. He felt he still owed Mitzi something, if only because she'd saved his final birthday in the flat from going down the tubes.

As a child, she had reminded Gregor of those fairies stuck onto the tops of trees in Christian homes throughout December. She was always smiling, whereas he was always raging. Mitzi babbled like an underground stream trickling along its course, whilst Gregor plunged over abysses, raged through culverts, crashed on rocks and flooded villages unfortunate enough to lie across his path. His ego did not leave him with enough room to embrace another human being in his heart, but Mitzi occupied the ante-chamber. He had often wondered why his father, who'd had so much going for him as a young man, hadn't married Mitzi. If she'd been his mother, Gregor thought, his eighteenth birthday might have panned out rather differently.

***

Wanda slipped the dress over her shoulders, fastening the buttons at the back. They were the kind of linen buttons that you only found in button boxes of a previous generation, difficult to fasten and, once in the holes, you couldn't get them out again. She'd worn the same dress every year. Grey suited her. As time went on, she'd had to let the waist out by a fraction and release the stitches in the shoulders, but the dress had worn well. It had never been in fashion, therefore it was never out of it. Whereas the costumes Mitzi wore, remained bizarrely young, the ones that Wanda favoured, had been ageless. Once, the colour had set off the dark hair that cascaded down over her shoulders. Now, she was a hard, metallic grey from top to toe.

She smoothed the satin at the throat. The high neck gave her a regality that Wanda found becoming. She secured her mother's necklace round her neck. Her fingers briefly circled one wrist where the bracelet should have been. She felt as if she had left off a vital piece of chain mail. Carefully, she combed her hair and swept it up into a roll behind her head. She stepped back from the mirror to examine the effect.

'The only thing that's missing is the mace and the tiara,' she'd heard Gregor mutter, scathingly, the first year.

Wanda brought the large oak carver from the study and positioned it at one end of the table, with a cushion on the seat to give her extra height. She made sure Gregor's chair, which was the same height as the others, did not have a cushion on it. She would not have Gregor looking down on her.

The heavy, aromatic scent of goulash drifted from the kitchen. She looked round her at the polished oak, the neatly folded serviettes, the gleaming silver. She had toyed with the idea of bringing out the album. All the photographs inside it, were of Abel. She had thought of showing some of them to Abel's friend if she turned up that evening, but he had been such a handsome little boy, she was afraid the gesture might backfire.

'So like his father,' people used to say. Nobody had suggested that he looked like Wanda. Wanda didn't care. When it came down to it, her younger son was hers. But for a cloakroom ticket he might never have been born.

When Wanda found the crumpled ticket in the inside pocket of her husband's coat, she'd been surprised that she was not consumed by jealousy. She thought that this was probably because her great fear wasn't losing Nathan; it was losing him to Mitzi. When she searched the lining, she found others.

She had never heard of Madame Julienne's, so one day she'd stood in the shadows opposite his office till the light went out and followed Nathan down the road and up a side street to the entrance set back from the road. She'd drawn her own conclusions from the people entering and leaving. Businessmen and whores. She knew the type. She'd seen them on the streets of Warsaw with their high heels and their scarlet lips.

So Nathan visits prostitutes, she thought. She felt she had been short-changed on an item she had paid for, though it wasn't likely Nathan would find a replacement for her in the brothel. It was sex that he was after. Well then, Wanda thought, I'll show him I could give him that too, if I wanted to.

She'd waited three days. Friday was their anniversary. The celebrations had been muted from the start. Once Gregor came along, there seemed less cause for them. That evening she had put a candle on the table and laid starched white napkins on the place mats. She did not ask Mitzi in to join them. Mitzi had her own life. She went out each morning to the council offices and came back every night at six o'clock. Occasionally, Wanda called out to invite her in, but for the most part Mitzi cooked her solitary meals and ate them in the kitchen by herself. Before he came home, Wanda had put on the necklace and tied back her hair.

'You look nice,' Nathan had said, hesitantly. Wanda pecked him on the cheek. He caught a faint whiff of her perfume and his heart sank. For some months they had existed in companionable silence, making no demands on one another. After Gregor's birth, he had felt he could reasonably withdraw from any carnal obligation. He'd fulfilled his debt to Jakob and would carry on fulfilling it. But if he could not find the key to making Wanda happy, that was not his fault.

Her reticence bewildered him. Although he wasn't sensuously

drawn to her, he thought he saw in her a recklessness, a longing to be swept away that, had he loved her more, he might have satisfied. He had set out to conquer her reserve with charm, but sensing her reluctance, he stepped back. Like boxers in a fixed match, they withdrew into their separate corners, meeting with a show of fisticuffs and sparring to keep up appearances, each looking forward to the moment when they could abandon the pretence and give themselves to other things.

There had been one occasion, which he was ashamed of, when he'd forced himself upon her in a sudden rage of bitterness and need, but the assault seemed to have left her unaffected. She lay stoically whilst Nathan thrashed about on top of her, increasingly aware that although alcohol had spiced his rage, it hadn't had the same effect on his performance. When he finally rolled over on his back, the sweat was running down his forehead. Wanda had not said a word but in her silence he could sense her victory.

He knew that by insisting on his rights, he'd forfeited them, morally, for good. In later years, whenever either of them looked at Gregor, with his greedy eyes and stubborn nature, they relived the violence of the act that had produced him and which Gregor seemed determined to revisit on them in his own inimitable currency.

It was in order to escape the sense of failure that had dogged him since his marriage, that he started going back to Madame Julienne's. He wasn't desperate for variety. He had no 'special needs' and Gilda who was his preferred choice was a thirty-something widow who had found a refuge doing something that she did well and without resentment, for a greater sum than she could have commanded in another job. She didn't sulk if months passed without Nathan coming in, but when he did, they chatted easily. In other circumstances, he would have been happy to come home to Gilda every night. The problem was that he would not have had a home to come to. It did not occur to him that evening that the vision of his wife attempting to seduce him, might be the result of her discovering his secret.

He sat down obediently in the arm chair, whilst she eased his shoes off. Nathan rested one hand on her head a moment and she leant her forehead on his knee. 'What is it, Wanda?' he said, anxiously. 'Is something worrying you?'

Wanda tossed her hair back in a show of carelessness: 'You don't remember what tonight is?'

Nathan made a show of thinking. 'Ah,' he murmured. 'Yes, now I remember.' He reached in the pocket of his coat and handed her a long, thin box. Inside, wrapped carefully in tissue paper, was a pair of beautifully tailored leather gloves. She touched them, reverently. She would never have bought anything as costly for herself. 'They're beautiful,' she murmured. 'Thank you.' Nathan leant across and kissed her.

'Happy anniversary.'

For once, their evening wasn't torn apart by Gregor. He had spent the best part of the afternoon down on the first floor with Miss Zellwig, practising the violin, though 'practise' wasn't quite how she would have described it. She had never had a pupil like him. She would play him tunes on the piano whilst he listened with his face a rictus of attention and then, with his large eyes glowing like volcanic rocks, he played the same tune back to her. She might suggest improvements, which he tried, but if he once decided they were not improvements after all, he tossed his head dismissively and went back to his own interpretation. When Miss Zellwig offered to accompany him, she became aware that, far from using the piano as a regulator for the speed, she was expected to keep pace with him.

'I do not think that he is teachable, your Gregor,' she said.

But at least, thought Nathan, he is occupied. He had been four years old when he discovered Jakob's violin inside the study. They could hear him crooning to himself as he experimented with the different sounds the strings made and the sequence in which he was able to wring music out of them. The minute that he put the violin under his chin, his energies were harnessed. He was in another world which they could only access through the sounds he made. It was as if, thought Wanda, everything that Gregor did was bigger, better or more horrible than anything that anybody else could do.

When she had cleared away the plates, she brought the brandy bottle from the study and the box of small cigars that Nathan kept there. He smiled, sleepily: 'It's been a lovely evening, Wanda. Thank you.' She felt suddenly suffused with pleasure. 'Have a little brandy,' Nathan urged.

She put her hand up: "You remember last time," she said, backing off.

'Six, seven years ago. You were a child then. Here,' he handed her the glass. 'I promise you will feel entirely happy afterwards.'

It was a promise that was irresistible to Wanda. She had long ago abandoned any hope of ever feeling happy, let alone entirely happy. She allowed the glass to brush her lips and took a small sip. As the scorching liquid crossed her tongue and burnt its passage down her throat, she felt the warmth begin to radiate out from the centre of her: 'You are right,' she laughed. 'I do feel happy.' She threw back her head. 'I feel so happy.'

Nathan got up from the chair and took her arm. The bed was cold when she got into it. She had felt Nathan's body next to hers. He'd raised her nightdress gently and unhurriedly and passed his hand across her breast. She'd felt a lingering residue of awkwardness that was in open conflict with a surge of longing to be utterly possessed. She didn't want to have to give permission or to feign restraint. She wanted to be freed from having to express an attitude, to lose herself entirely in the moment.

She clung on to him as if he were a rock and she a barnacle. She stroked and pummelled him, she touched him lightly, nibbling at his shoulder, kissing him between his fingers, tugging lightly at his beard and making tramlines with her fingers down his back. It was as if she had been taken over by another person altogether. She hoped fervently that the effects of alcohol would not wear off. She knew that she was acting like a harlot and she gloried in the fact.

She called his name and he called hers. She wondered if their voices would be audible to Mitzi in the room along the corridor. She hoped they would. She felt a liberation she had never felt before and never would again.

'I love you,' she cried, for the first and last time in her life, and in that moment she knew that another one of Nathan's sperm had reached its destination.

Afer his conception, Wanda's focus of existence had moved imperceptibly, but permanently, to her younger son. She knew that what had happened might have changed the way that she and Nathan acted with each other. But already, Wanda sensed that she had an alternative to Nathan growing in her womb, a creature she could mould entirely to her satisfaction, who was hers completely in a way that Nathan couldn't be.

She hadn't told him until she was several months into the pregnancy. She'd wanted to keep Abel to herself as long as possible. She even felt antagonistic to the midwife's gentle probing, as if this were an unwarranted intrusion on their life together. She had known from the beginning how he would look after he was born, not dark like her, but fair like Mitzi and her mother. He could easily have been mistaken for an Arian and this alone gave him an added value in her eyes. He had escaped the yoke that had destroyed so many of his antecedents. Wanda stroked the fuzz of fair hair and the pink cheeks. He was like a fragile piece of porcelain.

As Abel grew, his passive nature seemed to stabilise the household. He sat silently for hours in the armchair with a book in front of him that he could not yet read, his ears tuned to the rustle of the pages, listening to the sound his thumb made as he sucked it. Once he started walking, Wanda never took her eyes off him, removing obstacles from underneath his feet, confining any object that he showed an interest in to shelves above his head. He did not have a chance to hurt himself as other children did because his pathway through life had already been divested of potential dangers.

Wanda closed the album, letting her hand rest on it a moment. She was thankful that the time had passed when Gregor's influence upon her younger son was likely to affect her. She had held her breath as Abel got to sixteen and then eighteen and then twenty-one and then she had released it slowly. There would be no further crises, she'd decided.

***

Abel kicked his heels outside the college. If she hadn't got his message, Cressida would have already left. He dug his hands into his pockets so as not to endlessly keep looking at his watch. The flat was nearer to the library than the art school, but he'd thought it best that Cressida should not turn up without him. Although he had rarely been inside the homes of other people, Abel realised how unwelcoming his own must seem with its dark, heavy furniture, the mulberry coloured velvet curtains and the faded, gilt framed photographs of relatives who had been left behind in Europe or America. He couldn't bear the ghetto smell of Wanda's old fur coat, the laboured ticking of the clock that had passed back and forth across two continents, the high-heeled shoes and feather boa worn by Mitzi, that evoked the pre-war decadence of Berlin in the thirties, and the shrine with its bizarre appendages.

You wouldn't get an English family behaving in that creepy and obsessive way, he thought. It was ironic that the only anti-Semitism Abel had encountered, was the streak of it he had discovered in himself. He liked to think that he was English, even if the family he belonged to wasn't.

When he was a child, he had assumed as children do, that everybody's family was more or less like his, although he'd always known that there was something not quite right about it. Take his father's suicide. In retrospect, he saw that months before it happened ordinary events had taken on a sinister dimension. He'd heard Gregor and his aunt together in the kitchen on the night of Gregor's eighteenth birthday. He had not been able to make out the words, but he immediately recognised the tone of Gregor's voice, cajoling, with odd bursts of cruel laughter.

Curiosity would normally have prompted him to eavesdrop, but he was aware that what he heard might distance him forever from the innocence of childhood. Suddenly, there was a tiny shriek from Mitzi that reminded Abel of a rabbit he had seen, once, wriggling in a weasel's jaws, a cry at once shrill and despairing. He had pressed the pillow to his head and blotted out the sound.

When he woke up the next day, Gregor had already left for Oxford. In the weeks that followed, Mitzi seemed increasingly preoccupied. One night at dinner she announced that she had been invited down to Deal, where Mr Harpur had a cottage.

'Deal?' his mother had said, frowning. 'Where is this town?'

'On the south coast,' Nathan said. 'You'll like it, Mitzi. It's like Westgate; rather grand but in a run-down way.'

'But you are going there with this man who you hardly know?' insisted Wanda.

'Mr Harpur and his sister own a cottage there. He thought the sea breeze would be good for me.' A pained expression crossed her face. 'I haven't been myself, just lately.'

'I suppose that when you take your clothes off, it does not take so much time to get to know these people.'

'I've been working at the art school five years, after all,' said Mitzi, patiently. 'I do feel I know Mr Harpur well. He is a widower who lost his wife in tragic circumstances.'

'Are you hoping that he might be looking for another wife?'

'I know he isn't. He was very happy with the first one. He knows love like that can't happen twice in anybody's life.' She had looked quickly at his father, then at Abel. And then she had stared down at her hands. He was afraid she was about to cry, but it was more as if her head was bowed under the weight of something.

When she came back on the Monday evening, she'd seemed almost carefree.

'You enjoyed your weekend, Mitzi?' Wanda asked her, over supper.

'It was lovely,' Mitzi said.

'Here, it was not so good,' insisted Wanda.

'Here, it was perfectly all right,' said Nathan, smiling.

Abel looked at her. 'Did you see boats in Deal?' he asked.

'Yes, dear, there were a lot of boats. And seagulls.'

'Tell me more about the boats,' insisted Abel. He was into boats and water. Anything that offered an escape.

'I brought you back a postcard,' Mitzi said. She rummaged in her handbag.

Lynn Bushell

Abel had looked at the sailing boats and seagulls and the water stretching out behind them. He'd gone down the passage to his room and tacked the postcard to the pin board.

It was still there three months later when he heard his mother's shrill voice calling out, hysterically, and Nathan shouting from the hall where he was hanging up his overcoat:

'What is it, Wanda? What's the matter?'

'She has gone!'

'Gone where? Who?'

'Mitzi, she has left us!'

From that point on, Mitzi's absence was connected in his head with the flotilla of small boats. The freedom they embodied had acquired an edge.

His mother thrust the letter at his father, who leant heavily against the wall a moment after he had read it. He seemed drained of energy.

'Well,' he said, weakly, 'she is old enough to make her own decisions.'

'No,' hissed Wanda. 'When she make her own decisions, these decisions always they are wrong. Why she has run away? Why she has never brought the man here?'

'I expect she thought we wouldn't like him,' Nathan said.

'We do not even know that she is courting. There is no engagement. There is even not a wedding. She go off like someone burgling in the night.'

'Not quite,' said Nathan.

'She write that she wants to spare us. Are we spared now? Do we tell her, 'thank you, Mitzi, thank you for not sharing this news with us earlier?' She will be ruined. It is us who will pick up the bits of her.' She'd snatched the letter, reading it again, and started to walk up and down the room. 'It will be someone from the art school. Where else would she meet with men? No doubt he has already seen her without clothes. Why should he bother to treat Mitzi with respect when she does not respect herself? Who knows, perhaps this 'Mr Harpur' she is always going on about, perhaps he is the one.'

'I doubt it,' Nathan uttered, wearily. 'From all we've heard of Mr Harpur, I don't think he would encourage Mitzi to act recklessly.'

'Who, then?'

'I don't know.'

'She has not said anything to you?' said Wanda, her eyes narrowing.

'No.'

'You are sure?'

'You think I wouldn't tell you if I knew where Mitzi was? Of course I would.' He shook his head, distractedly, and walked past Wanda to the kitchen. She pursued him, worrying the letter in her hands as if she thought it might yet yield its secrets, and then threw it down.

'All right then, let her go. She will come crawling back here on her knees.'

'I hope you will resist the urge to crow, if Mitzi does come back,' said Nathan.

'Crow. That is a bird, na?'

'Yes, you know the ugly sound they make.'

'What are you saying?'

'It would be unseemly to make capital of her unhappiness, if in the end it doesn't work out. That is all I'm saying. We must be there if she needs us. Let us hope she doesn't.'

In the weeks that followed Mitzi's disappearance from the flat, it seemed to Abel that his mother centred her attention on him even more obsessively. He felt the full force of her love as if it were a blanket wrapped around him in high summer. He woke up at night and found her staring down at him. She sat beside his bed each evening till he feigned sleep and each morning she was there when he awoke. Once, he had overheard his parents arguing.

'It's not as if you've been abandoned, Wanda,' said his father. 'After all, you have your children.'

'Gregor is not here. Soon Abel will go too.'

'I doubt that.'

'Do you? Why?'

'Because I doubt that you will let him.'

'What choice do I have? When he is eighteen, if he want to go, he go. Like Gregor.'

'He is not like Gregor, though. Unless you let him go, he will still be here when he's forty.'

'You would separate us. Yes, I know.'

'It isn't that I want to separate you. He will always be your son, but you are suffocating him with love. He can't think for himself. His every action is determined by what you will think.'

'You want him to be selfish, like his brother?' Wanda threw out. 'You think Gregor is a good example to him? Gregor is a monster.'

'He is rather egocentric, certainly. But he is gifted. Gifted people can be difficult.'

'He is impossible. Like an electric current in the brain. He go through everybody like a dose. When Gregor go, I sigh, yes. With relief.'

'But still, with Abel it's important not to go too far the other way,' said Nathan, trying to maintain his patience. 'You must give the boy his head.'

'He is not yet eleven, Nathan. Abel does not have a head. He is a baby.'

He could hear his mother pacing up and down the room, neurotically: 'In any case, it is not Abel who is now the problem; it is Mitzi.'

'She can hardly be a problem if she isn't here. She isn't asking us for anything.'

'Not yet. She will, though.'

It was shortly after six o'clock one evening when he heard his aunt's voice in the hall. She went immediately to her own room. When his father came back from the office, Abel heard his mother whispering to him in the hall.

'How is she?' Nathan asked.

His mother answered him dismissively, then added: 'Something, it is not the same.'

'What?'

'I do not know. Something, it is missing." Wanda, so acutely sensitive to things when they went missing, was for once in a position to perceive a loss in someone else.

At dinner, Abel kept on sneaking glances at her. No one spoke. His father had insisted that he mustn't pressure her with questions. 'She is tired.'

'But she's just had a lie-down,' he protested.

'Mitzi's is the kind of tired that goes on for a long time,' Nathan said.

The silence round the table bothered Abel. It had been like this for months. He missed his brother, whose anarchic posturing restored the balance in the household, and he missed his aunt, whose innocent naiveté made even Abel feel that he knew something of the world. 'Did you bring something back for me?' he ventured.

Mitzi hesitated: 'I'm so sorry, dear, I didn't think.'

'It doesn't matter.' Abel shrugged his shoulders.

Nathan touched her hand, solicitously: "Let me pour you out a little wine." He moved the glass towards her, tipping the decanter. The extent of Mitzi's desolation wiped out any bitterness he felt at her desertion. He was shocked by her appearance. There were faint lines round her mouth and on her forehead which had not been there before; her eyes were vague and distant, as if she were gazing through a veil; her fingers fluttered at her sides, distractedly. He knew that this was his fault. He had not looked after Mitzi. He had left her unprotected. She had fallen foul of this man and now she was falling foul of Wanda.

'You will get a job now, I imagine,' Wanda said, as she began to clear the plates away. 'At least you will not be returning to that place where everybody take their clothes off.'

'They did say that I could have the job back,' Mitzi said.

'But now you are a married woman.' Wanda looked at her, obliquely.

Mitzi hesitated: 'No,' she said.

'You gave us the impression that you were.'

'It seems he wasn't free to marry.'

'What a pity that you did not ask him.'

Mitzi sighed.

'You thought he loved you and he didn't,' Wanda threw out, cruelly. 'I'm surprised it take as long as six months. I think I would have known sooner.' Abel heard his father clear his throat, but Wanda carried on. 'You have brought shame upon the household, Mitzi.'

'Wanda, there's no need...'

'Yes, there is need. She go off without saying anything, with some man we have never met, whom we would not like, and then later she come back as if nobody has been inconvenienced. She think she can take up where she leave off and nobody will notice. What will Mrs Pampanini say? Miss Zellwig?'

'Who cares what they say?' said Nathan, angrily.

'It matters, Nathan. And the social club. We have to live here; we have a position.'

'Oh, for God's sake, Wanda!'

'Always it is Mitzi who is wilful, who can get away with things, who does not have responsibility for anything. She come back thinking OK everything is all right. There is Wanda, there is Nathan. Always there is someone.'

Nathan's face was thunderous. Mitzi stared down mutely at her plate. There had been moments in the past months when she thought she was about to lose her mind. She could not speak to anyone about the thing that troubled her; not Wanda, she would only revel in her sister's fall from grace; not Gregor, he would blame her. Abel was too young and, although he was soothing company, he could not offer practical advice. The only person that she might have spoken to was Nathan, but he was the only one who put a value on her and she feared to lose it. She felt desperate to be on her own. She got up, stumbling as she let go of the chair. 'Forgive me, Wanda. I feel very tired.'

There was a stony silence after she had left the table.

'That was unforgivable,' said Nathan, finally. 'How could you, Wanda?'

'I do not know what you mean.'

'You know exactly what I mean – to start haranguing Mitzi about finding work, the minute she is back. You see how ill she looks. Are we so poor we can't afford the piffling amount of food that she consumes? There's nothing to her, as it is.'

'Of course,' said Wanda, carelessly. 'You always have the soft spot for my sister.'

'I love Mitzi. Are you saying you don't? We are all she has.'

'No,' Wanda said, triumphantly. 'She has this man who has now left her. Why can't he look after Mitzi? She is his responsibility.'

'You talk of her as if she were a package to be passed from hand to hand. I'm simply saying she is ill and we should give her time.'

'She is not ill, of course she isn't. She is, how you put it, 'mooning'.'

Abel had been woken in the early hours by the sound of Mitzi weeping. Somebody had gone into his aunt's room. Abel heard the door click open and shut quietly and the pad of footsteps crossing over to the bed. The racking sobs continued but now they were muffled and, above them, Abel heard his father's voice entreating gently:

'Don't cry, Mitzi. It will be all right now.'

***

Wanda didn't know what had possessed her that night. When she first saw Mitzi on the doorstep, she had felt a wave of pity. She thought she had never seen a human being so defeated. But before she had a chance to make a move, the pity was replaced by fear. If Mitzi could be brought to this, what might be waiting for the rest of them? She'd had a sudden urge to shut the door on her, to put a barrier between herself and the destruction Mitzi had unleashed. The moment that her sister crossed the threshold, she could see their lives unravelling.

That night she'd struggled to remain awake, assuming Nathan would soon join her. But he hadn't, and at last she fell into a restless sleep. She woke and saw that it was two o'clock. She stretched her hand across the mattress. Nathan wasn't there. The light out on the landing clicked on and then off again. She went into the hall. There was no longer any sound from Mitzi's room.

She put one eye up to the spy-hole and saw Nathan on the landing. He was staring into space, as if a scene were taking place in front of him that he was interested in, but not in an involved way. She watched as he took his jacket off and looped it carefully over the bannister. He slid the braces down over his shoulders.

Is he drunk? she wondered. Does he think he's somewhere else? His movements were coordinated and precise. He ran his thumb and index finger down the trouser crease, to make sure that it folded in the right place. Suddenly, she realised what he was about to do. She'd watched with fascinated horror as he gripped the bannister behind him. He was shaking with the effort of sustaining his entire weight on the narrow ledge.

She crept out of the door and stood behind him. She could see the dark hairs on his neck collecting beads of sweat and noticed how the veins protruded on his hands. So, she had thought, it's come to this. How dare he think of leaving her? She felt herself possessed of a demonic force, a sudden rage that once more something was about to be ripped from her grasp. She leant towards him, hissing in his ear, so that a small dart of saliva catapulted forward on his cheek:

'All right, then. Jump!'

And Nathan had.

***

'Guess who?' She took her hands from Abel's eyes and came round to the front of him. 'I'm sorry, am I late? I didn't have a chance to scrub up, I'm afraid.' She held her hands up and he smiled. The chipped green varnish wasn't thick enough to hide the dirt and paint beneath it. She had on a pair of denims and a man's shirt with the cuffs rolled up. Her fair hair had been chopped back even further in an urchin cut that took another five years off her age. She was the incarnation of a youth that Abel felt he'd been denied.

'I didn't think you'd come.'

'It isn't every day I get the offer of a free meal,' Cressida said, tactlessly.

'You look terrific,' he said, adding with an irony he hoped would pass her by. 'The dinner will be very casual.'

She looped an arm through his They crossed the pavement. Stuffed into her rucksack was a bunch of daisies evidently taken from the public gardens opposite the library since they had been bulked out with a branch of hawthorn.

'Who'll be there this evening, at the party?'

Abel hesitated: 'It's not really what you'd call a party, more a family reunion: my mother and my aunt; I mentioned Mitzi to you. And then there's my brother Gregor. We don't see him often. Once a year, in fact.'

'He lives abroad, then?'

'Gregor? He lives on a different planet.'

'Great.' she nodded, airily. They'd reached the market, where the traders were dismantling their stalls. She dropped his arm and walked ahead of him around the puddles in the rutted tarmacadam. When they came out at the far end, the apartment was ahead of them.

'I ought to tell you, there are things about my family that might seem a bit unusual,' said Abel, cautiously. 'My mother's Polish. Over there, they do things differently. She never properly adjusted to the English way of life.'

'Right.'

'Twenty years ago, my father fell into the stairwell from the top floor landing of our flat. My mother never really came to terms with it. This evening is the anniversary.'

She looked at him with interest: 'Dead, then, is he? Your dad?'

'Yes. It's just that sometimes when my mother talks about him, you might think that he was still around.'

'I get the picture.'

***

'Gott in Himmel,' Wanda said. 'You look as if the hedge has pulled you backwards.'

'Nice to see you, Wanda.' Gregor offered up his cheek. Wanda pursed her lips at it, distastefully. ' I tried to ring you earlier. There wasn't any answer.'

'I'm not answering the phone to strangers, Gregor.'

'What's the point of having a telephone, if you're not prepared to answer it?'

'The telephone is there for an emergency.' She looked at Gregor's scuffed shoes and the dead leaves clinging to his trouser legs. 'Where have you been?'

'I came across the park.' He looked around, uncomfortably. For all his efforts, it seemed he had still arrived first. 'Where's my brother?'

'At the library.'

'Nothing's changed then.'

'Only that you aren't with Gloria,' said Wanda, smugly. She did not want it to look as if she had an interest in his marriage, but she wished to know if she was still obliged to look on Gloria as family. 'Are you getting a divorce, then?' she asked, finally.

'I've got one, as it happens.' Gregor took his coat off.

'It was nice of you to tell us,' said his mother, stiffly.

'So that you could share the good news?' Gregor felt inside his pockets for his cigarettes.

'It is a big thing, a divorce. You need your family at a time like this.' He gave a short laugh. 'I am not surprised the marriage did not last,' said Wanda. 'Gloria was never one of us.'

'True. That was one thing she had going for her.' He went over to the window. Since he'd come into the flat, she noticed he'd avoided looking at her. He was more upset, perhaps, by the divorce than he was ready to reveal. She looked at Gregor's craggy profile, with its stubborn chin and it's determined swagger, and she felt a satisfaction mingled with an older, less familiar emotion.... pity.

'Maybe if you were a little more accommodating, you would still be married,' she said, turning to the table to prop up a serviette that had blown over in the draught.

He threw his head back. 'Thank you, Wanda,' he said, crisply, 'but I think I can get by without the marriage guidance.'

'It would seem you can't,' said Wanda, pointedly. She'd smelt the whisky on his breath and wondered where he'd spent the previous hours.

Gregor wandered restlessly around the room, as if he were afraid that anything he touched might bring his skin out in a rash. 'You've put an extra chair out.'

'There are going to be five of us.'

'You mean that father's still presiding over us.'

'No, not your father. Abel has a friend.'

'A girlfriend?' Gregor's voice changed timbre. 'How old is she?'

'I think Abel is the older by a long stick. But you will be able to decide.'

He dropped his overcoat onto the arm of the settee. 'I wouldn't mind a drink,' he said, although he was aware that it was probably the last thing that he needed.

Wanda picked the coat up, carefully, and took it out into the hall. She hung it on a peg. When she came back into the room, he'd lit a cigarette. 'You want I get an ash-tray?' Wanda said, reluctantly.

'Don't bother. I can use the fireplace.' Gregor flicked ash carelessly towards the grate, ensuring that it fell short.

Wanda looked at him with hatred and went through into the

kitchen, rooting at the backs of cupboards for the ash-tray that was brought out only for the anniversary. She closed her eyes and leant her head against the cupboard door a moment.

***

'So the sad day is arriving here again?' As Abel reached the second landing, Mrs Pampanini's door edged open. He smiled, wanly. 'Your poor father, all these years he might have been alive to watch his boys grow up. How is your mother?'

'Quite well, thank you.'

'You are not on your own, then?' Mrs Pampanini looked at Cressida, inquisitively.

Abel did not stop to introduce them. Cressida went up the stairs ahead of him, her small, tight buttocks moving rhythmically inside the faded jeans. At some point he supposed that he would have to make a pass at Cressida, if he was ever to push matters on, but he did not feel any urgency. This was in part because he feared to be rejected, partly because he was not sure how he would respond if she accepted him. He knew that at the heart of his pursuit of Cressida lay a determination to show Wanda that he had not been emasculated by her.

As they climbed the last flight, Abel wished that he could make the shrine evaporate or that his mother had decided not to celebrate the anniversary with candles and another bowl of hyacinths, but by getting rid of it entirely. He was not disloyal to his father's memory, but in keeping with the English way of doing things he would have welcomed a discreet urn in a place you seldom visited. He tried to shield her from the altar as they reached the top stair. Cressida glanced sideways at it. She put down her rucksack. Abel waited. She went over to the shoes and bent to pick one up.

'No,' he said quickly. 'Better not.' She looked up. 'It's just that my mother always puts them in the spot where he...my father.... where he fell.'

'Right.' She turned to the photograph. The candles on each side of it were newly lit and sent a pungent smoke into the air around them. She turned back towards the bannister and peered over the edge.

'He lost his balance,' Abel said.

She nodded. Her eyes moved towards the door. For a second Abel wondered if she was about to bolt back down the stairs and then they heard the front door slam beneath them. She was trapped.

'It's all right,' Abel said. 'They won't bite.'

In the parlour, Gregor heard the front door open and sent up a prayer of gratitude. His mother went into the hall. She bared her teeth in what she hoped would be mistaken for a sign of welcome and received the bunch of daisies with a tight smile.

Cressida looked round the room. Her eyes eventually encountered Gregor, who'd moved over to the window so that he could get a look at her first.

Abel guided her towards him. ' Let me introduce my brother.' Abel shook his hand. 'How are you, Gregor?'

Gregor didn't take his eyes off Cressida: 'Oh, you know. Bordering on the wonderful. You?' he asked, as an afterthought.

'Fine. This is Cressida; she's at the art school.' Gregor raised his eyebrows.

'It's my last year.' Cressida said.

Gregor nodded. He adopted the attentive pose, arms folded, one hand underneath his chin, of someone genuinely interested. 'And what happens then?'

'God knows. I'll have to get a job of some sort. What do you do?'

'Think,' said Gregor, smoothly.

She looked as if she expected him to carry on. 'And you get paid for that? Sounds cool.'

'I ought to add that I think very hard and that I do it rather well.'

'Gregor is a don,' said Abel, looking round him for a bottle. He's at Oxford.'

'Schopenhauer is my speciality. I don't suppose you've heard of him. No reason why you should. He was a miserable sod, by all accounts.'

She ran her tongue along her top lip, curiously. 'You're not much like Abel, are you?'

'No, I think for both of us.'

'You married?' she said, boldly.

'I'm not certain at the moment. Gloria, my wife or ex-wife, is behaving in a way that makes me glad the world is not yet ruled by women.'

'What's it like at Oxford?' Cressida accepted the glass Abel handed her, but kept her eyes on Gregor.

He refused the wine. 'No thanks, I'm holding out for something stronger.' He turned back to Cressida. 'It's better than it is here, entre nous. There are mad people there too, but they're less obsessive on the whole. You've seen the shrine? The milkman won't deliver to the top floor. It's been five years since we had an offer to put double glazing in and seven since we bought a poppy or a British Legion sticker. Mother might as well have gone for broke and put a cross on the door.' He turned round as the door flew open.

'Gregor!' Mitzi rushed towards him, kissing him on both cheeks, as if half a century had lapsed between this meeting and the last. 'Oh Gregor, it's so good to see you!'

'Hello, Mitzi,' Gregor held his cigarette at bay. They gazed at one another, fondly. 'You look well,' he said. 'I like the cardigan.'

'Oh, do you? Wanda thought it was a little colourful for, well, you know....'

'Don't let my mother bully you. It's very nice.'

With Mitzi in it, the room suddenly seemed crowded. Realising they were not alone, she turned to Abel and glanced past him to where Cressida was waiting.

'You've met Cressida already,' Abel said. 'She's at the art school.'

'Yes, of course,' said Mitzi. It was probably the first time Cressida had seen her with her clothes on.

'You were modelling for that tableau this week, weren't you?'

Mitzi flushed with pleasure. 'Yes, I was Olympia.'

'The choker was terrific.' Cressida said, diplomatically.

'How kind. The choker was my mother's. Well, our mother's. It was hers.'

They chattered on about the life class. Gregor had been sidelined. Anyone would think you only came to life when you took off your clothes, he thought, resentfully. He wasn't sure about himself. He was more painfully aware of his deficiencies when he took off his clothes, although if asked, he would say not removing them was just a matter of convenience; he had a lecture or tutorial immediately afterwards.

'You're here at last then, Mitzi.' Wanda put her head around the door.

'Yes, Wanda. Mr Harpur let me go a little earlier.' She caught the desperate look on Gregor's face. 'Does anybody want a whisky?'

Gregor's eyes closed rapturously.

'I will do it,' Wanda said, imperiously.

'But you'll only give me half as much and it'll take you twice as long,' said Gregor.

'Very well, I will bring in the glasses. If you want a whisky, you can serve yourselves. As you are here now, Mitzi, you can help me in the kitchen....if you're not too tired from posing for your Mr Harpur.'

'Wanda, you know very well I'm not just posing for Mr Harpur. I'm posing for the whole class.'

'You think that makes it better; that you take your clothes off for the whole class?'

'I think, after thirty years, we could stop arguing about it, Wanda.'

As the kitchen door closed, Mitzi turned to Gregor: 'I must speak to you,' she whispered, drawing him aside. She was afraid that if she did not speak now, it would be too late. 'I've had a letter. I'm not certain what to do about it.'

Gregor glanced down at the letter bunched inside her palm. He took it from her, slipping it into his jacket pocket. He was flattered that his aunt still came to him for help when she got letters with official headings. She had once paid income tax of sixty-five pounds on her earnings as a model with eleven five-pound notes, ten one-pound coins and an assortment of loose change. 'Just give the cash to me the next time,' he'd suggested, 'and I'll sign a cheque for you.'

'I'll look at it before I go,' he promised.

Mitzi frowned. It wasn't what she had intended, but at least it kept the envelope from Wanda's gaze. She glanced over her shoulder as her sister entered with a tray of glasses and saw this was not the case.

'Of course, if you have something you must talk about, then I can always manage by myself,' said Wanda.

Mitzi felt herself blush. 'No. It wasn't anything important.' She glanced back at Gregor and then followed Wanda out into the kitchen. Cressida went over to the jigsaw and knelt down beside it.

'Well,' said Gregor, turning to his brother, 'so you've struck gold.'

'Do you like her?'

'Who, your little girl? She's charming. Marry her. Get out of here.'

'There's no rush,' Abel said, defensively.

'No rush? Good God, you're thirty. What have you been doing all this time?' He threw a sly look at his brother. 'You're not still intacto, are you?'

'No,' said Abel. 'You made sure of that.'

'You realise there are other ways of doing it? Some of them, I have to own, are pleasanter, but that was probably because of you. It isn't much fun, buggering a toad.'

'It certainly put me off.'

'Oh come on now, don't be boring. You're not going to blame me for turning you into a queer?'

'I'm not queer,' Abel countered, hotly.

'Well then, get on in there. Mind you, I'm surprised you picked this evening to invite her.'

'Why? I wanted you to meet her.'

'Did you?' Gregor took the cigarette case from his jacket pocket, whilst he kept his eye on Cressida. He tilted his head sideways, to take in the fetching bottom with its matching ovals perfectly enveloped in the tight jeans.

Abel followed the direction of his gaze. 'You won't do anything to spoil it, will you, Gregor?'

'Me, old chap? Good heavens no.' He searched his pocket for the lighter.

Abel dug amongst the peanuts, moodily, and popped a handful in his mouth: 'Why can't we get along together, Gregor?'

'I thought we got on together splendidly.'

'You're all I have. I want to get along with you, but when I do I always have the feeling that it would be better if I didn't.'

'Schopenhauer's porcupines, old chap. Like them we rush together because we're chilly and rush apart again because we're prickly. Porcupines have no choice but to stick together – no one else will have them; but the instant those prickles come in contact with that soft flesh, they're away again.'

'You don't need anybody really, do you?' Abel muttered, glumly.

'Trust me, I have needs like everybody else. Unfortunately, there aren't many who can satisfy them. Gloria is one, but she has prickles of her own. What I need at the moment is a hamster, something soft and furry.'

'Something you can stick your prickles into.'

Gregor grinned.

'Oh God,' said Abel, turning towards Cressida. 'Look!'

Cressida had finished off the smile on the seducer's face, whilst they were talking. Gregor gazed down at the board a moment and then, turning with a wink to Cressida, he levered out a section, breaking up the pieces and distributing them randomly across the board. He stepped back

Abel gave a strangled gasp: 'I'll get another bottle,' he said, breathlessly.

Cressida picked up her wine and sipped it. She sensed there was more to this than just the desecration of a jigsaw puzzle.

'Is time to light the candles, Abel,' Wanda called out from the kitchen.

Gregor guided Cressida towards the table. Abel acted quickly to ensure that he was on the other side of her, thus leaving Mitzi and her sister sitting next to one another. Abel took the cork screw to another bottle and topped up the glasses. Gregor took the whisky bottle with him to the table.

'First we pray,' said Wanda. Those around the table bent their heads, except for Gregor who sat staring with a bored expression straight ahead of him and drained his glass as soon as it was over. Wanda ladled goulash out onto the plates and Mitzi handed round the vegetables.

'It's very interesting,' said Cressida, 'the shrine and everything.'

'In Warsaw cemeteries,' said Wanda, 'all the tombs have photographs and sometimes there are little shoes, if there are children in the graves. It is a tribute.' She regarded Cressida, obliquely. 'But you are not Jewish?'

'No, of course she isn't,' Gregor said, derisively. 'And nor are we, except by birth.'

He shook his serviette out. He was conscious of a buzzing in his head. I'm not myself, he thought, reflecting that in other circumstances, he might have enjoyed the break.

'Your name is Cressida?' said Wanda. 'Is an English vegetable, I think.'

'That's cress,' said Abel. 'It's the stuff that goes with mustard.'

'Is a funny name to give a child.'

'If it was 'Cress,' yes. But it isn't.'

'There is no need to be shirty with me, Abel. That is the right word?' Wanda gave a smug smile. She picked up her glass. 'To Nathan.'

Gregor filled his glass again. The others raised theirs. Cressida caught Gregor's eye and decided she didn't like the look in it. She moved her chair a little closer towards Abel's.

Gregor handed her the bread. These evenings had been more rewarding in the days when Gloria was present. She would wait until she saw his hand move underneath the table and then pass the vegetables, so that when he had served himself, he had to start again. He noticed Mitzi looking at him, mournfully. She'd hardly said a word since they sat down to table.

Cressida appeared to find the silence even more unnerving than the conversation. 'Did your train come into Paddington?' she said. 'One of the carriages derailed this afternoon.'

'I came this morning,' Gregor said.

'You came this morning!' Wanda looked up sharply.

'I had things to do.'

'Of course,' said Wanda. 'You would not come all the way to London just for us.'

'Too right,' said Gregor.

Cressida looked nervously between them. 'Anyway it wasn't serious. One casualty. A girl.'

'Just one?' said Wanda. 'Well, that is not serious.' Her voice was laced with irony. 'Except perhaps to who is waiting for her. Possibly her mother.'

'Obviously it would be serious to them,' said Cressida. 'I just meant if you put it next to something like the San Francisco earthquake, for example.'

'Yes, I see. Our mother, she was one of millions lost inside the camps. You do not think of individuals. This is the reason why it was so easy to do nothing. The authorities, they thought in numbers.'

No one spoke. 'Nice stew,' Cressida said, opting for a subject that she hoped was neutral.

'The recipe's been passed down in the family for centuries,' said Gregor. 'What we leave now, will become the basis of the same meal next year, like the Chinese cook-pot. It was difficult to get the full ingredients, occasionally. I gather we were once reduced to half an onion and some dock leaves. Ghetto soup, they called it.' Gregor smacked his lips together.

Wanda eyed him, darkly. 'For Gregor, life is funny business,' she said, smoothing out her serviette. 'Is not that way for everybody.' She dipped bread into the gravy. 'Was not funny at the time.'

'That's been the problem with our race,' said Gregor, philosophically. 'We have no sense of humour.'

'Nice though, that you get together.'

'This will be the last year.'

Wanda looked up sharply: 'What is this?'

'I think it's time we gave up the reunions. OK if he had died a normal death, but he was obviously so desperate to escape from us, he couldn't even wait to take his shirt off. Plus the little matter of his whereabouts that night.' He turned to Cressida. 'Has Abel told you why we're here this evening? Twenty years ago today, our father jumped off the balcony without his trousers on. Don't ask why. Your guess is as good as ours.'

There was an awkward silence. Cressida exchanged a look with Abel. He smiled, weakly. 'It's a funny way to go,' she said, reflectively, not noticing the look that Wanda shot at her. 'I would have taken tablets and then smoked a joint or two whilst I was waiting to drop off.'

Gregor grinned, delightedly: 'Sounds irresistible. Let's hear what you'd have done then, Wanda.' He sat back.

'I would not be so weak,' said Wanda, with an unexpected vehemence. Her hands were clenched in front of her.

'Oh, I don't know,' said Gregor. 'I'd have thought it took a certain strength of character to leap into the void.'

'And what about the people you are leaving?' Wanda said. You do not think there is an obligation there?'

So that's it, Gregor thought. We're here because she doesn't want us to forget he let her down.

'And what would you do?' Cressida asked.

'Drink myself to death,' said Gregor, amiably. 'Might as well get something out of it.' He poured himself another glass and passed the bottle round the table.

'Gregor, you forget yourself.'

If only that were possible, he thought. He glanced at Cressida. In truth, he could have done without the need to make advances to his brother's girlfriend, but he felt he had a reputation to maintain. For Christ's sake, he thought, couldn't I let this one go? I need a rest. I couldn't manage an erection if my life depended on it.

Mitzi was still picking at her food, distractedly. As Wanda started to collect the plates together, she attempted to make inroads on the goulash.

'You have not yet finished, Mitzi?' Wanda said, disparagingly.

Mitzi took a few more mouthfuls and put down her fork. 'I'm sorry, Wanda, it's delicious, but I don't feel very hungry. I had lunch in the refectory today.' She winced as she remembered.

'I was there,' said Abel. 'I called in to look for Cressida.'

'Yes,' Mitzi said. 'I saw you.'

Abel stared. 'Why didn't you come over?'

'I was halfway down a row,' said Mitzi. 'By the time I'd managed to get out, you'd gone.'

'Is this the place where you are spending lunches?' Wanda asked, suspiciously. 'The meat-paste sandwiches I make for you; these are not good enough?'

'They're fine. I didn't go down there to eat. I went to see if Cressida would like to come...' He stopped. His mother looked at him, with narrowed eyes. So this 'arrangement' hadn't been long-standing. Whilst she gathered in the plates, she kept her eyes on him. He felt the colour rising in his cheeks. She took the plate from Cressida, who looked as if she would have welcomed seconds, had they been on offer. She used the dessert spoon to scoop up the gravy. Hunger battled with politeness. 'Lovely.'

Wanda nodded: 'When the meal is over, Gregor will play one or two tunes on the violin,' she said. 'Is that so, Gregor?'

'If you say so,' Gregor yawned.

There was a sudden gasp from Wanda as she turned to take the crockery into the kitchen. She was staring at the jigsaw. She put down the plates and leant across the board, her fingers hovering. 'The songbird and the piece of carpet, they have moved' she said.

'Perhaps somebody nudged it accidentally,' said Abel. 'It's a bad idea, to put the jigsaw in the middle of the living room.'

'Gregor!' Wanda turned on him: 'Do you know who has done this?'

Gregor's rubicund lips bunched up in a mystified expression: 'Can't think who would bother,' he said. 'After all, it's just a jigsaw, isn't it?'

'No, Gregor. Is not just a jigsaw,' Wanda said. 'As Mitzi is not 'just' a model, na?' She looked triumphantly at Mitzi. 'That is sauce for the geese, right?'

'I'm afraid I might have knocked against the table when I came in with the vegetables,' said Mitzi. 'I remember feeling something brush against my legs. I'm sorry, Wanda.'

'No, this is deliberate,' insisted Wanda. 'There are seven pieces missing.'

Gregor peered over her shoulder: 'I expect they're in there, somewhere,' he said. 'Look, that's definitely a section of a wing.' He reached out. Wanda smacked his wrist.

'You do not touch the jigsaw, Gregor.' Wanda's hands were shaking as she tried to isolate the missing pieces.

Cressida came forward, tentatively: 'Can I help you find them?'

'No,' said Wanda, stridently. 'No, thank you.' She pressed both hands to her temples for a second and stood up. She went into the kitchen, closing the door after her. The others looked at one another.

'Is your family like this?' said Gregor.

'Not exactly.' Cressida looked nervously at Abel.

'Wanda's bite is worse than her bark,' said Gregor. 'She's unusual in that sense.'

'Should I go?' asked Cressida.

'Good heavens, no, she would be mortified. You've got to have your pudding first.' There was a clatter in the kitchen. Wanda came out with a steaming dish of jam sponge laced with treacle. She walked past Gregor with exaggerated self-control, her head erect, and placed it in the middle of the table. No one moved. She sat down.

Gregor heaved himself up. 'I'll be mother, shall I?' He began to ladle out the pudding into bowls. The portion he gave Wanda was particularly large.

'You know I cannot eat this,' Wanda uttered, coldly.

'Can't you? Why not? Do you the world of good.'

'You are determined to upset me,' Wanda said. You may be right, thought Gregor.

'I love jigsaws too,' said Cressida, unwisely.

'If you want to borrow one, of course you may,' said Wanda, in an effort to appear hospitable. 'Would you prefer 'The Haywain' or 'The Execution of King Charles'?'

'I don't mind. I don't bother looking at the picture anyway.'

'But is that not the whole point, to complete the picture?'

'Is it? I just find it restful, matching up the pieces.'

Wanda stared at her a moment and then bent her head over the bowl. They ate in silence. Even Gregor seemed to have run out of conversation.

'Gregor, it is time to play,' said Wanda, when they'd finished.

Gregor wiped the serviette across his mouth and threw it down beside his plate. He paused just long enough to make the others wonder if he was about to make a stand and then he got up. Jakob's violin was waiting on the dresser. Gregor took the violin out of its case and ran his finger tenderly along the neck, as if he were alone. He treated it as he would treat a woman, as an instrument of pleasure needing expert handling to release its best potential. He secured it underneath his chin, his small eyes passing round the table until they encountered Cressida's. He kept them there, aware that Cressida was making a symbolic link between the gaze that rested on her and the tightening of the violin strings.

Picking up the bow, he launched into a melody from Smetana.

The chatter ceased around the table. Wanda sat back with a satisfied expression. Mitzi's eyes were damp with sentiment. There was relief on Abel's face that for the next ten minutes he could see where Gregor's hands were. Cressida, well Cressida, unknown to any of them, had capitulated in that moment.

'It was nice to meet you,' Wanda said. She shook hands in the English manner, as opposed to kissing Cressida, who looked around for Gregor. She held out her hand to him. 'Bye.'

Gregor looked at it a moment and then took her by the shoulders and deposited a damp kiss on her left cheek. There, he thought, will that do? Can I go to bed now? Mitzi threw a haunted glance at him. 'I'll pop into your room to say goodnight,' he murmured. Mitzi nodded. It no longer struck him that he might be compromising Mitzi. She was just his aunt. Unfortunately, their relationship had stabilised too late. The stable door had bolted, as his mother might have said.

***

'You were particularly quarrelsome this evening,' Abel commented, when he'd returned from seeing Cressida back to her digs. 'What's up?' He had found Gregor with his feet up on the sofa and a tumblerful of whisky next to him. The others had retired to bed.

'Well, all this is a little self-indulgent, don't you think?' His brother swept his hand in the direction of the landing.

'I'd have thought you would be used to it by now.'

'The fact that it's been going on for twenty years without one throwing in the towel, does not mean that I haven't wanted to. That bloody shrine is an offence. It's time it went.'

'It's only a memorial.'

'No, Bunny, that's not all it is. It's turned into a stick that Wanda beats us with. You heard the way she spoke, this evening. Wanda doesn't care for Nathan, she just wants us to remember he abandoned her.

'Do you think papi meant to kill himself?' asked Abel.

'No,' said Gregor, taking out a cigarette and lighting it. He put back his head and blew a perfect smoke ring. 'Anyone who cared as much as him about appearances, would hardly take their trousers off and leave their shirt on.'

'What do you think happened?'

Gregor shrugged: 'Perhaps he slipped whilst he was practising the jump. Or maybe someone pushed him. Wanda, for example.'

'Mutti?' Abel said. 'She couldn't kill our father. It's against the law.'

'Oh grow up, Abel,' Gregor countered, irritably. 'Anyway, who cares? It's a bit much when you come home in a crisis and the only thing that anyone can talk about, is what another member of the family got up to twenty years ago.'

'It's you who kept on banging on about the suicide. What crisis?'

'Gloria has taken up with someone in the faculty. I wouldn't mind but this chap's only one stage further on in evolution from a pterodactyl.'

'I expect she'll soon get bored with him, then.'

'One can only hope so.' He held up the bottle. It was empty. He blew out his cheeks, pathetically. 'I married Gloria because she seemed robust enough to cope with me, now I suspect she's more robust than I am.'

'I suspect you're probably well suited.'

'So do I,' said Gregor, grinning. He looked at his watch.

'You won't be going back this evening, will you?'

'Too late,' Gregor muttered, gloomily.

'Why don't you stay on for a day or two?'

'I can't, I've got a dozen lectures to deliver this week. Anyway, the thought of staying on here, fills me with despair.'

'It's Mitzi I feel sorry for. She could have married once. She used to be quite pretty. This thing that she's got with Mr Harpur, you don't think it's physical?'

'I've no idea.'

'It's hard to think of Mitzi like that, isn't it?'

'Mmm.' Gregor eased his tie off and undid his collar stud. 'I don't suppose you fancy half an hour down the road before bed?' Faced with the prospect of a night alone, he'd found his stamina returning.

'Down the road?'

'That place dad used to go to.'

'You go there!' said Abel, flabbergasted.

'Every now and then. It's not my local, but it's quite a good place to relax in. I've been going there since I was eighteen; well, no,' he recalled his first attempts to storm the barricades, 'nineteen or twenty.'

'But they knew our father!'

'Absolutely. Special treatment. They're still feeling guilty. Guilt's a marvellous provider, when it isn't you that's suffering it.' After Nathan's suicide, he'd taken it upon himself to break the bad news to the girls at Madame Julienne's. This time he'd been confronted by a different woman when he rang the bell and he had profited from his mistakes the last time round. He'd managed to discover who his father's favourite had been and had the enviable task of comforting her when she broke down in his arms. Since then, he'd benefited from the introduction on a number of occasions and was sometimes entertained for nothing, out of deference to his father.

'Don't you feel odd, knowing papi spent his last night there!'

'No point in being morbid. Father probably had fifty first-rate nights before he had one that went pear-shaped. Come on,' Gregor punched his shoulder. 'You'll have fun.'

'I couldn't,' Abel said. 'I would be thinking of him all the time.'

'I promise you, he'd be the last thing on your mind. They're awfully skilled at making you forget yourself, these women.'

Abel shook his head. 'I'd like to, Gregor, but I'm not like you. I can't be casual about these things. I'd get involved.'

'I doubt it. These are not the sort of women you bring home for tea. You can't let Wanda get you down. She looks more like a praying mantis every time I see her. Tell me how you spent your twenty-first.'

'She made a cake and we had coq au vin.' And Mrs Allerton took all my clothes off, one by one, he thought, nostalgically, and ranged a line of petit fours across my stomach. Then she ate them.

'Wanda made a cake?' said Gregor. 'That it? No big party, no champagne, no presentation of the door key on a cushion, no relaxing of the house rules to accommodate the odd guest overnight?'

'No. Abel blushed.

'I rest my case,' said Gregor.

***

Mitzi jumped. She'd given up expecting Gregor that night, when she heard him leave the flat. She'd listened to the radio and, finally, she had prepared for bed. She was about to throw off her kimono when the door burst open. Gregor, breathing heavily and looking more than usually dishevelled, shook the letter at her.

'Mitzi, what in God's name is this?'

'It's a letter, Gregor.'

'I can see that. But what does it mean? Who sent it?'

'It's from somebody called Gaynor Tranter.'

'All right, Mitzi. I can read the bloody signature. Who is she?'

'It seems we're related,' Mitzi said, as if the news had come as a surprise to her, too. 'Or at least, that's what she thinks.' She pulled the loose kimono round her. Gregor waited.

'In what way does she think you're related?'

'She says I'm her mother,' Mitzi answered, simply.

He looked hard at her. 'And are you?' Mitzi nodded. Gregor stared: 'You're telling me you had a child you didn't know about?'

'Well yes, I knew about her, obviously. But all this happened years ago. I gave her over for adoption.'

'Without anybody knowing?' Gregor said, incredulously. 'How could you be pregnant, have a child and send it for adoption, without any of us noticing?'

'You weren't here,' Mitzi said. 'It was the winter you went up to Oxford. 'I went down to Mr Harpur's house in Deal and came back after it was over. The family thought I'd gone away with a commercial traveller. It was easier to let them think that there was someone else involved.'

'Well, and presumably there was. It wasn't an immaculate conception, I suppose.'

Far from it, Mitzi thought. She looked down at her hands.

'It wasn't Mr Harpur's?'

'Heavens no,' said Mitzi. 'Mr Harpur is a good friend and we share an interest in art. He is a gentleman. He wouldn't take advantage of me in that way.' Gregor raised an eyebrow enigmatically. 'No,' Mitzi murmured, 'Mr Harpur wasn't personally involved.'

'Who was it, then?' She looked at him. Don't answer, he thought, suddenly. Don't tell me. Mitzi gave a slight nod.

Gregor opened his mouth several times and closed it, like a goldfish in a bowl. He stared at her in disbelief. For twenty years he'd hardly given it a thought. Now, suddenly, it was as if a film caught on a ratchet for the past two decades had released itself and was unravelling before his eyes.

When he had finally got back to Primrose Hill, that evening, he'd found Mitzi in the kitchen.

'I thought you were going to be out,' she said. 'We could have organised a little celebration for you, if we'd known. An eighteenth birthday is a landmark.'

'I got bored and so I came home.' Gregor sank into a chair. The collar of his jacket was awry and he had taken off his bow tie at the second pub he'd visited. He scratched the stubble on his chin. It was three hours since he'd shouted through the letter-box at Madame Julienne's. It might as well have been three years, since he had still not got the thing he went for.

'Have you eaten?'

'No,' said Gregor, glumly.

'Have a bite to eat with me.' He watched her lift a portion of the chicken she'd been frying, onto two plates. She was standing with her back to him. His eyes passed vacantly across the rather pert behind. Her buttocks, like her breasts, were small and neat behind their screen of lace and taffeta. She was still pretty, though her blond hair had grown slightly gingery of late. It frizzed around her forehead like a halo that had fallen from the crown. He felt a genuine affection for her. Mitzi didn't judge him and, although he wasn't overly concerned by other peoples' criticism, it was nice to feel that he was genuinely liked by someone he had not tried to ingratiate himself with.

Mitzi glanced across at him. 'Are you all right?' He nodded. 'I'm afraid it's not much of a feast.' She put the plate in front of him and pushed a fork across the table.

Gregor took a mouthful, moodily: 'Do you think sex is overrated, Mitzi?'

Mitzi flushed: 'I don't know.'

'You must know.' He put another forkful in his mouth: 'You're thirty-five.'

There was an awkward silence. Mitzi bit her lip.

'Don't tell me you're a virgin!'

Mitzi's eyelids flickered: 'I'm not sure you ought to speak to me in that way, Gregor.'

'Why not?'

'I'm not sure it's right, between a nephew and his aunt.'

'There's less than eighteen years between us.'

'Eighteen years is quite a long time.'

'Are you?'

'Am I what?'

'Are you a virgin?'

Mitzi put a hand up to her cheek: 'Don't Gregor, please!'

'Don't what?' He went on chewing, but his eyes remained on Mitzi's face.

'Don't look at me like that.' She picked her fork up and attempted to secure a strand of pepper on it.

'Aren't you curious?' he went on, mercilessly. Mitzi didn't answer. Gregor took another mouthful. 'Shall I tell you what it's like?'

She looked at him, appalled: 'You haven't!' Gregor gave a sly grin. 'Does your father know about this?'

'What's my father got to do with it? I am eighteen, for God's sake.'

'But who was this girl?'

'What makes you think it was a girl?'

Her mouth fell open: 'Gregor!'

'How else can you find out what you like? I had to try both.'

Mitzi frowned. 'But Abel hasn't…' Gregor guffawed. 'You won't spoil his innocence,' said Mitzi, abjectly.

'It isn't such a bad thing, actually, to lose your innocence. It's better than preserving it until you get to thirty-five.'

'You don't know what the circumstances were.'

'Well, tell me.'

'No, I think I'd better not,' said Mitzi, firmly.

'Why not?'

'It would be disloyal.'

'To whom?'

'The other person.'

'Ah,' he said, triumphantly, 'so there was someone.'

'Once, yes.'

'And what happened?' Gregor pushed his plate away and leant towards her.

Mitzi sighed: 'He married someone else.'

'You could have slept with him, regardless.'

'No, I couldn't.'

'Why?'

'I'm sorry, Gregor, you don't understand.'

'Well, tell me. Make me understand.'

'I couldn't give myself to him and afterwards there wasn't anybody else I liked enough. There.' Mitzi drew back.

'Do you like me?'

'Well of course I do, you silly boy. But there is like and like. I'm saying that there wasn't anyone like that.'

'But if you don't know what it's like, how can you know how much you need to like someone for it to be enough?'

'It has to be a lot, that's all,' said Mitzi.

'So you don't like me a lot?'

She'd looked at him, despairingly. He had began to stroke her arm below the sleeve. 'You know I love you, Gregor. You're my nephew. How could I not? I cradled you when you were little.'

'Well,' said Gregor. 'Now it's time for me to cradle you.'

Out of respect for Mitzi and perhaps a modicum of shame, Gregor forced the curtain down at this point. He leant both arms on his knees and covered up his face. He was aware that neither of them had said anything for several minutes. Parting his fingers, he regarded Mitzi through the gap. Her eyes remained fixed on the space in front of them. He realised she'd been living through the same scene and he briefly wondered what it had been like from her perspective.

Mitzi had reached more or less the same point in that evening twenty years ago, as Gregor, but unlike him, she had not been able to forget what followed. She had looked down at the stubby fingers lined up on the pale pink of her forearm and felt more imperilled than she ever had before. She knew that Gregor had been drinking. She had never seen him in that state before. It frightened her, whereas it was his grasp on things that frightened other people.

'Well then, now it's time for me to cradle you.' He'd said it so straightforwardly that if she hadn't thought about the implications, she would not have questioned it. He gave her wrists a little tug.

'Oh dear,' Mitzi thought, hysterically. 'He's going to kiss me.'

Seconds later, Gregor's fulsome, rather moist lips landed on her own. She hadn't known how to respond. She knew that it was pointless trying to appeal to Gregor's sense of honour, his propriety, his moral obligation. These were qualities that Gregor didn't have.

I could try pushing him away, she'd thought. He's drunk. He might fall over. But she knew that if he did, he would get up again. At school, he'd had a reputation as a pugilist, both in the ring and out of it. He would take anybody on; it didn't matter if they towered over him. Gregor dug his teeth into the flesh and held on like a terrier. He'd never lost a fight, although the means by which he won, were frowned upon. Of course, he's foreign, they would say in explanation. It was entertaining to watch Gregor fight, but it was certainly not 'cricket.'

He had bent his head into her lap and Mitzi wondered for a moment whether he'd dropped off to sleep. She rested one hand, tentatively, on his forehead. She'd been careful not to make the gesture seem encouraging, although in the event it mattered little. Gregor was beyond the point where he required encouragement. Short, needy little sobs were coming from his throat.

She took his head in both hands, forcing him to look at her. She had expected to see tears of helplessness careering down his cheeks and was dismayed to see that he was smiling. It was a rapacious smile, as focused and unyielding as his eyes. When Gregor had decided that he wanted something, it was no use telling him he couldn't have it. Mitzi's nature thrived on compromise. Gregor didn't know the meaning of the word.

He'd given her a sudden wrench that pulled her off the chair and sent her sliding to the floor. He was immediately on top of her, his small hands moving quickly to remove those items that stood in between him and his goal. He seemed to know what he was doing. Mitzi was surprised at the dexterity with which he excavated all the layers. It was almost as if she had ceased to figure in the operation as an individual, a member of the family, his aunt.

She'd struggled feebly. She was terrified that someone might come back and find them in this terrible position, compromised for ever. They would be expelled from Paradise, condemned to darkness. Mitzi's feeling for religion was confused. She felt her mother's fate did not suggest a loving God. Although she did not think her mother was alive, nor could she think of her as dead. She felt a bit the same as far as God went. But she knew that having sexual relations with a member of one's family, was possibly the worst sin that one could commit and that the retribution would be harsh, regardless of whose fault it was.

'Gregor,' she said, making one last effort to release herself. 'Please don't.'

But Gregor's mind was wholly concentrated now. He'd buried his face in Mitzi's taffeta and, for the next few seconds, let himself be taken over. Afterwards, he lay still for a moment. Mitzi found her head trapped in between the back legs of a kitchen chair. One arm was pinioned underneath her. When he came to, Gregor had sat up, abruptly. There was no half way with him. He had the engine of a Peugeot, going straight from neutral into fifth gear.

He bent down to help her back onto the chair, but Mitzi felt that she would rather be alone. She turned her head away and Gregor pecked her on the cheek. He drew the frock down to her knees, obligingly, and gave her calf a little pat as he got up.

She'd heard him later, whistling snatches out of 'Götterdämmerung' as he threw clothes and books into a suitcase, ready for the early train to Oxford. Gregor's taste for Wagner irritated Wanda. She thought it was just another of the affectations he assumed in order to annoy her. She had been at pains to camouflage the family's German roots in favour of the Polish ones, but Gregor wasn't bothered either way. In other circumstances, Gregor's inclinations would have placed him firmly with the Master Race.

'I may not see you in the morning,' he had said. 'I'm going on the early train. But I'll be back at Christmas. Wish me luck.'

'Good luck,' she whispered.

When he'd gone, she sat there for an hour staring into space before she rearranged her clothes and cleared the dishes from the table. Then she turned the light out and went down the passage to her room, where she sat listening to the sound of Gregor getting ready for the next stage of his life.

All that Gregor could recall of the events that Mitzi had remembered in such detail, was a sudden surging of adrenalin, a sense of power and a freedom from responsibility more dizzyingly absolute than anything he had experienced before. His mood was quite restored. He'd felt benign towards the world in general and to Mitzi in particular. Good old Mitzi. He had had a cracking birthday. And he still had a bit of loose change in his pocket.

Oh the follies of a wayward youth......

He leaned back in the chair and took a deep breath. Mitzi was still staring at the space in front of her. Her eyes moved slowly round to meet his.

'It was you, dear,' she said, softly, answering the question he'd been fool enough to ask five minutes earlier.

'You're saying that that......incident?' He sucked his cheeks in and then let the air out in short bursts. 'Are you suggesting that this child is mine!'

She bent her head apologetically: 'I'm sorry, Gregor, but there isn't any doubt about it.'

***

Wanda finished tidying the sitting room before retreating to her own room. After Cressida had left and she thought everybody else had gone to bed, she'd heard the flat door close and from the window, she'd seen Gregor walking down the street. Perhaps he had decided to go back to Oxford early. Good. The thought of having Gregor there at breakfast, was like adding a PS to a tax demand.

She went into the living-room and opened all the windows, to let out the cigarette smoke. Then she systematically went round restoring everything to its original position, pumping up the cushions and replacing Gregor's photograph inside the drawer. When she came back into the room the next day, it would be as if the evening hadn't happened.

She had not enjoyed the dinner. Gregor had been more than usually obnoxious and she'd taken a dislike to Abel's girlfriend, with her youth and bright self-confidence. No, she did not want Cressida and her sort in the house. They made her feel that there was something odd about it, that what she regarded as the norm was not the norm at all. Why shouldn't they erect a shrine out on the landing, if they wanted to? But even she was starting to find Nathan's shrine an inconvenience. For Abel, it was an embarrassment; for Gregor, it was an excuse for jokes. She doubted whether Mitzi even noticed it was there, now.

Just as she was getting up to go to bed, she heard the key turn in the lock and Gregor's bedroom door clicked open. Wanda felt a wave of indignation. If he'd let himself into the flat, he must have borrowed Abel's key. She would have words with Abel in the morning. Since he left home, she no longer thought of Gregor as a member of the family, if indeed she ever had. She wouldn't have him coming in and out at will, disturbing everybody. She assumed he'd had an assignation. Judging by the route he took, she could imagine where.

She waited till the house was quiet again. She wasn't willing to risk meeting Gregor in the corridor. As she was passing Mitzi's bedroom, she heard voices from inside. At first she thought it was the radio, which Mitzi had on constantly. She hated silence, whereas Wanda wrapped it round her like a blanket. She could not bear people shouting, whistles blowing, even, though she kept it to herself, the sound of Jakob's violin with its disquieting reminders of a past age.

As she put her ear against the door, she realised it was not the radio in Mitzi's room, but Gregor. He was talking in a low voice that was menacingly gentle. He had never had to shout to get his point across. There was a breathless whispering from Mitzi followed by an oath from Gregor.

Wanda held her breath. The whispering took on a more insistent tone. She heard her own name mentioned. And then Nathan's............

***

'Oh, for Christ's sake, Mitzi!'

'I know,' Mitzi whispered.

Gregor let the letter drop between his knees. He felt increasingly surreal. He had a distant memory of that morning, rising from his bed with nothing more unpleasant to look forward to than the reunion. He looked at Mitzi. There was no doubt of the truth of what she said. It wasn't in her nature to dissimulate. In all her life, she'd had one lover and it happened, accidentally it seemed, to have been him. If they had let me into Madame Julienne's that night, he thought, we wouldn't be in this mess.

'Don't you think you should have told me at the time?' he said.

She sighed: 'It seemed unfair to burden you.'

He looked up. Mitzi suddenly looked very frail. He took a deep breath. 'I've behaved appallingly, haven't I?'

She gave a smile that was replete with all that she had suffered. 'Yes, dear, I'm afraid you have.'

'I'm sorry, Mitzi.'

She was staring at her hands. He fought the urge to put his arms around her. He knew what he was about to say, would need a large dose of philosophy to back it up. 'How many letters have you had from her?'

'I'm not sure. Two or three.'

'You haven't met her yet, then?'

Mitzi hesitated. 'No.'

'You mustn't, Mitzi.' Gregor looked away, in order to avoid the anguished stare that Mitzi threw at him. 'She's asking who her father is,' he reasoned. 'Incest is against the law. It's bad enough between first cousins, but an aunt and nephew...' Gregor shook his head. 'They'd take my Fellowship away. I wouldn't be allowed into the university. I'd end up wandering the Continent like bloody Oscar Wilde, sitting in cafés in Dieppe, waiting for somebody to offer me a drink. Things could get pretty hot for you, too, if it came out. I imagine you would have to leave the art school. There's a limit even there, to what they will put up with. Not to mention how your sister would respond?'

'My sister and your mother,' Mitzi whispered. 'Yes, I can imagine.'

'Better not,' exhorted Gregor. 'Better to let sleeping dogs lie.'

'But suppose our daughter needs us?'

'Frankly, Mitzi, if she's done without us for the past two decades, I imagine she's got someone else to help her.'

Mitzi didn't answer. She knew Gregor had a point. Her daughter would despise her if she ever found out who her father was and she would almost certainly reject her.

'I just feel so empty,' she said.

'But you must see, Mitzi, that it's not the way.'

'It's just that Mr Harpur...'

'Don't say you've told Mr Harpur.'

'Not about you, no. He knows about the child, though. He thinks....'

'It's not up to him to think, though, is it? It's not going to affect him one way or the other.'

'He's been very kind.'

'I'm sure he has, but maybe if he knew the truth, he wouldn't be so kind. You know the way the world works, Mitzi. Come now,' he began to knead her hands. 'You've done without her all this time. She's done without you. Write and say you think its better that you don't meet. Let her get on with her life.'

'But Gregor, aren't you curious?'

Of course I am, he thought. He knew that in the weeks that followed, he would think of little else. He'd wonder if she had his forehead, Mitzi's eyes, his brain, her nature... 'Yes, I'm curious, but I'm not suicidal. Not yet. You must put a rein on your imagination, Mitzi,' he said, somewhat hypocritically. 'If you were once to let her in, you would bring everybody down.' He turned her chin towards him. 'You're sure no one knows, apart from Mr Harpur?'

'Only Nathan.'

Gregor felt his knees turn suddenly to water. He let go of Mitzi's chin and held his hands out, impotently. 'Are you telling me you told my father!' His voice rose. He felt small beads of sweat erupting on his forehead.

'Only afterwards,' said Mitzi, startled by his tone. 'I wasn't going to, but Nathan asked me. He knew something terrible had happened. He said it would help him to protect me, if he knew the truth.'

'You didn't tell him it was me!'

'I'm sorry, Gregor. But he can't tell anybody, can he?'

'Mitzi, that is not the point!'

'I thought you said it was,' said Mitzi.

'Well, it would have been the point with anybody else. But not my father, damn it. What must he have thought of me?' He bunched his fists against his head.

'It happened after I came back. There was an argument. Nathan was upset because of something Wanda said. He came into my room that night, to comfort me.' She tailed off. 'Are you very cross?' she added, faintly.

'Mitzi, where do you suppose it leaves me, knowing that my father, having found out that his first-born had defiled the family name, went off at some point afterwards and killed himself? You're saying I as good as murdered him.'

'I'm sure he didn't die because of that.'

'How can you be? Did he come back and tell you that was not the reason? How soon after you had told him, did he kill himself?'

There was a pause: 'That night,' said Mitzi. Gregor groaned. 'But it was something else which might have made him do it.'

'Something else? What else?' He waited. Mitzi took her handkerchief out of her sleeve and toyed with it self-consciously.

'We had an understanding,' she said. 'Nathan and myself. I think we'd always had it.' Mitzi pressed the handkerchief against her cheek.

'You don't mean....'. Gregor struggled with the rather more robust interpretation he would normally have put on 'understanding.'

'It was never mentioned, not until that night. But it was......understood.' She nodded. 'I suppose that must have made it worse, in some ways.'

Gregor looked at her, ironically: 'Yes, I can see it might have done.' He felt as if the ground was sliding out from underneath him.

'Oh God, Mitzi.' He wrapped both arms round himself. It seemed that all his past sins had come back to haunt him, simultaneously.

***

'Gregor, I just don't believe this! Do you know what time it is!'

'It's half past two,' said Gregor, wearily.

'I've got three lectures back to back tomorrow. Tuesday is a heavy day for me!'

'It's only Marx and Engels. You could give those lectures in your sleep.'

'I know that you regard extemporising in the lecture hall as an alternative to going to the gym, but I prefer a mode of teaching that's a bit less hit and miss.'

'I need to talk to you.' He cupped his hand over the phone. 'This bloody dinner has turned into a Pandora's box.'

'I'm sorry, Gregor, but I'm not prepared to have a lengthy talk about your problems in the middle of the night. I'm very tired.'

'Can I assume that Cholmondeley's finally gone home?'

'If it will put your mind at rest, yes, we decided we could both do with an early night.'

Gregor settled in the armchair: 'Are you wearing those rough flannelette pyjamas with the thin blue stripe that make you look as if you've just come out of prison?' He bunched up his shoulders.

'No, I'm not.'

'I bet you're sleeping in your underwear, those long drawers with elastic just above the knee.' There was a short pause.

'George, I know this is the sort of conversation that we once enjoyed over the telephone when we were spending nights apart, but I would really rather go to bed.'

'You must be getting old,' said Gregor, irritably.

'Yes, I am. I don't dispute the fact.'

'At least say I can come round in the morning. I'm in trouble, Gloria; I've had some devastating news.'

'What is it?'

'I can't tell you on the telephone; I might be overheard. If it gets out, I could be ruined.'

'Wouldn't it be better if you kept it to yourself then?'

'It's not quite that simple. Really, you're the only person I can talk it over with.'

There was a sound behind him. He swung round. He had been sitting in the dark, assuming everybody else had gone to bed, but now he saw there was a strip of light under the hall door and a shadow moving back and forwards frantically in front of it. There was a tearing sound and then the splintering of wood. He stared. He wasn't of a nervous disposition, normally, but the events of that night had made inroads on his rationality. Could this be Nathan coming to exact revenge?

'I'll have to go. There's someone outside on the landing.'

'Go then, but don't ring me back in half an hour to tell me who it is. I don't care.'

'Can I call you from the station in the morning?'

'I suppose so, but I might not bother answering.'

'It's nice to know I can rely on you,' said Gregor, bitterly.

'You can't rely on me,' said Gloria. 'I don't have any obligation to you.'

'Let's just say, for old time's sake, I'll see you in the morning.' Gregor hung up.

***

Wanda broke the candles randomly and threw them on the floor. She took a pair of scissors, hacking at the starched, white tablecloth. She sent the hyacinths crashing to the ground, the rounded ovals of the petals scattering across the landing like confetti. She attempted to cut up the shoes. The leather uppers flexed, but would not separate. She smashed them on the bannisters.

'Whatever are you doing?' Gregor murmured from the door. His voice was calm. He felt that, given what he had already been through, finding Wanda going mad out on the landing in the middle of the night, was neither here nor there.

She turned on him, her eyes wild, her hair spilling out neurotically from its containment in the jade comb. 'I heard everything,' she uttered. 'Everything!'

He pressed his lips together, patiently. He felt so utterly detached from everything around him that he wondered whether he was in the early stages of a nervous breakdown. He picked up a bit of splintered wood: 'I hope you'll keep this for the aga.'

'Fornicator!' Wanda hissed. 'And with your aunt! How could you. You disgust me.'

'Really, Wanda, you must stop this eavesdropping. You'll just upset yourself. It happened twenty years ago. I dare say I was drunk. My memory of it is so vague, I must have been.' He ran his fingers through his hair and patted the pocket of his dressing gown, to see if he had left his cigarettes there.

'You think that is an excuse? You were so drunk you don't remember!'

'I admit I might have problems with it in a court of law, but why, if I'm the villain of the piece, is Nathan getting so much flak?'

'He is your father!'

'Well you're my mother. Why not cast yourself over the balustrade. You're equally to blame.'

'You think I care what you and Mitzi do together? You are animals.'

'Oh, come along now, don't go overboard. I had a one night fling with Mitzi twenty years ago. She was the only member of the family who showed a bit of life. I had a gorgon for a mother, a rabbit for a brother and a father who was never there. I felt a bond with Mitzi. It was never meant to go so far and God knows, if I'd known the consequences, I would probably have felt obliged to come back and do something practical to sort it out. She didn't tell me and I didn't know. The first I heard of it, was when you heard of it. The bit that really gets to you, I dare say, is the probability that that's why Nathan topped himself. He wanted Mitzi and I got there first.' He staggered backwards as she lunged towards him, bringing down the candlestick across his forehead. 'Oh, for God's sake!' He put one hand to his head, to stem the bleeding.

'You are like your father, sniffing bitches.' Wanda's face constricted, savagely. 'You will end up like he did, hanging from the balcony without your trousers on. Yes,' Wanda's mouth set in a grimace. 'That is how you will end up.'

'You really don't feel very motherly towards me, do you?'

'You are heartless,' Wanda said, contemptuously. 'You were always like that, even as a little boy. You were determined never to do what I wanted. You were not affectionate like other children. Even Nathan could not love you.'

Gregor's face twitched; 'But he didn't make it quite so obvious that he didn't.' He leant one hand on the balustrade. 'What do you think I'm looking for, when I go 'sniffing bitches,' as you say? It's not a woman that I need; there are a million of them, anyone will do. If I had had a normal childhood, I would probably be married to a placid girl and have three children. But I can't look for a wife like that until I've found my bloody mother.'

'I'm your mother, Gregor.'

'You detested me. You never let me near you!'

'All right, Gregor, come and have a cuddle.' Gregor drew back. 'There you are. You do not want to come. I offer you affection and you turn away.'

'I wanted it when I was six or seven.'

'Ah well, I am sorry. I thought that you wanted it tonight when you were twittering with Mitzi......sharing secrets.'

Gregor rolled his eyes. 'You're barking.'

'Yes, I have been driven mad!' shrieked Wanda. 'But no more. This madness, it is over. There will be no more reunion!'

***

'You think she means it?' Abel stood out on the landing. He was dressed for work, but Gregor noticed that the buttons on his shirt were out of line and that he hadn't shaved.

At some point during Wanda's outburst of the night before, they had turned round to find him standing with a shocked expression in the doorway. As the landing light kept cutting in and out, his silhouette against the open door reminded Gregor of a lighthouse blinking on and off. His face was pale with sleep. He'd woken, as so often in the past, to find that he was locked into a nightmare. His gaze passed from Gregor to his mother and then rested on the axe. 'Is anything the matter?'

In the presence of her younger son, the rage that had kept Wanda going, was already losing its momentum. She should have brought down the axe on Gregor's head whilst she still had the chance. The light came on again. Still no one spoke. Eventually, Wanda drew herself up. 'Go to bed,' she ordered. 'We will talk about it in the morning.'

'But the shrine...? And Gregor; what's the matter with his head?'

'The shrine is not important.'

'But it's been there twenty years!' protested Abel, horrified that what he'd hoped for all these years seemed to be happening at last.

'Is long enough, I think.' said Wanda. Abel looked at her, uncomprehendingly. 'Your brother will explain,' she added, finally, and stepping past him she went down the passage to her room.

'But why should she decide to sell up after all this time? You don't think it's to do with last night and the jigsaw?'

'I suspect there's more to it than that,' said Gregor, thankful that at least his brother had been spared the more salacious details. He had managed to palm Abel off with the excuse that Wanda was behaving menopausally, but it was clear he hadn't slept. He had the same lost look that he had carried with him through life, even when he wasn't lost. Or maybe, Gregor thought, he always had been.

If he hadn't been preoccupied with other things, he might have gone out of his way to jolly Abel through the present crisis, pointing out that this was just the sort of opportunity he had been waiting for. He would have furnished Abel with a couple of addresses and the phone numbers of half a dozen women more than anxious to help out. But Gregor had discovered when he went to look in his address book, that it wasn't there. He felt as if a life-line had been snatched away from him. He knew he wouldn't accidentally have left it anywhere; it was too precious. It meant more to Gregor than his research into Schopenhauer and the six or seven versions of the manuscript that he'd been working on for God knows how long.

Gregor kept the dog-eared archive, with its crinkly leather cover, in the left-hand pocket of whatever jacket he was wearing, so that he could comfortably rest his hand on it and use the other one to hold his cigarette, or shake hands, or in private moments satisfy himself in other ways. He searched his memory for the last time he'd been certain it was there. He had been waiting for a train at Baker Street. It must have been that bloody couple on the underground. They'd picked his pocket. To the casual attention of those thieving fingers, the worn leather cover with its studded flap, would have felt like a wallet. Gregor cursed. He couldn't bear to be the 'done-to' rather than the 'doer' It had put the final screw down on the coffin that was yesterday and now it looked as if today was catching up. 'I'd go at once, if I were you,' he said, 'before she makes her mind up that she wants to take you with her.'

'Odd, that after all this time, she doesn't. I feel quite hurt.'

'I expect she's looking for a consort and she thinks that you'll get in the way,' said Gregor. 'She'll be quite well off; it's not beyond the bounds of possibility that she'll take up with someone.'

'Come on,' Abel laughed. 'She's in her sixties.'

'She's a wealthy widow. Once she's managed to off-load the rest of us, the world will be her oyster.'

Abel shook his head. 'I can't believe its happening.' He looked round him.

Gregor kicked aside a table leg and picked up one shoe. Half of Nathan's face peeped out from underneath the shredded table cloth. The rest was scattered in small pieces on the landing.

'Poor old dad.'

'He got out just in time, if you ask me,' said Gregor.

***

'I've decided I shall go abroad. Perhaps the South of France or Italy, or possibly the East. I want the sun. I am full up with the English winters.'

Gregor turned his head. He had intended leaving without saying anything to anybody, but now he heard Mitzi in the kitchen with his mother. He sensed Mitzi was about to come in for the tail end of the blitz that Wanda had let loose on him the night before. He waited until Abel had gone down the three flights and then went back down the passage.

Mitzi, looking rather fetching in her Japanese kimono, glanced his way and smiled. She seemed oblivious to Wanda's stony face and the atmosphere of mustard gas that she was giving off. Relief at having finally told Gregor what she had been keeping to herself for so long, had apparently enabled Mitzi to sleep through the subsequent events out on the landing and emerge revitalised to face a new day. She took out a carton of fresh orange juice and brought it to the kitchen table.

'Italy,' she murmured, dreamily. 'That will be lovely, Wanda.' Gregor closed his eyes. 'You haven't had a holiday since we came over here from Warsaw.'

'That was not a holiday,' said Wanda. 'And in answer to your question, nor is this. I do not wish to come back ever.' She turned on her sister, her expression changing like a switch of channel on a television set. Her voice dropped to a savage whisper. 'All these years to mourn my husband and then to discover that my sister was his floozy!' She sat back and waited.

Mitzi hesitated with the carton in her hand. She turned, with an appalled expression. 'Wanda, I have never been a floozy. How could you say such a thing?'

'A woman who go off with someone else's husband? I believe the definition of that woman is a floozy.'

'Trust me, Wanda, there was never anything....'

'You took me for the fool!' The coloured spots on Wanda's cheeks had heightened and the pupils of her eyes dilated. She was warming to her theme. She caught her breath. She mustn't lose control. She'd had her moment of unbridled rage out on the landing.

Now her anger must be concentrated to achieve the maximum destructiveness. The revelation that, not only had her husband always wanted Mitzi, but that Gregor had, too, curdled inside Wanda's head like milk that has been simmering too long. Disgust and envy bubbled side by side and forced their way up to the surface. Even Gregor, who she'd thought incapable of loving anyone, had turned to Mitzi for affection and the satisfaction of his lust.

If Abel had not suddenly appeared out on the landing, bleary-eyed and anxious, as he had the morning following his father's suicide, she doubted that there would have been much left of Gregor or the shrine. The need to keep her younger son from the contamination all around them, had forced Wanda to withdraw her forces and regroup. She'd spent the whole night making plans. She wanted to be rid of all of them now, even Abel.

Mitzi gaped at her: 'I promise you....'

'You promise me!' spat Wanda. 'What is worth your promises? You have seduced my Nathan with your fluffy hair and empty head. He is a weak man, he cannot resist.'

'It's not true.' Mitzi looked at Gregor, shocked.

'Be careful, Mitzi. I know other things about you, about all of you. If I decide to tell these things you will be in big trouble. What you do now is not up to me. I do not care. The tortoise, she is slow, but she has caught up with the hare. I can do what I like and what I like is to sell up here and go somewhere else.'

'You're saying you will sell the house!' said Mitzi, breathlessly. Her gaze passed frantically between them. Gregor shrugged. 'What will become of us? We shall be homeless.'

'You'll be free,' said Gregor.

'But we won't have anywhere to go,' said Mitzi. 'All our memories are here.'

'Precisely. I do not want memories. I want a clean slate.'

Gregor took his glasses off and folded them, precisely: 'I presume you will be giving Mitzi her share of the proceeds from the sale.'

'Why should I do that? It is mine, the flat.'

'I think your father meant it to belong to both of you.'

'He didn't say so. Anyway, he left the flat to Nathan. On his death, the flat is mine.'

'And on your death?' said Gregor, mildly.

'I am not dead,' Wanda pointed out.

'But you are next in line,' said Gregor, with a pleasant smile. 'You could pop off at any time, especially getting so worked up. And then, presumably, the flat would pass to Mitzi. Or it might pass straight to Abel and myself, in which case we would naturally provide for Mitzi.'

'That is up to you. If you are worried about Mitzi, you can take her back to Oxford. That is a solution, na?'

'Not really. Women aren't allowed in with the Fellows. Oxford is a bit repressed on that score. Anyway, I think that Mitzi would be a distraction.'

'She is a distraction, it would seem, no matter where she is,' said Wanda. Gregor caught her eye at just the moment when he ought to have avoided it. 'Well, she can starve, then. I don't care. That's why I sell the flat now, so that I am not obliged to give her anything. She killed my husband, she has ruined me. What more she wants?'

'You probably owe Mitzi for the fact your marriage went on long enough for you to have us.'

'You think that is an achievement?'

'You do realise Mitzi is your last link with the real world.'

Wanda gave a harsh laugh: 'Mitzi in the real world!'

'She at least goes out to work. She meets real people, even if she isn't one.'

They looked at one another over the abyss. Though Wanda was infuriated by her inability to make a dent in Gregor's crust, she had at least brought Mitzi to her knees. She tossed her head. 'You'd better hurry, Gregor. You will miss your train and Mitzi will be late for her appointment in the real world. I shall call in lawyers. They will tell me what the house is worth. A pretty packet, is that what they say? The price of property has risen since we came here. Who knows, I may go to Monte Carlo, having nights on several tiles.' She gave a mirthless laugh.

There was a sob from Mitzi. Gregor's heart sank. 'Stop it, Mitzi,' he said, angrily. 'This is designed to make the two of us feel wretched because Wanda overheard me in your room, last night.' He turned on her. 'We all have secrets, Wanda. Secrets are just those facts that are more appropriately registered with one source rather than another. You wouldn't go into a grocer's, for example, if you wanted to make out a will.' He scratched the stubble on his chin. He needed a shower and a shave and, most of all, he needed Gloria. 'I don't confide in women very often. There's no need. They have a way of getting to the truth without me saying anything. I know I won't find anyone who understands me; it's too late and if I did, I'd probably repel them by revealing more than they could cope with. They'd be frightened by the sheer, raw, smelly odour of my need. The most that I can hope for is the odd night with a sympathetic soul with big breasts and a small mind who can overlook my ugliness, my Jewishness, my hopelessness, my lust, and wrap me up in their affection………Mitzi does that rather well.'

There was a long pause. 'Thank you, Gregor,' Mitzi whispered.

'It's a pleasure, auntie,' Gregor said ironically. He buttoned up his coat. 'And now we'd better make our way into the real world. You'll be late and I'll have missed my train, but 'out there' is our only hope. By all means go off, Wanda. You'll be dragging Granny's moth-eaten old fur coat after you.'

***

'Fares!' The conductor edged his way along the car and stopped in front of Abel who was hanging from the overhead strap like a carcass from a meat hook. Normally, he nodded and passed on. This morning, he seemed not to recognise him. He held out his hand and Abel rummaged in his jacket pocket. 'Madame Bovary' was still in there from yesterday; he'd used his bus-pass as a book mark. Out of habit, he tried not to lose his place, and then decided that it didn't matter anyway. He let the pages fall back. Yesterday, he had been passionately interested in the fate of Emma Bovary. Now he could only think about his own. His stop was coming up. He thrust his way past the conductor and got off the bus.

Schopenhauer's Porcupines

'You look a little tousled, Abel,' said Miss Quettock, disapprovingly, as he was hanging up his coat. He smoothed his hair down with his hand. The buttons on his shirt weren't properly aligned and made it look as if his head was on the slant. He noticed Aileen looking at him, curiously.

'You OK?'

'Not really.' If she'd had a bigger shoulder, Abel thought, he might have cried on it. He felt as if the ground had been pulled out from underneath him. All these years, whilst he had been berating Wanda for her eccentricities, he realised he had needed her in order to feel normal. Now that she was being normal, he was not sure where it left him. 'Normal' was, he saw now, simply what you happened to be used to. Anything that went on long enough became the norm.

It wasn't so much the destruction of the shrine that shocked him, as the violence with which she'd done it. She was angry with his father. Or perhaps she was so furious with everybody else, that she could not help but include him. But how could a dead man be responsible? He wasn't sure if he was outraged on his own behalf, or on his father's. He knew there was more to it than her deciding that the shrine had been there long enough. It might have been there long enough; no one denied that. But you didn't put a bowl of hyacinths on an altar one day and then slice the heads off with an axe the next. At some point in the evening, something critical had happened.

Abel went back over the events of that day. Could it have been his insistence on inviting Cressida that had precipitated Wanda's outburst, or his brother's bullishness, or Mitzi's wearing of the scarf that he was sure he'd seen inside the sewing room. He'd sometimes wondered whether Mitzi knew about the sewing room. Perhaps she and his mother were in league with one another.

He'd been staring at the order form in front of him when it occurred to him that it was in a foreign language – all the letters were encryptions; ancient Greek or possibly Egyptian. He looked at his fingers with the pencil clasped between them. What a funny way to hold a pencil, he thought, if that length of wood with graphite running through it was indeed a pencil. P..e..n..c..i..l. 'Cil' was French for eye-lash. 'Cil.' He murmured it. 'P..e..n..c..i..l'. Abel tapped the point a few times on the page and noticed how the space between the dots was charged with electricity and how the dots seemed to be jumping up and down.

'Is anything the matter, Abel?'

Abel didn't answer. He'd forgotten how to. His eyes moved along his wrist, across his cuff and up his arm. He wore a black and yellow check shirt. He saw how the black lines formed a grid. He was behind it, as if he were trapped behind a fence. 'Trapped,' he said.

'Abel?'

He could hear the letters stuttering behind his teeth, like prisoners trying to get out. Tra...tra..tra.... His head nodded up and down. Somebody on the other side had looped their fingers through the wire. He felt it shudder. Tra...tra...

'Aileen! Could you come here quickly, please!'

Whose voice was that? He looked up, stupidly, and saw a face approaching him from several hundred miles away. 'Tra...' he said.

'All right now, Abel, up you get. We'll move him to the office,' said Miss Quettock. 'It's a bit more private.'

Arms supported him on each side. Abel didn't want to go. He didn't like change. But perhaps it didn't matter, because suddenly he wasn't trapped behind the wire any more. He'd floated up over the fence and he was looking down now at Miss Quettock in her penguin suit and Aileen with her irritating lisp and her engagement ring, manoeuvring some awkward old aged pensioner out of the seat he'd occupied too long inside the library. If he had only spread a copy of The Guardian out on the table, no one would have bothered him.

'This is a LIBRARY,' Abel had explained once. 'I'm afraid that if you want to sit in here, you have at least to look as if you're reading.'

Maybe the old man had dropped off. Or perhaps he'd died whilst he was sitting there. That happened sometimes.

'Shall I call an ambulance?' said Aileen, panicking.

'Good heavens, no,' Miss Quettock said. 'He's just a bit off-colour. Come along now, Abel. Pull yourself together.' Abel felt a sharp slap on his cheek that pulled his brain back, temporarily, into his body. 'Abel, look at me.'

'No,' Abel uttered. He could not bear coming back behind the fence if it meant looking at Miss Quettock.

'Are you sure he isn't having some sort of a fit?' said Aileen, fearfully. 'I thought he looked odd when he came in.'

Abel felt a sharp slap on the other cheek. Why was Miss Quettock hitting him? What had he done now?

'What's he saying?'

'Heaven knows. I think we'd better get him home. I'll call a taxi.' She leaned forward, staring into Abel's eyes. 'Don't worry, Abel, you'll be all right. You just need a little rest. We'll get you home.'

He gabbled something.

'What was that?' said Aileen.

'I think he just said he hasn't got a home.'

***

'So how was it with Cholmondeley?'

'It was very pleasant, since you ask.' She put a cup of coffee down in front of Gregor and went over to the dressing table. 'Cholmondeley is a far more interesting person than you think.'

'I have spent time with Cholmondeley, Gloria. I was the one they asked to shepherd him around when he arrived here for his interview. I promise you, there's nothing interesting about him. He secured the job because he said he didn't drink, he wasn't interested in politics and they assumed he wouldn't fornicate with students or seduce the Dean's wife.'

'I expect they thought that having somebody like that already in the faculty, they'd better be a bit more careful next time. Drink your coffee, you've got seven minutes.'

Gregor yawned. He'd managed to secure a corner seat when he

got on the train, so that he was supported on two sides, but just as he was settling down, a family with a small child got into the carriage. Gregor found his gaze drawn irresistibly towards the child. He'd always thought of childhood as a waste of time and he regarded children in the same light. He had never wanted one and Mitzi's news had not inspired a change of heart, although he was aware that having oneself replicated in the world had its advantages, numerically at least. Somewhere on the planet was a creature who was half him. He had a suppository for his genes. It was in this confusing frame of mind that he had stumbled down the pathway from the buttery, unsure how he would cope if Gloria refused to let him in. He took two sugars and then spooned an extra one into the cup. 'The fact is, Gloria, I'm in a bit of a conundrum.'

'You've got problems.'

'You could say that.' Gregor hesitated. For the first time in his life, he ran the risk of finding his behaviour reprehensible. 'Remember Mitzi?'

'Your aunt. Like the seed head of a dandelion. One puff and she's all over the place. Still, she was an improvement on your mother. Did she ever manage to complete that jigsaw of the Tower of London?'

'Yes. This year it was the turn of the Pre-Raphaelites. Some nineteenth century seduction scene. Unfortunately, Abel brought his girlfriend and she finished off the face of the seducer.'

'I can imagine what your mother will have said to that.'

'She's selling up the flat and going on a tour of Europe.'

'I'd have thought that was a bit over the top, even for her.' Gloria went over to the dressing table and began to smooth foundation on her face.

'The jigsaw wasn't the deciding factor. She discovered that I'd had a tumble in the hay with Mitzi, twenty years ago.'

'Christ, George, you're such a shit.' She smoothed the lipstick round her mouth.

'I wish you wouldn't call me George. You know it's not my name. The 'G' is hard, like yours.'

Schopenhauer's Porcupines

'You've no objection to me calling you a shit, then? How you can lecture year in, year out, on the categorical imperative, and still behave as if there is no moral law, defeats me.'

'Schopenhauer is my speciality, if you remember; Kant is just a sideline. Come on, Gloria, I need somebody I can talk this over with, who isn't biased.'

'Well that lets me out. I'm definitely biased.'

As she pursed her red lips in the mirror, Gregor found himself diverted momentarily by their resemblance to a cow's bottom. 'You're not being very philosophical.'

'Philosophy's not going to protect you. Even Schopenhauer has his limits.' Gloria sat back and turned her head from side to side, to study the effect.

'He did say that desire preceded thought.'

'He also said, if I remember rightly, that aesthetic contemplation was the way to deal with it. I think he meant instead of, not as well as.' She turned, briskly, on the stool and smoothed her skirt down. 'Anyway, what's brought it to the surface after all this time?'

'It seems that after I'd gone, Mitzi found out she was pregnant and she disappeared for six months. When she came back, Wanda took her in, but with such bad grace that my father finally decided he had had enough. He went to Mitzi and confessed that he had always had a soft spot for her. Mitzi felt if he had told the truth, she had an obligation to as well. He couldn't take it. Next day, when she went to bring the milk in, Mrs Pampanini found him lying face down in the stairwell.'

'Go on.' Gloria leaned forwards. She had pieced together Gregor's family history over the years as if it were a weekly series in a magazine. Until she met his family, she'd suspected Gregor of inventing them. 'What happened?'

'Mitzi felt she couldn't make it worse for Wanda by revealing what had passed between them. Nathan was the only person who knew everything, apart from her, and he was dead. Unfortunately, now the girl has managed to track Mitzi down and is already asking who her father is, so Mitzi thought she'd better tell me what had happened. No one talks to Wanda, but she manages to find out most of what she needs to know by listening at doors. In one go she discovered Nathan had betrayed her, that I'd slept with Mitzi and she had a love child, and that Nathan had found out about it and had topped himself in consequence.'

'Sounds like a full day.'

'Nemesis was written right across her forehead. She attacked the altar with an axe and then announced that she was selling up. The idea is to punish Mitzi by leaving her alone and destitute, and Abel by cutting him loose too late for him to usefully do anything about it. I knew Wanda was a bitch, but I'm surprised she was prepared to jettison the toad.'

'He was the only member of the family who bore some resemblance to a human being,' Gloria said, drily.

Gregor touched the plaster on his forehead. 'What concerns me is that Mitzi may agree to see the girl and if she does, the whole affair will come to light.'

'But only if she tells her you're the father.'

'Gloria, you don't know Mitzi very well. She's capable of keeping secrets if she has to, but she's quite incapable of guile. If she was asked directly, she would own up.'

'It's an interesting problem.' Gloria sat back. 'I'm not surprised you'd stoop to incest, actually.'

'I've never had to stoop.'

'There isn't anything with Wanda that I ought to know about?'

'No. I did bugger Abel once, though, and I don't think he's forgiven me.'

There was a pause. 'I have to say this, Gregor, I think it might be a service to mankind if you were put away. Do you think there are other families in the UK as dysfunctional as yours?'

'I would have given you support, if you'd been in this sort of mess.'

'Believe me, George, I'm not the sort of woman who would go round sleeping with her aunt. It wouldn't happen in our family. For what it's worth, I think you're right. If Mitzi sees the girl, your cover's blown. In that case, you can either brave it out, which is a course I wouldn't recommend, or start applying for a job abroad. Australia is fairly liberal. Most of the inhabitants had criminals as antecedents anyway.'

'I'd actually quite like to see the child myself. I can't imagine what she'd look like.'

'Nor can I.'

'If she were me, but taller, it would be all right.'

'But what if she were Mitzi, only shorter? She's not likely to turn out a raging beauty, that's for sure. She might be clever but if she takes after you, she'll never find a husband. Frankly, I'd keep out of it. Lie low and hope she disappears again.'

'Mmm.' Gregor looked at Gloria's exposed knees. 'How long till your lecture?'

'I ought to be going.'

'Can I stay here till you get back?'

'No.'

'Please, Gloria. I need to put my head down.'

'Put it down inside your own rooms, then. You can't stay, Gregor. I'm expecting Cholmondeley.'

'Christ, you might give the poor sod a day off.'

'He doesn't want a day off.'

Gregor got up sullenly: 'I suppose I'll have to wait until it runs its course, this thing with you and Cholmondeley.'

'You might have a long wait. We shall probably be getting married in the spring.'

'For God's sake, Gloria, you can't be serious.'

'I'm nearly forty, Gregor, and I have to think ahead. When I'm an old aged pensioner I shan't want somebody who beats me to a pulp and then expects me to walk three miles up and down their back.'

'You'd rather vegetate with Cholmondeley in a little cottage by the sea? You realise I could get him sacked. I'm his superior in the department.'

'If you do, I'll tell the Dean you had a fling with 'Mrs Dean', as well as half a dozen of the students, and that you've a taste for S & M, as well as incest. Don't even think about it, Gregor. It's an own goal.' Taking Gregor's arm, she shunted him into the corridor. As he walked back across the Old Quad, he saw Cholmondeley coming in the opposite direction.

'Hello, George,' said Cholmondeley, pleasantly. 'How's life?'

'About as bloody as it gets,' said Gregor.

'Well, that's why we took philosophy, no doubt. To try and make some sense of the incomprehensible, to find an explanation for life's bloodiness.'

'Is that why you took up philosophy?' sneered Gregor. 'If a student had said that, I would have failed him.'

'That's the difference between us, I suppose,' said Cholmondeley.

***

Wanda put a cup of tea in front of him. He stared at it. A week ago, if he had been sent home in this condition, she would have insisted that he go to bed. She would have made a beef broth that she spooned into his mouth, asked whether she should call a doctor, brought him books and magazines and pressured him to take the next week off, to make sure he was better.

'Could I have some sugar, please?' he asked, pathetically. She pushed the sugar bowl towards him. There were deeds and lawyers' letters laid out on the table. Looking at them upside down, he realised he was looking at the leasehold contract on the flat. He'd hoped his mother's threat to sell up had been made in anger and that, having had time to consider, she would see how utterly impossible it was. His mother followed the direction of his gaze.

'You are upset,' she said. 'This is the reason why you are not well. I understand this. You have lived here all your life. You do not want to be alone.'

He didn't answer. All his life he'd wanted to be on his own if it meant freedom from his mother. Now, the idea terrified him. He sat with his head bent. Wanda watched the wave of brown hair fall across his eyes and fought the impulse to reach out and draw it back. This was the moment when she could retract with honour. She could say she had decided not to sell up after all, for Abel's sake, because he could not bear the thought of leaving Primrose Hill, of leaving her. She could pretend she had forgiven Mitzi for the way she had behaved and then make Mitzi pay forever for the privilege of being able to remain there. Gregor might guess that it was her own fear that had paralysed her, but the others would accept her change of heart as being for the general good. They would applaud the gesture as magnanimous.

But Wanda didn't feel magnanimous. The only feeling she had now that was more powerful than fear, was anger. Her resolve was strengthened two or three days after the reunion when she'd received an unexpected visit from the person she wished least of all to see again. She only knew that it was Mrs Allerton because as soon as Wanda heard the bell ring, she went over to the window, waiting for whoever was below to give up and walk back along the street where she could see them. She'd expected it to be the man who'd called before, but there was no van parked below. The bell rang once more. Wanda let out an exasperated sigh. If she'd been living there alone, she would have had the doorbell disconnected. What right did the outside world have, to continue persecuting her? She wished that they would go away and if they wouldn't, well then, she would go.

She gave a low gasp when she saw the buxom figure in the gaberdine and green hat walk along the road a little way and then cross over. She felt weak with indignation. Mrs Allerton! For her to come here, after all she'd put them through. It was as much her fault as anyone's that their lives had been made impossible, that Wanda was now forced to sell up and go somewhere else in order not to be tormented by the kind of people Mrs Allerton epitomised. Once she'd destroyed the shrine, the rest was easy. She might quake with terror at the thought of other people trampling over territory that had been hers, but now the ground was scorched in any case. The sooner she left Primrose Hill, the better.

Abel sat forlornly at the kitchen table.

'It's not easy for you, Abel, but is time you made your own arrangements,' she said, firmly.

'What arrangements?' Grease spots floated on the surface of the tea. She hadn't even washed the cup before she gave it to him.

'Finding somewhere else to live. That is the first thing. I will give you an allowance. You can rent a room somewhere.' She shrugged her shoulders. 'Maybe even two rooms.'

'Where will you go?' Abel pinched his nose above the bridge.

'I do not know yet. Maybe I will find a nice place on the Continent and then when I am settled down you can come out and visit me.' He looked up, hopefully. 'But this is in the future,' Wanda added, quickly. 'You must make your own way, Abel. You cannot rely upon your mother all your life.'

'Why?' Abel whispered.

'Why? Because this is not good.'

'No,' he said, desperately. 'Why are you doing this? Why now?' She hesitated. 'Was it me? Did I do something wrong? Was it because I brought someone to the reunion?'

She gave a short laugh. 'You think I would go to all this trouble just because you bring an extra person to the table?'

'Why then? Is it Gregor?'

'Always it is Gregor, but no more than usual. No,' Wanda put her hand up before he could go on to ask whether Mitzi was to blame. 'There are things, Abel, that you do not understand, that I too cannot understand.

'What things?'

'It does not matter. These things go back to when you were not yet born. Is not your fault.'

'But if it's not my fault....'

'Like in a war, is not just those who are deserving who get killed. When it is over you cannot remember how it started, only how it ended. But is not the end yet.' Wanda drew herself up in the chair. 'You need to buck up, Abel. You are young man still. This is an opportunity. You must not hide your light under a bushel. Drink your tea now.'

***

'I suppose I ought to look on it as an adventure,' Mitzi said, but she was glad that Mr Harpur stopped short of agreeing with her. She was trying not to panic, but the more she thought about the future, the more weight the past seemed to assume.

She'd managed to retrieve one half of Nathan's face before the remnants of the shrine were swept away, his clothes and shoes stuffed into dustbin liners for the Oxfam shop, the wedding album dumped into a skip, the photographs that had been on the dresser and the mantelpiece ripped into shreds.

Since the reunion, she'd hardly slept and when she did, it was invariably Nathan whom she dreamt about. She had been waiting all these years, she realised, for precisely this to happen, for her sin to reap the punishment that it deserved. When he had come into her room that evening, he had found her with her suitcase on the bed. She couldn't stay here now; she knew that.

'I thought if I came back it would be the same,' she said, 'but I see now that it will never be the same. It's better if I go.'

'At least stay here until you have recovered,' Nathan urged her.

'I'm afraid that if I stay here, I may not recover,' Mitzi murmured.

'But this is your home.'

She smiled, ironically. He took her hands in his. He kept his voice low, but not low enough that Abel, in the next room, could not pick up snatches of the conversation.

'This man who has treated you so badly, Mitzi, did you love him?'

'No. At least,' she hesitated. 'Not in that way. I was fond of him.'

'I thought he must have swept you off your feet.'

'Well in a sense, he did.' She flushed, remembering the tussle on the floor under the kitchen table.

'Was it him who left you?' Mitzi bit her lip. 'I'm sorry, Mitzi, I don't want to pry. I just feel that I have to know in order to appreciate what you've been going through.'

'Yes,' Mitzi said. 'He left me.'

It was strange, thought Nathan, how in spite of her distress, a calm seemed to have settled on her that he'd never seen in her before. She still had the ability to move him with her beauty. 'Would you rather he had stayed?' He forced himself to ask the question.

Mitzi put a hand up to her cheek. She wasn't certain how to answer him. She didn't want to lie, but she could hardly tell the truth.

'I've been alone for some time,' she said, quietly. 'I stayed until the loneliness became unbearable. And then I came home.'

Nathan noticed how the last word seemed to fade: 'We've disappointed you,' he said. 'We've let you down.' He threw his head back. 'This is not a home, not in the real sense.'

'It is your home, Nathan,' Mitzi said. 'At least you know that you belong here.'

He laughed harshly: 'I have fewer rights than any of you.' For a second, Mitzi thought he was about to say more. Then he stopped. 'Well,' he said, wretchedly, 'it hardly matters now.' He looked at Mitzi. 'When I married Wanda, Jakob made me promise to look after her. I can't default on that. And she has been a good wife. She can't help the way she is. But Mitzi,' he leaned forward and his voice dropped, 'I'm not sure that I could bear to go on living here alone with Wanda. Do you understand?'

'Yes,' Mitzi whispered. 'Yes, I understand.'

'If you had found a man who made you happy, I think I'd have come to terms with that. Yes, yes, I hope I would.' He nodded, as if he still needed to convince himself of this. 'But for you simply to go elsewhere, just because you don't feel you are wanted here and for us both to go on being lonely and unloved, but separately...' He tailed off. Mitzi sensed the struggle going on inside him. She could feel the pressure of his thumbs against her palms. 'You don't have any contact with this man, now?'

Mitzi hesitated. She felt honour bound to tell the truth if she was asked, although she was afraid she might have reached the limits of his tolerance already.

'Mitzi?'

'Yes,' she said, 'from time to time.' He frowned. 'Believe me,

Nathan, there is no need to be jealous. He just happens to be where I am, occasionally.'

Nathan paused. 'Is this man known to me?'

She closed her eyes, as if she hoped to white the question out by doing so. 'Please, don't ask me to talk about it any more,' she said. 'It was a terrible mistake and I have paid for it.'

She could see Nathan wrestling in his mind. 'You're keeping something from me, Mitzi. If it is to spare my feelings, don't. I know whatever happened wasn't your fault. But I have to know who did this to you. It's important that you tell me everything. I won't judge. God knows, I'm in no position to. Our whole lives up to now have been a lie. It's time to stop. Who was he, Mitzi?'

Mitzi looked away. She made a helpless gesture with her hands. Her voice, when finally she spoke, was barely audible.

'He was your son,' she whispered.

She could not get rid of the expression on his face when she had told him. It was as if he had put a wall between himself and what she said. She'd realised in that moment that she should have kept her secret, that it wasn't always right to tell the truth. She saw his brain attempting to make sense of it. Twice he began to speak and stopped.

'It isn't true. You're lying,' he'd said, harshly.

'No,' said Mitzi, gently. She could not back down now. She had told the truth and that was it.

For months after that dreadful evening, she'd felt paralysed with shock whenever she came back into the flat or left it. She had hurried down the stairs without allowing herself time to think about the figure tensing itself in the corner of her eye. She'd smelt the rancid mixture in the air of terror and excitement and was half-repelled, half drawn by it.

She'd never told another soul. When Gregor came home for the funeral, she kept her silence. She had wondered if he would refer to their last meeting, but he didn't. He had probably forgotten all about it. He seemed to regard his father's death more as an inconvenience. He'd had to miss two lectures, to attend the funeral.

He wanted to get back to Oxford. He had borrowed five pounds from her for the cab fare and that was the last she saw of him until the anniversary came round, the next year.

Mrs Allerton had been a godsend in those bleak days afterwards. When Mitzi took a closer look at her, she'd realised that, for all her motherly concern and ample bosom, Mrs Allerton was probably no more than twenty eight or thirty, but she seemed to know about the kind of loss they'd suffered, how one always blamed oneself. But, Mitzi thought, in her case she knew that the agony was justified. She was to blame.

Her agitation at the thought of leaving Primrose Hill had been augmented by the news that Mr Harpur was retiring at the end of that year although, without him, she doubted that she would have wanted to stay anyway .

'I'd hoped to have a few more years,' he had confided, 'but it would mean taking courses in a thing they call computer graphics. I'm a little old for that. In any case, I think that forty years is long enough to be in one job.'

'But you're such an inspiration,' Mitzi remonstrated. 'It seems such a pity.'

He smiled, philosophically. 'The truth is, that the students who are coming to the college now, don't want to learn about the treasures of the past, still less to analyse them. Painting is a lost art; they aren't interested in it any more. I think I might prefer to go off on a pilgrimage for three or four months, whilst I still can. When I was a young man it was my ambition to retrace the route the pilgrims took to Santiago da Compostela, taking in the churches and cathedrals on the way. My wife and I had planned to do it when we first got married. Sadly it was not to be. It's taken me a long time to get round to it, but it seems now may be the moment.'

Mitzi nodded wistfully. So she was losing everything. Within a few days, her entire world had turned upside down. She set herself to search the windows of the newsagents for vacant flats, but when she went to look at them, they were so squalid and depressing in their hopelessness that she could not endure to look at any more. She wasn't certain what would happen to her when the moment came for her to move on. She suspected that, in spite of what she'd said to Mr Harpur in the studio, she might just sit down on the pavement with her suitcase and remain there.

***

'Hi. Remember me?'

'Of course I do,' said Gregor, buying time. 'You're Abel's girlfriend.' He secured the dressing gown, protectively, around his waist. It was his favourite outfit when he wasn't going anywhere. He'd had some of his best, although not always his most academic, thoughts when there were no restrictions on his circulation.

'It's impossible to find the rooms in this place,' Cressida said, irritably. 'All those windy little staircases and passages. Why don't they knock them down and put up modern buildings, or have proper signposts?'

'I suppose because a large proportion of the Fellows would prefer that no one found them.'

She walked through into the study. Gregor's table lamp was on and there were papers scattered on the bureau. Cressida picked up a page and looked at it.

'Don't touch that,' Gregor said. 'Please.'

'I'm just interested.'

'Are you? Do you warm to the idea of life as evil, futile, full of suffering?' Cressida shrugged. Gregor waited. 'Do I take it you're not canvassing or selling poppies?'

'No, I came to look you up.' He gave a low groan. 'You did make a pass at me, for Christ's sake!'

'Did I?'

'Underneath the table. You were fumbling with my knees.'

'Good God, I ought to be ashamed, at my age. If I tell you that I had a loose nerve in my leg and I was trying to control it, would you buy that?'

'Are you saying you weren't groping me?'

'If I were ten years younger, like my brother, and I wasn't still half married, I admit I might be seriously tempted, but my life is rather complicated at the moment.'

'I'm not complicated.' Cressida sat down on the settee and folded her legs under her.

'I know that you're not, but the situation is.'

'Because of Abel?'

'Partly.'

'Abel understands. I've told him that I'm going off for six months with a group of friends. We're hitch hiking through Europe.'

'I expect that pleased him.'

'I'm just saying that we aren't an item.'

'So you think he thought you were?'

She gave a smile that you could strike a match on. Poor old Abel, Gregor thought. I hope he doesn't think it's my fault. Cressida was rummaging inside her knapsack for a cigarette. She swept the hair back from her forehead, carelessly.

As recently as ten days earlier, reflected Gregor, he would have accepted her arrival on his doorstep and the implications of it, cheerfully and without hesitation. She would have filled up the space between one lecture and the next like an exotic entrée. She had that delicious combination of self-confidence and ignorance, an innocence that cried out to be plundered. I could teach her something, he thought. I could change her whole life in the course of half an hour. Once, the idea would have thrilled him. Now, it left him with a feeling rather like dyspepsia. She was the same age as his daughter, he thought, dismally, and it occurred to him that practically the whole of Oxford was the same age as his daughter. In one fell swoop, he had lost the lot.

It wasn't what you were that mattered; it was what you thought you were. Or rather, what you thought you weren't. He'd been a father for the past two decades and been unaffected by it. He had sailed on under the impression that he was a free man, without obligation, whereas all the time he'd had a child. If she was twenty, she was probably a student. She might even, God forbid, be one of his. As someone who regarded incest as a waste of valuable resources, it disturbed him to consider that he might have inadvertently been guilty of it twice.

I'll have to put a rein on my excesses, he decided. But there was another factor creeping in. Since learning that he was a parent, Gregor had begun to feel like one. The revelation had impaired his appetite. He looked at Cressida and knew that if he took her into bed with him, he would get out of it again, dissatisfied. Not only would he feel he'd had a snack when he was looking forward to a decent meal, but he suspected he would not enjoy it anyway.

It's over, he thought, sadly. A whole generation, half the female population of the country and two thirds the female population of the university, was suddenly beyond his reach. Respectability was staring Gregor in the face. The loss of his address book now seemed like a portent. Change was being forced on him.

'You're not adopted, are you?' he said, feeling that he'd better ask.

'No, why?'

'Just checking.'

Cressida took out a tin and rizla papers.

'Dear heart, please don't roll your joints in here. They'll never wear it. I'll be struck off.'

'Serves you right.' She grinned. 'I thought that you'd be pleased to see me.'

'I am pleased to see you. I'm just not sure what you want from me.'

'I fancied going somewhere for the afternoon. I've never been to Oxford. Can you take me out in one of those boats with a blunt end?'

'No, I'm sorry, Cressida, I'd like to make your afternoon a pleasant one, but there are things I must attend to.'

'Liar.'

Gregor glanced down at his watch. There was a footfall on the stairs outside. He rearranged his face into a smile.

'Am I disturbing something?' Gloria said archly.

'Not at all. Meet Cressida, a friend of Abel's.' Gregor put another glass out and poured whisky into it. He rummaged for his wallet and took out a ten pound note. 'There, go and buy yourself an hour on a punt and please, when you get back to London, don't tell Abel that you've been here. Half the family's not talking to me as it is.'

'You're trying to get rid of me!'

'There's nothing I can do for you. Believe me.'

'You could talk to me about philosophy.'

'You're better off without it. Trust your instinct.'

'Shall I come back later?' Cressida inclined her head to take in Gloria.

'You wouldn't find me in. I've got an early evening lecture.'

'Sod this,' Cressida said, looping her bag over her shoulder. She screwed up the ten pound note and stuffed it in her pocket. 'See you.'

'See you,' said Gregor, wearily. The door closed. He and Gloria regarded one another. Gloria went over to the window. Cressida had paused to read the 'Keep off the Grass' sign, before striding off across the lawn.

'Where did she come from?'

'She's a little number Abel hit on when she came to change a library book.'

'She knows her own mind, doesn't she?'

'She thinks she does. She'll meet someone who'll change it for her and she'll never be quite sure of anything again.'

'You mean you, I suppose? That's why you're in your dressing gown.'

'No, actually, I don't mean me. The dressing gown is accidental. I have absolutely no interest in Cressida. It would be like seducing a puppy: all teeth and bounce, no substance.'

'When did you want substance in a woman?'

'All the time. That's why I married you.'

'Are you deliberately trying to be nice to me, Gregor?' Gloria put down the glass. 'I gather you met Cholmondeley in the Quad. He said you seemed depressed.'

'I'd really rather not have Cholmondeley's sympathy.'

'He thought you might decide to top yourself.'

'And have you come to stop me, or to tell me where to find a rope?'

'I thought I'd better pop across. I didn't want to spend the next ten years consumed by guilt.'

Gregor nodded at the empty glass: 'Another?'

'No thanks. I hate drinking in the afternoons.'

'Remember when we used to take a bottle of that Greek liqueur to bed with us on Thursday afternoons, when neither of us had tutorials.'

'I do. The headache lasted through the weekend.' She scanned Gregor's mantelpiece and turned a couple of the invitations over.

'I've still got a bottle tucked away.'

'If I were you I'd drink it. It could go off whilst you hang about for somebody to share it with.'

'I wouldn't dream of sharing it with anyone but you. It's one of my most treasured memories.'

She shot a glance at him. 'I think you ought to see a doctor, Gregor. You're not normally this sentimental.'

Gregor spread his hands out. 'Why won't you come back to me?'

'We know that doesn't work. We had eight years of it. It was a good try.'

'I was younger, then. I wasn't able to appreciate what being married meant. I didn't feel sufficiently committed.'

'What's changed?'

'I have. All these revelations have unnerved me. I feel that I ought to make amends. There's not much I can do for Mitzi and, apart from pushing women Abel's way, there's not much I can do for him. Wanda is beyond help, so there's no point agonising over her, but you and I do have a future, Gloria.'

She looked at him, suspiciously.

'I would be faithful. Promise.'

'I would knock your teeth in, if you weren't.'

'Well there you are. At my age, keeping one's teeth is a priority.' He noticed Gloria was still not any nearer to the door. He tactfully removed her jacket to a peg. She wandered over to the window. Gregor lightly cupped her shoulders from behind. 'Admit it, you'd be bored to death with Cholmondeley. At least you and I find one another stimulating.' He drew out the last word with insinuating emphasis.

She tossed her head. 'It seems ridiculous to go through the palaver of divorce and then go back to being married. Suppose, after a few weeks, you've recovered and you're back to being Gregor?'

'Then, as promised, you can kick my teeth in.'

Gloria went to retrieve her cigarette case from her bag and noticed Cressida's tobacco tin perched on the arm of the settee: 'What's this?'

'I believe it's known as a recreational drug.'

She eased the lid off, fingering the resin and sniffing her fingers: 'Do you know, I've never tried this.'

Gregor smacked his lips together: 'Would you like to?'

'Will she mind?'

'I hope she's half way back to London by now. The ten pound note I gave her should cover the purchase of another half ounce.'

'Do you roll it in the same way as an ordinary cigarette?'

Gregor smiled. He came and sat down next to her. Taking a rizla paper, he tipped the tobacco out of one of Gloria's cigarettes and mixed it with the resin, easing it along the length of paper. His little lizard's tongue licked the rizla paper down its length. 'I can't imagine how you spent your youth if this is really your first joint.'

'Seems a pity to have left it till it's nearly legal. It takes away a bit of the excitement. Still, it's quite a novel way to spend an afternoon.'

Gregor lit the joint and passed it to her. Gloria drew deeply on it. They were silent for a moment, puffing away, companionably.

'Gregor?'

'Yes?'

'I think I'd like to go to bed.'

***

'Happy birthday, Abel.' Wanda placed the cake in front of him. The single candle glimmered wanly. Abel blew on it half-heartedly. Mitzi bunched her shoulders up. For Mitzi there would always be some reason to find life worth living. She had given him a present of a blue and white scarf that went three times round his neck and dropped below the knees. From Wanda he'd received the first instalment of his annual allowance. That day being Saturday, he'd spent it going through the local papers, making lists of rooms. He'd favoured somewhere near the college but when he told Cressida that he was looking for a place to live, she had responded absently. She would be giving up her own digs anyway, once she had graduated, and she planned to spend the summer travelling, she said.

Since the reunion, she'd hardly said a word to him. He wondered which bit of that dreadful evening was responsible for putting the kibosh on their relationship. When Abel asked her if she'd like to help him celebrate his birthday with a visit to the cinema, she told him she had things to do. He had already told his mother he'd be going out and she had organised an early tea, so he'd decided to go on his own. He would prefer to spend an evening in the darkness of the cinema than in the twilight world of Primrose Hill, which looked a little like a holding station with its crates and rolled-up carpets and its air of imminent abandonment.

'You like the cake?' asked Wanda.

Abel turned the dense mass over in his mouth. These days, he'd noticed that his mouth was always dry, as if his vital substances were draining out of him. He nodded. 'Very nice.' He pushed the plate away. 'I'd better go.' He took the scarf and wound it round his neck. His aunt smiled, sentimentally. It was so easy to make Mitzi happy that it was a pity so few people bothered trying.

'Have a lovely evening,' she said, genuinely.

It was not a film that offered much scope for escape. A violent robbery in which a policeman got shot and his pregnant wife miscarried. Abel ate his popcorn, thinking of the birthday twenty-one years earlier when he had sat with Mrs Allerton beside him, watching 'Star Wars.' She had given him a bag of popcorn that lay open on his lap so that he didn't have to let go of her hand to put it in his mouth. He'd felt completely happy sitting in the darkness. All the critical events in Abel's life until that moment, had been finite, partial, painful, isolated, or shot through with the inevitable question 'What next?' Mrs Allerton had turned and smiled at him and he had felt a rush of joy.

He screwed the bag of popcorn in a ball and threw it on the floor. Heaving himself up out of the seat, he stumbled to the aisle and out into the rain. He had imagined that if he and Mrs Allerton were ever to run into one another, they would be consumed by the embarrassment they'd felt that day when Wanda had discovered them. He'd been expelled from Eden and, historically, he saw that there was no way back. His innocence had been destroyed. It was because of this that Abel had resisted the desire to creep back to the house in Belsize Park during the years that followed, to see whether Mrs Allerton still lived there.

So it's come to this, he thought, as he stood in the shadows opposite the little row of terraced houses. I'm behaving like my mother. In the half light it was difficult to see if anything had changed. The garden was a wilderness, but then it always had been. Having grown up in his mother's regimented household, Mrs Allerton's untidiness delighted him. His gaze passed lovingly across the peeling orange shutters. He felt a nostalgia so intense, it reinforced his fear that Mrs Allerton was just a figment of imagination. In reality, she would be old now. But he didn't care how old she was. It hadn't mattered when he was eleven and it didn't matter now.

A light went on inside the parlour. Abel caught a brief glimpse of a painting on the far wall of a field of poppies, which he recognised from ten years earlier. A second later, two unseen hands whisked the curtains shut.

It wasn't until she had passed him that he registered the figure on the bicycle. He heard the high pitched whine the brakes made as the wheels slowed down. He looked at the familiar back, encased in its unfashionable gaberdine, the auburn hair bunched carelessly in at the neck with strands escaping at the sides. He had already taken the first step towards her when it struck him that, if Mrs Allerton was outside on the pavement, someone else was inside. She had propped the bicycle against her thigh, in order to negotiate the latch.

The gate had never opened properly. He could remember struggling with the catch himself. Presumably his mother, when she came there that day, must have also had to raise the gate with one hand and align it with the fence in order to unlatch it. He imagined her lips pressed together as she wrestled with the final hurdle separating her from Abel and his happiness.

The front door opened. Abel saw the silhouette illuminated in the beam of light. The young man ran towards her down the path. He kissed her on the cheek and turned the bicycle around. He can't be more than twenty, Abel thought, aghast; the same age he had been when he and Mrs Allerton had started their affair. He had a sudden vision of the young man lying with a well of brandy in his belly button. All at once, the oxygen had drained out of the air.

They disappeared into the house together. Abel pulled his collar up. He realised in that moment what a sour harvest Wanda must have reaped from all her years of eavesdropping on other peoples' lives. The dusk had turned to darkness and he felt a drizzle in the air. Abandoning the shelter of the doorway, he stepped out into the rain.

***

As Wanda dragged the final tea chest out into the hall, she caught a glimpse of her reflection in the mirror, which she had forgotten to remove from its position half way up the wall. She looked away instinctively. Since the reunion, she had avoided mirrors. She was not sure who she would see looking back at her. In decimating Nathan's shrine, she had destroyed the past. When you destroyed the past, you ran the risk of going with it.

Abel had already moved out. She'd expected him to be the last to leave, but once he'd had his birthday, he no longer seemed to care what happened to him. Or perhaps he'd reached the limits of his desolation and some instinct for survival had cut in. She felt a pang of jealousy. A part of her was tempted, even now, to rein him in again, to stay there or to take him with her. Abel was her love child, but she knew that every time she looked at him, now, what she would remember wouldn't be the night of his conception but the years of lying and deception on each side of it. She could not jettison the rest and still keep Abel.

She had booked a passage on the Orient Express. She wanted to see whether its romantic reputation lived up to reality. She'd bought herself some clothes: dark suits, large hats with veils, a cloak with inside pouches. With the thoroughness she brought to doing jigsaws, Wanda was now planning her departure to the East.

'But wont you vorry, going back to that place where your mother has been missing on the railway station?' Mrs Pampanini had insisted.

'I'm not going back to Poland, Mrs Pampanini,' Wanda said.

'There are still Nazis there, they say. I read it in the paper.'

'There are Nazis everywhere,' said Wanda, thinking that she had met several in the area round Primrose Hill.

After consulting lawyers, she'd agreed to sell the house with Mrs Pampanini in it. After all, she was the one who had discovered Nathan in the stairwell. She had history on her side. She'd offered to maintain the shrine herself, or what was left of it. But Wanda had no interest in the shrine. 'It does not matter,' she said, nonchalantly. 'It is time to move on.'

Mitzi's room reflected nothing of the urgency that Wanda felt to bring the curtain down on life at Primrose Hill. When she looked round the door, that morning, she'd seen half a dozen cardboard boxes, drawers with underwear and stockings hanging out of them, a pile of dresses on the bed and hangers strewn across the floor. If anything, it seemed to have more in it than before. For her part, Wanda was determined nothing would remain inside their former home once she had left. She could have summoned the removal men to help her with the crating-up but the frenetic round of packing and the constant physical exertion it required, kept other thoughts at bay.

She saw how her reflection in the mirror seemed to shift, as if there were another face behind it and the two had not quite locked together. After half a century of immobility, she sensed that everything was on the move. For fifty years she had remained imprisoned by the memory of her mother. She had clung to what was left: her father, Nathan, Primrose Hill, her son. And now, with one amazing gesture, she had cast them all adrift. She marvelled at her own temerity. She wasn't sure if what she felt was terror or exhilaration, but she saw that, having made the gesture, there could be no going back. She dragged the tea chest to the landing and then, making her way back along the passage, she removed the mirror from the wall.

The only room left, was the sewing room. She was still agonising in her own mind over what to do with the collection. She could make a trip down to the Oxfam shop with Mitzi's clothes. This was where most of them had come from in the first place and in time, no doubt, her sister would retrieve them piecemeal without even noticing. She might donate the tins and packets to the Shelter down the road. They would be grateful and she would derive some satisfaction from the knowledge that she had been generous. It wouldn't be the same degree of satisfaction that she got from hoarding them, but she could hardly take a hundredweight of sugar, fifty packs of tea and half a dozen jars of chocolate spread onto the train with her. 'These things I do not need,' she told herself. 'I am a wealthy woman. I can buy more.'

But still she had hesitated. The collection represented her security. It was a guarantee that she would never want for anything. It started when her father died. The morning after Jakob's funeral, she had been wandering blindly down the Goldhawk Road. Her heart seemed to be weighted down with concrete. She'd felt full and empty at the same time, as if something huge and alien were gnawing its way through her. It had started raining. Suddenly the drizzle turned into a deluge.

She had gone into a supermarket. She did not have any money on her and she hadn't brought a shopping bag. She wandered up and down the aisles, distractedly. It was a Saturday and she was jostled on all sides. Nobody seemed to realise she had lost her father. Wanda felt a sense of absence so acute, she had to fill it up with something, or she knew that she would fall into the void.

She'd seen a tray of petit fours in presentation packets: delicate, small squares of marzipan with gelatine and almonds on the top. She reached out and slipped one into the pocket of the fur coat. It was as if she'd been thrown a life-line. Instantly, she'd felt a rush of power. She walked down the aisle and out onto the pavement without looking either right or left. The rain had stopped as suddenly as it had started. As she walked, she curled her fingers round the box. When she got home, she put it underneath a pile of linen in the sewing room. She had no wish to eat the petit fours. It was enough to know that they were there, that they were hers.

She had been adding steadily to the collection, ever since. Except for that unpleasant episode when someone had accused her of not paying for a packet of Earl Grey, no one had ever challenged her. She wondered whether it might be more satisfactory just to leave the things there in the cupboard, shut the door and go away. But she could not afford to raise suspicions. Someone might ask questions. They might wonder why so many of the books in there had glue marks on the inside cover. What if they came after her?

She fetched a large, deep canvas bag. She would feel better, once she'd made the first trip to the Shelter, and she would reward herself with little treats each time she came back. She took down the key ring from the hook behind the kitchen door and crossed the bedroom to the sewing room beyond it. Fumbling for the light switch, she discovered that the bulb had blown.

She gave a low hiss of annoyance. There were no spare bulbs left. She would have to take the one in Abel's room. She was about to fetch it when she realised there was something tacky on the floor. Her shoes were sticking to the lino and she heard a crunching underneath them. She took off her shoe and dabbed her finger on the leather sole. As she adjusted to the dim light, Wanda saw that there were crystals on the floor. She held the door back to let in the light behind her. Sugar. Underneath the sewing table, was the shredded packet it had come from.

Had a mouse been in there? But how could a mouse have forced the cupboard open? She put out a hand and felt her way across the room. She gagged. A hoard of rodents working full time, could not have achieved this devastation. All four of the cupboard doors were open and she saw that two were hanging from their hinges. Coffee, flour, tea and pasta, all had had the cellophane ripped off them and the seals torn. She made out a kilner jar of pears preserved in brandy, smashed with shards of glass embedded in the fruit, the brandy leaking out across the floor. Even the tins had been thrown down and stamped on, so that they were dented.

In the cupboard, she could see a dark stain on the sheets, occasioned by the jar of coffee essence oozing through the wooden slats that formed the shelves. She stared around her, disbelievingly. She could still feel the anger in the air. Whoever did this, had not wanted to acquire the objects. They had simply wanted to ensure that she no longer had them. This was somebody who hated her.

***

Abel tipped the remnants of the bowl of muesli in the bin and looked on, dully, as the milk began to soak into the rubbish. It was half-past eight. He closed the lid and grabbed his jacket. As he let himself out, he picked up the postcard from the mat. It was a picture of the Pantheon. He tucked it in his pocket. He had had a string of other cards from Cressida, none more than two lines long, none that suggested she was missing him or asking what his flat was like. Bed sitter, rather. By the furthest stretch of the imagination, it could not be called a flat. Her postcards left him feeling more dispirited because they endlessly reminded him that, out there, was a better and more interesting world, where people did things.

He had tried, initially, to feel excited at the thought of having his own space at last. The room looked horribly abandoned, when he saw it first, and it had all the drawbacks of a place where many people stayed, but not for long. The cooker was encased in grease, the walls were pockmarked with the rusty legacies of nails and there was a settee that had hard lumps protruding through the base so that, to sit on it, you had to ease your bottom down between the bumps or perch on top of them.

He'd done his best to make the place look homely, putting up the posters that had graced the walls at Primrose Hill and scattering his own possessions round the room. But it seemed rather pointless to have left his old life, just to recreate it here. Inside his room, he heard the sound of other peoples' lives all round him: women shouting, children crying, traffic in the street outside, the noise of sirens wailing in the city. None of it impinged on him.

He had expected that when Wanda went, the two things she would take would be the fur coat and the clock, the things that locked her to the past. But she'd insisted that he have the clock: 'You will need something that will wake you in the mornings.'

'I can soon get an alarm clock, mutti.'

'No, it is this clock that you must have. It is an heirloom. Heirlooms must be passed down.'

Abel had smiled tightly: 'But I haven't anyone to pass it down to.'

'You will find someone. You must strike whilst your iron is hot, ja? Take the clock. I do not want it.'

Abel didn't want it either. It depressed him, when he put his key into the lock each night, to hear the mournful sound reminding him of yet another wasted day. He might have gone to university; it wasn't too late, theoretically. And yet, in practice, he suspected that it was, that when he got there, he would find himself as isolated as he was here and with less excuse. The trouble was that Abel did not want a crowd; he wanted someone who was his alone and for whom he was everything. This was the role that Wanda had fulfilled in childhood and continued to fulfil long after child psychologists would have suggested it was time to stop.

He had deliberately not invited her to see the room. He knew that, once she'd been inside it, he would see it through her eyes rather than his own. Now that the flat was up for sale, however, and his mother was about to leave the country, he had felt obliged to see her once more. Wanda had stepped, gingerly, into the room and sniffed the air. She looked around her, nodding as if what she saw confirmed her worst fears. 'You have heard from Cressida?' she asked, observing the small charcoal sketch of Abel's head and shoulders pinned above the gas-ring.

'Yes.' He gestured at the row of postcards on the mantelpiece and hoped that Wanda wouldn't pick one up and turn it over. 'She's been hitch-hiking through Europe. That's a record of her journey so far. She's just crossed the border into Italy.'

'How thrilling.' Wanda swept her hand across the sofa, felt the lumps and looked round for a chair. 'So Cressida will go to Italy and then, when she return, you will get married.'

'No,' said Abel. Sometimes, in the past weeks, he had wondered whether even now this might be possible. But the moment he heard Wanda say it, he knew that it wouldn't happen.

'I thought that was what you wanted.'

Abel filled the kettle. 'You can't always have the things you want.'

His mother grunted. She picked up the book on Abel's bedside table. Since the night of the reunion he hadn't managed to read more than half a dozen pages of his 'Madame Bovary'. He'd reached the point where Emma, in despair, goes to the pharmacy for arsenic. He wasn't sure he had the stomach for a death scene. Whilst she stayed there on his bedside table, there was still a chance she might survive.

His mother tossed the book aside, but went on staring at the cover as it lay there. Abel wondered if she were about to ask him for a résumé. He doubted she would find the downfall of a French, romantically-inclined adulteress to her taste, though unlike Abel she would welcome her come-uppance. She reached out her index finger to the book and nudged it so that it lay four-square on the table.

'She was not the one for you, my Abel.' For a moment he thought she meant Emma Bovary. She turned towards him. 'Anyone could see. She was too...in your face.'

He gave a dull laugh: 'Where did you pick that up?'

'It was what she said, that she was sorry if I thought that she was in my face.'

'I didn't know you'd had a conversation with her.'

'Well, of course. I had to find out how she felt about you. There is no smoke without fire, eh?' Wanda gave a thin smile. 'It is good I learn these English sayings. Everyone speak English on the Continent.'

He felt the skin across his forehead stretch: 'You mean you asked her?'

'I am sixty, Abel. Finally the time comes when I have to, how you say it, pass the baton.'

Abel slammed the tea-pot down: 'I'm not a baton, mutti.'

'You think that I do not care about your wishes, but I do. I want you to be happy.'

'You can't ask a girl what her intentions are! We're friends, that's all.'

'Yes, that was what she said. But it was not what you said. You said you were keen on her.'

'I may have said that, privately, but not to her.' He poured the tea. The pot was shaking in his hands.

'You are upset,' said Wanda.

'No, I'm angry.'

'She cannot help if she does not love you.'

'I'm not blaming her; I'm blaming you.'

'I cannot help it either, if she doesn't love you. But is better, in the end, to know these things.'

'Not always.'

'Painful it is, when one is not loved.' Her mouth constricted in a tight line. 'But the heart recovers. Every dog…'

'Don't!' Abel uttered. 'I can't take another bloody proverb.'

'Proverbs, they are wise. They tell you things.'

'But only if you get them right.'

'You criticise my English,' Wanda drew the cup towards her,

primly, 'but I am the only one who bother to take English lessons. I know that one has to integrate. Does Mitzi go? No. Gregor? He cannot be bothered. They think that they do not have to make the effort, that they are above these things.'

I'm going mad, thought Abel. Why did I invite her here? He looked at Wanda's bent head as she sipped her tea, her long chin pointed at the cup in front of her, as if she'd cast a spell on it. That's how she used to look at me, he thought.

'There are a couple of nice ladies at the English class. Perhaps you ought to join. There will be space when I go.'

'I don't think I would have got a job as a librarian, if I could not speak English properly,' said Abel.

'There is always room for an improvement. They are Polish ladies. You would be well cared for.'

'I suppose you've interviewed them.'

'Don't be silly, Abel. You must meet them first.'

'You're sure it's necessary? Why don't you just sign them up? Why bother asking me what I think?'

Wanda took a fig roll from the plate. Her teeth bit into it, immaculately. 'That has always been the trouble with you, Abel. You are never picking women who are suitable.'

'Gregor always seemed to think they were.'

'They might be suitable for Gregor. That is not the point.' She dabbed the serviette against her mouth. 'Gregor does not take these women seriously. He cannot be damaged by them. You are not like that. You want a woman who will be reliable, who knows what things you need, who will not flirt with other men when you are looking in the opposite direction.'

'They don't make girls like that, any more.'

'Of course they do. The ladies at the English class...'

'Oh, fuck the English class and fuck the ladies in it.'

Wanda straightened her back. She put the cup back on the tray. She'd wondered briefly, following the desecration of the sewing room, if Abel might have been responsible. Perhaps she'd driven him too far. Perhaps he had found out about the sewing room and wanted to get back at her for what he felt she'd taken from him. In the end she had dismissed the idea. Abel was not capable of violence on that level. He might lose his temper but, like an elastic band, it didn't stretch beyond a certain point. No, she decided, Abel could not be the culprit. She'd resisted a brief impulse to pick up the book on Abel's bedside table, to make sure there were no glue marks on the inside cover.

Mitzi? The idea of Mitzi going on the rampage was absurd, although there was that scarf, the one she had been wearing on the morning of the anniversary. If, as she had suspected, Mitzi had retrieved it from the sewing room, then she had been the last one in there. It was hardly credible, however, that she would proclaim her guilt by flaunting something she had taken.

That left Gregor. He was more than capable of violence and destruction, but he lacked a motive. Since he'd always hated her, there was no reason to assume that he would suddenly decide to demonstrate it now. Besides, she had to own that Gregor was more subtle. He had weapons in his arsenal that were far more effective than the smashing of a few jars.

She'd gone down the list of people who had been to the apartment since the night of the reunion. The family lawyer, Mr Spriggett, was exempt. There was that pushy young man who had come to take the details of the flat before they put it on the market. He had asked what was behind the door in Wanda's bedroom and she'd said it was a cupboard. The removal men had spent the past month tramping in and out and she had had a visit from the auctioneers. That was the trouble when you let in people from outside. You never knew what sort of person you were dealing with. As soon as strangers crossed the threshold, she felt that the flat and all that it contained had passed beyond her grasp. She did not care about the sewing room or the collection any more. Whoever was responsible for decimating it, had ultimately freed her from the need to find a home for everything herself. She simply put the whole lot on a skip, together with the two halves of the bracelet and the six remaining charms. The missing charm had been the lynch-pin holding them together and without it all of them were lost.

She looked at Abel's sullen profile. He might not have been responsible for the destruction of the sewing room, but there was definitely something not quite right about him. Wanda pursed her lips. 'You have not been yourself just lately, Abel. Maybe you are going through a crisis of the middle life.'

'I can hardly be going through a mid-life crisis at the age of thirty-one.'

'Is not an easy time for you; you have to move house, then you lose your friend. Your expectations have been disappointed.' Wanda hesitated. This might be the last time she and Abel talked to one another. She did not want them to part on bad terms. She wished him to know that she had suffered too, that they had that in common. 'I know what this means,' she said. 'My heart was also broken.'

'Really?' Abel said, indifferently.

'I loved a man who did not love me.' Wanda sighed. The pain had not decreased over the years. She felt it as acutely as she had that night outside the study. 'He loved someone else.'

There was a slight tilt in the slant of Abel's head: 'Was this before you married papi?'

'No,' said Wanda. 'This man was your father.' Abel turned his head to look at her. His mother went on staring at the tray. 'Still, that is in the past,' she said, determinedly. 'The water has passed underneath the bridges.'

'If he married you, it can't have been more than a passing fling.'

'But he was bribed to marry me. And it was not a passing fling.' Her voice had taken on an edge. 'He was unfaithful from the moment that he married me until the moment when I saw him jump.'

'You saw him jump?' said Abel, flabbergasted.

Wanda frowned. She hadn't meant to go so far. 'I heard him coming up the stairs. I watched him through the spy-hole as he climbed over the bannister.'

'You didn't try and stop him!'

'To what end?' She was confused and disappointed by his interest in the details of his father's death. The suicide was not the point. What she had wanted him to understand, was how she had been wronged. 'A man decides to kill himself, what can one do?'

'For heaven's sake, he might have been depressed or drunk. The next day, he would probably have felt quite different!'

'Maybe,' she said, shortly. 'We will never know.'

She wanted him to do it, Abel thought, with sudden insight. It was her revenge. 'If you were there,' he said, 'Why didn't you go down?'

'I could not bear to see him like that, broken up, without his trousers.'

'But you didn't care if Mrs Pampanini saw him like that!'

'Mrs Pampanini is not family. Does not affect her in the same way.'

'What if he was still alive!' said Abel, frantically. He felt he wanted to take Wanda by the arms and shake her.

Wanda shrugged: 'So far? I do not think so.'

'You could surely have dialled 999. You didn't have to go down there yourself.'

'One is confused when these things happen. I went back into the flat and shut the door.'

'How could you!' Abel uttered, desperately. He had a vision in his head of Nathan's semi-naked body splayed out on the hall tiles, of the click as the light switch turned itself off in the stairwell and of Wanda turning her back, decisively, upon her husband. 'Couldn't you at least have woken Mitzi up? She would have done something.'

There was a long pause. Wanda looked at Abel, calmly: 'It was Mitzi who your father was unfaithful with.'

***

She ran along the corridor, her wild hair flying, her coat billowing behind her. Students turned and stared. Some shook their heads and touched their foreheads. One stood back and made a sweeping gesture with his hands. His friends laughed. Mitzi didn't care. She felt like jumping in the air. She'd had to take her leave of Mr Harpur quickly, or she would have thrown her arms around him. It was all so unexpected. And yet, in an odd way, it seemed pre-ordained. They had been taking down the props and folding up the carpet of fake grass in preparation for the end of term. The rooms that Mitzi rented were above a launderette, so she'd elected to take home the sheets for washing. In the past, she'd left her Chinese slippers and kimono in the dressing room so that, when she came back the next term, she would feel that she belonged there, even if the students she had known had moved on.

This time she was less sure that she would be coming back, although she didn't know what she would do instead. She had to have a job. The small allowance Wanda gave her paid the rent but did not even cover for the basics when it came to living.

There had been a farewell lunch for Mr Harpur at which other members of the staff had praised him for his years of service, his encyclopaedic knowledge and his old-world courtesy. She knew, and so did Mr Harpur, that the people who paid tribute to him looked on these things as anachronisms, although Mr Harpur had responded charmingly. When they presented him with garden vouchers and applauded him, she made up for the rather lack-lustre applause by clapping so hard that the people in the row in front of her turned round and stared.

'Well, that was very nice,' said Mr Harpur afterwards. He gave a rueful smile. 'I'm not sure what will happen to the garden whilst I'm on my way to Santiago da Compostela. Maybe I should wait until I come back before cashing in my vouchers.'

'I'd be very happy to pop in from time to time,' said Mitzi, 'just to keep an eye on things. I've never had a garden, so I'm not sure what to do there; you would need to leave instructions. But I can at least make sure it's watered.'

'That's kind, Mitzi,' he said, mildly, and then added. 'but it isn't what I had in mind.' He smacked his lips together, absently.

'Of course, if there is something else that I can do for you whilst you're away, you only have to say.'

'There is.' He cleared his throat. He had the folded sheet of fake grass on his knees and went on stroking it, distractedly. It wasn't used to lying down and, like the students who had passed through Mr Harpur's hands over the years, sprang up when it no longer felt the pressure of his hand. 'The fact is, Mitzi, it occurred to me that you might care to come along.'

'Along where, Mr Harpur?'

'On the pilgrimage.'

She stared at him. 'You're asking me to come to Santiago da Compostela with you?'

'Does the idea not appeal to you?'

'Why yes, of course, but....' Mitzi frowned. 'I'm sorry, Mr Harpur, I don't understand.'

'It suddenly occurred to me when I was looking through the brochures and I thought, why not? Why shouldn't you come too? It would be pleasant to revisit all these places in the company of someone as enthusiastic as myself.' He went on folding up the fake grass into ever smaller squares, until the plastic stalks began to push their way out, breathlessly, on all sides.

He glanced briefly at her through the double lenses of his glasses. 'It's been my ambition for so long, I'd almost given up the thought of actually doing it. I wasn't sure at my age how I would adapt to foreign travel, though I've always loved France, in particular. The whole thing would be so much more rewarding if there were the two of us. Please say you'll think about it.'

Mitzi looked about her, desperately. 'I'm touched that you should think of such a thing,' she said. 'You've always been...so kind. I owe you such a lot.'

'You owe me nothing, Mitzi,' Mr Harpur said. 'I did what any friend would do.'

'That isn't so. I'm overwhelmed that you should ask me, but it's no use, I can't possibly accept.'

'Might I inquire why not?'

She hesitated: 'I would rather not say. Only that the reasons make it quite impossible.'

'Are you afraid you might not be back here in time to start the new term?'

'No, it isn't that. The fact is, I'm not sure that I would want to come back to the college anyway if you weren't there.'

He gave a grunt: 'That's what I thought. Perhaps you feel you can't give up the room you've rented?'

'No,' said Mitzi, feebly, 'No, it's not that either.'

'Could the reason be financial? Mitzi, listen to me,' he insisted. 'I've lived modestly for forty years. I have a pension that is more than adequate, a house that's paid for, nobody to leave my money or possessions to, no children that need help, no dogs or cats that have to be considered….'

Mitzi tried to interrupt, but he put up a hand to silence her. 'I can assure you, Mitzi, that my motives are entirely selfish. I would relish the companionship of somebody I know well and who knows me, who won't feel obliged to fill the gaps in conversation, somebody who knows when to be silent.' Mitzi bit her lip. It was a knack that she had taken quite a long time to acquire. 'And most important, someone who won't rush me. I'm an old man now. I need to take things slowly. One cathedral at a time, no more. If it takes six months to arrive at Santiago, well so be it. It's the journey, after all, that matters just as much as the arrival.' He sat back and looked at Mitzi. 'You would make an old man very happy if I could persuade you to say yes.'

'Oh, Mr Harpur….' Mitzi spread her hands out.

'Good.' He gave the grass a final pat. 'That's settled then. I'll go ahead and book the tickets, shall I? Waterloo to Paris, supper on the train, a hotel in the capital and maybe three days to see Notre Dame? The pilgrims would have travelled there on foot, of course, but I think we could be a little more indulgent.'

Mitzi sniffed.

'Oh, please don't cry now. This is not the moment.' Mr Harpur patted her hand briskly. 'Shall we finish clearing up?'

'There is just one thing,' Mitzi said. 'The letter that I showed you.'

'Ah yes. Have you come to a decision about that yet?'

'Yes,' said Mitzi. 'Yes, I have.'

***

'For God's sake, Abel, I've been ringing you for half an hour. Couldn't you have answered?'

'I was upstairs in my room. The telephone is in the passage.'

'Gloria said you had called. Is everything all right?'

'No,' Abel muttered, shakily. 'It isn't. Mother's been round here for tea.'

'I sympathise. It must have been a miserable experience. Still, you'll get over it.'

'She said something whilst she was here. You won't believe this, Gregor, but she saw dad jump.'

'I always said that, didn't I? I bet she pushed him.'

Abel put a hand up to his mouth, in part because he feared the words that he was forming there and partly to conceal them from another tenant coming down the passage. 'Did you really think that?'

'It depends. Sometimes my view of human nature sinks so low, I can imagine anything.'

'The thing is, Gregor, that apparently he had been having some sort of a love affair with Mitzi all those years and Wanda knew about it. So, in theory, she would have a motive.'

Gregor licked his lips. He sensed that caution might be wise.

'I asked her why she hadn't shouted out for Mitzi after he had jumped. That's what she said, that it was Mitzi father was unfaithful with and that it had been ever since they married.' Abel bit his lip. 'It's quite a shock, eh?'

'Mmm.'

'What do you think we ought to do about it?'

'Do about it? After twenty years, there's not much point in doing anything.'

'But mother might have been responsible for papi's death. We can't just carry on as normal.'

'We were never normal, Bunny.'

'It's all right for you,' said Abel. 'You weren't close to mutti to begin with.'

'Nor were you. Our mother could put Messalina in the shade. She's dominated you for thirty years. You're free now. Go off and enjoy yourself.'

'I reckon mother put the lid on my relationship with Cressida,' said Abel, bitterly.

'I'm sure she did, but now you've left home, why not have another go at her?'

'She's on her way to Ankara with half a dozen of her friends.' He leant his head against the wall. 'I don't know what's the matter with me, Gregor. I've been feeling really odd. I've got this tightness round my throat and there's a buzzing in my ears.'

'It's perfectly straightforward. You don't want to hear what Wanda has to say and you won't swallow it. You'll come to terms with it in time.'

***

'How is he?'

'Like a lemming looking for a cliff. I don't think Abel understands the concept of free will. He's buckling underneath the strain of it.'

'It's not uncommon.' Gloria broke two eggs in the pan and lapped the oil against them, as if she were coaxing sea water into a moat she'd just dug on the beach. A pinafore was tied around the flannel dressing gown. She fed a second slice of bread into the toaster.

Gregor leaned back in the arm chair, with his eyes half-closed, and listened, rapturously, to the sizzling and clattering. It conjured up a vision that was cosily banal. For once, he felt no urgency to move on. He could feel his member stirring slightly, like a slug responding to the warmth of early summer whilst still comfortably cocooned in sleep.

'It turns out he'd invited Wanda round for tea and she let slip that Mitzi and our father had an understanding. Abel thinks it would have been enough, with somebody of Wanda's disposition, to provide a motive for a late night tussle on the landing. Father never put up much resistance. If she'd made it clear she wanted him to jump, he'd probably have done it to avoid an argument.'

'I wish I knew a few more men like that.' She took the smoking slices from the toaster and began to scrape them in the sink: 'It's rather late to start resuscitating all that now though, isn't it?'

'Of course it is. I've told him to forget about it, get on with his own life. Trouble is, he hasn't got one. Abel needs a woman.'

'Wives are usually more reliable.' She looked at him, obliquely. 'Even if they are less fun.' She turned her back on him and took two plates down from the rack. She gave a short yelp that declined into a savage purr as Gregor pressed himself against her back and wrapped his fingers round her waist. She stuck her buttocks out, obligingly, whilst rummaging inside the cutlery drawer, and then dropped the knife that she was holding and curled both hands round the taps. She sounded like the engine of a deux-chevaux he'd had once, stuttering on the ignition and erupting suddenly into a roar that seemed to come from somewhere else, until the whole car started rattling.

As they puffed their way back to normality, the phone in Gregor's pocket started to vibrate. At first, he thought it was the legacy of their exertions and, as always when things carried on too long, he felt a stab of irritation.

'Better eat your toast before it cools down and goes rubbery,' said Gloria, giving her buttocks a quick shake so the dressing gown fell back across them by itself. It was another of the things he liked about her. There was never this appalling need that other women had, once you had finished with them, to be stroked and cuddled and have nice things said to them. Whilst Gloria was busy at the sink, he held the phone inside his pocket, trying to decipher what was written on the screen. It was a London number.

'Take this.'

Gregor took the plate she handed him and sat down at the table. Gloria sat opposite. She'd wound her hair round in a loop, securing it with what looked like a knitting needle. As she bent her head, the loop sagged to the side.

She tore a piece of toast in half and dunked it in the fried egg, taking small, quick bites and running her tongue round her lips. 'Eat up.'

'I get more pleasure out of watching you.'

'You should have said so, earlier. I wouldn't have bothered doing two lots.'

Gregor lifted his egg, carefully, onto the slice of toast and started eating his way round the yolk until the golden orb was isolated, like a sun against a cloudless sky. He moved the bacon from the outer edge towards the centre, where it nudged against the circle, ominously, like a landscape threatened by a line of storm clouds.

Gloria looked on whilst she continued disinterring the remaining shreds of bacon from between her teeth. She glanced up. Gregor held her eyes. He raised his knife and fork, suggestively, suspending them above the threatened egg. The tip of Gloria's tongue poked out from between her teeth and curled against her top lip. As he went into a nose dive, Gregor felt his inner thigh vibrate again. He scooped the egg into his mouth in one go and ate noisily.

'Is that it?' Gloria said, scathingly. 'I thought you were about to show me how to eat an egg without breaking the yolk.'

'You can't eat an egg without breaking the yolk, Gloria.' Gregor wiped the bacon round his plate. It had been too long underneath the grill and was already brittle. He sat back and poured himself some coffee. Gloria collected the remains of burnt toast and went over to the window, scattering the crumbs across the ledge outside. Two pigeons in full flight, crash-landed on the sill.

'You shouldn't feed them,' Gregor muttered, peevishly. He didn't like it when he didn't have her full attention. 'They'll come back and bring their friends.'

'Why shouldn't they? It's not as if we're short of bread.' She pushed a crumb towards one of the pigeons.

'You'll be giving them a full English breakfast soon.'

'I reckon this one's pregnant. She needs feeding, don't you, precious?' She reached out and and scratched the feathers on its neck.

'You don't spoil me like that,' said Gregor, sulkily.

She glanced over her shoulder, curled her index finger, saucily, under the bird's extended beak, then shooed them both away. She sidled round the back of Gregor's chair and leant across him, resting one cheek on his head. She slid her hand under the robe and wrapped her fingers round the dark hairs on his chest. 'Why don't we have a walk this afternoon in Norham Gardens?'

Gregor frowned. 'Why ever would we want to have a walk?'

She gave the hair a light tug: 'It's what people do on Sunday afternoons. It's the one day of the week they spend together.'

'Fine. Why don't we go to bed?'

'We've only just got up.'

'Come here.' He held his arms out. Gloria came round the chair and curled up on his knees. He rocked her gently.

'Do you reckon Abel's going to make trouble?' she said, nibbling at his ear.

'I can't see anybody being interested, after all this time.' He reached into his pocket for his cigarettes.

'You don't care that your mother might have pushed your father off the top-floor landing?'

'Whilst I'd happily see Wanda banged up for the next ten years, it won't make any difference to my father.'

'There is such a thing as justice for its own sake.'

Gregor stroked her inner thigh with one hand, whilst the other held the cigarette. Somewhere, deep down, he realised that the phone was still vibrating. Wedged between their thighs, it felt so far away that Gregor wondered if he were imagining it.

He looked, stealthily, at Gloria. Her eyes were shut. He moved his hand a fraction and she raised her eyebrows. As the hand continued creeping up her thigh, her lips pursed and she started to emit short pants. She parted her legs slightly and he realised the telephone was in between them and that now, without its padding, the vibration was more audible.

Whilst he was concentrating on the task in hand, he wondered who might need to get in touch with him so urgently. Since losing his address book, he'd relied on the women in it, phoning him. Although still revelling in his restored relationship with Gloria, he nonetheless felt there was something missing from his life without the option of philandering. He'd bought another book and was painstakingly restoring numbers as they came to him, but it was still a fraction of the size of the original and as an archive it was woefully inadequate. He lowered Gloria onto the rug where she lay flapping like a beached whale.

'Are you going?'

'Time I did a bit of work. I'll call for you this afternoon. We'll have that wander in The Parks. I'll treat you to an ice-cream.'

'Mmm.'

'Pity I can't cross the Quad in slippers and a dressing gown. This endless dressing and undressing is extremely time-consuming.' Gregor pulled his trousers out from underneath the chair. 'I'll see you later.'

'Haven't you forgotten something?'

Gregor pursed his lips. He went down on his knees and kissed her on the cheek: 'OK?'

'Fine, but that isn't what I meant. Now that your mobile's served its purpose as a sex aid, you can turn it off.' She looked at Gregor, quizzically. 'We wouldn't want your batteries running down just when you're on a roll, now would we?'

***

Abel looked at his reflection in the glass above the sink. He hardly recognised himself. Since Wanda's visit, he had felt detached from everything around him. He no longer thought of Cressida, which was as well because the postcards ceased when she crossed over to the Balkan coast at Brindisi. They'd reached the end of the mantelpiece and the end of their association, simultaneously.

He was not obliged to be alone, of course. The art school was just down the road; there would be other Cressidas if Abel cared to look for them. The girl he'd seen that lunch-time in the park, had been back to the library since then and the way she looked at him suggested she would welcome an approach. But even if he made friends, even if he went out, Abel sensed that it would only make him more aware of what was absent from his life.

At work, he did his tasks mechanically, without enthusiasm. Even the old ladies sensed his disaffection. Ever since she'd had to foot the bill that morning for a taxi to send Abel home, Miss Quettock kept her distance from him, too. If it had not enhanced his sense of isolation, he might have been grateful, but increasingly she gave him jobs to do that kept him by the photo-copier or in the back room. Even Aileen took care when she spoke to him, as if a wrong word might precipitate another crisis. She was reticent about the wedding plans she had discussed so fulsomely before. She didn't want to find herself obliged to add a madman to the list of guests.

Each night, when Abel made his way back to his digs and let himself in, he felt like a half-emerged grub turning back into its chrysalis. He might have once had the potential to become a butterfly, but somewhere on the way the process had been interrupted. He was neither one thing nor the other.

He no longer bothered cooking for himself. Sometimes, he finished off the toast left over from the morning. Once, he'd pierced a large tin of condensed milk and sat on the sofa, pouring it into a spoon and ladling it onto his tongue until the tin was empty. At the start, the sweetness of it comforted him, bringing solace to the lonely outposts of his being. When he'd finished off the tin, he sat there in the dark for quarter of an hour before rushing to the downstairs toilet to be sick.

He would have gone to bed as soon as he got home, but if he turned the light out too soon, he would only have the same dilemma in reverse, reluctantly emerging from the comforting cocoon of sleep at half-past four or five o'clock, no longer tired enough to go back into it.

At night he found the clock an unexpected consolation. In the daytime he felt chivvied by it, but when all the city sounds had ceased he listened to it in the darkness and retraced its passage through the centuries. It linked him to the past and seemed to promise him a future. Wanda had been right. An heirloom, something passed on over generations, gradually became inseparable from you, like an alter ego. He could understand, now, why his grandmother had gone back for her father's letters and why Wanda wore her mother's fur-coat, year in, year out, till it fell apart.

He bought a television set for company and, for a while, he took an interest in the Soaps and the brief glimpses they afforded him of lives that often seemed to Abel as pathetic as his own. Then he remembered they did not exist outside the set. He wondered what could have persuaded anybody to invent them and it struck him that perhaps this was a way of offering his own life up to ridicule. He turned instead to Game Shows, which he could at least participate in without feeling that they reinforced his own inferiority. He found his general knowledge far superior to most of the contestants. All those years in which he had immersed himself in Wanda's stolen library books, had given him an education that no university could match.

He had brought several with him when he moved, including the one he'd given Gregor for his birthday, all those years ago. Predictably, his brother hadn't bothered taking it and, worried that his mother might discover it, he hid it underneath the mattress in his bedroom. He could never bring himself to throw a book away, no matter how incriminating it might be.

He tried to pull himself together. One weekend he set himself to clean the cooker. He had spent all morning on his knees, his head inside the oven, a scouring pad in one hand and the oven cleaner in the other. At some point, he'd felt himself begin to drift off and came round to find his forehead resting on the rear wall of the oven and a pool of neat bleach underneath his nostrils. He had forced his way out of the narrow space. He didn't want to die like that, but for the first time it occurred to him that maybe dying wasn't such a bad idea.

***

'I didn't think I'd cry,' said Gaynor. 'I felt OK until I was coming up the path.'

'That's often how it is,' said Mitzi, who could easily have cried as well.

'I worried more that I might not feel anything at all.'

'I'm glad that didn't happen.' The first thing that struck her when they met were Gaynor's eyes. They were like pansies. She had dark hair, tied back loosely with a green scarf. She was very pale and Mitzi wondered whether she was prone to headaches. She imagined Gaynor cooped up in a little room with an electric fire, a pile of books and endless cups of coffee, eating poorly and deprived of fresh air. Anyone would think I was her mother, Mitzi thought.

As she and Gaynor looked at one another, Mitzi had an overwhelming sense of the fragility of youth and the appalling ease with which it could be brought down. 'Oh my dear.' She held her hands out and her daughter's face had crumpled. She fell into Mitzi's arms.

Although she'd felt uneasy about disobeying Gregor, whose instructions not to see her daughter had been so specific, once she had left Primrose Hill it was as if she'd left behind her obligation to the people in it. Wanda had rejected her, her nephews had their own lives, she no longer had a home and soon she would not have a job. But what she did have suddenly, miraculously, was her daughter. No, decided Mitzi, she would not allow this final chance of happiness, however dangerous, however fleeting it might be, to pass her by.

They had discovered Gaynor lived in Gravesend. 'Just a few miles down the coast from Deal,' said Mr Harpur, when he had suggested that they use the cottage for a rendezvous. Whilst she was waiting in the cramped space of the living room for Gaynor to arrive, she lit the fire and then, appalled, she watched an ant crawl down the log she had thrown onto it. The flames were licking round the wood. The ant turned, frantically, and ran back in the opposite direction. Mitzi gave a whimper of distress. She held a spill out to the ant, but it reacted to the new threat by retreating to the hollow in the bark it had emerged from. Mitzi grasped the poker, wedged it underneath the log and tipped it out into the hearth, where it lay smoking.

There was no sign of the ant. How many other tiny, microscopic creatures had the log been home to? She had wanted to warm up the room, to welcome Gaynor with a cosy fire, but now the room was filled with smoke and she did not dare put another log on. She debated whether she should prop open the window and let in the cold air, or hope that the smoke would disappear before her daughter got there.

It was such a novel thing, to say 'my daughter.' Since the day the nurse had taken her away, when she had no more substance than the blanket she was wrapped in, Mitzi had not dared to say those words. She had occasionally, when her mind was wandering, imagined what her daughter would be like at seven, at eleven, at sixteen. She half dreamt and half dreaded that, when she was eighteen, she might come to find her. She could understand the helpless, suffocating love that Wanda felt for Abel. After all, he was there to remind her. Mitzi managed no more than the merest glimpse before the tiny bundle was removed from sight.

When Gaynor came into the room, she'd sniffed the air. 'I'm sorry for the smoke,' said Mitzi. 'The fire isn't drawing very well. It's been some time since it was last lit.'

'Apple wood,' said Gaynor, breathing deeply. 'What a lovely smell.' She looked round. 'Is it your house?'

'No,' said Mitzi. 'It belongs to a dear friend. He suggested we should meet here as it's not too far from Gravesend.'

Gaynor frowned. 'It's strange. I have the feeling I've been here before.'

'Well, in a sense you have,' said Mitzi. 'This is where I spent the winter before you were born.'

'My first home.'

Mitzi smiled: 'I'll put the kettle on.'

'Can I look round?' She scanned the bookshelves. 'There are lots of art books.'

'Mr Harpur, that's the man who owns the cottage, is a teacher,' Mitzi said. 'He will have read them all.' She watched as Gaynor took a volume on Italian frescoes over to the window and stood silhouetted in the light. She glanced up, suddenly, and gave a quick smile that had echoes of so many lives behind it, that it was like leafing through a family album. Mitzi wished she could have seized and tucked away the moment so as to retrieve it later, when she was alone again. 'You said you were a student?'

'Yes, I'm at the L.S.E. I'm reading economics.'

'Heavens. That sounds difficult.'

'It isn't really.' She stood in the kitchen door, observing Mitzi as she spooned the tea into the caddy. 'Odd, you're not a bit as I imagined.'

'What did you imagine?' Mitzi asked her, gently.

'I suppose I thought you'd look like me.' She hesitated. 'Do I take after my father?'

Mitzi drew breath. 'There's a bit of both of us there, I suppose.' It turned out Gaynor's parents had been in their forties and already had one child, a boy of nine, when they adopted her. They'd told her she was not their child when she was eight, but that her parents hadn't wanted her and they had. Mitzi made a helpless gesture with her hand. Whilst her adoptive parents were alive, said Gaynor, she had worried that they might be hurt if they knew she was looking for her mother.

'That was why I waited. Though I was afraid I might be too late.'

Mitzi shook her head: 'I always hoped that one day you would come back.'

'I'd already started looking, in a vague way. It was your name on the birth certificate and the address was Primrose Hill. In fact it's Camden, so that was a bit confusing, but when I discovered you were still there and the other names were different, I did wonder if you might be living with my dad. That's till I saw the ages of the men and realised neither of them would be old enough.' The irony of this was mercifully lost on Gaynor.

When she asked, inevitably, why her mother hadn't kept her, Mitzi looked away. She'd always found it difficult to lie and, if she owed the truth to anyone, she owed it to her daughter. 'You have to believe me, that if there had been a way of keeping you, I would have done.'

'My father had abandoned you?'

'No. But he couldn't marry me.'

'He was already married?'

Oh dear, Mitzi thought. This was the way the conversation had gone that night when she had confessed to Nathan. 'Both of us had obligations that we had to honour.' Mitzi realised Gaynor's eyes had strayed towards the finger which, in other circumstances, would have had a ring on it. She curled her fingers up, protectively. 'What sort of little girl were you?' she asked, to move the conversation back to Gaynor.

'Would you like to see some photographs?'

'I'd love to,' Mitzi said, enthusiastically, and Gaynor took the scrap book from her rucksack and arranged it on her knees. The snapshots had been individually fixed with corners stuck onto the thick black pages. Captions in white ink identified the time and place.

As Gaynor turned the pages, Mitzi found herself absorbed into a life that had run parallel to hers for twenty years. She was there in the audience when Gaynor played a sheep at the Nativity, with papier mâché head and cotton wool balls stuck onto her dress. She clapped when Gaynor won the history prize at school and played 'The Rambler' at a Brownie concert. She saw Gaynor's room in Gravesend with its Che Guevara posters and its CDs strewn across the floor, along with socks and sneakers, an untidy teenage room that shrieked normality. It was a world away from anything that Mitzi had experienced.

A family group showed Gaynor with her brother and adoptive parents on the beach at Broadstairs, where they'd gone for holidays. The boy was making castles in the sand whilst Gaynor smashed a spade against them and was sent off to fill buckets from the sea to put into the moat. There was a table cloth spread out over the sand nearby with the remains of sandwiches and cake. The Tranters, both with white hair although Mr Tranter didn't have a lot of it, had been reclining in adjacent deckchairs. Mr Tranter had The Daily Mail propped on his knee whilst Mrs Tranter oversaw the building of the keep from a respectful distance, offering advice that no one took. So this was how real families lived, thought Mitzi.

Gaynor had glanced up at her and hesitated. 'Is it too much? Shall I stop?' Her eyes searched Mitzi's face.

'No.' Mitzi shook her head. 'No, please don't. It's……..It's wonderful.' She'd pressed her lips together. 'It's so…..so.' She had given up the search for any word that could do justice to her feelings.

Gaynor pressed her hand: 'I'm sorry you weren't there.'

'Me too,' sighed Mitzi.

***

The train erupted from the tunnel with a whoosh that made her ears pop. Wanda stirred the glass of iced tea. It occurred to her as they were rattling through the countryside, that she had not been on a train since she was nine. She had expected to feel apprehensive, but in fact she felt quite safe inside the first-class carriage with its plush seats and its dated elegance. She found the sound and rhythm of the swaying carriages exhilarating. She was grateful for the broad-brimmed hat that she was not expected to dispense with, even in the dining car, and which allowed her to observe the scene around her whilst remaining hidden. She felt as if she were on the film set of a silent movie, acting out a part with characters and costumes that she could put on and off at will. She wasn't locked inside herself, as she had been at all the other crucial junctures of her life.

She'd noticed people looking at her, curiously, but they looked away as soon as Wanda caught their eye. The English, with their natural reserve, responded instantly to hers. The fact that she looked foreign was enough to put them off. She might have trouble later on, as she encountered people who were foreigners themselves, but over sixty years she had acquired a mask of such determined isolationism that few cared to try and make a dent in it.

She took the postcards from her bag and toyed with the idea of sending one to Abel, but she did not want to end up on the mantelpiece with Cressida. Of course, she'd known that wouldn't last. She could have told him so at the beginning. Abel wasn't looking for a partner; he was looking for a mother. That was why she had been so appalled by Mrs Allerton. If she had simply been a fatter version of herself, her son's association with her might have been less threatening. But she represented everything that Wanda wasn't. She was uncontainable. She seemed to overlap the boundaries of her own existence. She leaked into other peoples' lives. The very air around her was contaminated by the lost souls she was meant to rein in. Wasn't she a social worker, after all? As far as Wanda could determine, Mrs Allerton's solution to a problem was to offer tea and sympathy and, if that didn't work, to ratchet up the 'sympathy' until the 'problem' was submerged beneath it.

Wanda doubted that her methods followed the official line. She'd wondered whether to complain to the authorities and have her struck off, but she was suspicious of officials and she did not want to draw attention to herself. In any case, once she had found them that day, shame had done the rest. The trouble with Abel was that he had always had a tendency to see things through the eyes of other people. It was only when he looked at them through her eyes, that he saw these things for what they were.

Whilst she still mourned the loss of Abel, Wanda was surprised how little she regretted losing everybody else. It had been a relief to get away from Gregor and to know they did not have to meet again. The ribbon that attached her to her sister had snapped unexpectedly and Mitzi too had disappeared from view. She rarely thought of Nathan, though she made a point, when booking herself into hotels, of explaining that she was the widow of a wealthy businessman. She noticed she got better treatment when she did.

She checked the time. She'd changed her watch, the minute they'd left Waterloo. In England, darkness would have fallen and lights would be going on inside the flat. If there was anybody there, of course. The agents who had come to put a value on it, had advised her that it might be difficult to sell. It was the sort of property the English didn't care for these days: too much space under the ceilings, too much opportunity for draughts and people didn't like the atmosphere. Of course, you didn't rate a house according to its atmosphere, but still these were the sort of things a buyer took account of.

'It feels foreign,' said the agent and she overheard him say it was the sort of scent you found on railway stations on the Continent. And then there was the history. They might have cleared the shrine away and swabbed the tiles out on the landing, but the fact remained that from this landing somebody had thrown themselves into the stairwell. People might not be averse to tragedy but they would rather not live cheek by jowl with it, in case the bad luck rubbed off.

Wanda hadn't liked the young man. Did he want to sell the flat or not? Of course he did. He was just pointing out that it was not a seller's market and she might have to be patient. Although Wanda could live adequately off the interest from the capital she had invested, she was still reluctant to expend large quantities of money without the security of having sold the flat. She was relieved when it was taken by another family of immigrants, a large and boisterous extended family of Jamaicans who put in an offer far below the one that Wanda had in mind. Once more, she felt she had been robbed of something. She had tried to push the offer up, but they responded, artlessly, that they were not in a position to pay more and clearly felt no obligation to.

'You have the choice,' the agent said. 'You can accept, or you can wait and hope you get a better offer.' Grudgingly, she had accepted, but the feeling that she had been swindled, chafed at her.

Had all the recent revelations not come simultaneously, Wanda doubted that she would have found the strength to smash the

Schopenhauer's Porcupines

edifice she had so carefully created. There were terrifying moments when she wondered if perhaps the past was still there underneath the rubble, perfectly preserved and waiting to be resurrected. Would she end up digging through the debris with her bare hands?

Normally, a pot of coffee and a Continental breakfast were enough to reassure her that her current life had more to offer. Though she still missed Abel, she saw now how cloying their relationship had been, how Abel was the one who'd held her back. She'd spent two decades in the flat in Primrose Hill with nothing more exciting to look forward to than the reunions. I might have travelled round the world, she thought. She might have spent the intervening years on trains like this one, junketing across the Continent in a protective capsule. She delighted in the landscape rushing past, she took a hedonistic pleasure in the fawning service of the flunkeys on the train, she revelled in the power money gave her and the little luxuries that it provided.

No, she thought. She would not write to Abel. Not yet, anyway. She put the postcards back inside her handbag. Signalling a waiter, she asked for another iced tea and a tray of pastries.

***

As he stood there in the dark, a dull light from the street lamp outside filtered through the open door onto the hall, illuminating the familiar pattern on the tiles. The light clicked on and Abel pushed the door to, silently He crossed the hallway and began to mount the staircase. Inside Mrs Pampanini's flat he heard the murmur of the BBC World Service. He crept quickly past her door and up the next flight to the landing at the top.

He'd half expected to discover that the shrine had been restored. He'd even wondered whether he might still find Wanda there. But no. He rested one hand on the railing and looked down. There was a lingering trace of something in the air. It was a smell of absence. The sharp scent of hyacinths, the reek of fear, the whiff of perfume from the costumes Mitzi wore, the cooking odours percolating from inside the flat, the scents that testified to life, had all been swept away. The flat was empty of its human cargo and it seemed that Nathan's ghost had finally departed with it.

I'm alone, thought Abel. He'd come looking for his father, but if he had failed to find him whilst he was alive, it wasn't likely he would find him now. Perhaps, if he had been a little older or his father had been younger, or if Abel had been more assertive, less a 'mother's' boy, they might have forged a link with one another. Although Nathan had occasionally taken both the boys to football matches, it was Mitzi, always half a child herself, who usually organised their outings. Nathan had remained a shadow from the start. The only way that Abel could connect with him, was by becoming one himself.

He gazed into the darkness of the stairwell. Clasping one hand round the rail, he looped his leg over the balustrade. He needed to know what it felt like, to have just that narrow ledge between himself and nothingness. He pressed his heel against the uprights. There was barely room for him to keep his balance. Gingerly, he looped the other leg across. His palms were skidding on the rail.

This was the closest he would ever come to feeling what his father felt. He forced himself to look into the void and what he saw was emptiness; the kind of emptiness he felt inside him. He had been aware of it, the first time, sitting on the swing that evening in the park, when Mitzi had forgotten him. His loneliness, he realised, did not depend on being on his own. It was there anyway. He came to the conclusion that he had been born with this essential missing 'thing,' like a genetic defect. Maybe he would not feel empty when he reached the bottom. Maybe, in the instant when he leapt, his father would be there.

There was a click that sounded so loud in the silence, Abel jumped and almost lost his footing on the ledge. The light went out. He whimpered in the darkness. Suddenly, the flat door opened on the landing down below and Mrs Pampanini came out in her dressing gown. She stood a moment looking round, as if she couldn't fathom what it was that had disturbed her. Abel pressed himself against the balustrade. He wasn't sure what he would do if Mrs Pampanini turned the light on and looked up and saw him. She might well regard a re-run of the same scenario that she had witnessed twenty years ago, as rather tasteless.

She turned back into the flat again and closed the door. The seconds passed whilst Abel stood there, paralysed, like someone half way up a mountain who looks down and recognises in that instant how precarious their situation is. His legs were trembling with the strain of trying to maintain his balance on the narrow ledge. He knew that, if he stayed there any longer, they would give way. Suddenly he panicked, scrabbling with his hands and feet to gain a purchase on the ledge and throwing himself bodily across the balustrade.

He lay there on the tiled floor, staring up into the lantern roof which, as a small boy, he had thought of as the vault of heaven. Pigeons scratted at the moss and dead leaves in the cracks. Their webbed feet pattered on the glass like rain drops. Abel used the rail to hoist himself onto his knees and pulled his shoes on, tying up the laces, shakily. He slid his arms into his jacket. He did not dare turn the light on, but as he was steadying himself to go back down the stairs, the front door slammed and someone at the bottom switched it on again. He listened to the footsteps as they crossed the hall and climbed the first flight, past Miss Zellwig's flat and on up to the second landing, then the third.

'Hey, man.' The black face broke into a smile as he saw Abel waiting at the top. 'You not find anybody der?' He hammered on the door. 'Rose! You got someone out here waitin'.'

Abel heard a high-pitched chattering inside the flat; small bodies tumbling over one another to be first to welcome the intruder. When the door was flung back, they came out at him like brightly coloured bullets from a gun. A woman in a yellow blouse with very white teeth smiled at Abel dazzlingly. 'You waitin' long?' she asked. 'I tell you, Charlie, dat bell don' work.'

'It's all right; I didn't ring,' said Abel, quickly, thankful that he hadn't been discovered earlier. 'I wanted to stand outside on the landing for a moment, that's all.'

They were looking at him, curiously, but without suspicion, as if there was nothing odd about a man they'd never met before who hung around on other peoples' landings. Abel nodded down the hall. 'I lived here,' he explained. 'My family had this flat for fifty years. I came to say goodbye.'

'You only jus' this moment met us an' you wan' say goodbye?' said Charlie, cheerfully.

'I meant the place. I came to say goodbye to the apartment,' Abel stammered. 'This was where my father died, you see.'

Five round, black faces with dark eyes surrounded by a ring of white, were staring up at him.

'No problem. Come on in.' Rose gathered them together, shooing them inside, and beckoned Abel. 'Lesia! Put the kettle on.'

'No, really,' Abel said. 'I don't want to disturb you.'

'You not doing' no disturbin,' Rose insisted.

Charlie put a chair out for him. 'Dis de house where you were born, man?'

'Yes,' said Abel. 'My room was the bedroom at the end.'

'That's ours,' a chorus of small voices cried. He looked around the kitchen. Children's' drawings had been selotaped onto the walls. A string of garlic and two strings of onions dangled from the pelmet. There were magnets covering the fridge door and above it, in a wicker basket, was a jumbled pile of mangoes, peaches, oranges. Wherever Abel looked, he saw bright colours, chaos, love.

'It's nicer than it was when I was here,' he said.

'Oh, get along now,' Rose protested, bashfully.

'I heard the flat had sold, but I thought no one had moved in yet.'

'Las' week,' Charlie said. 'We reckoned we'd move in and let de place grow round us.' One of the smaller children clambered onto Abel's knee.

'You don' feel sad, now that you aint here?' Rose said.

'Not at all,' said Abel. It had done him good, he realised, to see the flat like this, with someone else's stamp on it. You couldn't blame a place for making you unhappy. Places, like animals, were a reflection of their owners.

'Come see our room,' urged the children, tugging at his jacket.

All except the eldest, who stood back and looked at Abel shyly. She might want him to see their room, too, but she would never ask. She was about eleven and when Abel caught her eye, she blushed and looked away. He let himself be chivvied down the passage, the remaining children hanging onto him as if asserting rights of ownership over whichever bit they happened to have hold of.

'You don' tire de gentleman now, Clovis,' Rose called. 'Dinner will be on de table in ten minutes.' From the kitchen came the smell of peppers sizzling in a pan of garlic. In the bedroom, Abel saw the colourful array of bricks, charts, rag rugs, cushions, splodgy renderings in tempera of Rose and Charlie, and potato cuts of animals with square heads. In amongst the pictures on the pin-board, he saw one he recognised: the postcard of the boats in Deal that Mitzi had sent and that, somehow, had been left behind. It wasn't out of place amongst the other cards, but it had lost its potency. He knew exactly what he'd felt when, as a small boy of eleven, he had lain in bed and looked at the flotilla of boats bobbing on their moorings, but he didn't feel it any longer.

'Boats.' The smallest of the children pointed at the postcard.

'Yes.' The child broke into peals of laughter, as if he'd said something hugely funny. Abel laughed, too. She began to pull him back along the corridor towards the room that had been Wanda's. He resisted but the other children had closed ranks behind him and were jostling him along the passage. 'Cheneil wan' you to see her room.' Abel hesitated. He had never been invited into this room whilst it was his mother's.

'Don' look at de mess in there.' Rose called out from the kitchen.

He stood at the entrance to the sewing room and looked at what had been his mother's secret hideaway. The cupboards were still lined along the far wall, but the doors had been removed and the double shelves converted into bunk beds. Cheneil vaulted up the ladder, rolling over on the narrow mattress, giggling with her plump legs in the air. The darkest recess of the kingdom Abel had grown up in, had been swept clean of its dour legacy. Light flooded in. It's as if we were never here, he thought, and wondered why he didn't find the idea more disturbing. He felt as if he had been released from prison and was taking his first walk out in the open air.

'Why don' you stay for supper?' Rose asked and the children clapped their hands.

'Yes, yes,' they shrieked.

And so for once he didn't spend the evening on his own. At table, they bombarded him with questions about how his grandfather had made the trip from Warsaw with his two young daughters, how they had adapted to the English way of life, who'd lived in the apartment, what they did, which rooms they'd occupied. They told him how Rose had come over from Jamaica with her widowed mother, ten years earlier, and taken up with Charlie who had come a generation earlier. They argued over whether it was better to be black, or white but with an accent. They congratulated Abel on not having any accent. 'You de real thing, man, an English gentleman,' said Charlie.

Abel laughed. He'd never felt at home with anybody except Mrs Allerton, but here with Rose and Charlie and their children he felt he had broken through the crust that separated him from other people and discovered something on the other side that he identified as a capacity for happiness. When he eventually left the flat at midnight, he stood on the landing looking at the space where Nathan's shrine had been and where a row of small red boots had now replaced the leather shoes with their immaculate white uppers.

'Bye, dad,' he said. 'You'll be all right now.'

***

The jug was small and silver, with a delicate relief of berries and acanthus leaves around the base. The overhead lights were reflected in the hinged lid. As she leant across, she saw the shadow of her own face on the surface. Wanda ran her finger lightly over it. A waiter came along the car and asked if he could take the tray.

'No,' Wanda said. 'Not yet,' and he apologised and went away. She poured a little of the tea into her cup, but it was cold now. Soon, the waiter would come back. He would ask whether there was something else she wanted. She picked up the jug and held it in her fingers. On the underside, there was a hall-mark.

A Dutch couple, with a little girl, came down the centre of the dining-car and sat across the aisle from her. The woman smiled at Wanda, distantly. The waiter came back and they ordered tea and cakes. The train went through a tunnel and the lights came on inside the carriage, ricocheting off the silver jug. The woman settled down to read a magazine. The man was fussing round the little girl. But it was not her father whose attention the child wanted. She looked past him, sullenly, to where her mother turned the pages of her journal. She knew that her daughter's eyes were on her; there was an attentiveness in her determination not to look up, that could not be justified by what was on the page in front of her since, having scanned it, she immediately went on to the next one. The girl sidled over to her mother and slipped one hand into hers. The woman patted her, half-heartedly, and went on reading.

Wanda found her interest caught between the three of them. She wondered what had caused the woman to withdraw affection from the little girl and why her daughter valued it above her father's. Had the man been guilty of a distant indiscretion that the child was being made to pay for? Was the father so devoted to his daughter because he too felt excluded? Why do those we love, so rarely love us in return? she wondered. They love other people, who in turn look elsewhere for affection.

After Mitzi's birth, her mother had seemed lost to her. Her disappearance on the railway station did no more than rubber-stamp the loss. But she had something Mitzi didn't have: her mother's fur coat. The most difficult decision she had had to make, was not if she should leave her youngest son behind her when she left, but what to do about the fur coat? She felt it no longer represented her. It was old-fashioned, moth-eaten and scruffy, and to Wanda's nostrils, newly sensitised by the refreshing novelty of ready money, it smelt noticeably of the ghetto. She could hardly claim to leave the past behind and take her mother's fur coat with her. When she found the lining on the inside, parting at the seams, she bunched the coat up in her arms and pressed her face against the collar, taking in a last, long, lingering whiff of family history before she dumped it on the skip, together with the decimated contents of the sewing room.

The next day, she went back and rescued it, consumed with panic in case someone else had found it in the middle of the night and taken it away. She'd hurried upstairs to the flat, past Mrs Pampanini's door, and once inside, had shaken out the coat, which smelt a lot worse after being on the skip all night. She wrapped it in a dustbin liner, sealing up the opening before putting it into a trunk. She now had so much luggage that she'd worried about what would happen when she had to leave the train.

The woman yawned and let the journal sink onto her lap. She closed her eyes. The child still mutely kept her in its line of sight. The man had given up his efforts to divert her. Having poured himself another glass of tea out of the pot, he settled down to looking at the countryside as it flashed past them.

Wanda studied his reflection in the window of the car. There was a heaviness about him, now that he'd been forced back on himself. He needed other people, to confirm his own identity. So did his daughter. Now, she had lost both her parents, Wanda thought. The girl had slid into the seat beside her mother and was playing with a small doll she had brought with her, pretending to force crumbs into its mouth and scolding it when it refused to eat them. Suddenly, she gave its arm a sharp twist and it came away. She gave a shrill laugh that, to Wanda's ear, was too high to be natural. There was a faint air of hysteria about it.

The man glanced at her and looked away, uncomfortably. The woman's eyes had opened. She was looking at the doll. The child glanced up at her. There was a silence in which everyone, including Wanda, waited to see who would break it. Finally, the woman made a tutting sound and went back to her magazine. The man went back to looking at the landscape. The child started to undress the doll to see if she could reconnect the arm and Wanda, feeling unaccountably distressed, looked round for something else to focus her attention on.

The waiter came back down the car. He glanced at Wanda and then turned towards the other table. When he saw the doll in two halves, he put down the tray and threw his hands up in the air, theatrically. He held the body up and peered into the hole left by the severed arm, commiserating in Italian, hunching up his shoulders,

Schopenhauer's Porcupines

making gestures that suggested he was weighing up its chances of survival and would put them at no more than fifty/fifty. Picking up a pastry fork, he gingerly inserted it into the hole and hooked it onto the elastic band inside the body. Drawing it out, carefully, he slotted it around the severed limb. The arm sprang back immediately into its original position. He held up the doll, triumphantly, and kissed it on the cheeks.

The girl received it back, politely. When the waiter wasn't there, she'd get her own back on it in some other way. She started putting on its clothes: a frilly blouse and miniature, embroidered waistcoat. Wanda looked away. She felt as she had sometimes when she came out of the theatre or the cinema, as if her own life were a pit she was about to step back into, stripped of colour and the comforting proximity of other people. Empty.

Having been congratulated by the parents of the girl, the waiter had begun to stack the plates and cups onto the tray. Whilst he still had his back to Wanda, she leant out across the table, picked the little silver jug up from the tray in front of her and slipped it in the inside pocket of her coat. She rose unhurriedly and left the carriage.

***

In the months that followed Mitzi's meeting with her daughter, they had met again on two or three occasions, either at the cottage or in London. Mitzi hoped she wasn't waiting for an introduction to the other members of the family. She knew that it would not be easy to maintain the frontier that divided Gaynor's life from hers. Once she had graduated, Gaynor planned to find a flat in London. In between, if she could find someone to go with, she was hoping to spend three or four months travelling and was working in a shoe shop at weekends, to make a little money. It was just as well, thought Mitzi, that they weren't still living in the flat in Primrose Hill, which would have left them more exposed to one another's scrutiny.

She'd furnished Gaynor with a rudimentary history of the family background in America, then Europe. She'd described her mother's disappearance on the railway station and her father's efforts to provide a home for them in Primrose Hill. She had been careful not to mention Gregor in all this, although she was surprised at how much Gaynor seemed to know already. When she said 'my cousin', once, and Mitzi had looked up at her, inquiringly, she'd added, artlessly. 'The one at Oxford.'

Feeling that it would be better not to start a conversation that might lead to Gregor, Mitzi nodded, mutely. If he'd met her, she knew Gregor would have said something and so, presumably, would Gaynor. Gregor wasn't someone you could overlook.

Her first impression of her daughter, had suggested that she didn't take particularly after either of her parents. Individually, her features, other than the eyebrows which she'd certainly derived from Gregor, were refined. The chin was delicate and slightly pointed. From the eyes down, she looked like the second fairy in the Sleeping Beauty story, kindly rather than attractive, positive, not fey, the one whose gifts would make up for the malice of the first. She had a thin, straight nose, lips that were generous rather than too large and an expression that was wistful, even when she smiled. It was the eyebrows, in the end, that did for Gaynor. Given the genetic possibilities of an amalgamation between her and Gregor, Mitzi thought, the consequences might have been a lot worse, but whoever was responsible for dishing out the genes, had not done Gaynor any favours. Mitzi's heart went out to her.

Once they had passed the stage of feeling that they had to talk to one another, Gaynor often brought her books down to the cottage for a weekend and sat at the table, studying, whilst Mitzi sewed. She didn't share her mother's taste in fashion. For the most part, she wore plain skirts with thick stockings underneath and woollen pullovers in blue or brown that Mitzi guessed came from a different corner of the Oxfam shop that was her own source of materials. She'd started knitting her a loose-ribbed pullover, reflecting Gaynor's taste in colour rather than her own, but she could not resist incorporating into it a sheep in white wool with a cloud above its head. 'It seemed a shame to waste the wool,' she said, and Gaynor smiled her wistful smile and kissed her mother on the cheek.

Whenever they worked separately in the same room, Mitzi took an opportunity to sneak a glance at Gaynor's bent head and to marvel at the miracle that had restored her daughter to her. After Gaynor had looked up and caught her mother's eye on two or three occasions, Mitzi realised she was being contemplated in the same way and, deciding that her daughter's needs must take priority, she concentrated on the sheep instead.

She found that Gaynor liked to cook and, in the afternoons, they sometimes made a cake together, spreading the ingredients across the table without bothering to measure out the quantities and laughing, recklessly, as they tipped nuts, sultanas, mixed spice and whatever else was readily available, into the mixing bowl. They made a batch of gingerbread men to leave for Mr Harpur and, when they were cutting out the last one, Mitzi gave it a white halo with some icing sugar and incised the rims of spectacles around the currants that were eyes. She added caraway seeds to represent the buttons on his jacket and a glacé cherry for the handkerchief he carried in his pocket.

'Mr Harpur, I presume,' said Gaynor, laughing.

They took walks together arm in arm along the beach and stood in silence looking at the sea. Once, Mitzi, gripped by sudden terror at the memory of the last time she had walked along the beach alone, grasped Gaynor by the arm and leant her head against her daughter's shoulder for a moment. She had not yet told her about Mr Harpur's invitation to accompany him on his pilgrimage to Santiago. She had not met Gaynor at the time and never dreamt they would become so indispensable to one another. The departure date was several weeks away, but Mitzi was increasingly preoccupied to wonder how to break the news to Gaynor and increasingly concerned to wonder if she wouldn't seem to be abandoning her yet again.

It wasn't Mitzi's only worry. She had managed, so far, to skirt round the issue of who Gaynor's father was, but she knew that eventually this would have to be confronted. Gaynor's odyssey to find her parents couldn't end until she had found both of them.

'I had a good life with the Tranters,' she explained, 'but there was always something missing. They were very kind to me. They treated me the same as Derek. We got lots of hugs. They seemed to have forgotten I had been adopted; I was theirs. Except I wasn't.' She had looked at Mitzi. 'Every time I had an idea or a feeling that I knew would not have come from them, I wondered where it could have come from. Knowing who my parents were, was crucial to my understanding of who I was. Do you understand?'

'Yes, dear,' said Mitzi. 'I do understand.'

She'd hesitated before telling Gaynor what she did to earn a living. She guessed that the Tranters wouldn't have approved and maybe, therefore, Gaynor wouldn't, either. In the end, she had no choice. Her daughter asked her what she'd done when she left school.

'I worked for some years in the council offices,' said Mitzi, hedging, 'as a clerk. But I had always hoped to go to art school. I think papi would have let me, but he died the year before I would have gone and Wanda....well, she didn't think it was a proper thing to do. By that time she was pregnant, so the family needed my wage. I was there for thirteen years.

'What made you leave?'

She took a deep breath. 'One day I was going past the art school on my way home and I...went in.'

'You enrolled?'

'I asked them whether I could work there as a model and they said yes.'

'Golly.' Gaynor gave a little laugh. 'I'd traced you to the art school, but I never dreamt you worked there as a model. How exotic.'

'No,' said Mitzi, truthfully. 'Not really.'

'Is that what you're doing now?'

'It was, until the end of this term. Mr Harpur has retired and I'm not sure I would enjoy it quite as much without him.'

Gaynor nodded. 'It's about the people rather than the places, isn't it?'

'Yes, in the end I think it is. If Mr Harpur had been head clerk in the council offices, I dare say I would still be there.'

'I'd like to meet your Mr Harpur,' Gaynor said.

'Why not?' said Mitzi.

In the end, there was no need to engineer a meeting. Mr Harpur turned up at the house one Sunday afternoon with a bouquet of flowers and a cake. He'd stopped by on his way to see his sister. He was anxious, he said, not to interrupt them, merely to assure her that he was delighted she and Mitzi had agreed to use the cottage.

Gaynor kissed him on the cheek and Mitzi saw him blush with pleasure. She had furnished Gaynor with as many details as she could, regarding Mr Harpur. He'd been married, she said, to a woman he loved very much but who was ill and needed constant care and, when she died, he'd reconciled himself to living on his own. He had no children and his sister was his only relative. She'd tried to mention those things that would make him sympathetic to a younger person and she seemed to have succeeded. Over tea, her daughter mentioned Giotto's 'Lamentation,' which she could remember seeing in a reproduction.

'You've not been to the Scrovegni Chapel, then?' said Mr Harpur.

No, said Gaynor, but her parents had once taken her to Venice and she'd seen the Tintorettos in the Barbarigo Palace.

Mitzi, glancing anxiously between them, realised there was no need to be apprehensive. Gaynor had inherited her father's charm, albeit, thankfully, of a less calculating kind. As she washed up the dishes, Mitzi heard them laughing in the other room. She'd wondered whether Gaynor really knew what Giotto's 'Lamentation' looked like. In that instant, she had won a place in Mr Harpur's heart. He never failed to ask for news of her and Gaynor did the same. The people most important to her happiness, were friends with one another.

***

'Hello, Abel?'

In the seconds before Abel raised his eyes, he wondered what would happen if he looked up and discovered Mrs Allerton was not there, standing at the desk in front of him, that this was just another aberration of a mind beyond recall.

The evening he had spent with Rose and Charlie in what Abel now considered their flat, had destroyed the past for Abel more effectively than Wanda had when she destroyed the shrine and made them homeless. He felt liberated from his old life without having found a new one. When he was with Rose and Charlie, it was not a problem. They shared their life with him so completely, that he could forget he didn't have one of his own.

The member of the family he identified with most, was Lesia. Always standing on the outside of the circle, looking at him shyly with those dark eyes, saying little, she reminded Abel of himself. She was suspended in that creaking hammock between childhood and whatever followed it, a victim of whatever breeze blew, swaying one way then the other, waiting to see which direction she would settle in and coming to rest somewhere in the middle, not from choice but simply from the pull of gravity. He played games with the other children, but he talked to Lesia. He brought books back from the library for her and encouraged her to read the stories she could live in.

For the first time, he felt useful and appreciated. But it only worked when he was with them. Then, he was like litmus paper; he was able to absorb their happiness. But he could not create his own. For it to be a part of you, you needed to have been exposed to happiness when you were young, he thought. It was a habit that could be acquired, like any other. Every time he went there, he felt he had been injected with a vital substance, like a stem cell that had not quite 'taken' and was not yet growing independently inside him. He could lose himself in Rose and Charlie's loving and chaotic household, but no matter what he did, he knew that at the heart of him there still remained a vacuum.

He leant one hand against the counter, to support himself. A queue was forming on the far side of the desk and Abel sensed the people in it, watching him expectantly. He glanced up. Mrs Allerton was smiling, calmly, at him. He looked round and gestured Aileen to take over from him. Mrs Allerton moved down the counter and he moved down, too. 'How are you?' he said, breathlessly.

'I'm very well.' The laughter lines around her eyes had deepened and the auburn hair had flecks of grey in it, but otherwise she seemed unchanged. They stood and looked at one another for a moment. 'I don't want to bother you at work,' she said. 'I know you're busy. It's just that...' She took an envelope out of her pocket, passing it across the counter to him. 'Quite a long time back, I saw your mother in the market. She was shopping. I'm not sure if she saw me, or not. When she was getting out her purse, she dropped something. I saw her go down on her knees and I'd have gone across and helped her, but I wasn't sure she'd welcome an approach from me.'

The idea that his mother would have welcomed anything from Mrs Allerton, made Abel wince. 'Yes.' Mrs Allerton smiled. 'That's what I thought.' She waited whilst he took the envelope and slid his thumb under the flap. 'She seemed a bit upset and she was clearly in a hurry. When she'd gone, I noticed someone who'd been in the queue behind her, bend down and pick something up.' She nodded at the envelope and Abel looked inside it. He tipped out the silver charm and held it in the palm of one hand.

'I thought it might have some sentimental value, so I offered to return it. I went to the flat in Primrose Hill twice, but your mother wasn't in, the first time, or perhaps she wasn't answering the door. The second time, the lady in the flat below said there was no one there.'

'That's right.' He stared down at the silver charm. 'My mother sold the flat. She said she didn't want to live there any more.'

'Good heavens.'

'Something happened. I'm not sure what. We'd just had a family reunion. We had one every year. That night she suddenly decided she had had enough of it.' He shrugged.

'That must have come as quite a shock.' She went on looking at him, keenly. Abel kept his eyes fixed on the counter. The account he'd given Rose and Charlie of his family and their life in Primrose Hill, had airbrushed out the worst excesses of his mother's dictatorial regime. He hadn't told them that his father had committed suicide and that for twenty years there'd been a shrine out on the landing. He avoided anything that might have cast a shadow over the uncomplicated optimism of their lives. He was afraid the shadow might engulf him too.

'Yes,' he said, coughing to disguise the tremour in his voice. 'Still, it was time we had some space away from one another.' Abel kept his eyes down. He saw Mrs Allerton's hand moving imperceptibly towards the counter, stretching out towards him as if moving of its own volition.

'So you've got your own place now?'

'I've got a bedsit up in Kentish Town. It's not a very up and coming area, compared with Primrose Hill, and it takes longer for me to come in each day, but I've been there three months, so I've acclimatised.'

'And how do you like living on your own?'

'It feels strange, going home and finding no one there. I'm still not used to that.'

'No,' Mrs Allerton smiled, sympathetically. 'It's quite a hard thing to adapt to, being on your own.' She hesitated. 'It was you I saw, the other evening, Abel, wasn't it? Outside my house?'

He blushed: 'I'm sorry.'

'No, no, don't be sorry. I just wondered why you didn't come across. I waited for you.' She looked, searchingly, into his face. 'You know you're always welcome, Abel. You don't have to stand out in the rain.' She touched his sleeve.

'I wanted to find out if you were still there,' he said, wretchedly. 'I felt so lonely.'

'But when you discovered that I was....?'

'You weren't alone, though,' he said, harshly. 'There was someone else there.'

'Anthony?' She gave a faint laugh. 'You'd have liked him, Abel. He's my nephew. He was starting university this term. I put him up whilst he was looking for a room.' She paused. 'You didn't think...?' She put a hand up to her mouth and gave a stifled laugh. 'You didn't think that it was something else? Oh, Abel.' She regarded him with helpless tenderness. He hung his head. 'There wasn't anybody after you,' she murmured, lowering her voice. 'There wasn't really anyone before you, either. Nobody important. And there isn't likely to be anybody now.'

'I've missed you,' Abel said, compulsively.

'I've missed you, too.'

'I thought because you didn't come into the library any more, that you'd decided it was over.'

'I thought, when you didn't come back to the house, that you had.' They laughed, shyly.

'It was an appalling thing my mother did, that day,' said Abel. 'It was unforgivable.' Now that the circle of his silence had been breached, he felt an urge to go on talking to her.

'I did think that, maybe afterwards, you might feel more inclined to get your own flat,' Mrs Allerton said, quietly.

He glanced round. Miss Quettock was observing them, acutely, from the desk. He took a book and turned the pages back, as if he were explaining something.

'I'm disturbing you,' she said, divining his discomfort. 'I must go. Perhaps we'll run into each other sometimes, from now on.' She paused. 'I hope so."

Abel saw from the expression on Miss Quettock's face, that he could not continue talking: 'Maybe we could meet up for a cup of tea,' he said.

'I'd like that very much.'

'I don't know that I ought to ask you round to my place. It's a bit chaotic at the moment. We could go out to a café.'

'There's a little tea-room just along the road from me,' said Mrs Allerton. 'They opened it last year. Why don't we meet there?'

'That sounds lovely.'

'Let's say four o'clock on Sunday. And if it's a nice day we might walk down to the river.' Abel smiled. She tapped his hand. 'Take care now.'

Abel watched the buxom figure, with its bosom that was starting to look rather matronly, negotiate the swing doors of the library. She secured the green hat on her head and crossed the street towards the bus stop. Abel turned back to the desk. He tried to keep his face straight, but he couldn't stop the grin invading it. On Sunday afternoon he would be back in Mrs Allerton's embrace and this time he would not let anybody prise him out of it.

***

She'd passed them once more in the corridor, but this time none of them acknowledged her. The little girl's hand clung onto her mother's jacket. From her other hand, the doll hung limply by one arm. It looked dead, Wanda thought. She'd never liked to play with dolls, unlike her sister who gave weekly tea parties for hers at which they sat with straight backs, staring stupidly ahead of them, whilst Mitzi poured pretend-tea into cups so small an ant could not have got a decent drink out of them.

Mitzi loved pretending. Wanda couldn't see the point of it. Why bother trying to convince yourself of the reality of something, when you knew it wasn't there? The only real bit, sometimes, was the cake, which Sophie cut into minute squares, one for each doll and one each for Mitzi and her sister. Mitzi ate hers delicately, pausing to exclaim ecstatically about the taste, the texture, the exquisite decoration on the top. Occasionally, it was no more than a bit of rye bread. Once, it was a pebble. Wanda spat it out.

'You can't do that,' said Mitzi. 'Spitting's rude.'

'I don't care. This cake's horrible. I hate it.'

'Babou thinks it's lovely. Look, she's smiling.'

'Babou's stupid. So are you. If you eat stones, you'll die.'

'I won't,' said Mitzi. 'You're the one who'll die.'

As they squeezed past her in the corridor, she caught the doll's eye. It had that blank, weary look of disappointment people often wore in middle age. She closed the door of her compartment and sank down into a seat next to the window. Since their first encounter in the dining-car, she had felt vaguely threatened, not by them particularly, not by anything particularly. She was just uneasy. She felt she was waiting and that when whatever she was waiting

Schopenhauer's Porcupines

for, eventually happened, she would recognise it as the thing she'd been expecting all her life.

She shivered. When she'd first come back to the compartment, she had felt the drop in temperature. She'd checked the lever by the window. It was turned to maximum. She wrapped the shawl around her knees. The clothes she had brought with her in her overnight case, weren't warm. What she needed, was her mother's fur coat.

When a guard passed down the corridor, she called him. 'It is cold in here, I think.'

He checked the dial: 'It's on at maximum.'

'Perhaps the heating isn't working. It does not feel cold to you?'

'No, madam. I think if you were outside you'd find it very warm in here by contrast.'

'But I have no wish to be outside.'

He smiled: 'Quite. Better off here where it's nice and warm.'

'But this is what I'm saying. Is not nice and warm. Is chilly.'

He smiled, patiently. 'I'll organise a rug to be brought down to you.'

'No thank you. I would like to fetch a coat out of my trunk, please?'

'If the trunk is in the luggage car, I'm sorry but you can't have access to it on the journey. It could be behind a dozen others. There's no way of knowing.'

'I would know.'

'But passengers are not allowed into the luggage car. It's sealed off.'

'You mean I can't have my own belongings?'

'Not until you reach your destination.'

'But I want my fur coat now. I'm needing it. I'm cold.'

'As I said, I'd be pleased to organise a rug for you.' He cleared his throat. He had a thin moustache and small, dark eyes that looked at Wanda distantly from underneath the peaked cap. On his uniform lapel, there was a badge and, round his neck, a satchel and a portable machine for stamping tickets.

He is just a railway supervisor, Wanda thought, a public servant. But she was intimidated by the uniform. The man was backing out into the corridor. He would not give her back her coat. If she had worn it underneath the other one, she would be nice and warm now. Wanda hated being cold. She thought of the five winters she had spent in Warsaw, when they put their outdoor clothes on over their pyjamas and wore mittens without fingers when they sat down at the table.

She had left all that to go to England and now she was going back. She clutched the shawl around her shoulders. She had felt protected in the railway carriage. It was like a smaller version of the flat in Primrose Hill. Now, she felt danger all around her. She heard voices raised inside the next compartment. Somebody was shouting. Every now and then, another voice broke in, a reedy, thin voice, like a shard of glass. She didn't know which was the more unnerving.

Wanda put her hands over her ears, but she could not block out the sound. It seeped under her fingers, curling round the hollows of her ears. She did not want to know what they were arguing about. But, suddenly, the man swore and she recognised the dialect as Schwabing. They were Germans. They came from the part of Germany her father's parents had been born in, but which had rejected them as 'untermensch' in consequence of Sophie's.

Wanda wasn't sure if she was trembling out of fear or indignation now. She wondered, for the first time since she'd left, what she was doing there. She'd thought the Eastern Bloc would be a place where she might meet with others like herself. She'd never mastered English. She had tried to speak the language, but still people looked at her as if they didn't want to understand; as if they wanted to confirm her in her foreignness.

She had looked forward to a new start somewhere else, but it had been the journey that preoccupied her. It had barely crossed her mind that they might actually arrive somewhere and that the 'somewhere' might not live up to her expectations. Why had she not given more thought to her destination? She could hear the painful thudding of her heartbeat underneath the woollen shawl. I'm going in the wrong direction, she thought. In her panic to get out

Schopenhauer's Porcupines

of England, out of Primrose Hill, she had turned back the way she'd come. But East was not the only option open to her. With the money from the flat, she could have gone back to America. It was the last place where she had been truly happy, where it did not matter being Jewish because half the population came from Eastern Europe. There might still be neighbours, friends in Iowa who would remember her. She could have bought a little house out in the suburbs, with a garden. In America, they would not think it strange for her to wear her mother's fur coat, or that she spoke English with an accent. Everyone spoke English with an accent in America.

Why had they left? Why, why, when half the world was fleeing in the opposite direction to a safer place, had they rushed into the inferno? It was Jakob's fault. If he had loved us, he would not have done it, Wanda thought. My father hated us. He wanted to be free of us.

No, that was not true. He had made a terrible mistake. And now she was repeating it. I must go back, she thought. It's not too late. I must get off the train. She listened to the thudding of the wheels over the sleepers. As the rhythm changed, it sounded like machine gun fire. Lights strafed the carriages. She wiped away the condensation on the window and peered out. It was snowing. She could see the silhouettes of trees and, every now and then, an isolated house. The couple in the next compartment had stopped shouting. She could hear their voices, muted now, exhausted, edgy. They sped through a small town with a railway station that consisted of a small hut with a white fence round it and an old man on the platform, waving at the driver.

It was nearly midnight. She had had no supper and she wondered if the dining car would still be open. When she had gone in for breakfast, she had seen the waiter looking at her with an odd expression. He had laid the table carefully, depositing the side plate and the serviette just to the side of her and polishing the cutlery with an exaggerated care. He glanced at her before he put each item on the table and when he had finished, he paused, looking down at the arrangement, then at Wanda, before asking her what she would like. She'd asked for grapefruit and a boiled egg. It came with a little silver teaspoon. She'd already taken two of them, but this time, when she'd finished, she replaced it by the egg cup. Once she'd drunk her coffee, she went back into her carriage. She did not like being stared at in that way.

But she would have to go back to the dining car at some point. She did not feel hungry, but already she felt that familiar space inside her that cried out for something. In her pocket, she felt for the spoon she'd left there, yesterday. She put her thumb into the silkily smooth hollow of the bowl and traced her finger up along the stem, towards the crest. What passed between the nerve-ends of her fingers and the spoon, was love. She knew that it was intimately bound up with possession, but still, love was what it was.

There was an almost imperceptible deceleration in the rhythm of the wheels. She looked out. There were still trees all along the route but, in the gaps between them, she saw buildings. They were coming to a town. The voices in the next compartment suddenly erupted, as if they were arguing in rounds and, having rested in the interval, had gone into the ring again. Inside her carriage, Wanda rocked in agitation. Should she call the guard? But if it were the same man as before, he wouldn't listen to her. He would say he couldn't interfere.

I can't stay here, thought Wanda. Maybe she could move into another carriage. Half of them were empty, although if the guard came round again, he might insist she come back to the seat that had her name on it. But then at least she could explain that she had wanted to escape the noise made by the couple in the next compartment. He would have to act, then.

She went out into the corridor. The blinds were down in the adjoining carriage but the voices carried on, relentlessly, behind them. There was so much anger that she feared she might herself become a victim of it, if they found her there. She hurried down the corridor and was about to cross the narrow passage linking one car to the next, when suddenly the wheels locked in a drawn-out screech and skidded on the rails. They must be coming to a station.

She pulled down the window and peered out into the darkness. Sleet blew back into her face. She saw lines criss-crossing each other. There were trains parked with their lights out and, a hundred yards away, a railway workman going down the track, banging the wheels. The echo resonated, thinly, and was swallowed up into the darkness.

The broad brim of the fedora acted like a shelf to keep the snow out of her eyes, but she was blinded by the alternating dark and light. The train was moving at a steady pace into the station. There would be a sign to tell her where she was. She curled her fingers round the sill. The train was almost at a standstill now, progressing at a slow crawl down the track. She leant out. She was getting wet and she could hardly feel her fingers.

When she heard the faint click, Wanda knew immediately what had happened. She knew, too, that this was what she had been waiting for. So she had come to the right place, after all. She needn't have spent all those hours wondering about her destination. In the end, it didn't matter where she caught the train or where she left it. It was not a matter of geography.

It was exactly in the instant when the carriage door clicked open, that the engine of the train went up a gear. There was a mild jolt, just sufficient to make Wanda lose her grip. The door swung back. Her body followed it. She lost her balance and as she fell out onto the track, the train accelerated, thudding past her, on into the darkness.

***

'People think that as an architectural event, it's not worth visiting,' said Mr Harpur. They were gazing up at the façade of Orléans cathedral. 'But it has a fascinating history: struck by lightening, plundered, burnt down, blown up. Once, it even fell down on the congregation.' A faint murmur of excited indignation rippled through the small group of disciples that had clustered around Mr Harpur as he gave his unofficial tour. It was the same in every city. Mr Harpur, in his white suit and his straw hat, with a guide book underneath his arm, would stand in front of the cathedral, pointing out the interesting features to his two companions, and would gradually find himself the centre of attention. When he'd finished and moved on, his audience moved with him.

Anxious not to lose her altogether, Mr Harpur reached back through the crowd and held his arm out. Mitzi took it, gratefully. She looked around for Gaynor. She was gazing at a gargoyle on a corner of the west façade and making pencil notes inside the guide book. Mitzi had decided her enthusiasm must be genuine since Mr Harpur now had the attention of so many others, he was not dependent on them any longer.

His proposal had saved Mitzi from a terrible dilemma. As the date for their departure drew near, she'd been torn between excitement at the prospect of the trip through Europe and anxiety at leaving Gaynor on her own. When she told Mitzi she would like to travel 'if she could find somebody to go with,' Mitzi realised that the latter might be the more difficult condition to fulfil. She didn't think she could have borne to go abroad and leave her daughter by herself, but if she didn't go, she'd feel she'd disappointed Mr Harpur. Possibly he was aware of Mitzi's difficulty, or perhaps he genuinely relished the idea of Gaynor's company.

'Of course, she's young. I don't suppose she'll want to stay with us the whole time, but why shouldn't she come out to join us, once she's graduated?'

'Are you certain?' She felt humbled by the inexhaustible supply of goodness Mr Harpur seemed to have at his disposal.

'If I'd wanted to go on my own, I could have done so any time. To have your daughter come back after twenty years, is cause enough for celebration, and what better way of celebrating? Why not ask her?'

So she had. The only thing that had preoccupied her in the days before they left, was whether she was duty-bound to tell her daughter who her father was before they left, or risk a rupture on the journey that might prove more devastating in its consequences. She had held back, partly out of deference to Gregor, partly because at the start she'd told herself she needed time to get to know her daughter better, before gauging how to tell her. It was no use. Now that she and Gaynor had a close relationship, it would be even more impossible to tell her. There would never be a 'right' time. She would simply have to wait till Gaynor asked her outright and then hope the revelation would not blow their lives apart.

It had been Gaynor, Mitzi realised, who they had to thank for Mr Harpur's sudden popularity. It was her air of fascinated curiosity that by-standers found irresistible. Invariably at his elbow, following his gaze, not interrupting till he'd finished, Gaynor was the student he had longed for all his life. She had her father's intellect, her mother's sense of wonderment and, possibly a legacy the Tranters had passed on to her, respect.

'I think, when we get back to England, I might write a book,' said Mr Harpur one night, over supper.

'That's a wonderful idea,' said Mitzi.

'Possibly 'A Pilgrim's View of the Cathedrals'. At the moment, all the information is in different places. If it was amalgamated, it would be much more accessible.' She nodded. 'And then, next year maybe, we could go through Italy and look at the Giottos. Would you like that, Gaynor? That's of course if you aren't doing something else. At your age, I appreciate a year is quite a long time.'

'I would love to come.' She squeezed his hand and he smiled, modestly.

'You seem to have worked miracles,' said Mitzi, once, when all that they could see of Mr Harpur was the straw hat in the centre of the group. 'You've made him very happy.'

'Well, why shouldn't he be happy?' Gaynor said, as if it were the simplest thing imaginable to make someone happy. And perhaps it was. A pity one can't do it for oneself, she thought. At Chartres, as they'd passed beneath the south porch, he had pointed out the rows of devils pushing souls towards the pit and weighing others in the balance. On the face of one, she saw a grin she thought she recognised and had a brief reprise of the seduction underneath the kitchen table. She had been so happy in the past weeks that the circumstances leading to this point in time had all but been forgotten.

She'd swayed, waiting for the wave of anguish to sweep over her again. The seconds passed and nothing happened. The guilt she had suffered for the past two decades, seemed to have evaporated whilst she stood there. In the midst of so much history, her own seemed insignificant. She could not alter what had happened in the past and she could only face the future when she got there. For the first time in her life, she was entirely taken up with living in the present.

Since she'd joined them on the journey, Gaynor had not asked about her father and, although he was her confidante in most things, Mitzi had stopped short of telling Mr Harpur his identity. With customary diplomacy, he'd never asked. Unburdened by her apprehension and enjoying his new role as mentor, he was more relaxed and jovial than she had ever known him.

Their days had assumed a pattern that was blissfully predictable. They rose late, breakfasting together, unless Gaynor opted for an extra hour in bed. Together, they spread maps and brochures out across the table and drew up a plan for that day. When the sun went down, they sat out on the terraces of pensions under the bougainvillea and chatted, with a background chirruping of crickets, until darkness fell.

As they progressed from one cathedral city to the next, they started to encounter other pilgrims travelling the same route, whom they met again as old friends later in the journey, or as former acolytes delighted to meet up again with The Professor. Gradually, the pilgrimage appeared to Mitzi to assume the quality of life itself, with its disrupted friendships and reunions, its retribution and its absolution.

'It's not easy to maintain an attitude of scepticism, faced with so much beauty,' Mr Harpur had remarked one day, as they were crossing over into Spain.

For Mitzi, who had never known the luxury of scepticism, beauty merely reinforced her faith. She wasn't limited to anything as narrow as religion. She believed in everything. The one event that in the past had dented her belief - her mother's disappearance on the railway station; even this now seemed to fit into a pre-determined pattern. Mitzi saw that, without tragedy, the human spirit would not need the consolation of religion and without religion, beauty of the kind that now surrounded her, would not have come into existence.

They engaged a passer-by to take a photograph and stood there with their arms around each other. In the cloistered silence of a chapel on the route to Santiago da Compostela, Mitzi felt that she had come to terms with life at last.

***

'I think I'd better go down there and break the news to him myself.'

'It isn't like you to consider anybody else's feelings.'

'Abel is my little brother. Certainly I care about his feelings.'

'Do you think he'll mind?'

'Mind? That's a curiously pallid word to use when you're referring to the death of someone's mother.'

'It's a pallid word for yours, I grant you. Given that your family seem particularly prone to falling from a great height, I think you should watch your step.' She threw a sideways glance at him. 'Whatever was she doing, leaning out of a carriage window in the middle of the night in some godforsaken outpost of the Eastern Bloc?'

'Perhaps she felt in need of fresh air.'

'Just as well you weren't there. You'd be suspect number one.'

'I dare say when the police have finished interviewing all the other passengers, they'll find that the majority will have been more than happy not to have my mother as a travelling companion.'

'Still,' said Gloria, reflectively. 'She was your mother.'

'It's not like you, Gloria, to state the obvious.'

'You're an orphan,' she said, thoughtfully.

'Boo hoo. Why don't we go back now to your rooms and I'll lay my little head against your chest and suck my thumb and cry. I've no doubt that's how Abel will react.'

'You're not expecting me to come to London with you?'

'Good God, no!' said Gregor, rather more emphatically than he'd intended. I was not implying it was your chest he'd be leaning on.'

They turned the corner by the pond and walked towards the buttery. A crowd of students passed them and looked back over their shoulders. Gregor gave his gown a flourish. Two weeks earlier, a photograph of Gloria and Gregor had been printed in the college magazine for freshers underneath the heading 'Things To Look For When You Come To Oxford.' Somebody had photographed them from a ground-floor window as they crossed The Old Quad after lectures. Gloria was looking like a ship in full sail, her cloak billowing behind her. Gregor, several inches shorter, black from head to toe and with his short arms waving in the air, looked like a cockroach on its hind legs.

It was Cholmondeley who had pointed out the photograph. He had been outraged more on Gloria's behalf than Gregor's. 'Bad enough to have the bloody paparazzi after you when you're a film star. You would think that in a place of learning, you'd be safe.'

But Gregor wasn't in the least perturbed. He'd never wanted to be safe. He had become a legend in his life-time. Students queued outside his door to get into his seminars. There was a waiting-list of undergraduates who wanted him to supervise their theses. He'd been asked to speak at the first union debate that year on the subject 'Virtue Will Hurt You.'

'Careful, Gregor,' Gloria advised. 'Don't go too far.'

'You're right,' said Gregor. 'I'll speak for the opposition.'

'That'll tax your intellectual capacities,' said Gloria, drily.

As they passed the porter's lodge, he was already planning what he'd do in London, once he had off-loaded the unpleasant duty of informing Abel he no longer had a mother. Since their reconciliation, he and Gloria had settled amicably back into an edgy domesticity, enlivened by the fact that they were still officially estranged. I dare say I shall have to make an honest woman of her in the end, thought Gregor, but he wasn't in a hurry. He had everything he wanted at the moment, plus the freedom marriage tended to curtail. He gave her bum a little pat as they went past the buttery.

'I think it's time I saw my mother,' Gloria said, thoughtfully.

He looked at her, surprised. 'I didn't know you had a mother.'

'It's not easy to arrive on earth without one.'

'What's she like? Why did you never introduce us?'

'She's a psychoanalyst.'

'Good heavens.' Gregor looked at her with interest. 'Would you say you'd had a balanced childhood?'

'No, I wouldn't. On the whole her patients got more out of her than I did. Still, I ought to make my peace with her before she dies. She lives alone.'

'What happened to your father?'

'He's a bit like you. My mother was his second wife. He's now on number five.'

'I don't see the comparison. I'm only on my first.'

'That's where you differ. Dad thought he should do the honourable thing. He married them.'

'You'd rather I had half a dozen wives in tow?'

'I'd rather you had nobody in tow, except me.'

'You've got Cholmondeley.'

'So have you.' They laughed, conspiratorially. Gregor knew that Gloria was keeping Cholmondeley as a fail-safe, rather than a spare part. Every now and then, if she saw Gregor's focus of attention wandering, she would go off with Cholmondely for a weekend, but she always came back like a hungry child to table. Now that Cholmondeley had apparently adapted to his role as sous-chef, he and Gregor got on rather well. They even had a drink together, periodically, though Cholmondeley hadn't much to offer, one to one.

'He's like a book you give up halfway through but keep on picking up again by accident, said Gregor.

Since the last reunion, he hadn't heard from Mitzi. He felt guilty that he hadn't kept in touch; he knew the depths of Mitzi's grief at having to reject her daughter's overtures, but after all she had the art school, she had Mr Harpur... As time passed, he felt less guilty. Now, he felt no guilt at all. He'd even started taking what he passed off as 'a fatherly concern' in certain of the female undergraduates.

If he left early on the Friday, he would have that evening to himself, which didn't necessarily imply he would be by himself. Then, on the Saturday, he could collect the violin he'd left in Cheapside for the bridge to be repaired, find Abel, get the latest news of Mitzi and return on Sunday night in time for supper.

When the consulate had asked about repatriation of the body, he'd said no. Like soldiers on the battlefield, he felt that Wanda should be buried where she fell. When told that it was without precedent and therefore might well be considered inappropriate to bury someone on a railway track, it took all Gregor's patience to explain that he had not meant to be taken literally. 'Just take my mother to the nearest cemetery and put her in the ground,' he said. 'I'll foot the bill for anything beyond what she was carrying in small change in her handbag.

'You don't want the family to be there for the committal?'

'No,' said Gregor, finally. 'The ceremony for my father lasted twenty years. I'd like to think it was sufficient for the two of them.'

'Unfortunately, the authorities will not be able to release the body until they've completed their investigations. There is, too, the possibility that Orient Express could be at fault if they discover that the door fell open at the crucial moment.

'Sounds more like an Act of God.'

'We'll naturally keep you notified of the results of the investigation.'

'As you wish,' said Gregor, stifling a yawn.

'Your mother's ticket listed Bucharest as her intended destination. Do you know if she was planning to remain there?'

'I can't answer you on that one, I'm afraid. My mother didn't talk to me about her plans.'

'We found a number of small items in her luggage, Dr Silver. Things that wouldn't normally have been there.'

'What things?'

'Things that seem to have been taken from the dining car: spoons, egg cups, jugs, that sort of thing. Of course, she might have been intending to return them but I wondered if your mother had, well, any sort of problem?'

Gregor snorted: 'Just between ourselves, old chap, her problems went a little way beyond an egg cup.' There was silence at the other end.

'In your view Dr Silver, had you reason to suppose your mother might have cause to want to end her life?'

'I think she would have gone on living, just to spite the rest of us. She once said she regarded suicide as weakness.'

'Still, it seems the case could be more complex than we thought.'

'Tell me,' said Gregor, carefully, 'when she was found, what was she wearing?'

'A black skirt, a woollen jumper with a jacket and a black fedora.'

'No sign of a fur coat?'

'I shall have to check, but no, I don't think that was on the list.'

'That's it, then. I can tell you, categorically, that there's no possibility my mother would leap out onto the railway track without her mother's fur coat. It would be poetic justice for her to end up there, but without the fur coat, no. You will, however, find it somewhere in her luggage. It would be a kindness to my mother if you could arrange to have her buried in it. I know that would be a comfort to her.'

'I'll do what I can. Perhaps you could assume responsibility for passing on the news to other members of the family.'

'Of course.'

'We'll send her luggage back as soon the inquiries are complete. Would you prefer to have it sent on to the family address in London, or should we put Oxford as the destination?'

'You have an address for her in London?'

'NW1. It's the address on all her luggage. I believe that's Camden Town?'

'It is. Yes, why not send it there?'

'Does Mitzi know yet?' As they climbed the staircase, Gloria took out her key. They ran the last few steps.

'I've no idea where Mitzi is,' said Gregor, fumbling underneath her gown. She pushed him off. 'Oh come on, Gloria, cut the crap. I know you're wearing those silk directoire drawers. How your students manage to contain themselves, I can't imagine.'

'That's just it. You can imagine; they can't.' She drew back and rearranged her skirt. 'I think she ought to be informed.'

'For God's sake, Gloria, are we obliged to stand here in the corridor whilst we discuss my obligation to my family? I'll make sure she knows. I'm sure my mother only fell out of the railway carriage, knowing it would ruin Mitzi's holiday, and certainly, if that was her last wish, we ought to honour it. Now get inside or there could be another accident.'

***

With hindsight, Mitzi wondered if what had occurred to her much later, might not have occurred to Mr Harpur somewhat earlier. They had been sitting by themselves, one evening, after Gaynor had excused herself to have an early night. Whilst fireflies flitted through the darkness, Mitzi sipped her wine and Mr Harpur filled his pipe.

'I can't think that I've ever been so happy,' she said.

'Not a bad idea of mine, then?' he said, evenly.

'I'm only sorry that your dear wife wasn't here to share it.'

Mr Harpur sucked his pipe, reflectively. 'Yes,' he said, 'though I like to think a bit of her is here. I think of her a lot, you know.'

'I'm sure you do.'

'But one can't live entirely in the past. The fact of having you and Gaynor here has made me realise that the present is still something to be cherished. To be honest I feel younger than I have for years. That's Gaynor's influence, I dare say.'

'Yes, I dare say.' They sat silently a moment.

'Has she talked about her plans for when we get back?'

'I imagine she'll be looking for a flat in London.'

'That'll make it easier for you to see her.'

'Yes.'

He picked up on the doubt in Mitzi's voice. 'There's an alternative, of course. If Gaynor were to stay in Gravesend, you could go on meeting at the cottage. You could do that anyway, but if you wanted to live there instead of London, I know that my sister would have no objection.'

'What a kind thought. I'm not sure yet, to be honest, what will happen once we get back. Gaynor's young. She might prefer to make her own way.'

'I expect she will, but she can make her own way and still want to see her mother.'

'Yes, well let us hope that's how it works out.' She'd tried not to look beyond the pilgrimage. Real life, she felt, might not be as forgiving. She suspected she'd been given a reprieve, an opportunity for happiness that she must cherish, knowing, as she did, how easily it might be whisked away.

'I often wondered what it would have been like to have children,' Mr Harpur murmured.

'Me too,' Mitzi said, ironically.

'You don't regret what happened?'

'Not what happened; only how it happened.' Who it happened with, was probably more pertinent. But when she looked at Gaynor, she was so much like her father that regretting it, was tantamount to saying she wished Gaynor had been someone else, or had been nobody at all. So much of what she loved in Gaynor was what she had loved in Gregor, but in him it seemed the genes had rioted. There was too much of everything in Gregor.

There was no doubt in her own mind that if Gaynor were to meet her father, she would know immediately who he was. She must warn Gregor she was still in contact with their daughter. He would need to take steps to protect himself, although it wasn't easy to see how he could protect himself or what excuses he could give if Gaynor once decided that he should be taken to account. In such a situation, she feared more for Gregor than her daughter. Gaynor might be shocked, disgusted, angry or contemptuous, but Mitzi did not think she would be damaged irretrievably. She was sufficiently clear-sighted to accept that she was not responsible for what had happened and although she might have been condemned genetically, she had the wherewithal to live an independent life, to forge a destiny that wasn't yoked to her beginnings, as had been the case with every other member of her family. Despite her drawbacks, she would be a match for Gregor, probably the only female who had ever been a match for him, apart from Gloria.

It was no accident, thought Mitzi, that it had been Gloria who'd netted him. He didn't want an easy conquest. He did not, like Mitzi, hanker for a quiet life. Maybe, then, in spite of everything, he would win Gaynor over and the two of them would find that they were drawn together by a common heritage. It was the outside rather than the inside world they had to fear. When Mitzi thought about the future, she felt as her medieval ancestors had done, convinced the world was flat and that at any moment they could tumble over into the abyss. Yet here, in spite of being face to face with everything she feared, she'd had the curious impression in the past weeks that in Gaynor's mind at least, the problem had already been resolved.

'I've noticed,' Mitzi said, 'that lately Gaynor has stopped asking who her father is?'

He grunted. 'That's good, isn't it? It's what you were concerned about.'

'That's true,' said Mitzi, thoughtfully. 'Of course, she might ask later, but she seems less 'driven' since she came out here.'

'Art does have that effect sometimes,' said Mr Harpur. 'One becomes aware that history has outlived us; that what seemed important, isn't so important after all.'

'I'm sure you're right,' said Mitzi, pensively. She took another sip out of the glass. She had been standing in the square in front of the cathedral, watching pigeons scratting on the pavers, when she'd looked up and seen Mr Harpur and her daughter walking arm in arm across the square towards her. Mr Harpur had been pointing at the cupids in the fountain. He'd made some remark and Gaynor laughed and leant towards him, so that for an instant their heads touched. As Mitzi watched, she saw them suddenly from Gaynor's viewpoint rather than her own and, with a jolt, she realised what had happened.

She put down the glass, but kept her fingers round the stem as if to give herself some fragile purchase. She glanced sideways. Mr Harpur knocked the ash out of his pipe bowl on the iron leg of the table. He was humming, mildly, to himself.

'I only wondered,' she said, tentatively, thinking how ironic it was, to come all this way to get away from one dilemma, only to discover it had turned into another. 'I just wondered if perhaps she wasn't looking for her father any more because she thought she had already found him....' She tailed off. The silence seemed to ebb and flow between them.

'Would it matter very much, if that turned out to be the case?' His head inclined towards her.

Mitzi gaped: 'You wouldn't mind?'

He paused a moment before answering, but Mitzi felt he had already given it some thought. 'Your daughter, Mitzi, is the one I never had. Of course, one wouldn't want to be dishonest. If she asked me outright, I would have to say she was mistaken, but I don't think that she will, somehow. You introduced me as a friend. If Gaynor wishes to believe there's more to it, then who are we to interfere?' He tapped the pipe against his teeth. 'We've never talked about this, Mitzi, and I don't think that we need to now, but I'm assuming that you're worried Gaynor might be disappointed or upset if she were to discover who her father was.'

'I don't think she'd be very pleased,' said Mitzi.

'Then why don't we leave things as they are for now? She's a delightful girl. If you want my advice, you'll let her set the pace. I've noticed that the young prefer this.' He wrapped one hand round the pipe bowl to make sure it wasn't too hot, before dropping it into his pocket. 'At the very least we shall have had this time together. It's a happiness that she can build on, even if it doesn't last forever, and we're not deliberately misleading her. I think she'll recognise we have her interests at heart.'

He looked at Mitzi. She was sitting, with her head bent. She did not know what to say. The longer Mitzi lived, the less she understood, but still she felt an indescribable relief. The lights went out behind them in the pension.

'Perhaps we're keeping them awake,' said Mr Harpur, chuckling. He checked his watch. 'In three days, we shall be in Santiago. In the old days, pilgrims used to celebrate by taking off their clothes and running naked down the shore into the sea.'

'Good heavens,' Mitzi murmured.

'I suppose they looked upon it as a kind of baptism. It might be better not to mention that to Gaynor, either. Being young, she's bound to want to try it and she might expect us to go in with her.' He leant across and laid his hand on Mitzi's. 'I hope I've not spoken out of turn, my dear. I just feel we should let things take their course.'

The hand remained there. Mitzi nodded.

***

Abel's pale face crumpled. 'It's not possible. I can't believe it.'

Gregor nodded. 'Takes a bit of getting used to, doesn't it?'

'Whatever was she doing, wandering about in the middle of the night like that?'

'Search me, old chap.'

His brother's horrified reaction to the news, made Gregor realise how inadequate his own had been. If Wanda had to die, he had thought irritably, why go all the way to Bucharest to do it? Falling from a train, left all sorts of unanswered questions. Privately, in spite of their antipathy, he would prefer her to have stayed alive. He'd lost his whipping-post. From now on, he'd have nobody to gripe at. 'I suppose I'll miss the old bird, too,' he said. 'She'd been around a long time.'

Abel was still staring into space, his face a medley of emotions threatening to erupt onto the surface. Gregor shifted. It was hard to empathise with someone else's feelings when you had none of your own. His were like tics cavorting on the surface of his mind. Occasionally, he was bitten, but more often when one got too close he simply batted it away.

He fought the urge to yawn. He hadn't had much sleep the night before. He'd booked into a hotel north of London, where he had arranged an assignation with a Romance languages professor. She'd turned out to be a disappointment. Gregor had suggested varying the usual routine and she'd pretended to be shocked. When she eventually complied, she spoilt it with a fit of nervous giggling. She had kept her glasses on and in the frenzy that ensued, they'd fallen down her nose and then hung dangling from the cord around her neck, the lenses banging into him with every thrust.

He'd left her tied by both wrists to the bed rail, gone out for some air, and kept on walking till he reached the station. It had taken him an hour and a half. He caught the last train into London, but it stopped at Hebden where it shunted down the track into a siding. After half an hour, when the lights went out and Gregor saw the driver walking off into the dark, he realised that the train would not be going any further. It was half past midnight. Gingerly, he'd made his way across the sleepers to the nearest platform, eerily aware of the resemblance of his present situation to his mother's final moments.

He had found a poky little waiting room at one end of the station, where he waited till the morning. Gregor didn't need a lot of sleep but when he was awake, he liked to feel that he was usefully employed, and sitting in a waiting room in Hebden in the middle of the night seemed a particularly useless way to spend his time. He also felt a mild attack of guilt. He'd walked out on the Romance languages professor in a fit of boredom when he realised he no longer cared if she was shocked or not, or even if they carried on with it. He'd rather have been sparring energetically with Gloria or even, he thought dismally, continuing to work on the revisions to his current draft of Schopenhauer. Shit, he thought, I must be getting old.

It hadn't been straightforward, tracking Abel down. He'd left the digs that he was in and when he checked the library, thinking he might catch him, Gregor found that he'd already left. He had been planning to return to Oxford once he'd furnished Abel with the bad news, but on hearing he was lodging with a Mrs Allerton, he was intrigued.

His brother seemed to have gone off into a dream. 'We shouldn't have allowed her to go off like that,' he muttered, brokenly.

'When did you last try to stop Wanda doing anything?'

'She can't have wanted to end up in Bucharest.'

'Oh, I don't know. I think the Eastern Bloc would probably have suited her quite well. For once that fur coat wouldn't have looked out of place.'

'How will we get her home?' said Abel, as the practicalities began to dawn on him.

There was a pause as Gregor sought a diplomatic answer. 'I'm afraid they had to keep her in the fridge whilst they conducted their investigations. These things take time. They're obliged to wait for a post mortem to establish cause of death. The railway company will also have to be investigated, to determine if the lock was faulty. In the end, I thought it best that they should bury her out there.'

'But she'll be all alone!' said Abel, horrified.

'She did elect to go there on her own,' said Gregor, reasonably.

'That doesn't mean she'd want to stay in Bucharest forever.'

'But she did seem fairly certain that she didn't want to be in Primrose Hill. Why don't you have a whisky?' Abel nodded vaguely. 'Shall I fetch one?' Gregor rose. He rooted in the cupboard, noticing that there were half a dozen miniatures of Babycham in there, as well. He poured a liberal amount of whisky into one glass and another, smaller measure for his brother.

'Here's to mother.' Abel was still staring, trance-like, into space. 'Come on, old chap,' said Gregor. 'Don't go catatonic on me.'

'I was just remembering what she was like when we were children.'

'Is that wise?'

'She always seemed, I don't know, disappointed.'

'I doubt I fulfilled her expectations, but I'm sure that you did.'

'I don't mean with us. I meant with life in general. As if she felt it had let her down. She'd had a hard life, Gregor.'

'I suppose it had its off-days, but I don't think it was any worse than most.'

'Odd, that she lost her mother on a railway station and that's how we lost her.'

'Life does seem to throw up these coincidences.'

'Then, the fact that she and father both fell to their deaths, is strange.'

'As Gloria remarked, it's something of a family trait.'

'Does Mitzi know?'

'That's partly why I'm here. I thought you might know how to get in touch with her.'

'She sent a letter with some photographs, though that was weeks ago.'

'Oh well, no point in ruining her holiday.'

'She ought to know, though. Wanda was her sister.'

'I think we've established that, but given how her sister treated her, I don't think Mitzi will be too down-hearted.'

'You don't understand,' said Abel. 'It's the fact that you belong to somebody that counts, not how they treat you. Mitzi will be devastated.'

'Right. But wouldn't it be better if she put off being devastated till she got home?'

'It's so......unresolved,' said Abel, tearfully. 'I can't accept it.'

'Give it time.'

'Time won't make any difference. We need something to hold on to, something tangible. We need to try and get her back.'

'I'm sorry, Abel, but it's too late. I've already given them the go-ahead to bury her. She's probably already underground. You wouldn't want her disinterred now, surely?'

Abel shuddered: 'Sorry, Gregor, do you reckon you could pour me out another whisky?'

'Absolutely.'

'I suppose we'll have to come to terms with it.' He sighed and took a large gulp from the glass. 'We can at least create some sort of a memorial.'

'Please don't suggest we build another bloody shrine.'

'Of course not, no. But don't you feel there ought to be a stone or something? How about a plaque?'

'Where would you put it?'

'I suppose it ought to go in the apartment. That was where she spent the most time.'

'I'm not sure the present tenants would consider that a good idea.'

'I don't think they would mind.'

'You've met them, have you?'

'Yes.' He hesitated. 'I went over there one evening after mother left. I needed to be there once more, to say goodbye. I couldn't move on. I'd thought that the place was empty; then I realised that it wasn't.'

'Who's there?'

'It's a family from Jamaica. Lots of kids. They laugh a lot. They're nice. I'll ask about the plaque then, shall I?'

'If you feel it's necessary.' Gregor looked round. He saw Abel's slippers casually placed beside the fender, half a dozen books left open on the bureau, Abel's glasses draped over a chair back. He seemed to be thoroughly at home there. 'Is this your place?'

'Not exactly. It belongs to Mrs Allerton.'

'I gathered she was in the picture somewhere.'

Abel looked at him, suspiciously: 'Who told you that?'

'Miss Quettock. I went looking for you at the library. You hadn't given me a forwarding address.'

'You know that mother found us once? I had been spending Wednesday afternoons here and one day she followed me. She found us eating melon sandwiches in bed.'

'You're talking about you and Mrs Allerton?' said Gregor, curiously. He'd assumed, in spite of indications to the contrary, that the relationship with Mrs Allerton was one of mutual convenience and certainly platonic. 'Melon sandwiches. You filthy beast. I bet you were sharing a plate, too.'

'Mrs Allerton made everything we did seem innocent. That's what I liked about her.'

Me too, Gregor thought, remembering the evening he had met her bringing Abel back from tea. As they had shaken hands, he'd taken in the broad expanse of bosom in the floral patterned dress and felt his spirits rise.

'You're Abel's brother?' she had said. 'I've heard so much about you. My name's Mrs Allerton. I've been brought in to look after your brother, whilst your mother makes arrangements. I'm so sorry about Mr Silver. What a tragedy.' She'd placed her hand on Abel's head. He'd looked up and his eyes met hers, adoringly.

Oh get off, toad, thought Gregor, irritably. He had taken in the fulsome head of auburn hair, the soft mouth and the full lips. She had nice eyes, welcoming and pardoning. The latter was particularly useful. Gregor felt a stirring in his loins: 'Will you be staying?' he'd inquired.

'No, but I will see Abel into bed before I go. I always do that, don't I, Abel?' She smiled down at him. 'We always have a story.'

'Lucky Abel,' Gregor murmured.

'You can come and listen, if you want,' she'd added, teasingly.

He eased a hand under the waistband of his trousers. 'Last time we met, you were still with Cressida,' he said at last.

'Yes.' Abel bit his lip.

'I don't suppose she's still about?'

'She comes into the library every now and then. She married one of the boys she went off hiking with. He's teaching at the art school. He took Mr Harpur's place.'

'She was a great girl, Cressida.'

'Yes,' Abel said. 'She told me that you thought so.' Gregor frowned. 'She said you'd groped her knee under the table that night.'

'Did she also tell you that she followed me to Oxford? She turned up at tea time with a tin of wacky baccy. It was very awkward. I'm afraid I sent her packing. Sadly for her, she left the wacky baccy on the sofa when she left, so Gloria and I got stoned on it. I do owe that to Cressida. Without it, Gloria might never have come back to me. I swear that Cressida was never in my line of sight, though.'

Abel shrugged: 'It hardly matters anyway. She never wanted me.'

'I often wondered why you picked the girls you did,' said Gregor. 'None of them were ever quite you.'

'Quite a few of them were you, though.'

Gregor hunched his shoulders: 'It was never serious with any of them. Honestly, it never went beyond a fumble.'

'But the point was, that they never wanted me afterwards. They all felt you were more exciting. You were dangerous.'

'I was indifferent. That's what drew them.' They were silent for a moment. 'Bunny, you're not still cross, are you?'

'No, of course not,' Abel answered, unconvincingly.

'I'm sorry if I hurt you. I would hate to think you wouldn't feel at liberty to introduce me to your friends because you were afraid I'd filch them off you.'

'Do I take it that you're back with Gloria now?'

'Tight as tics.'

'I can't imagine you deciding to be faithful.'

'Nor can I. I didn't say that I was faithful.'

'But I thought that was the reason you broke up, the first time. You were cheating.'

'That's a term that only somebody who didn't understand, would use. I wasn't cheating, I was just exploring other ways of doing things.'

'With other people.'

'There's a limit to how long you can continue working on your own allotment. Once you know the layout, where the grass ends and the vegetables begin, which bits you can walk up and down on and which bits need netting over them to keep the birds off, you can either get the deckchair out and sit there looking at it, or you can go off and see if someone else has got a rare plant you can take a cutting from.'

'Is Gloria unfaithful, too?'

'Of course not, Abel, don't be stupid. She's a married woman; or she will be.'

'You're a hypocrite.'

'I'm not. I'm just a man. This thing with Mrs Allerton, it's not a real relationship, I take it; melon sandwiches aside.'

'I don't see what it's got to do with you,' said Abel, bullishly, 'but yes, it is a real relationship. It's probably the realest one I've ever had.'

'But have you thought, old fruit, she must be pushing fifty.'

'No, she isn't. Anyway, that sounds a bit conventional for you. You buggered me when I was eight.'

'You keep on harking back to that.'

'It made a big impression on me.'

'But you still refer to her as Mrs Allerton.'

'Why wouldn't I?' said Abel. 'It's her name.'

'But even you must see it is a little….odd, if your relationship is what you say it is.'

'You don't know anything about it,' Abel threw back. 'Mrs Allerton and I, well all right, Stephanie, can please ourselves. We don't need your approval.'

'No, you don't. But there's a chance you might need other peoples.' It's a bit, you know,' he made a tipping gesture with his hand.

'It's what I'd call her, if I were a lodger. Since she has a job, we have to be discreet.'

'But that's not really why you do it, is it? You prefer to think of her as Mrs Allerton and that's a bit rum, given that you're thirty-one.'

'You've done a few rum things yourself, Gregor.'

'Yes, I have.' He hesitated. You don't know the half, he thought. 'You see this as a permanent arrangement, do you, you and Mrs Allerton?'

'Yes.'

'Does she have a family?'

'Her husband was a merchant seaman. He went off when she was twenty-six.'

'But she's still married?'

'I suppose so.'

Excellent, thought Gregor. Abel glanced up. He had heard the gate swing back. A moment later, Mrs Allerton appeared inside the door. As Gregor hauled himself up from the chair, he caught the faint scent of gardenia. He braced himself and turned. He had to look up, slightly, to encompass Mrs Allerton's face, but he took in the breasts first. They appeared to have sagged marginally, but he was relieved to find that Mrs Allerton was otherwise unchanged.

She scanned his face and hesitated: 'It's not Gregor?'

'Yes, it is.' He smiled expectantly. He saw her eyes pass fleetingly to Abel's face and back again.

'What a surprise. However did you find us?'

'I asked at the library. Miss Quettock told me Abel had moved into digs here.'

She exchanged a glance with Abel. 'We thought it would probably be easier to call it that. There might be some who'd take exception, me a social worker and a young man who was under my protection, although obviously that was some time back.'

'I'm still under your protection,' Abel said, and Gregor had a sudden urge to hit him.

'Well, congratulations,' he said. 'It's about time Abel got himself a life.'

'We're very happy,' Mrs Allerton said, giving him a look that had an element of prayer in it. She put her bag down.

'Gregor's brought some devastating news,' said Abel, as if saying it was costing all the self-control he had. 'Our mother's died in Bucharest.' He stuttered on the 'd'. His bottom lip was trembling.

Mrs Allerton looked stunned. She stared at Abel, then at Gregor, as if needing outside confirmation. Gregor nodded. 'Oh my dear.' Her mouth fell open. 'Oh, you poor boy.' She came forward with her hands out and encircled Abel with her arms. He leant his head against her chest. She glanced up and caught Gregor's eye. He gave an enigmatic smile.

'She fell onto the railway track,' said Abel. 'The door opened accidentally.'

This time the look that Mrs Allerton exchanged with him was tinged with scepticism. She began to speak and stopped. He sympathised with her dilemma. He could not imagine Wanda willingly adapting to her son's choice of companion. She might not have wanted Abel any longer for herself, but that did not imply she would have welcomed Mrs Allerton, a fact that Mrs Allerton undoubtedly appreciated. She made do with patting Abel's head, consolingly. 'To think whilst we were here, all that was going on so far away. This is a sad day, Gregor.'

'Isn't it?' said Gregor, wondering what lengths he had to go to before he could qualify for comfort, too.

'At least you have each other; that's a blessing.'

Gregor looked discreetly at his watch. He'd left it too late to get back in time for dinner. Mrs Allerton glanced up: I'm sorry, Gregor, I'm afraid I'm being inhospitable. You will stay on for supper, won't you?'

'Thank you. I should be delighted.'

She squeezed Abel's shoulder and unfurled his arms from round her waist. 'I'll go and do the supper, dear. We'll have a chance to talk about it, later. You take care of Gregor, now. Perhaps he'd like another drink.'

'It's nice to see the uniform still fits,' said Gregor, as they listened to the welcome clattering of saucepans in the kitchen.

'What does that mean?' Abel blew his nose.

'That is what drew you in the first place, isn't it?' He saw the colour rise in Abel's face and laughed.

'We get along together. She's a lovely person.'

'I don't doubt it.'

Mrs Allerton brought in a tray of glasses and a bowl of peanuts. 'I'll just go and change,' she said. 'The supper won't be long. Perhaps you'd lay the table for me, Abel, if you're up to it.'

'Of course.' He fetched the cutlery and laid a place for three. As Gregor watched him, he felt unaccountably that there was something he'd missed out on which his brother, notwithstanding all his handicaps, had not. When Mrs Allerton came back into the room, ten minutes later, she had on a slightly newer-looking skirt, but of the same cut and material, a freshly laundered white blouse and the same dark stockings. Gregor snorted gleefully. The only item missing, was the hat.

The conversation at the table, was desultory. Though Gregor tried to introduce some life into it, Abel seemed determinedly preoccupied. He hoped that Mrs Allerton would not suggest his brother stay the night. He would prefer to come to terms with what had happened to their mother without Gregor's input. Wanda's death, far from uniting them in grief, seemed merely to have pointed up the differences between them. Looking at him, Abel was acutely conscious of how little he and Gregor had in common. Had he known that they had Mrs Allerton in common, he might have preferred that they had even less.

And yet, he is my brother, Abel thought. Genetically, we share more than we share with anybody else. He caught his eye and Gregor gave a quick smile. It was not complicitous, but in that instant Abel realised that Gregor had seen through him and that, for the first time, so had he. He didn't need a plaque in Wanda's memory in order to accept that she had gone. He needed it in order to be certain that she wasn't coming back. How terrible was that?

He stared down at his plate. His first reaction had been disbelief, but underneath it he had felt a tenuous relief, a longing to believe that finally the link between them had been broken. Was that what he had in common with his brother? After Gregor left, he would tell

Mrs Allerton. She would explain that it was not unusual to feel relief as well as grief when someone dies, that these things aren't straightforward, that what mattered wasn't what had happened in the past, but what would happen in the future. For the first time, Abel felt he had a future.

'I think we should make a point of meeting like this once a year,' he said, 'to raise a glass to both our parents.'

'Excellent idea,' said Gregor, grateful that his brother was emerging from the coma he'd seemed to be sliding into.

'Don't you think that's what we ought to do?' said Abel, turning automatically to Mrs Allerton. 'Continue the reunions but here instead of Primrose Hill?'

She hesitated. 'Yes, of course.' She nodded. 'It's important for you boys to stick together.'

Gregor pursed his lips delightedly. She'll pay for that, he thought. He wondered what had happened in the last ten minutes, to turn Abel round. He had the look of someone coming out of a confessional, although he doubted that whatever secrets Abel had would call for absolution. He's a funny blighter, Gregor thought, but he felt almost warm towards his brother.

'I'll look out the letter Mitzi sent from Santiago.' Abel left the table and went over to the bureau. Underneath the letter was the envelope that Mrs Allerton had handed to him in the library that day. He tipped out the charm. A low relief in silver of a bearded hermit carrying a child across a river, had been stamped onto the disc. St Christopher. In Spanish under the relief, he read 'Si en San Cristobal confias, de accidente no moriras'.

Should he have tried harder to return it to his mother? Abel wasn't superstitious, but his mother was. To travel without her St Christopher must have seemed like deliberately tempting fate and, not for the first time in her life, fate had responded. Abel curled his fingers round it. It felt warm inside his palm. He held it for a moment and then tipped the charm back in the envelope and shut the drawer. There would be time for all that, later on. He handed Gregor Mitzi's letter. Gregor fumbled for his glasses.

'Borrow mine,' said Mrs Allerton. 'They're good enough for photographs.' She rose. 'I'll get the dishes out into the kitchen.'

Gregor looped the glasses round his neck and hooked them on his nose. His face creased as he looked into the radiantly happy eyes of Mitzi. She looked quite beside herself, as if she would continue staring at the camera with that bovine look of pleasure, even after it had been switched off. His gaze moved sideways to encompass Mr Harpur: white hair, white suit and a little bow tie that was also white, though dotted with grey circles, that brought some relief to his appearance. Looks a dull cove, Gregor thought, but good enough for Mitzi. She'll be all right now. The photograph had obviously been taken outside one of the small pensions where they'd been staying. You could see the hotel in the background, with the bougainvillea above the door. His gaze passed to the woman standing next to them, whose features, fuzzy though they were, appeared uncomfortably familiar.

'Christ!' said Gregor, 'It's the girl outside the buttery!'

'What?'

'Who is that they're with?' He thrust the photograph at Abel and then wrenched it back, so he could look at it again.

'The woman on the left? I think she said it was an English student who had joined them en route. They met up in France and then again when they crossed over into Spain. Mitzi writes about her in the letter. Both of them have taken quite a shine to her.' He peered over his brother's shoulder.

Gregor saw there was a smudge where he had rubbed his thumb against the face, as if he had been trying to erase it. He could see the features all too clearly in his own mind, though. If you put his and Mitzi's genes together in a sieve and shook them vigorously, what came through the holes was bound to look like this. The slightly long nose and the lips that were a little too thick for a woman, eyes that had a message, though in her case it was rather scrambled. She had Mitzi's height, at least. It was too early to know whose brain she'd inherited, but she'd been bright enough to track her mother down and she was clearly onto him. Had Mitzi lied when she said she had never met her daughter? Gregor felt a new respect for her. So Mitzi wasn't such a push-over. The girl's head was inclined towards her. They were gazing, laughingly, into each other's eyes.

He looked at the pale, smiling face of Mr Harpur, searching it for signs of guile. There were none. In so far as it was possible to be outside the circle, that's where Mr Harpur was. His eyes and mind were firmly fixed on the cathedrals. He would spend his evenings pouring over brochures and his days examining the hollows in the flagstones made by pilgrims' knees. He felt he could leave Mr Harpur out of the equation. It was that girl whom he had to reckon with. She could destroy me, he thought, with a flutter of excitement. It was years since anyone had had him by the balls like that. The thought brought back an image of himself and Gloria, but he dismissed it. He must concentrate.

The truth was not an option. He could always put the blame on Mitzi, he supposed. He'd been an innocent eighteen year old and she was thirty-five. But anybody looking at her, even now, could see that Mitzi wasn't worldly. She was one of Nature's innocents. It didn't matter what you did to her, she wouldn't come to the conclusion that the world was evil, only that the people in it were misguided.

Gregor wondered what effect the scandal might have on his delicate relationship with Gloria. I should have married her, he thought. I'd better do it quickly. As my wife, she'll be more likely to be understanding. If I go down, she'll come with me. 'What time is it, Abel?'

'Half past ten.'

'I think I'd better make a dash for Paddington. Perhaps I could put through a call to Gloria. I said I'd let her know when I was leaving London.'

'Help yourself. There's an extension in the hall.'

He lit a cigarette and dialled. The ringing seemed to echo at the other end, as if there were no other objects in the room except the telephone. He looked round for an ash tray and eventually used the drawer to flick his ash into. Behind him he heard Mrs Allerton and Abel talking in low voices as they sat together on the sofa.

'Come on, Gloria,' he muttered. 'Wakey, wakey.'

Finally, the answer phone cut in: 'There's no one here to take your call at present and if that's you, Gregor, please don't bother ringing back. I've gone to Birmingham with Cholmondeley.'

'Birmingham!' said Gregor, as if it were an expletive. 'What's this, Gloria? I said I would be back on Sunday. It's your wifely duty to be waiting for me.' He broke out into a sweat as Gloria's voice cut across his own.

'I've had a call from a Ms Bottomley, a Romance languages professor. She resented being dumped and left to pay the bill for your hotel on Friday night. False economy, Gregor. You ought to know better. I should warn you that Ms Bottomley will probably be bringing charges for assault. Apparently, she spent three hours tethered to the bed rail before summoning the hotel staff to cut her free. She's not in a forgiving mood. Friday, incidentally, is when you were supposed to be in London comforting your brother. Does he know his mother's dead yet, or have you decided not to bother telling him? Not that I care. Ms Bottomley has the distinction of being the last of your paramours that I shall have to deal with. You'll find your belongings in a dustbin liner outside your rooms. There's an address book in amongst them that was underneath my bed. No doubt it's a replacement for the one you lost and said you wouldn't bother to replace. Just as well you did. I dare say you'll be needing it.'

'Oh come on, Gloria! At least let's talk about this. Is it really likely I'd choose someone like Ms Bottomley to be unfaithful with? Whatever she's been telling you, she's lying. She came onto me. The woman's a hyena. If I'd stayed there any longer, she would have been feasting off my corpse.........' The line went dead.

'Shit!' Gregor banged his head against the wall.

'Did you get hold of Gloria?'

'No. It seems Gloria's in Birmingham.' He sank down in the armchair, breathing through his nostrils. Abel threw a glance at Mrs Allerton, which she mistakenly interpreted as brotherly concern.

'You're very welcome to stay over, Gregor, if you'd rather,' she said, hesitantly. 'Nothing worse than going back to empty rooms, I say.'

'True,' Gregor sniffed, forlornly.

'I'll just go and turn on the electric blanket. Maybe you would like a brandy with your coffee?'

'Very kind.' He sat immersed in thought as Abel sulkily put out the glasses. Mrs Allerton went through into the kitchen and came back, a moment later, with the brandy bottle. Mitzi's photograph was on the coffee table, angled so that all three of the figures in it, seemed not to be laughing at the camera, but at him. He lit another cigarette. 'Did Mitzi say when they'd be coming back?'

'They thought some time in August. They'll be staying for the Festival. For Mitzi, it's the highlight: fireworks in the square, a carnival procession and a feast for fifteen hundred pilgrims laid on by the city fathers. Mitzi is beside herself. For penance, Mr Harpur's taking her to Mass.'

'Don't tell me Mitzi's now decided she's a Catholic.'

'You know Mitzi.' Abel laughed. 'She finds it difficult to say no.'

Gregor shot a glance at him, but irony was not in Abel's arsenal. 'The money's lasting, then?'

'She says they won't have much left by the time they get to England, but at least she'll have a place to live. She's leasing Mr Harpur's cottage down in Deal. She's quite excited at the prospect.'

Gregor nodded. I suppose that girl will come back with them, he thought. She won't have pursued them this far, just to back off now. She knows that Mitzi is her mother; soon she'll know that I'm her father. She'll know, even if she isn't told, because the truth is in the air and gravity means that it has to come down somewhere. So my days are numbered. At some point, I shall be called on to explain myself. I can't bear blusterers or self-apologists. I shall confess, or plead the Fifth Amendment, but I shan't say sorry.

Mrs Allerton had sat down next to him. 'I see you've brought your violin,' she said.

'It was my grandfather's. I picked it up this morning from the musical repair shop down in Cheapside.'

'I remember when you played that piece by Handel at your father's funeral,' she went on, heedlessly. 'It was a really memorable occasion.'

Yes, it was, thought Gregor.

Mrs Allerton flushed suddenly, as she too recollected other ways in which it had been memorable. He had been gratified to note from Mrs Allerton's expression, when she first arrived, that she recalled that night in all its questionable detail. Gregor only wished that he could.

'Maybe you could play your violin tonight?' she ventured, 'as a tribute to your mother. We would like that, Abel, wouldn't we?' She took his hand.

Why not, thought Gregor. It was how he'd solved his problems in the past, unravelling a Beethoven Sonata or a composition by Corelli. It reacted on him like a good whiff of ammonia, clearing the unnecessary debris from the brain. He took the violin out, twanging each string as he tested it for tightness. Wedging the bar underneath his chin, he sailed into a Bach Partita. He knew that as long as he continued playing, the dilemma that he found himself in, would be held at bay. Music, in that respect, was like sex. He could throw himself in, like a swimmer at the deep end of the pool. The trouble was that he had no choice but to surface after sex, whereas with music he was like a deep sea diver, exploring the rocky hollows and the rich life on the sea bed, meeting curious, exotic shoals that brushed his body as they passed him.

He turned so that Mrs Allerton was in his line of vision. She was swaying, not exactly in time to the music, but at least it was affecting her. There was an awkward moment, when she realised he was watching her. She tried to smile in an encouraging, but hopefully detached way, as she had been taught to do on courses she'd been sent on by the social services. She hadn't felt this threatened for a long time. The fact that part of Gregor's mind was with the group outside the pension in Santiago and another part with Gloria and Cholmondeley up in Birmingham, did not prevent the rest from pulling her within its orbit. She was worried that the spare room wasn't spare enough. It lay between the room she shared with Abel and the bathroom.

I expect I'm wrong, she thought. All that had happened such a long time in the past, he'd probably forgotten all about it. But as she connected with the beady glance, she knew that he had not forgotten. 'That was lovely, Gregor,' she said, as he put the violin away. 'Your mother would be proud of you. Perhaps you'd like another brandy as a nightcap before Abel shows you where your room is. It's a small house; no chance of you getting lost.' If she had meant to make a point here, it was wasted on him.

He looked over at the pleasant, middle-aged face with its laughter lines, the kindly eyes, the capable, consoling hands, the simple, unaggressive personality, a cosy port in what was promising to be a Force 9 gale. Ridiculous, he thought. This is a woman who is old enough to be our mother, Abel's mother, anyway. Perhaps, if we had had a proper one, neither of us would be here now.

His eyes passed to Abel with his long hair and his drooping cardigan, his handsome face with its benign expression and the soft, bewildered eyes that gazed at Mrs Allerton with such devotion. Wanda could not have prepared him better for the life he had now. Abel needed a protective presence that was utterly secure, a lap to lay his head on and a cleavage big enough to hide in.

Gregor felt a wave of envy, fuelled in part by a reluctant recognition that, no matter how desirable it seemed, this wouldn't do for him. The rollicking that he had had with Mrs Allerton, the evening of the funeral, had been one of the pleasanter experiences of his life, but it was unrepeatable. In any case, however much he might have wanted to usurp his brother's place, he could not bring himself to take away from Abel the one person in his life who seemingly had given him some happiness. It was a parting of the ways. In spite of Abel's plan to carry on with the reunions, he doubted they would meet again. If Gregor's future lay with anyone, it lay with Gloria. She was his only hope.

The problem is, he thought, that I have difficulty being anyone except myself. Most people could be anybody but themselves. When you had stripped away the various personas, there was nothing there. But at the core of Gregor, there was an eternal flame that couldn't be extinguished. It dictated every gesture that he made, each argument he propagated, every woman he seduced. It was the echo of this flame in Gloria that held the two of them in thrall.

Together, their flames made a bonfire bright enough, he still hoped, to incinerate small primates like that hedgehog Cholmondeley, who had taken refuge in the pyre. I could make do with Gloria, thought Gregor, if I can persuade her to make do with me.

He held his glass out. Mrs Allerton picked up the brandy bottle and came round to his side of the table. She leant over him to pour and Gregor closed his eyes deliriously. As the fulsome breasts swung past his face, he felt for one brief moment as if destiny was cradling him, not stretching him on some unseen rack.

'To the future.' Abel raised his glass. A whisky, several glasses of a Pinotage that Mr Allerton had brought back from a trip to Cape Town, plus the brandy, had begun to do their work on Abel. Cushioned between Mrs Allerton and Gregor, he felt pleasantly protected, like a seal surrounded by warm water, bobbing on the waves. If he had taken his reflections further, it might have occurred to him that these conditions were precisely those preferred by sharks. 'Cheers.'

'Cheers, old boy. Here's to it.' Like a whisper, Gregor felt the downy presence on his cheek, as Mrs Allerton leant over him. 'Here's to it.'

***